PRAISE FOR THE MIDAS LEGACY

"Readers . . . will find *The Gimirri Invasion* thoroughly absorbing, unpredictable, and powered by strong forces that both enlighten and create an incredible page-turner."
~D. DONOVAN, SR. REVIEWER, MIDWEST BOOK REVIEW

"This bold new entry in The Midas Legacy series builds on the excitement and intrigue of the first book and raises the stakes even higher, creating a captivating page-turner . . . a novel that's impossible to put down."
~BETH CASTRODALE, AWARD-WINNING AUTHOR AND EDITOR OF SMALL PRESS PICKS

The Gimirri Invasion is a thrilling second installment in The Midas Legacy, filled with high stakes, rich emotions, and an ever-expanding world. Betrayal, heartache, and rising tensions kept me turning the pages late into the night. I'm already counting the days until book three!
~ JINX MORELAND, "OREGON FAMILY ADVENTURES"

"*The Curse of King Midas* . . . stands out as an unforgettable work . . . exemplifies remarkable storytelling and critical depth, making it a noteworthy addition to any literary collection."
~SHAWNA THOMPSON, READER VIEWS LITERARY AWARDS

"A gripping fantasy that blends classic myth with contemporary storytelling finesse . . . a standout in the genre . . ."
~FORAM VYAS, READERS' FAVORITE BOOK AWARDS

THE GIMIRRI INVASION

Also by Colleen M. Story

THE MIDAS LEGACY

The Curse of King Midas (Book I)

∽

STAND-ALONE FICTION

Rise of the Sidenah

Loreena's Gift

The Beached Ones

∽

NONFICTION

Overwhelmed Writer Rescue

Writer Get Noticed!

Your Writing Matters

∽

For more information, please see:

colleenmstory.com

masterwritermindset.com

COLLEEN M. STORY

the
GIMIRRI INVASION

THE MIDAS LEGACY BOOK 2

MIDCHANNEL PRESS

Books may be ordered through booksellers or by contacting the publisher at:

Midchannel Press
P.O. Box 131
Iona, ID 83427 www.midchannelpress.com
Email: publisher@midchannelpress.com

To receive Colleen M. Story's email newsletter, register directly at www.colleenmstory.com/newsletter. Writers may prefer her writing newsletter at www.masterwritermindset.com/newsletter.

Cover Design: Damonza.com

Map by: BMR Williams

Ebook ISBN: 979-8-9926172-0-7
Hardcover ISBN: 979-8-9926172-2-1
Paperback ISBN: 979-8-9926172-1-4

Library-of-Congress Control Number: 2025903918

Originally published in hardcover in the United States by Midchannel Press in 2025.

Around the eighth century BC, a group of nomad equestrian warriors named the Cimmerians (*Gimirri* in this book, as in the Akkadian language) first appeared in Assyrian records. Some scholars believe they were driven out of their homes by another nomadic group named the Scythians, who had established themselves on the Pontic Steppe, which is now modern-day Ukraine and southern Russia.

The Cimmerians, now without a home, journeyed south and battled in Urartu—King Sargon II of Assyria's rival to the north. The nomads experienced some victories there, and word spread of their fierceness. It is thought that the danger they presented compelled King Midas, ruler of the neighboring Kingdom of Phrygia, to declare peace with Sargon in 709 BC, perhaps in the hopes of forming an anti-Cimmerian alliance.

The Cimmerians tried to cross the Assyrian frontier in 705 but were defeated by Sargon's forces. Despite this victory, Sargon himself was killed in another battle later that year against the Cimmerians in Tabal, south of Phrygia.

The Cimmerians then turned their attention to Midas' kingdom, raiding and plundering as they traveled toward the capital city of Gordium. They attacked the city, some believe around 696 BC, though other records put the attack later around 679. (The date of 696 is used for the purposes of this book.)

The Gimirri Invasion continues the tale told in Book I of The Midas Legacy, *The Curse of King Midas*, following the history of that time and the threat posed to Gordium by the Cimmerians.

PROLOGUE

716 BC

On the road between the Assyrian Empire and the Kingdom of Phrygia

Elanur Savas shivered, rubbing her arms. The sun had set hours ago, leaving the night's chill to gnaw at her unease. They had traveled too far north. She'd suspected it for a time. Her child companion, Little Bird, had journeyed from the Assyrian Empire to the Kingdom of Phrygia alongside Elanur's son, Emir Alkan, only a few moons ago. Elanur had trusted the girl to remember the way. Foolish, perhaps, but she'd had little choice after escaping King Sargon II's city of Durukin.

For fifteen straight days, they'd trekked over hills and flatlands, begging for food and water from the villages they passed, their sandals thick with dirt. Now and then, they'd come across a grove of trees where they could rest and take shade, but often, they'd traveled under the hot sun. Elanur's skin burned red, and her body felt like a giant swollen ache. She longed for a bath, but the road before them stretched on, dry and unforgiving.

"Little Bird?" She wanted to stop for the night, but ever since the northern mountains had risen as cone-topped shadows on their right, Little Bird had stepped up her pace. She, too, seemed agitated, her little body taut with worry.

They were lost.

"Little Bird, my feet," Elanur called again. "I need to stop."

She knew when it had happened—the wrong turn. They had come to an intersection three days before. The girl had seemed hesitant about which road to take. Neither went directly west, which was where they were headed, toward the great city of Gordium. Elanur had dreamed of reuniting with her brother, King Midas, in his grand castle. She'd pictured him as she'd last seen him at the Battle of Karama, allowing the vision of their reunion to spur her onward. But Little Bird had chosen the road that veered slightly north, and now their future seemed less certain.

"Please, Little Bird."

The girl returned to stand before her, her face a shadow in the night. She'd disguised herself as a boy before, back when Emir was still alive, a protective response to her perilous life as an orphan. She'd revealed her true identity to Elanur only after the battle, and now Elanur wondered how she'd ever seen the child differently.

"I need to rest," Elanur said.

The girl scanned the area, then circled Elanur as if creating a protective boundary. Finally, she returned and sat down. Elanur could feel her gaze lingering. Sometimes, it was uncomfortable, these silences. Elanur had learned enough of the mute girl's hand language to communicate during the day, at least somewhat. But at night, without the flicker of firelight, they were left with only silence. That or Elanur's one-sided conversation, which she sometimes engaged in to feel more comfortable.

"Do you think we took the wrong road?"

The girl made a flurry of hand motions Elanur couldn't make out, then rested her arms on her knees and sighed.

"It's all right. We'll get there."

Elanur rubbed her ankles, willing the circulation back into her feet. She'd worried when they left Durukin that they might end up this way. The girl had brought no supplies. But when faced with the choice of following the one who might lead her to her brother or staying where King Sargon might repossess her as his slave, she'd chosen to follow. She was still quite certain it had been the right decision, but she would be glad to see her brother's capital city on the horizon.

The throbbing had just begun to subside when Little Bird got up and pulled on Elanur's arm.

"Already?"

The girl persisted.

"Why are you so worried?" Elanur asked. "Is it dangerous here?"

Little Bird grabbed her other arm, pulling with urgency.

"All right, all right. I'm coming."

She struggled to her feet and instantly regretted it, the blisters stinging worse than before. If only they could find water. She could soak them. Wrap them. There was some extra fabric on her skirt she could use. Even without water, she was considering binding them when she felt a faint vibration in the ground beneath her. A subtle, distant sensation, it grew more noticeable by the moment.

Hoofbeats.

Elanur grabbed Little Bird's hand, and the two darted off the road and raced toward the northern hills beyond. The riders approached swiftly, slowing as they drew near. Elanur flattened herself alongside Little Bird, both still as sticks.

The riders halted.

Peering through the grass, Elanur counted five of them: muscular warriors with long dark hair, thick beards, and heavy animal pelts shielding their broad shoulders. Three carried torches that cast long, menacing shadows. One turned her direction, and a shiver ran down Elanur's spine. His face was more intimidating even than King Sargon's—something she hadn't believed possible. His features were sharp and angular, as if chiseled from stone rather than shaped by flesh. The horses were just as imposing, each as formidable as Sargon's giant piebald, a rare sight in Durukin.

The group hesitated for several moments, the three with torches venturing from the road as if searching for something. Thankfully, they seemed to have somewhere they needed to be, for the one in front soon barked a few strange words, and the men took off at a gallop. Within moments, they were gone.

Little Bird gestured for Elanur to follow her back to the road. When Elanur caught up, the girl reached out and took her hand.

"It's all right," Elanur said, squeezing. "We're going to make it."

They trudged on until the sweat on their palms loosened their hold. Eventually, a distance opened up between them again, Elanur's bloody feet no match for Little Bird's youthful steps. As the dark loosened its grip and the first light of dawn crept over the eastern horizon, they entered a shallow canyon flanked by rising hills. Elanur focused on putting one foot in front of the other, the child soon disappearing from sight up ahead. The gray sky induced a trancelike state and Elanur's eyes grew heavy, weariness spreading over her body like a warm blanket. The ground rose to meet her and relief flooded her body. She surrendered to the dirt and fell fast asleep.

LATER THAT MORNING, in the murky depths of her dreams, Elanur sensed a distant rumble seeping into her consciousness, then a woman's stern and commanding voice. These sensations quickly faded, leaving another comforting silence, before a cloud of dust spewed across her face, filling her nostrils. She sneezed herself awake and blinked against the bright sunlight.

A horse's brown leg came into view.

A man with a gravelly voice said something in the same strange warrior's language she had heard the night before. Another man with a thinner voice answered. The first man responded, and all the rest laughed. Elanur sat up, quickly realizing she was surrounded by the intimidating riders.

"Little Bird?" Her voice broke as panic seized her body. Scrambling to her feet, she twisted desperately, scanning for any sign of her companion. But the child was nowhere to be seen. Neither was there any other woman.

She backed up, seeking an escape, but the warriors blocked every exit. Leathery faces stared down at her with appraising expressions. Then, one by one, the men turned to look behind them. In unison, they dropped their heads to their chests and pulled their mounts in reverse, creating a clear path.

Elanur started down it but quickly halted, for a new rider appeared. He sat astride a massive black stallion, its glossy coat rippling with power, its nostrils flaring. The man's sleeveless shirt and leather vest revealed muscular arms, his intimidating form blocking the sun, his face in shadow. He said something she didn't understand and gestured for her to come closer. Elanur longed to flee, but she was trapped, so she obeyed. The warrior's thick legs encircled the stallion, leather boots covering his feet and ankles. An iron medallion, carved with a geometric design, dangled from his neck.

He spoke once more.

"I don't understand," Elanur said.

His gaze flicked to the road ahead. He seemed to have recognized her tongue, though she guessed he was no closer to understanding her than she was him. After a pause, he pointed at himself and said, "Ilker."

His name? Elanur placed her hand on her chest and said, "Elanur." The men laughed. She looked around at them, confused. Did they find her voice amusing?

The leader glared, and the warriors fell silent. Dark eyes rested upon her again. Elanur waited, her spine like curdled cream.

Once more, Ilker pointed at her, then at himself. When she didn't respond, he gestured to his men. Before Elanur could protest, she felt herself being lifted by two powerful hands, one under each of her arms. She wriggled fiercely, but the men maneuvered her as easily as they might a small child, placing her on the saddle in front of Ilker. Then they were off, all of them trotting down the road she and Little Bird had traveled, headed west. Elanur squirmed, trying to get free, but Ilker's arm was an iron band around her waist, unyielding. She turned her head this way and that, hoping desperately that the child had escaped.

There was no sign of her.

The horses shifted into a steady canter. Tears stung Elanur's eyes. She had been only two years old when King Sargon had stolen her from her village, killing her mother and wounding her brother. Now, all these years later, men were taking her away again, forcing her to abandon someone she cared about. She clenched Emir's whistle in her pocket.

No. Not again. She would escape. She would return to find Little Bird.

PART ONE

CHAPTER
ONE

696 BC
(20 years later)
Gordium, Capital City of Phrygia

Princess Zoe awoke with a start.

"No, Anchurus! Don't!"

Her father was shouting again.

She threw off the blankets, grabbed her robe, and dashed barefoot across the chilly stone floor of her room. In the hall, she found her two guards staring up at the ceiling.

"How long?" She addressed Ozan, the shorter one, a fresh-faced young man with a ready smile, though he wasn't smiling now.

"It started a few moments ago, Your Highness," he said.

"Call Pembe," she told him, referring to the head cook. "Warm goat's milk. Quickly. Dogan," she said to the second guard, a taller, older man with a chin that jutted forward. "Come." She flew up the hall, Dogan on her heels. When they reached the third level, they heard King Midas shouting again.

"He wasn't supposed to be there!"

Zoe slowed as she approached. King Midas' two guards stood at attention on either side of the door. "Open it," she commanded.

The one on her left knocked and announced, "Princess Zoe, Your Majesty."

"I couldn't stop him!" Midas shouted. "Don't you think I tried?"

Zoe reached past the guard and lifted the latch. Two steps inside the room and she paused, searching. No lamps were lit. Dogan retrieved a torch from the hall and joined her.

"Father?" Zoe called.

"Zoe, you must not. You will *not* go there!"

"Father, it's me. I'm right here."

The bed was empty, the blankets rumpled. The nightstand's usual vase of roses had spilled onto the floor, its water pooling on the stone.

"Father?"

Dogan's flame illuminated a face. Zoe stopped, startled. Her father sat on the couch on the far side of the room underneath the window. He looked pale, his fig-brown hair splayed about as if he'd been pulling it. He wore only his nightshirt and undergarment, his feet bare on the floor, shoulders hunched.

"Father? Are you all right?" She took a careful step toward him. Dogan placed the torch in the wall harness near the window and left. "Father?" She crouched in front of the king. "What is it? What did you see?"

Midas reached a weak hand toward her. "Zoe. My girl. You're all right."

"Of course." His hand felt cold. "I'm right here."

"She was going to take you. Throw you into the chasm."

"She didn't take me." Zoe's heart clenched. Again, he'd dreamed of the Battle of Karama. It had been nearly twenty years since the goddess Katiah and her half-sister Denisia had defeated him in the worst of ways. "It's over," she said. "We're safe now."

"Anchurus?" He looked at her with hope in his eyes. When she said nothing, he dropped his gaze. "No. He's gone."

10

Zoe's heart ached. The pain over her brother's loss had eased over the years, but for her father, it seemed to have resurfaced with a vengeance.

The room filled with new light as Dogan entered carrying an oil lamp, Ozan close behind him with the goat's milk. Behind them, the commander of the king's guard, Rastus Volkan, appeared, his sharp features catching the glow.

"Your Highness?" he said.

"He's all right," Zoe said.

Rastus offered a hand to the king, his blond hair illuminated by the light. "Your Majesty."

Zoe hung back while the older man cared for her father as he had for so many years. Loyal Rastus. He was still handsome despite his age, his hair smooth on his head, though there was a little less of it on the crown.

"Leave it there," he said to Dogan, pointing to the nightstand on the opposite side of the bed. Dogan placed the lamp and left, Ozan on his heels. Rastus offered Midas the cup of goat's milk.

"Drink it, Father," Zoe said. "It will help you sleep."

Midas shook his head. "I don't deserve rest. She said so, and she's right."

Zoe pressed her lips together. It wasn't the first time he'd spoken of a "she." When the nightmares started, Zoe had believed them only the symptoms of age. But lately, it was getting worse.

"Who's right?" she asked.

Midas rested his back against the headboard. "I apologize for waking you. Go back to bed now." He lifted his gaze to Rastus. "Both of you. There is much to be done tomorrow."

Rastus bowed and obeyed, but Zoe lingered. When the commander closed the door, she sat on the edge of the bed, holding the milk in her hands. "We have to talk about this," she said. "It's taking a toll on your health."

"I'm an old man," Midas said. "Few kings live sixty years."

"Perhaps. But you need your sleep. And this . . ." She gestured into the center of the room. "This isn't normal."

He gazed at her with tired eyes. "You could take another room."

"I like my room."

"You've always wanted a larger one."

She shrugged. "It's grown on me." The milk felt warm under her palm. She offered it to her father again, but he turned away, so she downed it herself in a series of gulps. "You don't know what's good."

He smiled weakly. "Go to bed. Let me rest."

She embraced him, then blew out the lamp by his bed. "Goodnight, Father."

Back in her own room, Zoe studied her favorite painting of her mother, Queen Demodica. It hung on the west wall and showed the softer side of the queen's expression. She had died when Zoe was only seventeen years old—over twenty-two years ago now.

"He's getting worse," she said to the image. "I'm worried someone is harming him."

Follow your instincts, Zoe. You're a bright girl.

She could hear her mother saying that. She crawled into her bed and stared up at the canopy. Thankfully, no more shouts came from her father's room. Still, it was early morning before she could finally go back to sleep.

It FELT as if Zoe had just closed her eyes when the warning horns shattered the stillness. Blaring from the castle turrets, they signaled danger in the city. Her heart sank. She threw a linen dress over her head, the fabric brushing hastily against her skin. She feared she already knew why the horns had awakened them.

Another attack.

"What word?" she asked Ozan as she stepped into the hall.

"The south side of the city, Your Highness," he said, blinking tired eyes.

She hurried up the stairs to her father's strategy room. Inside, she found King Midas, Rastus, Baran—the supreme commander of the king's army—and the king's three advisors sitting around the large conference table. King Midas looked tired but in control, his gaze lifting briefly to hers before he addressed Baran.

"They came from the south?"

"As far as we can tell, Your Majesty." About ten years younger than the king, Baran was wrinkled and bald, with a tightly trimmed gray beard, but still had the upright posture of a soldier. "Others say they sneaked between the dwellings in the middle of the night, then waited to attack at dawn."

"How many have we lost?" Princess Zoe asked.

Baran looked behind him to see the princess. "No way to tell yet, Your Highness," he said.

"How much damage this time?" Zoe asked.

"Some dwellings on the south side have been destroyed," Baran said, "and some livestock stolen. We're not sure how many yet."

Zoe's face fell. "Father, this must stop. This is the fifth attack in the same number of moons. We've lost at least ten citizens. You must summon the soldiers."

Midas turned his attention to his three advisors, who sat opposite him beside Baran. "Have you learned more about them?"

Aster, the lead advisor, was the first to answer. Gray tinged his wavy dark brown hair, but he, like Baran, remained fit and muscular, his brown eyes intense. "They are from the northwest, Your Majesty, the far northwest."

"Northeast, then?" Midas had long ago grown used to interpreting Aster's strange way of speaking the opposite of what he meant.

"We don't believe they are the same attackers that King Sargon II repulsed before he died," Aster continued.

Midas scowled at the mention of King Sargon II, his long-time enemy, and the former ruler of the eastern kingdom of Assyria. "Now they seek their fortunes here," he said.

"They employ unusual tactics, Your Majesty," Baran said. "Sneaky. Cunning."

"And quite agile on their horses," added Gediz, the newest advisor. A doughy man in his thirties with a broad nose and spiraling curls about his head, he had been in the king's service for only a year. A gift from the king of Lydia, or so the messenger had said, Gediz was one of a long line of temporary advisors the king had employed in his efforts to replace Fotis, the original lead advisor lost in the great Battle of Karama. "They leap on and off even while the beasts are moving."

"Stunning new information for the king," Aster said in a low undertone.

"You told him that last time," the second advisor, Xander, whispered to Gediz. Once the youngest of the three, Xander was now in the middle age-wise, sporting some gray strands himself amid the brown about his ears and even more weight on his belly.

"It is important information," Gediz grumbled, his voice like a bleating goat's.

"As are all your astute observations," Aster said.

Midas shifted his attention to Xander. "Do you know how Sargon defeated them?"

"We can't say he *defeated* them, Your Majesty," Xander said. "His army outnumbered them, from what we know, but he only pushed them out of his territory."

"Rumors do not tell of one of these warriors killing Sargon in a later battle," Aster said.

"That's nonsense, Your Majesty," Gediz said. "It is recorded that Sargon died in his battle to subdue . . . uh . . . yes, in his battle with Tabal."

"Of course, none of these nomad warriors were allied with Tabal at the time," Aster grumbled at him.

"Well," Gediz sputtered, "I wasn't there!"

"Difficult to be reminded of such a tragedy," Aster said.

"Men," Midas said, holding up his hand. "The task at hand. You believe these are the same warriors who carried out a series of attacks against Assyria, which Sargon repelled."

When the advisors nodded, he rubbed his chin.

"They call them the Gimirri, Your Majesty," Xander said. "From their homeland, perhaps?"

The sound of the horns blowing again interrupted the conversation. Zoe got up and, standing on her tiptoes, looked out the window behind her father's chair. "Oh, no!" she said. "Fire, Father. I see smoke!"

Baran glanced at the king.

"Go," King Midas said. "And Baran, they must come no farther. If you must take castle guards, do so."

Baran bowed and fled the room.

"Castle guards?" Xander said, looking nervous. "But who will protect the castle?"

"The king has great faith in you," Aster said with a sly glance.

"Surely the king doesn't expect his advisors to fight?" Gediz whispered.

"All the time," Aster said. "I'm sure they told you that before you traveled so far to join us."

"Rastus," Midas said, ignoring the advisors' banter, "send the king's guardsmen to take over the castle defense positions."

"Your Majesty," Rastus protested, "you are our most precious—"

"Now, Rastus," Midas said.

Rastus bowed and left the room.

Zoe stared at her father. "You would leave yourself defenseless rather than recall the army?"

"We don't need an army to fight off a few nomads," Midas said.

"But they have breached our borders several times, and now, it seems, with increasing numbers." She came back to the table. "Gordium is in need. The kingdom is in need."

Midas raised one hand. "We have lived in peace for twenty years. I will not disrupt everyone's lives over a few skirmishes."

"Skirmishes?" Zoe's eyebrows shot up. "Our people are losing their livestock. Their homes. Some of them, their lives. If you will not call back the army, then we must finish the wall on the south side."

"That would take years," Xander said.

Midas sighed and glanced at his daughter. "You may get started with your planning. When you have it finished, bring it to me."

"I've already done so." She turned toward the king's nearby cabinet. "I believe those are the plans, that parchment?" She pointed to the third shelf.

Midas directed his attention to the advisors. "You three. GAX." He paused, the strange-sounding acronym hanging in the air. "See if you can sneak your way out to observe how these . . . Gimirri, did you say?"

Xander nodded, sitting forward in his chair.

"See how they fight. I want all the details you can gather."

"Now, Your Majesty?" Xander said in a small voice.

"He *does*!" Gediz whispered, his eyes bugging from his head. "He wants us to fight!"

"He is aware of your agile skills with a sword," Aster said.

"Not fight," Midas said with a sideways glare at Gediz. "Observe."

"But to observe, Your Majesty, we must . . ." Gediz stammered, "get close to them, as they say."

"How insightful," Aster murmured.

Midas shifted his gaze to Xander. "Before you report back, I need you to check on Katiah's tomb. There have been rumors of rumblings in the earth. You must ensure it remains secure."

"You haven't heard something, Your Majesty?" Aster asked.

Midas got up from his chair. "A precaution. Hurry, before Baran's men chase the invaders out and you lose your opportunity."

The three advisors made their way to the door. "Surely he doesn't mean for us to go into the thick of battle?" Gediz muttered.

"Not us," Aster said, "just you."

Xander shut the door behind them.

Alone with his daughter, Midas turned to her. "You are unhappy."

Zoe's shoulders sagged. "I just don't understand why you're so hesitant. We need our soldiers."

"Our kingdom has thrived for twenty years without soldiers. Our farmland has tripled in size. We have more food than ever before, and your storage designs and the men's hard work protect us from drought and famine. I thought that would make you happy."

"It does! It has." Zoe pressed her hands together. "But if these warriors destroy the city, all will be lost."

"If we call the soldiers back now, just before harvest, we may lose a substantial amount of food stores." Midas moved to his strategy table. By habit, he chose the black rider figurine, the one he'd used to represent Sargon all those years before the great battle. "They are a few meddling nomads, looking for plunder. We can manage them without demanding our farmers leave their fields."

"The women and children would step up to manage them." Zoe approached, looking over the table.

Midas set the Sargon figure down and picked up another. It was supposed to be a generic representation of the commander of Midas' army, but it resembled Prince Anchurus. "We will manage this," he mumbled.

Zoe's gaze fell to the bottom shelf of the cabinet where her father had always kept his sister, Elanur's, doll. He'd hoped for a reunion at the Battle of Karama. He'd gotten one, but it had been cruelly short. "May we start on the temporary barrier, at least? We must protect the city."

He placed the Anchurus figurine where Gordium rested on the map. "Very well," he said.

Zoe left the room, her thoughts restless. She should be happy. She'd gained permission to build the temporary barrier on the south side. It would help deter future attacks, but a nagging fear clung to her—that it wouldn't be long before the harvest would be the least of their concerns.

CHAPTER

TWO

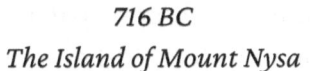

716 BC
The Island of Mount Nysa

Little Bird pressed her fingers to her temple. Pain radiated from the knot above her ear, sharp and unrelenting. She sat awkwardly on her hip in damp earth, small stones biting into her knee. Pushing her hair away from her face, she took in her surroundings.

Elanur? They'd been together on the road. Elanur had fallen into a heavy sleep. Unable to wake her, Little Bird had curled up nearby and closed her eyes. Then . . . what had happened? A rumble of hoofbeats. Dust across her cheeks. She'd leaped to her feet and then *whap*. Something had hit her hard on the side of the head.

Now she was here. Wherever "here" was.

Bracing herself against the ground, she stood. Her vision blurred and the world tilted. It was dark, but ahead, a faint gray light veiled the horizon. Dusk? But they'd stopped not long before dawn. Could she have lost an entire day?

Underfoot, dirt and stones crunched against a foundation of

solid rock. A chill passed over her skin, the air crisp with a wild type of salt and a distant sound, unmistakable: crashing waves.

Rock walls marked the space to the left and right. Ahead, a narrow road bordered by wiry trees and lush ferns stretched into the twilight. She made her way toward it, but as she drew closer, a strange structure came into view—a lattice of tangled branches and thick stems covering the cave entrance. Feather-soft leaves enhanced the weave, their pungent aroma sharp in her nose.

She pressed her hand against the barrier, trying to push through, but her arm slid in only as far as her wrist. She explored its edges— standing on tiptoes, crouching low—but the crisscrossing branches formed an unyielding cage.

Elanur? She peered through the vines, but it was growing dark and all she could see were the shadowy shapes of the closest trees. Even the outline of the road was fading.

In the opposite direction, a deeper darkness awaited her. She moved to the left wall and dragged her fingers along it, letting it guide her to the back. There, the rock felt lumpy, like big boulders placed one on top of another. They must have fallen in at some point. She continued to explore until she reached the right wall, then returned to the front barrier once more to watch the last of the sun's gray shadow disappear. A knot formed in her stomach.

She was trapped in a cave somewhere near the ocean, and there didn't appear to be a way out.

She explored again. Perhaps she had missed something, but there was only damp earth, black rock, and the occasional water drop falling on her head. Eventually, she retreated to the back wall. Shrinking into a dark crevice, she started to cry. Emir would have told her to stop, that brave boys didn't cry, but there was no one here to see. And she wasn't a boy. She'd never told him. She didn't know how he might have reacted. She hadn't been bold enough to find out.

Thinking of him only made her cry harder. Dreadful *Katiah*. Had she not killed Emir, Little Bird would be with him now. Instead, she was . . .

where? The ocean was far away from the road she and Elanur had been traveling on. It didn't make sense that the warriors would bring her here. So who? She wondered over that question until she finally fell asleep.

SOMETIME LATER, she awoke with a start.

She'd heard something.

She dared not move, her breathing shallow. Beyond, soft light filtered in, its warm yellow glow heralding morning. The barrier was still there, its interwoven branches casting fractured patterns across the rock floor. She waited, listening.

Then she saw it. A shadow inside the barrier. Fear gripped her body. This must be her captor. He'd appeared seemingly from nowhere. Drawing her knees to her chest, she wrapped her arms around them. The back of the cave was dark. Maybe she could stay hidden.

"Good morning," the captor said.

A woman's voice.

"I'm not here to hurt you. You don't have to be frightened."

A feminine, honeyed tone. The voice sounded familiar, but it didn't inspire sweet memories. This was the woman who had changed everything. She had cursed the great King Midas. At the Battle of Karama, she had chanted the strange words that tore open the deep cavern. She had caused the chaos that split the armies, required Prince Anchurus' sacrifice, and whisked Emir away, tearing him from Little Bird's arms.

"Do you remember me?" The captor took a few steps inside the cave.

Emir. Little Bird wished for him desperately. He would have been able to disable the captor and free them both.

"I brought some breakfast."

Little Bird's stomach growled. She hadn't eaten since the day before. Or was it two days?

"I am Denisia," the captor said. "I've brought you to my home on Mount Nysa. I think we can help each other."

Little Bird dared not move.

"I remember you, you know. From the castle." The goddess set something down on a tree stump Little Bird hadn't seen before.

Yes. The goddess had attended Princess Zoe's birthday party. Her grandfather had interrupted the music contest after Emir had performed his triumphant winning song.

"You were dressed as a boy back then," Denisia said. "Why did you disguise yourself?"

There was no sense in hiding any longer. Little Bird sat forward and, using her hand language, said, *Boys safer.*

The goddess didn't understand. "You cannot speak?"

Little Bird shook her head.

"At the great battle, you cried over Emir. Yet you didn't . . . cry."

Little Bird saw again the bolt of light shoot from Katiah's hands. She squeezed her eyes shut. *Katiah!*

"There." Denisia pointed at Little Bird. "That's why I brought you here."

Little Bird opened her eyes.

"You loved Emir, didn't you? I loved the prince. Do you remember Prince Anchurus?"

The valiant prince had ridden his horse into the chasm to save everyone. Little Bird said nothing. If the goddess hadn't created the chasm in the first place, both the prince and Emir would still be alive.

"So you see," Denisia said, "we have something in common. We both lost someone we loved that day. I brought you here because. . ." She paused and looked down. "Perhaps you could tell me your name?"

Little Bird had no slate. She crouched and drew a shape in the dirt.

Denisia came over to look. "Bird?" she asked.

Closer up, she looked disheveled, a pale green scarf over her head and a light linen wrap over her shoulders. But she was the goddess Little Bird remembered. That gave her some hope. Denisia hadn't seemed a mean goddess. Perhaps she would let her go soon. Little Bird nodded.

"A kind of bird?"

Little Bird shook her head.

"Just bird?"

Little Bird cupped her hands together and held them close to her mouth.

"Little? Little Bird?" When the girl nodded, Denisia stood straight again. "Very well, Little Bird. I am the goddess Denisia. How do you say that in your language?"

Little Bird shrugged. She'd never had to say Denisia before.

"You come up with a way to say it. Then you can teach it to me."

Little Bird had no desire to invent a way to say the goddess' name. *What happened Elanur?* she signed.

Denisia frowned. "I don't understand."

Little Bird drew a figure in the dirt.

"Oh, you mean Elanur."

Where? Little Bird signed.

Denisia removed her scarf, twisting it around one hand. "I didn't need her. I let the warriors take her."

The warriors! Little Bird recalled the frightening men.

"They like me, and I may have use of them in the future. So, we made a deal. They were to find you for me, which they did. I didn't need Elanur, so I was happy to let the leader have her. He's an ambitious one."

No! Little Bird ran toward the cave entrance, but it was no use. There was no escape, no way to find Elanur.

"You must forget about her now," Denisia said. "I brought you here because I think you can help me."

Little Bird stared out at the horse Denisia had tied to a nearby tree. Poor Elanur. Captured by the warriors. Little Bird felt guilty for having fallen asleep. If only she had awakened earlier.

"I want to bring Prince Anchurus back," Denisia was saying. "If I can do that, I may be able to bring Emir back, too."

Little Bird whirled around. *Emir?*

"They're dead, I know. But the dark goddess can bring them back. King Midas has her locked up in that tomb—"

The king? Little Bird walked back toward the goddess.

"What?" Denisia's eyes narrowed as she studied the girl's face. "King Midas? Back in his capital city of Gordium, surrounded by his servants, of course. As if nothing happened. His son plunges into the chasm and King Midas gets to go back to his privileged life living on the hill with his lovely daughter." Her voice had grown thin, mocking. "Oh, don't look at me that way. He appears the gallant king, but he's not. It was his fault the prince died. His stupid desire to defeat Sargon. The witch lied to me, you see. She lied about everything going back to as it was *before*. She was sorry for telling me that, don't think she wasn't. In the end, she was sorry."

The goddess' words came quickly, her cheeks red with rage. Little Bird stared at her, her lips parted.

Denisia stopped talking. With a roll of her shoulders, she composed herself. "So. Katiah." She draped her scarf around her neck and flipped her hair back. "Midas has locked her away. If we can find her, bring her back, she could help us. You knew her, didn't you?"

Little Bird shook her head. She had seen Katiah kill Emir. That was all.

"I don't think that's true." Denisia crouched and lifted Little Bird's chin. Up close, she smelled like old sweat and pine needles. "I saw you when Emir died. You shook your fists at Katiah. You were angry with her."

Little Bird made a gesture for a bolt of light.

"That bolt was meant for Elanur. Katiah didn't mean to kill Emir. Still, you had a right to be angry." She released her and stood up. "But it wasn't just anger, was it? You seemed to know her. It was like you had gotten angry with her before."

Little Bird stared into Denisia's mud-brown eyes. Something

shifted in her belly. Then a dark and horrifying image flashed in her mind. Anguished faces, so many faces staring up at her from somewhere far below, hands reaching toward her, clawing, their mouths open in silent screams. She retreated until she felt the rock against her back.

Denisia watched her with a fascinated expression. She seemed almost bemused. "You *do* know something." She came forward and bent at the waist to keep Little Bird at eye level. "It's all right. It's only you and me. You're safe here."

Little Bird wriggled away from her and tried to get through the barrier. Three times she ran into it, but it was unforgiving. She darted to the back of the cave and curled into a ball against the boulders. For many moments she crouched there, trembling. When she heard nothing, she peered out to see Denisia standing by the entrance.

"This is good," Denisia said. "There is something here for us to explore. We will start tomorrow." She smoothed the fabric of her dress and backed away. As she passed through the barrier, the vines twisted around her, melding grotesquely with her face. Green and brown tendrils merged with flesh, reshaping her into half human, half plant.

Little Bird shuddered, recoiling into the darkness.

"You're hiding a secret, Little Bird," Denisia said, her voice suddenly like the wind, "a secret I intend to root out. Imagine if you could see Emir again." She turned, mounted her horse, and rode away into the clear night air beyond.

It took a long time for Little Bird to stop trembling. Even then, she remained huddled in the shadows, haunted by the memory of Denisia's viny face.

Later, in her dreams, she saw Katiah throwing the bolt of light at Elanur, Emir moving into its path just in time to save his mother's life.

"No!" she screamed, and then, with a quick twist of her hand, set Katiah on fire.

CHAPTER

THREE

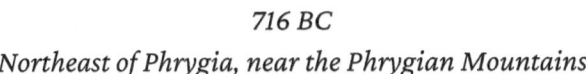

716 BC

Northeast of Phrygia, near the Phrygian Mountains

E lanur had spent two days perched in front of Ilker. He was a broad-shouldered, muscular man, his thighs twice the size of hers with arms thick as young tree trunks. She was grateful, at least, for the saddle; she'd expected a nomad like him to make her ride on the horse's rump.

He hadn't spoken since he'd seized her. Neither had he taken advantage of their nearness to grope her, though his arm had grazed her breast a time or two as he reined. Still, she was glad to be riding with one like him rather than any of the alternatives she saw around her. The one called Draris, with the jutting chin and missing teeth, had leered at her multiple times, then had gestured toward the younger, homelier man named Khogu, who often rode beside him, until the two were laughing in that frightening way some men laughed about women. Both of them were thick with muscle too, like every one of these warriors. Elanur would have no chance against any of them.

They rode relentlessly, journeying west for a short time on the same road she and Little Bird had traveled, then turning north onto a narrow path that wound back and forth like a snake. By the first evening, they were climbing and had been climbing ever since, the steady incline interrupted occasionally by a drop into a valley or ravine. They stopped once the next morning for a brief rest. Ilker offered her some dried meat and a drink from his waterskin. Despite her distaste, she had accepted. She'd been a slave long enough to know that depriving herself wasn't the way to freedom. She had to stay strong.

The second day had been one of steeper climbs, the path filled with jutting rocks and thick forests. The men kept up a jolly banter, teasing one another, though Elanur didn't understand their strange language. Occasionally, they broke into song, and it was those times when she could snatch a few moments of escape, at least in her mind. Intimidating as they appeared, the warriors had sonorous voices, and when they sang together, they lifted her mood despite her circumstances.

On the third morning, they stopped once again for a brief rest. This time, they found a small lake surrounded by towering pine and oak trees. Elanur longed to soak her feet, but with toothless Draris leering about, she had to satisfy herself with a quick splash of water on her face and hands. They'd just finished eating when the rain started. The men hardly noticed, but Elanur was soon soaked through and shivering. She was glad when they mounted up again, for Ilker's warm body was protective at her back. Inside the forest there was little light, and with the storm upon them, it seemed almost as if they were traveling at dusk.

It wasn't until sunset on the fourth evening that they finally reached their destination. Cold, wet, and aching, Elanur was like a doll in the saddle, staring blankly at the horse's mane and imagining her days with her young son Emir when he used to play his oud, his bare feet swinging back and forth as he strummed his rhythms from atop a rickety stool. The men, also weary from the journey, had fallen quiet over the last leg of it. When they suddenly began shouting and whooping, Elanur startled from her stupor. Looking up, she saw that the forest had given way to a broad expanse of green meadow. Wildflowers swayed among the grasses as far as she could see, the land rolling into more hills beyond, twin mountain peaks posing in the background, the dark clouds drifting over it all in a bustling rush to the northeast.

Ilker moved his horse into a canter, the men rushing toward a camp in the distance. Tents of various sizes lay strewn about the flatland between the hills, herds of sheep and goats grazing peacefully around the perimeter until they heard the approaching men. Then they all headed up and started running in the opposite direction. A group of people dressed in leather clothing gathered at the southern edge in welcome, women, children, and old men, some younger as well, adolescents from the look of them. Elanur observed them all with anxious eyes. At that moment, she felt farther away from her world than she ever had, her painful muscles taut with fear.

She glanced back, seeking any sort of tie to the life she'd known, but only the forest and clouds remained, the ominous storm bearing down upon her.

AT THE CAMP'S EDGE, the warriors dismounted and rushed to greet family members with enthusiastic hugs and raucous laughter. Elanur stood where Ilker had left her, watching as the young boys tied the horses to wooden posts, then stripped the beasts of their gear, saddles, bridles, and storage bags before brushing them down. She longed for escape, but there were no other villages, and her chances of making it out in the wilderness alone were slim, particularly with no supplies. She would succeed only at provoking her captors, and right now, she needed them to survive.

Little Bird, Elanur thought. *I shouldn't have fallen asleep.*

For a long while, she stood there, the tribe seemingly unconcerned with their newcomer. Finally, as the boys began to release the horses into the pastures, Elanur spotted an older woman walking toward her. She wore a black cloak with a loose hood over her head, her shoulders rounded and her gait slow, as if she had to be careful not to stumble and fall. As she came closer, she lifted her gaze to Elanur. A few wisps of gray hair framed her face, wrinkles deeply marring the skin under her eyes and over her cheeks.

"Bri," the woman said with a thick tongue, pointing at herself. Elanur kept silent, the only form of rebellion left to her. The woman repeated the action. When Elanur still said nothing, the woman reversed her finger and pointed again. "Ela-nuur," she said with effort, raising gray eyebrows.

So Ilker had remembered her name. The old woman's attempt to pronounce it was so sincere that Elanur relented. "Bri," she said.

The old woman nodded, her lips pressed in a type of smile, though it wasn't friendly. More like they had reached an agreement. She gestured for Elanur to follow and walked back into the camp.

Elanur obeyed, happy at least not to be bound in any way. The vast expanse of rugged land around them was binding enough, she supposed. They passed multiple tents, the men packing away their supplies while setting aside the treasures they had collected on their travels. The rain persisted, but light enough that the cooking fires burned unhindered, the setting sun casting an apricot glow across a strip of horizon.

At the north edge of camp, they continued on toward two larger tents in the distance, both positioned on a small rise to the right. Bri must have an elevated position in the tribe, Elanur surmised. In front of the first tent, an adolescent girl with light brown hair tended to what looked like venison rotating over a spit. Another with darker hair and a younger face spread blankets on the grass under an open shelter made with four posts and a thatched roof. Some horses that had been set free grazed behind the rise, the sheep Elanur had spotted earlier having settled into a close-knit herd to the northwest. Bri gestured for Elanur to sit down on the blankets. Elanur obeyed, well aware she was being watched by the two young girls as they performed their duties. Bri slipped inside the tent, allowing the flap to close behind her.

The meat emanated a succulent scent, the fire crackling happily underneath it. The older girl poked at the logs while keeping the spit turning. Elanur glanced at her, noting the muscles in her upper arms and the ease with which she moved, her body well adapted to living in the mountains. She had a round face with fleshy cheeks, her long hair the color of wheat. Elanur worried it might catch fire, with how closely the girl was working to the flames, but just when it seemed inevitable, she would toss it away. Back in camp, most of the men were sitting with their families around similar fires, their voices jovial as they told their stories. Elanur shivered but dared not move from where Bri had left her.

By the time the old woman emerged again, Elanur couldn't stop her teeth from chattering. Bri set a lit candle down in the center of the blanket and said something to the younger girl. A child a couple of years older than Little Bird with doe-like brown eyes, she disappeared and returned with a heavy blanket. Elanur accepted it gratefully, wrapping it around her shoulders. The rain had stopped, the candle flame flickering with the evening breeze. Bri gestured in flowing motions over the flame—a ritualistic prayer of some kind?—then drew a circle in the air around her. The younger girl poured milk into cups and filled bowls with cooked carrots while the older girl dished up the meat. Finally, both of them sat down on either side of Bri, Elanur placed opposite the old woman. Bri gestured for them all to eat.

The flavors exploded on Elanur's tongue, the milk a salve on her turbulent stomach. She ate everything they gave her and accepted more meat when the older girl offered it. When they finished, she had stopped shivering. The younger girl gathered up the bowls and disappeared around the back of the tent. When she returned, empty-handed, Bri nodded at her and pointed to Elanur.

"Ela-nuur," she said.

One by one, the girls said her name as best they could. Then Bri gestured to the older girl. "Goakina," she said. Elanur repeated the name. "Hastet" was the younger girl's name. Once they were all introduced, the old woman folded her hands in her lap and closed her eyes. The girls followed suit. Elanur watched the three of them, confused. They sat like that for a time, the candle casting out its seedy scent. After several moments, Bri looked up, her gaze pointed into the camp.

Elanur turned and found Ilker approaching. It startled her, not only because he was such a powerful, intimidating man, but because in that moment, in the yellow-orange glow of the firelight, he appeared handsome. She'd had little chance to see his face before, having sat in front of him for the entire journey, but now as he strode toward them she noticed he had large, dark eyes and thick, wavy hair with a furry beard and mustache. There was something distinctive in his features, something wild but held in check, like a black wolf staring down from atop a jutting rise.

She ducked her head by instinct. Bri didn't get up and didn't bow. When Ilker stopped near the edge of the blanket, she addressed him in their language. They talked back and forth, Elanur sneaking glances upward. Ilker, at one point, turned his gaze on her. Then he nodded and left.

Bri spoke to the two girls, after which Goakina came and extended her hand. Elanur glanced at Bri, who nodded for her to take it. Goakina led her around the back of Bri's tent to a second, smaller tent. Elanur understood. This is where the slaves slept. She'd never been a slave to a woman before. They walked inside. She found bedding for three already prepared, wool blankets and furs placed upon thick animal hides. Goakina gestured to the one on the far left. That would be Elanur's. She realized she was invading their space and nodded in gratitude. It was better than being left outside. Then the girl picked up something from the corner and gestured for her to follow.

They traveled across the grass to the east and down a gradual incline to a narrow creek. Goakina tucked soap into Elanur's hand

and gestured for her to wash. Elanur obeyed, splashing herself with the cold water, then changed into the knee-length, sleeveless dress and undergarments the girl had brought for her. The dress, made of thinned animal skin, was soft and comfortable. Back at the tent, Goakina took her soiled clothes from her, exchanging them for a heavy wool cloak. It was itchy against her skin but felt deliciously warm. Elanur clutched it about her as Goakina led her once more back to the front of Bri's tent, where the blanket and candle remained, the older woman having retreated inside.

The cooking fire cast a golden glow into the night, many other fires lighting up the camp beyond. Goakina joined Hastet on the blanket. Elanur stood nearby, unsure what to do with herself, until Goakina gestured for her to join them. They were cleaning animal skins, likely preparing them to be used for clothing or perhaps weapon sheaths. Hastet handed her a scraping tool, giving her a little smile. Elanur went to work. This she knew how to do. She'd done it many times before in Sargon's service. She finished her piece before the other two, so she took up another. Goakina smiled at her then, clearly pleased that Elanur would be useful. The smile brightened the older girl's serious face, making her more attractive in the firelight. Elanur kept at her work. She was doing what she always did. Keeping busy. Accepting her fate. But inside, she was screaming. Captured again. She had vowed to herself it would never happen, and yet, it had. *I must find a way to escape*, she told herself, *and soon.* Little Bird could be in trouble, and she was out there all alone.

CHAPTER

FOUR

696 BC
Gordium, Capital City of Phrygia

"We can't go down there like this." Gediz paced in the middle of the advisors' room. "Those . . . *men* will spot us. You know they'll see us."

"The king did not emphasize the need for haste." Aster was already changing clothes at the south side of the room, his space surrounded by his predecessor's historical records stacked high on tall wooden shelves.

"Come, Gediz." Xander was also changing his clothes, though he wasn't as fast as Aster. His bed rested on the north side where similar shelves filled with spices, minerals, crystals, and dried plants stood fully stocked. "All we have to do is sneak around. You should have seen what we did in the great Battle of Karama."

"The Battle of Karama," Gediz said in a mocking voice. "Despite all your bragging, I have yet to hear anything great about it. And I have seen no examples of this bravery you're so happy to boast about, either."

"Today, perhaps?" Xander said.

Aster slipped his dagger into its sheath on his belt and headed for the door.

"Wait!" Xander stepped into a pair of leather sandals, drained a cup of water, and hurried after his friend.

"I'm not ready!" Gediz said. "You must allow me to prepare."

The two glanced back to see the curly-headed man standing by his bed in his underclothes. "The warriors will tremble," Aster said.

"I said I'm not ready!"

"Take your time. The king will be pleased when you fail to accompany us." Aster strode out the door, Xander tight on his heels.

"But . . ." Gediz stared after them. "Aren't we supposed to be a team?" Grumbling, he threw on a long tunic and, still wearing his castle sandals, hurried after them.

THE SUN WAS SHINING BRIGHTLY OVERHEAD, the air already turning warm. If not for the nomads, it would have been a wonderful day to visit the market, as there were early vegetables to enjoy. Instead, the morning breeze brought the smell of smoke and charred wood and thatch to the advisors' nostrils, filling the atmosphere with the scent of dread.

Aster took the lead down Castle Road. Xander did his best to keep up, his brow soon shiny with perspiration. From their elevated position near the castle gate, they could see the dark smoke blackening the sky on the south side of the city. The breeze bent the plumes toward the fields beyond, a sight that made Xander nervous. If the fields caught fire, the crops would be ruined. Then there were the sheep. A fire could be devastating to the herds.

"Will you slow down?" Gediz was struggling to put on his cloak as he half jogged, half shuffled down the road after them. "This is so unconventional, unconventional! A king's advisors do not go charging down the hill to meet invaders."

"The king's guards will have the warriors chased off soon." Xander spoke the words with a confidence he didn't feel.

"If the guards are doing such a wonderful job," Gediz said, panting audibly now, "then why do we need to be out here?"

Aster stepped up his pace as if daring the new advisor to fall behind. Soon they entered the main part of the city where the wealthier citizens lived. Stone and wood dwellings lined the roads and alleyways, but they were strangely empty. No children ran about playing. No mothers scraped hides or washed clothes. Xander spotted a few faces peering from the doorways as they passed.

"Should we take better care to hide ourselves?" he asked Aster.

"We must not hurry before they have gone."

Xander didn't want to come face-to-face with one of the warriors. They were nearly twice the size of normal men, he'd been told, and quick with their swords.

At the intersection where Castle Road joined Market Street, Aster continued on a narrower path south. Here, dwellings of mudbrick, thatch, and straw provided shelter. The ragged tents of old were no longer around, thanks to Princess Zoe's rebuilding efforts. Aster led them in a general southwest direction, taking shelter behind dwellings and then hurrying forward before taking shelter again. There were shouts up ahead, men's voices and now and again a screaming woman or child. A shiver ran up Xander's back. He pulled his dagger out of its sheath and clenched it tightly in his palm.

"You have a weapon?" Gediz said behind him.

Aster paused at the edge of a narrow goat pen. Xander peered around his shoulder. They were close to the west end of the city, with only a few remaining dwellings between them and the hills beyond. To the south, the fighting raged. Swords clanged and arrows flew, horses thundering about, their hooves kicking up dust. Smoke filled the air, but Xander could see only edges of flame, small fires burning tentatively as they sought more fuel. Then he spotted a flicker near the fields.

"Fire," he said to Aster. "It will take the crops."

"I'm not charging out there like a fool," Gediz said.

"You appear the epitome of intelligence sitting here," Aster said, before dashing forth. Xander followed to a heap of dried grasses beyond. When he looked back, Gediz was still crouched behind the goat pen.

"He's not really working out, is he?" Xander said.

"A brilliant deduction," Aster said.

"How many have we had now?"

"Important to discern at this moment." Aster leaned forward to better see the clearing beyond.

Two of the king's guards lay dead, one with his head near sliced off. A few steps away, three of the nomads fought with two more guards. The king's men were hopelessly outmatched. They stood on foot, valiantly trying to best the warriors on horseback, but the rumors were right. Each warrior seemed a third again the size of the guards. Leather armor covered their wall-like chests, their thick hair knotted with pieces of bone and feathers, their brows fierce as slabs of rock. Their horses, too, oozed power from their hides. Midas' men fought hard, shifting and playing off of one another, but it was clear they would not win.

Aster crept forward, unsheathed one of the dead guards' swords, and slipped away before Xander could stop him. Sneaking up on the closest nomad, he struck the horse on the hindquarters. It squealed and bucked, its hips rising so suddenly that it tossed its rider onto the ground.

It was all Midas' men needed. While Aster finished off the fallen nomad with a swift strike to the neck, the nearest guard turned to battle the second warrior while his companion kept the first one busy. Two more guards soon joined them. After a fierce skirmish, another nomad was dead, the third fleeing the scene.

The guards ran back into the city, seeking more warriors to fight.

Aster ducked behind a wooden wagon beyond. When the way was clear, Xander joined him.

"They're so big!" he said.

"They do not work in teams," Aster said. "One not together with the other."

"You got all that from that?" Xander pointed to where the men had been fighting.

"The king did not task us to observe," Aster said. "I see you were paying attention."

"I was!"

Aster crept forward until he could see beyond the wagon. There were three more warriors up ahead, though this time they fought against two of Gordium's citizens as well as two guards. As Xander watched, he could see that Aster was right. The nomads worked together to split the group, then distracted them with strange calls and whistles, circling like wolves in a pack. Xander checked behind him, but could no longer see Gediz. When he looked forward again, Aster was gone.

"Aster!" he whispered.

Leaning out from the wagon, he spotted his friend with a flaming board in his hands, running headlong into a herd of scared sheep. Blatting and bleating, they were stampeding toward the city, two of the mounted nomads herding them from behind.

"Oh, for the love of the gods," Xander said. He soon found where the lead advisor had gotten his weapon. A small, wheeled cart lay smashed on the ground, the wood splintered and broken. Xander grabbed a long, jagged piece, lit it in the burning grass up ahead, and targeted the second warrior's approach. Waving and shouting, he tried to look threatening. Undeterred, the nomad thundered toward him with a glowering countenance the like Xander had never seen. It was as close as a living man could come to resembling a demon from the underworld, the face smeared with mud and the eyes wide and crazed.

"No!" Xander yelled at the oncoming sheep, waving his flaming board. "Go back. Go back!"

On his right, Aster did the same, but they were no match for the heavy mounted warriors and their frightening voices. Xander threw the burning piece of wood, whirled, and ran back toward the city. Sheep soon surrounded him, cloven hooves stabbing his feet. He flowed with the herd, moving toward the smoke and fire beyond.

"No," he whispered.

Up ahead, the nomads were slaughtering the sheep. They hacked and stabbed even as they continued to direct the animals into the flames. Blood sprayed all over the ground, white wool painted red. Frightened bleats slashed the air. Baby lambs cried for their mothers while running about in circles. Sheep ran into the city with their hides burning.

Xander stumbled and fell onto his bottom. He was shaking, his feet covered in hoof-shaped bruises. He spotted one little lamb running west. A nomad chased it down and, leaning low on his horse, slaughtered it. The man uttered a series of celebratory shouts, thrusting his ax into the air. Other nomads answered his zealous cries. Horses' hooves rumbled the ground, smoke mixing with thick dust. For a long while, Xander didn't move.

Gradually, the sound of hoofbeats receded, the warrior calls growing less frequent. Aster's face appeared out of the gray.

"Are you not all right?"

Xander shook his head. "They're killing them. All of them. For no reason." Tears flowed down his cheeks. "The sheep didn't do anything."

Aster grasped his arm and pulled him over the abandoned carcasses. "They are not food," he said. "Without food, a city does not grow weak. It is not an effective tactic. Come."

Aster led them east until they came to a small mud dwelling that had escaped the fires. Behind it, three pigs huddled together under a leaning shelter, their pebble eyes peering out from under long eyelashes.

"Is it slowing down?" Xander asked.

"They do not seem to be nearly finished," Aster said.

"Finished? With what?"

"What they did not come to accomplish."

"Which was?" Xander stared at his friend in disbelief.

"To make the citizens feel safe and secure."

Xander wiped his forehead with the back of his hand, then looked down to see his palms covered in blood. He cleaned them as best he could on the ground. Smoke saturated the air, but beyond, the crops were untouched. He let his gaze roam over the golden stalks of wheat and the green leaves of the peas and beans. Never had they needed barricades around the fields, nor a stone wall on the south side of the city. For the first time in his life, Xander realized the home he loved was not as invincible as he thought.

"Dare we try to go back?" he asked.

"We may not discover more if we go now."

Xander didn't wish to encounter another warrior, but Aster was right. It was their mission to observe. He fell in line behind his friend as they made their way north. Sheep carcasses obstructed the road, now and then accompanied by the dead body of a man or woman. Xander nearly vomited twice. He glanced back. "We lost Gediz," he said.

"A tragedy."

"I miss Fotis."

Aster uttered a short hum in the back of his throat.

They returned to the castle unscathed and were climbing up the stairs when Xander stopped. "Katiah's tomb," he said. "We were supposed to check it."

"We have little information to give the king," Aster said. He paused inside the entrance, searching for a guard, but there was none. "He must not be up there," he said, pointing to the ceiling.

Xander groaned. King Midas liked to watch over the city from the turret, which was many steps up. "Are you sure he wants to be disturbed?"

"You would not prefer to take a nap first?" Aster asked.

"All right, all right." Xander rolled his eyes and followed. As they climbed to the second level, then the third, his melancholy returned, the image of the bleating and dying sheep one he couldn't get out of his mind. Worse were the two little children crying over their dead father in the alleyway near a hut burned to ashes. By the time they reached the narrow stairs to the turret, he was panting and dizzy. He pushed on, pausing only when he saw Aster's back in front of him.

Beyond, the king stood looking out the window, his hands resting on his belt. Xander gazed at him with weary eyes. The pair waited for the king to invite them in. Then, a brilliant light descended from the heavens, cleaving the king in two.

"Oh!"

Xander blinked and looked again. The king's body glowed as if possessed by the sun, the ground seeming to erupt underneath him. Xander brace himself against the wall, but the rock was still. He heard a sizzling sound, accompanied by the rumble of oncoming horses' hooves. When he looked up again, the castle was crumbling, fire erupting at its edges. From the clouds beyond, four Gimirri warriors emerged atop phantom horses, thundering toward them like the fiercest of storms.

"No!" Xander exclaimed, and fainted straight away.

CHAPTER

FIVE

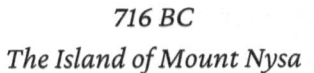

716 BC

The Island of Mount Nysa

The second morning of her captivity, Little Bird searched for any escape routes she might have missed. When she found none, she returned to the barrier to look out. She knew the largest space between the ropelike vines. It was on the right side, near the cave wall, a square about the width of her forearm and level with her knees. It was as if the vines had granted her a small window, but no more, fearing she would attempt to wriggle through. Beyond, the road dropped off about ten steps from the cave entrance, its descent hidden from her. On either side of it grew tall ferns and windblown elms that blocked the view, interspersed with proud pines, their branches retreating in deference to the ocean breezes.

Denisia had left a waterskin. Little Bird took a drink, then replaced it on the tree stump. She walked along the rock wall, studying the bugs in the stone crevices—black beetles and centipedes and little brown flies. The boulders at the back of the cave were more defined in the morning light, but she found nothing between them, not even an air gap. She tried climbing them twice, but they had been tightly compressed when they'd fallen, as if a giant had slammed them down with his fist and then pressed again to be sure they were well stacked. There weren't enough footholds to get very far.

During her exploration, she found a flat rock with a sharp edge. It was like the one Princess Zoe had given her at the castle only a few moons ago so she could draw on a slate, the only way she and the princess had been able to communicate. Little Bird used it to make her first two marks on a far-right boulder. Here, she would keep track of her captivity. Every time she made a mark, she would picture Princess Zoe's face. One day, she would get back to her, King Midas, and Elanur. Poor Elanur!

She tucked the drawing rock under the boulder and returned to the front of the cave. To the right stood one tree that was different. Its trunk emerged from a crack in the rock itself, curving up toward the sky, large, triangular leaves the color of moss. This was the tree Denisia had used to secure her horse. Little Bird reached out, but it was too far away to touch. She was trying again, stretching her fingers, when she heard the soft thud of hoofbeats.

Her captor.

She stepped back and waited, nerves on edge. Soon, she could see the goddess approaching. She wore a cream-colored linen dress and carried a bag in her hand. Full of food, Little Bird hoped. She took another step back, anxiously clutching at her dress.

"Hello." Denisia tied her horse to the same rock tree, approached the barrier, melded into it and appeared on the other side. It was an unnerving thing to watch, the way the branches and stems disappeared into her body and reappeared again behind her.

"I found fresh berries today," she said, lifting the bag.

Little Bird bowed her head until her captor set the bag on the tree stump.

"I'm later than planned," Denisia said. "It was a difficult day."

Little Bird glanced up with her most innocent, curious face.

"My grandfather," Denisia continued. "He's . . . not well." She clasped her hands together in front of her and looked around. "It's tiring to talk this way. We need chairs. I'll have to bring some. Maybe a mattress too. Would you like that?"

Little Bird forced a smile onto her lips, though she didn't relish the idea of having to stay long enough to need a mattress.

Denisia pulled a small leather pouch from her inside pocket. "What we talked about yesterday. Your secret. It's time to root it out." She withdrew a cup from the same pocket, set it on the tree stump and poured water into it. Next, using a smooth, sticklike piece of wood, she mixed in the contents of the pouch—what looked like a greenish-brown, lumpy powder. "Drink this."

Little bird took the cup, sniffed, and scowled.

Denisia's face hardened. "Drink it now, or go without your meal."

Little Bird glanced at the bag on the stump, back at the cup, then into Denisia's stern face. Moments passed. She was trapped. There was no escape, and the goddess was her only source of food. She looked into the cup again and grimaced.

"Very well." Denisia snatched the bag and headed out.

Little Bird grabbed the cup and swallowed the concoction, grimacing as it bumped down her throat. When Denisia glanced back, Little Bird showed her the empty cup. Denisia lifted her chin, replaced the bag of food, and directed Little Bird to sit on the ground across from her. With the same stick she had used to mix the concoction, she drew a strange pattern in the dirt and began chanting. It reminded Little Bird of the goddess's words at the Battle of Karama. Was Denisia going to open another chasm? She tensed, ready to flee at the first sign of trembling, but the rock remained solid. Her vision, however, blurred. Her head, too, felt lighter, as if it were floating above her neck. Then she heard something, or thought she did. A faint sound, like it was coming from inside the boulders at the back of the cave.

Little Bird! A female voice.

Little Bird blinked. She was standing on a pathway in a forest, the dirt covered in rich red wood shavings. The voice came from up ahead. She could hear it more clearly now, but couldn't identify who it belonged to. She ran up the path and sensed another presence beside her.

"What do you see?"

Little Bird jumped. The goddess came back into view.

"Tell me! What do you see?"

A raven had been flying alongside her, a bird with the most startling blue eyes.

"Speak, child!" Denisia said.

Little Bird signed. *Trees. Path.* When Denisia didn't understand, she drew them in the dirt.

"A path in a forest?" When Little Bird nodded, Denisia said, "What else?"

Little Bird pointed to her ear.

"You heard something?"

Little Bird nodded and signed her name.

"Someone was calling you?"

Little Bird nodded.

"Was it her? Was it Katiah?"

Katiah? Little Bird frowned. Why would the dark goddess be calling her name? She shook her head. *I don't know,* she signed.

Denisia sighed, tucked the cup back into her pocket, and stood up. "At least the spell worked."

The spell?

"Next time, I'll bring something stronger, something that will take you more deeply into your memories." She turned to leave. "Eat your meal. I'll be back tomorrow and we'll try again."

Little Bird stood up, swaying, and eyed the bag on the stump.

The goddess made it to the barrier before she paused. "You must concentrate and tell me everything you see and hear. If you try to hide something, I'll know. Do you understand?"

Little Bird nodded, all the while thinking of the raven.

Denisia rode away. Little Bird stumbled over to the tree stump and dove into the food pouch. She found raisins, two slices of bread, some cheese, a handful of berries, and five dried strips of lamb. She conserved only two of the meat strips.

Her head clearing, she rested against the back boulder and gazed at the barrier. Her vision was still blurry, her head spinning from Denisia's distasteful mixture. Suddenly, the vision she'd had the night before flashed in her mind again. Inflamed human faces entreated her, claws reaching out to touch her skirt. She shuddered, clenched her eyes shut, and brought to mind the song Emir had sung on their journey from Durukin to Gordium. It was a merry tune, one he had said reminded him of his mother. Over the many days they'd traveled, Little Bird had learned it too. She could only mouth the words, but she imagined Emir's rich voice coming from her own throat.

Little girl, little girl, where do you go,
Tripping along in your skirt just so?
The creek wants to know if you'll follow it there
Down the hill to the river and on if you dare
To the wild lands green where the horses will run
And the long desert roads beaten brown by the sun.

CHAPTER

SIX

Somewhere in the deep, dark underworld

Emir Alkan opened his eyes to darkness as black as the deepest night. He blinked, trying to clear his vision, but nothing changed. He rolled onto his side. A powerful pain stabbed his chest. He touched his shirt, but there was no sticky wetness, no blood. The air around him felt cold and damp, the sound of a hollow wind whispering past his ears. He rose and walked a few steps to his right, then several more to his left. Nothing impeded him.

"Hello? Is anyone there?"

The words fell dead at his feet. He chose right again and walked, one hand out. After ten steps, his fingers touched a rock wall. It extended as far as he could reach above him and all the way to the floor. He turned and moved again, finding the same thing on the other side. A tunnel, it seemed. The boy had led him through a tunnel on their way out of the city of Durukin.

"Boy, are you there?"

No answer. He returned to the opposite wall and, dragging his right hand alongside it, started walking. The boy had accompanied him to the city of Gordium. He remembered playing the oud and a crowd of people applauding. King Midas was there. He had proclaimed Emir the winner. Emir had slept on a mattress in a comfortable room filled with wine barrels. The boy had been there too. But then something had happened. A fight with . . . had it been wolves? Emir touched the back of his neck, but the skin was smooth, unscarred. The king had nearly died, but for the water Emir brought him. But the princess . . . something had happened to the princess. Memories passed through his mind in blips, there and then gone.

He walked for what felt like half a day. There was no light and only the hollow sound of air against rock. Other memories returned. His journey with Katiah and the golden sculpture of the princess. His fight with Baris Olgun. Witnessing the two armies coming together at the Battle of Karama. His mother riding at King Sargon II's side. He had planned to save her, to get her away from Sargon somehow. He was trying to recall what happened next when a sound caught his attention.

A scuff in the dirt.

"Who's there?" a man said.

Emir's hand went to the hilt of his sword.

"Speak!"

It was a commanding voice, familiar. "Prince Anchurus?" Emir said.

A pause. "Alkan?"

"Yes!" A swell of relief passed over Emir's body.

"Where are we?" Anchurus asked.

"I don't know." Emir looked around, but he couldn't see Anchurus. "Your Highness," he added.

"The king? The princess?"

"I don't know." Emir took a few steps toward the voice. "We must be in a tunnel of some sort. A dungeon?"

"I don't remember being captured."

Emir wanted to touch him, grasp his arm, prove to himself that the prince was real. "I woke up back there." He pointed, then realized the silliness of that. "About a half a day's journey."

"I woke up here."

"How long ago?"

"Not long." He waited a beat. "You said you came from that direction?"

"From behind us." Emir turned and stared into the dark. "Well . . ."

"There has to be a way out of here," Anchurus said.

"I'll follow you."

The two men started again, both hovering close to the wall, one behind the other, Emir's mind racing. How had he gotten here and why was Prince Anchurus, of all people, here with him?

CHAPTER

SEVEN

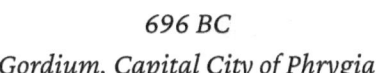

696 BC
Gordium, Capital City of Phrygia

The morning after the attack, King Midas' three advisors left the castle once more. This time, they didn't venture into the city. Guards and citizens alike were cleaning up the carnage. Families retrieved their loved ones for burial beyond the north wall. The dead animals they dragged to the south side, having already salvaged all the meat they could. The rest of the carcasses had to be hauled out the east gates and on to a clearing where the citizens could burn them without fear of the fire spreading to the crop fields. It was hot, dusty, stomach-churning work, and Xander was glad not to be anywhere near it. Instead, they were off to complete the second task the king had given them: checking on Kati-ah's tomb.

For twenty years, the dark goddess of the underworld had been trapped underground. Her resting place had been created for a member of the royal family, having been dug deep into the base of one of the northwestern hills. But when King Midas killed her—or at least incapacitated her with his golden sword at the great Battle of Karama—he had ordered the tomb repurposed. Workers dug even deeper and laid great slabs of stone onto the floor, reinforcing both the base and the walls to ensure no force, mortal or divine, could break through. It was the most secure space they had, so there the goddess went. Since then, Midas had built new tombs for the royal family directly north and northeast of the castle, creating a wide perimeter around the goddess.

Xander walked behind Aster as usual, the three advisors forming a line as they traveled out of the castle grounds, past the abandoned soldiers' quarters and horse pastures, along the wall to the west gates, then back on the narrow road at the base of the western hills. It would have been quicker to have traveled through the secret underground tunnel to the north side of the castle, but that was forbidden, except under the direst emergencies, to avoid the risk of being seen emerging from the hidden hole in the ground.

To the north, wild grasses shimmied, evergreen bushes tickling the earth like whiskers. Now and then, Xander cast a glance back toward the city. Gratefully, they were too far out to see any details of the cleanup, save the smoke from the carcass fire burning east of the great wall. It towered high, its snaking trail black and menacing, the scent of charred meat fouling the air.

"Why are we walking all this way?" Gediz complained. "Surely the king would offer his advisors a wagon, or at least some horses?"

"The king thinks only of his advisors' comfort," Aster said.

"No king expects his trusted advisors to trudge for hours on foot," Gediz said. "Did you request a wagon?"

"Our thoughts are ever focused on your convenience," Aster said.

"Best leave it alone." Xander glanced behind him. Gediz looked sweaty and disheveled, his cream-colored cloak mussed with dust.

"I don't see why this is necessary. The dark goddess is in a tomb. You don't have to *check* a tomb. Dead is dead. This is a poor use of a king's resources, I say."

"Your opinion is most appreciated," Aster said.

"This is the dark goddess we're talking about," Xander said. "The king is wise to use caution."

"She's been trapped for what, twenty years?" Gediz said. "If she was going to get out, she would have by now."

"There have been rumors of rumbles as of late," Xander said.

"Rumbles?" Gediz asked.

"In the earth. Tremors."

"So the ground rumbles now and then. What does that have to do with a dead goddess? In a tomb?"

"Your intellect is astounding," Aster said. "I am humbled in your presence."

Gediz grumbled.

Xander walked on, hoping Gediz would let it drop. Aster was irritated enough. He didn't need the little troll making it worse.

"There must be a way to get her out," Gediz continued in his bleating voice. "Otherwise, there would be no reason for your concern."

"Hopefully not," Xander said. "We did put a spell on it."

"A spell?"

Aster glared over his shoulder.

"A little magic," Xander stammered, remembering that Aster didn't trust the third advisor with detailed information.

"What sort of magic?" Gediz asked. "Could anyone, you know, break it?"

Xander glanced up the road. They were getting closer. "It's meant to be unbreakable," he said.

"What sort of spell was it? A . . . what do you call them . . . enchantment? Or divination?"

Xander jogged to catch up with Aster.

"You are much too secretive," Aster said.

"I wasn't thinking," Xander muttered. "But he *is* an advisor. From King Kandaules?"

"So the messenger did not say," Aster murmured.

Xander looked back, but Gediz had fallen behind. "Would a messenger lie?" he said in a low voice.

"It is beyond the realm of possibilities."

"I'll be more careful," Xander said, "but he won't be able to find the tomb again anyway, if he should ever try without us. The spell will take care of that."

Aster nodded his acknowledgment and let Xander take the lead. As the one who had cast the spell in the first place, he was the only one it didn't affect. They approached the turn where the road angled northeast, beginning its long trek to the mountains and the sea. Xander left it behind and headed toward the heart of the tallest hill west of the castle. Here there was a slight incline, the ground rising to meet them as they climbed. His breath came more quickly, perspiration breaking out on his forehead. He'd been traveling this way for years, but it took more effort now. He felt the stiffness in his knees most of all.

"Hey!" Gediz called. "Slow down!"

Xander turned to see the third advisor had left the path and was trying to catch up over open ground.

"Watch out!" Xander called. "There are cacti!"

"I can't hear you!" Gediz called.

"Of all the . . ." Aster began. "A king's advisor . . ." He stopped in exasperation and stared back at the little man. "The king must not dispense with him immediately!"

"The king is not in the best of shape to be approving a new advisor now," Xander said.

"But he is simply . . . acceptable!" Aster threw up his hands. "We have no challenges right now. We do not need wise men. He must not be replaced!" Aster took Xander by the shoulders. "Your vision does not ring true?"

Xander looked into worried brown eyes, flashes of the vision from the day before invading his mind. The king, fallen in a burning castle, the Gimirri thundering toward him. "I'm afraid it's much like they usually are," he said.

Aster turned away, his hands coming to his cheeks. "There must not be something we can do."

Xander continued up the path. "We will figure it out. Come. Let's finish this task."

"We do not have to warn the king about your vision."

"As you said, he has enough on his mind."

"The king must not be warned. He must not prepare."

"I don't know," Xander said. "He is already haunted enough."

"Haunted?" Aster asked.

Xander slowed as the ground leveled off, the surrounding brush fresher than the rest of the vegetation, even after all these years. There was no mound or marker of any kind. The king had wanted the tomb to remain hidden, particularly from Katiah's loyal followers. Xander searched for the entrance. He knew it was in the space where the wild grasses didn't grow. Something to do with the dark goddess' presence beneath it, he surmised.

There—he spotted the rectangular-shaped dead spot. He withdrew the brush from his pocket and swept the dirt aside. Aster used his hands to help, and soon the two had cleared the slab of limestone. Aster set it aside and they cleared off more dirt to reveal a much larger plank of wood. With effort, they lifted that too, revealing a hole in the ground and a set of descending mudbrick stairs. At their base, a heavy wooden gate blocked access to a stone wall. Xander pulled a key from his pocket and started down the steps.

"The king's night disturbances," Aster said, following him. "You do not expect something besides age?"

"His pain seems closer than ever." Xander slid the key into the notch on the gate. A single lift and the bolt released. He pulled it open and turned to Aster. "Perhaps you can convince him to allow one of us to stay with him overnight?"

But his friend wasn't looking at him. Aster's face had fallen, his mouth open as he stared past Xander's head.

Xander looked at the wall behind the gate. "Oh no," he said, for there in the stone, stretching from the upper right corner to the lower left, was a long, dark, sinister crack.

"Rumbles, eh?" Gediz said.

They both whirled to see him peering down from the top of the stairs, a satisfied smile on his face. He gestured toward the fracture. "Doesn't look like your spell is helping much."

Zoe left the castle early to go into the city. It was a somber, smoky morning, Gordium more subdued than she could ever remember seeing it. Gone were the children who usually played outside their dwellings, their mothers instead keeping them close inside. No men gathered by the roadside to chat. Here or there she spotted someone, but they were always busy about some unsavory task, such as fixing a broken-down animal shelter or cleaning blood off the stones.

A bucket of fresh water in her hand, she followed the main road until she came to the intersection at Market Street. No traders had set up their tables on this day. The inn on the south side looked quiet and empty. To the east, the great carcass fire burned, belching black smoke into the sky. She turned left and started up the road, pausing where the first table usually stood. Men trudged by her, their faces streaked with dust, their eyes red from the ever-present haze. Most carried carts with dead sheep in them, some with dead pigs and goats, the flesh ruined by flies and other insects, the meat bruised and punctured by the warriors' weapons. A few hauled dead men, women, and even a couple of children out to the burial grounds beyond the north wall, families treading in single-file lines with their gazes down into the dirt.

Zoe spotted Commander Baran standing near the gates and made her way toward him.

"This is no place for a princess," he said as she approached. "You should return to the castle, Your Highness."

"You must be thirsty." Zoe set her bucket down and handed him a ladle full of water.

He took it gratefully, his face stained with sweat and ash. "The king has many servants to carry water."

"Look around you, Commander," she said. "The city has suffered a terrible blow. We must rally the people. Help them believe their king will protect them. Even the most loyal of citizens have had their faith shaken by this." She paused as another family walked by, this one with no wagon or cart. Instead, four young men were carrying a dead man between them, three women and six children following behind, the women clutching flowers. Many of them bowed when they saw Zoe.

"There is talk of abandoning the city," Zoe said, "with some seeking to move west to Lydia." Four castle guards approached with a wagon full of dead sheep. Zoe gave them all water, then motioned them onward. When they passed, she rejoined Baran.

"King Kandaules is no King Midas," he said, continuing their conversation. "Word of his depravity spreads far and wide. Any citizen who chooses him over our leader is a fool."

"Nevertheless, there have been no attacks on his capital city of Sardis."

"Not yet." Baran nodded to some of the guards as they moved through the gate. "Besides, if you had the choice between Gordium and Sardis, which would you choose?" When Zoe said nothing, Baran added, "The citizens are loyal. They will survive this." He bowed to the princess and then turned to follow the last wagon out.

Zoe watched the commander join the crowd at the fire beyond. The scent of scorched wool and blood filled the air, dust settling in her throat. They burned on the far side of the river, using it as a boundary to keep the city safe from any straying embers. She waited for a while, allowing her gaze to blur over the rising smoke, then turned and walked back, passing more mourning families on the way. Many bowed low when they realized who she was, some breaking out in tears and dropping to their knees to touch her skirt. She patted their hands and offered assurances, but by the time her water had run out, she was near tears herself. This had to stop.

Setting a determined gaze on the castle on the hill, she took a moment to regain her composure, then started for home.

CHAPTER

EIGHT

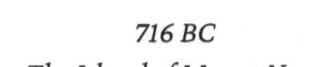

716 BC
The Island of Mount Nysa

After the spell that included the distasteful concoction, Denisia didn't return to the cave for many days. A girl named Cemile brought Little Bird her daily meal. She had a stout build with thick brown hair, pudgy cheeks, and hazel eyes, and appeared to be fourteen or fifteen years old. During her first few visits, she stared at Little Bird as if she were a wild animal. It wasn't long, though, before she was smiling as she passed food through the barrier. When she'd finished, she would wipe her hands on her sand-colored dress, wave, and leave.

Little Bird tried to keep herself busy, but her days became lingering experiences in solitude. She wondered what was keeping the goddess, particularly when she'd seemed so intent on discovering whatever secret she thought Little Bird held. As the marks piled up on the boulder in the back of the cave—twenty, thirty, then forty—she despaired at her prolonged captivity. During those times, it was better to think about anything else but the marks on the stone.

And then he came with two chairs.

She heard him before she saw him. Highly attuned to sound, she'd already adapted to the whistles, rustling, and drips in the cave. The wind moaned in distinct tones, depending on where she was standing. The beetles and other bugs clicked when they walked across the rock at night. So it was that when she heard footsteps on the path, even when they were still a good distance away, she sensed it immediately. It was as if the air changed direction. She turned toward the entrance. It was too early in the day for the goddess and the gait too relaxed for Cemile. The footsteps came closer, the sound of soft moccasins on dirt like huffing breath.

The first thing she saw was his hair. Thick and wavy, it sat like a fur rug on his head. She giggled at the thought, but then the rest of him came into view and she grew serious again. He moved with an angular sort of grace, his long legs striding confidently forward. Tall and athletic for a boy of about twelve, he carried one chair in each hand, holding them out from the sides of his body as if they weighed near nothing. When he spotted her, he smiled. It sent a shock through her, as if a beam of light had shined in her eyes. He had a golden-brown tan, full eyebrows high on a heart-shaped face, and a thick nose bridge between his cheekbones. She wanted to smile in return, but it was so surprising to see this boy coming toward her with such a friendly expression that all she could do was stand and gape.

"Hello," he said as he got closer. His voice was lower than she'd expected. "Goddess Denisia commanded me to bring these." He set the chairs down just outside the barrier and stood back. "I guess you need them to sit on?"

Little Bird managed a nod. She wondered what the goddess had told this boy about her. Surely he must think it strange to have a girl trapped in a cave?

He let his gaze trace the breadth of the barrier. His smile faded.

He rested his hands on his hips. He wore baggy trousers and a loose linen shirt with a brown hide jacket. The day was cool so far. Little Bird had her blanket over her shoulders. He glanced at her again. "My name's Verin."

It was one of the many times Little Bird would curse her inability to speak. She moved as close to the barrier as she could, pushed her hands through two openings that were big enough, and signed her name. *Little.* She tucked her hands as if over a small stone. *Bird.* She formed her fingers into wings and flapped them.

The boy watched. "Little Bird?" he said.

A smile broke out on Little Bird's face. No one ever got it right the first time.

"Little Bird. Yes. The goddess Denisia told me you wouldn't speak to me. But there's more than one way to speak, isn't there?"

Yes! She showed him again. *Little. Bird.* He copied her correctly. She nodded and withdrew her hands.

"How do you say chair?"

Deep brown eyes. Long dark eyelashes. It was easy to get lost in them. Little Bird demonstrated. One hand flat. The other bent at the knuckles.

"Well, Little Bird." He signed her name. "I just brought you some chairs." He signed chairs.

Little Bird made her sign for thank you, both hands pressed palm to palm.

"Is that 'thank you?'" When she nodded, he said, "How do I say 'you're welcome'?"

She showed him: open palm over one's heart, then extended in an arc toward the other person.

"You're welcome," he said while signing. "This is fun. I've never learned a new language before."

Little Bird had never thought of it that way. Languages people understood. No one understood her way of communicating except Emir, and he was gone. The kind King Midas had learned a few words. No one else had ever tried. They'd just looked at her like she was strange. But this boy. *Verin*. She thought for a moment, then pointed at him. Once she had his attention, she formed her hands into a "V" shape, then clasped them both together and brought them into her chest.

"V-in," he said. "Verin?" When she nodded, he smiled. He signed it again. "Verin. Well, Little Bird"—he signed it—"I'm happy to have brought you some chairs." Signed. "Thank you"—signed again—"for the chat. I have to go back now, but if Denisia wants something else brought to you, I'll be the first to volunteer."

Thank you, Little Bird signed. She didn't want him to go. When he turned his back and walked away, she felt the sting of tears in her eyes. She shook them away. Silly. She'd just met him! She clenched her jaw tight until the rug of wavy hair was gone, but she couldn't tear her gaze from the path until the sun rose high in the sky.

A FEW DAYS after Verin's first visit, Little Bird was playing with her collection of stones when she heard hoofbeats. She'd gathered over forty small rocks together, trapping them in a hole she'd dug at the back of the cave. They were all different sizes, many dark gray or black, but she'd found a few lighter gray ones and even one with a bluish-gray shade that, so far, was her favorite. When the hair stood up on the back of her neck, indicating the goddess' approach, she shoved them back into the hole and covered them with a thin layer of dirt. Then she stood up, slapped the dust off her hands and dress, smoothed her hair with her fingers, and approached the barrier. Cemile hadn't come that morning. Little Bird wanted nothing more than food, but she was certain Denisia would demand something from her first.

Riding up the path, Denisia appeared slumped and tired. Her head was down, her auburn hair done up in its customary bun, though several strands had come loose to dangle about like stray twigs. She was an elm tree having been blown about in a storm, weathered and weary. At the cave's edge, she dismounted, melted through the vines, then glanced at the tree stump.

"Oh no. I forgot your dinner."

Little Bird deflated, her stomach a hollow. Not another whole day without food!

The goddess pressed her fingers to her temple. "This is so hard. I should just let you go."

Yes, let me go, Little Bird thought. *Please.*

Denisia turned away, clutching her arms about her. "Trying to find the goddess and take care of *him* at the same time that I'm taking care of you."

Taking care of? Is that how her captor saw it?

"The good news is, I now know where Midas is keeping Katiah. I have spies everywhere, you know." She raised an eyebrow at Little Bird, as if in warning. "It's not far from the castle. Unfortunately, it didn't help much. She is encased in a stone tomb. They even lined the floor with it, so I can't get through." She heaved a heavy sigh. "It seems King Midas took every precaution."

Good, Little Bird thought. King Midas was wise.

Denisia ran her hands through her hair, grasping the bun on the way to undo it. Long auburn locks fell onto her shoulders. Little Bird recognized her opportunity. She walked over and, reaching as high as she could, smoothed the hair back. Using her fingers as a comb, she worked her way gently through the ends of the strands, carefully separating them until they laid more evenly along the goddess' back. She finished and stepped away.

Denisia cranked her head around. Her eyes were a lighter brown than Verin's, but they held a soft emotion. "You're a kind child, aren't you?" For a moment, she looked vulnerable. Even frightened. Then the hardness returned. She crossed to the right side of the cave, reached through the barrier and pulled the chairs in, setting one across from the other. "Please." She gestured. "Sit down."

Little Bird obeyed. Dried stems, interwoven and stretched over the wooden frame, formed the seat. She drew her legs up into a cross-legged position.

Denisia sat opposite her, then leaned forward and gazed into Little Bird's eyes. "All right. We're going to try again." She reached into her pocket and pulled out a pouch.

Little Bird groaned inwardly, her stomach clenching in hunger. She drank the concoction, and when the goddess started chanting, closed her eyes and drifted off into another dream world.

Many moons later, during the cold season on the Island of Mount Nysa

LITTLE BIRD WAS LAUGHING. It was sunny out and she was in the middle of a meadow filled with yellow and white flowers. Her cow, Tubba, a gentle red and black animal with a shiny hide, grazed happily nearby. Little Bird had milked her earlier that morning, but now it was afternoon and she was jumping rope. It magically twirled on its own, arching over her head and slipping easily underneath her feet. She made it to forty-three jumps before she tripped. The rope fell. Little Bird leaned over to catch her breath.

"Not bad," a woman said. "But your record is fifty-one."

Little Bird knew what her record was. She didn't need reminding. She looked out over the meadow, her gaze drifting toward the afternoon sky. Over there lay the Red River and her path to escape.

"That's all you can tell me?" Denisia said, intruding upon the dream.

Little Bird blinked. She was back in the cave. Her heart fell. The meadow had been so pretty, the sun warm on her face.

"Well?" Denisia asked.

Little Bird pointed her index fingers at each other and then pulled her hands apart, ending with a twirling motion to show the rope moving.

"Yes, yes, you were jumping with the rope." Denisia was getting better at understanding Little Bird's signs. "And you were in a meadow with grass. And a . . . what? A horse?"

Little Bird made the motions for milking a cow.

"A cow. Yes. Is that all?"

Little Bird put her hand by her mouth and flapped her fingers.

"Someone was speaking? The same woman from before?"

Little Bird had heard a voice several times now. The first time, calling her name. Another time, it had been humming a tune. This time, the voice had been more subdued. Was it the same voice? She shrugged.

Denisia stood by the barrier. Rain fell gently outside the cave, soaking the edges of the rock. They'd spent many moons together going into Little Bird's dreams, the goddess casting spells using concoctions, fragrances, and chants, sometimes drawing symbols in the dirt or using rocks to mark out a space into which Little Bird had to stand, sit, or lie down. Little Bird found herself in different places in the dreams, sometimes in the forest, other times in the meadow, and occasionally in a wooden cabin. Once she walked alongside the Red River, searching for something, though she didn't know what. She played with her animals, her cow and pony and sometimes, the black raven. She never told the goddess about him. It seemed best not to.

She pointed to the dead flowers Denisia had set on the ground near the entrance.

"You want to try again?" the goddess said.

Little Bird nodded eagerly. She didn't understand where the dreams were coming from or how Denisia was bringing them about, but they were preferable to being in the cave alone with her captor.

"Very well," Denisia said. "Sit down."

Little Bird settled herself on the chair once more. The goddess chanted three strange words, made swirling motions over the flow-ers, then wafted perfumed oil under Little Bird's nose. The scent was heady, one that made her feel dizzy. Picturing the meadow in her mind, she listened for the woman's voice. *Please let me go back,* she thought to herself.

The goddess' chants dimmed in her ears. Behind her eyes, darkness deepened. Sticks crackled under her feet. In the distance, a wolf howled. She touched something rough, a tall cedar tree, her palm against the reddish-brown bark of the trunk. It had to be dusk. Gray and muted blue colored everything in shadow. The wolf howled again, closer this time. She wasn't afraid of it, but she didn't want it to find her. She hurried to the next tree and the next, flitting between them like an owl. After a time, the sound of the rushing Red River reached her ears. The wolf was gaining ground. If it found her, it would not harm her. But she didn't want to be found.

After a brief run, she reached the river's edge. The view was limited beyond the bank, but she knew this river. A deep red color, it competed with the shades of the sunset, as if to see which could carve the most striking line from east to west. Fast and wide, it was the only river that traveled from the depths of the forest to . . . where? All she cared was that it flowed the direction she wanted to go, which was away from here. She jogged upstream and down, trying to find where she had tied her wooden boat. Kartal would be here soon. The name came to her suddenly. The swiftest of the three wolves, he would find her first and she would be punished for sneaking out.

She hurried back upstream. The boat had to be there. But it was getting dark. When her chest burned with breath, she spotted it. There! She traced the rope with her hands to the tree, loosened the knot, and pushed the boat into the water.

"What have I told you about that?" a feminine voice said.

"Stop!" Denisia shouted.

Little Bird jumped. The dream vanished.

"She spoke to you again, didn't she?"

Little Bird slumped forward in her chair.

"No, no, no." Denisia clapped her hands until Little Bird looked up. "Tell me what you saw."

Little Bird made the sign for a river and a forest. She explained it was dark, and she'd been running.

"But someone spoke to you," Denisia said. "I almost . . . heard it. Who was it?"

Little Bird shook her head.

"The same as before?"

Little Bird tried to remember. The tone of the woman's voice had been different again. It wasn't yelling, nor was it exacting. It sounded more . . . what was it? There had been a tremor in it—only a slight one, but enough to make it echo a little.

"Well?" Denisia asked.

Little Bird shrugged. How could she be sure?

Denisia threw up her hands. "You are hopeless! Surely you can tell if a voice sounds the same or not?"

Little Bird shrank from her.

"Was it the dark goddess? Was it her?"

Little Bird stared at her captor's face. Her fair skin was damp, her cheeks red. Water droplets clung to the strands of her hair that had escaped her bun. Wide hazel eyes glared at her.

"Answer me!"

Little Bird thought of the dark goddess, and how she'd killed Emir. She remembered storming toward her, wishing that she could scream at her, that she might, when she extended her hands, strike *her* with the fierce light and see how she liked it. But all she'd been able to do was throw a handful of dirt. Her thoughts whirled from that night to all her dreamworld experiences. Did she know the dark goddess? Had she known her before?

I don't know.

"You stupid child!" Denisia turned her back. "How long is this going to take? We get so close and then . . ." She clenched one fist in the air. "I know it's her. It's got to be her." She glanced at Little Bird. "The way she looked at you at the battle. I don't understand why you can't remember."

Outside, the rain fell more heavily. Little Bird wished it would

69

stop. The goddess didn't like getting wet. She would linger until it let up.

Denisia plopped into one of the chairs. Leaning her elbows on her knees, she pressed her fingers together. "I need you to reconnect with her, Little Bird. I have a feeling you're using these visions to escape."

Little Bird blinked innocently.

"She can't release Anchurus or Emir as long as she's buried in some tomb. Imagine Emir in the underworld, suffering. Who knows what's happening to him there? Don't you want to rescue him from his torment?"

Little Bird stared at her. Emir in torment?

"Surely you know something about the underworld?" When Little Bird didn't respond, Denisia continued. "It is not a nice place. Dark. Lonely. And there are evil creatures there. Creatures who do as they like with no one stopping them. Anchurus is down there, and so is Emir. It is where people go when they suffer a death that is . . . *wrong.*"

Little Bird stared at the goddess, her body suddenly cold.

Denisia approached her. "You have to try harder. Only she can help us rescue them. Do you see?"

The vision flashed in Little Bird's mind again, the horrific one with the red faces and long fingers reaching out to her, the mouths open in unheard screams. She squinted her eyes shut.

"We're trying again," Denisia said.

She started chanting. Soon came the perfume under Little Bird's nose. Her stomach twisted. She tried to imagine another pleasant dream, a green meadow or thick forest. She pressed one fist into the other palm, fighting to direct her mind. This time, she would control it. She focused on Emir's face, remembering when they'd stayed in King Midas' undercroft, when she'd lain near his warm body and slept the most peaceful sleep she could remember.

"Stop it!" Denisia shouted.

Little Bird jerked awake.

"You said you would cooperate!"

Little Bird blinked. *I am,* she signed.

"You're blocking it!"

Blocking it?

"Don't try to trick me. It won't work."

Little Bird stared at her, confused.

Denisia came nearer. "What did you see this time?"

Little Bird hesitated. It wouldn't make the goddess happy. But she had to tell her. *Nothing,* she signed, and Denisia slapped her across the face. The blow reverberated through her head, a startling array of white and dark lights bursting into rays before her eyes. She pressed her hand to her cheek.

Denisia grasped Little Bird's upper arm. "You think you can trick a goddess?"

Little Bird shook her head.

"I've warned you enough. You will either cooperate or you will starve up here!" She flung Little Bird away with such force that she fell out of the chair. Then she pulled her hood over her head, cast a last angry glare over her shoulder, and disappeared through the barrier.

Little Bird went without food for three days after that.

CHAPTER
NINE

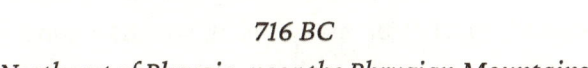

716 BC
Northeast of Phrygia, near the Phrygian Mountains

By the time the warm season had started to fade, Elanur had grown accustomed to life in the warrior's camp. She understood some of their language, at least enough to get by and to know that they called themselves the "Gimirri." She also knew what was expected of her on a daily basis and that she could manage these expectations. It was a simple existence, filled with regular routines involving the cleaning and storing of food, the making and repairing of clothing, and the addressing of various injuries and illnesses that came up, often in connection with the warriors' return to camp.

They never stayed for long. Seven days after she'd arrived, Ilker took fifteen men and left again. The women and children gathered at the south side to watch them go, the remaining men cheering the warriors on. Elanur was glad Draris was one of those leaving. Ilker took Khogu, the skinny one, too. The ones who were left were not to be feared. She had a position with Bri and her girls, which meant she was protected.

She had thought about trying to escape on her own, but she was never alone long enough to pack any supplies. One girl was always with her, which she was certain Bri had ordered on purpose. Elanur had no desire to embark on another arduous journey without being prepared. If the Gimirri hadn't seized her, she mused sometimes, she and Little Bird may have perished on the road to Gordium. Now, she worried the girl hadn't made it.

I should never have fallen asleep.

While the warriors were gone, it was a peaceful life for the women. They went dutifully about their daily chores and gathered at night around the central fire to eat and laugh and sometimes dance in worship of their gods. Elanur enjoyed the company of the girls as well. Goakina was generous in teaching her the ways of the camp. Hastet preferred to chatter away, as if she had long wished for someone to talk to. Elanur was delighted to discover the girl spoke the same language as she did—something Hastet kept hidden from the others. But whenever the two were alone, the girl would talk and talk, never exhausting herself. Elanur soon realized that Hastet had been stolen too, just as Elanur had been, and that Hastet and Goakina were not really sisters. They had been put together for Bri's benefit, to help the old woman carry out her healing duties to the camp.

Bri herself remained a mystery. Though Elanur had determined the older woman was a healer and that her skills gave her many privileges, she had discovered nothing about her past. Bri left Goakina to manage Elanur's duties and would only nod when she met Elanur in passing. Elanur often wished she could talk to her, but so far, that had proven impossible. After a time, it grew less important, for she realized that despite Bri's elevated position, the old woman would never help Elanur escape. For that, Elanur needed to find someone else.

Which led her to think about Ilker. She'd seen him watching her many times since she'd arrived, as if he had stolen her for a purpose other than helping Bri. She knew what desire looked like in a man's eyes, but she'd seen something in Ilker's that puzzled her, something that seemed like genuine curiosity. King Sargon II had only ever desired her for the thrill she provided him. Ilker was no different, she told herself, but Ilker *was* different, and captor or not, she couldn't help but be intrigued. She thought perhaps if she made him feel sympathetic toward her, he might allow her to return to her own world. It was a long shot, but the most powerful man in the camp was interested in her. All she had to do was find the courage to do something about it.

AFTER ANOTHER MOON cycle had come and gone and the air was starting to cool, the sounds of shouting awakened Elanur. She blinked her eyes open to see Goakina was already getting dressed. The older girl shook Hastet's shoulder and told her, "Come." Hastet groaned and pulled her blanket up over her face. Goakina shifted her gaze to Elanur in an unspoken order, then left.

Elanur dressed quickly, uncertain what all the shouting was about. Outside, the other tribe members gravitated toward the south edge of the camp. The warriors had returned, the men dismounting and handing their horses and stolen treasures to the boys. Elanur sought the source of the alarm, but noticed nothing out of place. It was still dark, with only the central fire burning, a few young men setting torches around it. They did the same when preparing for a camp meeting. Strange, to have a meeting now, in the middle of the night? She paused, unable to see where Goakina had gone. Bri was nowhere in sight, either, but everyone else was gathering in the central circle. Elanur hesitated to join them until Hastet, sleepy and mussy-haired, showed up at her side.

"They've brought children," she said in their shared language, gazing up at Elanur with dull, sleepy eyes. "Now the families must take care of them."

75

Children? Elanur thought.

Hastet took her hand and together, they walked to the fire. Spotting Goakina, they went to join her, only to find the older girl sitting next to Thom, one of the young men typically left behind to hunt for the tribe. A warning glance sent Elanur to another space a few steps away. There, they sat on the ground and waited. Two young warriors danced around the fire, now and then lifting their arms to the sky to ask for blessings from their gods.

Hastet continued to glance at her sister as the tribe collected around the fire. The women and young children, some still asleep, came first. Once the men finished unloading the treasures they'd brought back from their journey, they joined their families. Eventually the young boys came too, the horses grazing in the pasture beyond. Elanur hadn't seen Ilker. Usually, he was one of the first to enter the camp upon their return. Another sign that something strange was going on.

The buzz of human voices increased in volume as the men greeted their mates and children. Their chatter was so fast and mixed that Elanur understood only pieces of what they were saying. So many of the Gimirri words she still didn't know, but she caught those that meant "triumph," "power," and "weapons." They were bragging about the bounty they had stolen, certain it would help make the tribe stronger. Things had gone well for them, it seemed, so why the middle-of-the-night gathering?

Gradually, they all quieted until the space around the central fire became still. Elanur sensed a tight anticipation in the air. She looked behind her, but it was too dark to see anything. Everyone waited, all eyes focused on the flames.

"I hear them," Hastet whispered.

The girl was shaking. Elanur pulled her close. She was uncertain at first what Hastet was talking about. Then she heard a whimper, soft and pitiful. A call for "Mama." Someone was coming. Her shoulders tensed, her breath caught in her throat. As she gazed to the south, Ilker, Khogu, and Draris came into the light, ushering a group of small children before them, all three men holding infants too young to walk. One toddler, a girl with black wavy hair, was whimpering, but the rest were quiet, staring at the tribe with frightened eyes. The men herded them into a clump near the fire for all to see. There were ten total, counting the three infants in the men's arms.

"Babies this time," Hastet said under her breath.

Ilker began to talk, addressing all the tribal members. Holding tightly to the girl's hand, Elanur listened carefully. She gathered he was boasting about the goods they had secured for the people, and how the new children would add their youth and strength to the Gimirri. He turned this way and that to show off his prize, an infant with a pale face and smooth sandy hair that peered out of his blanket with tender eyes. At Ilker's urging, the other two men followed suit, showing off the babies as if they were items to trade at the market. The toddlers and young children huddled together nearby, the oldest of them maybe five, a frightened boy who held a younger girl in front of him, both hands on her shoulders. Elanur recalled her older brother, Karem, riding to save her as King Midas at the Battle of Karama. Her stomach twisted.

"Who will take them?" she asked Hastet.

"Whoever wants to," Hastet said. Gone was the sparkle in her personality. No longer did she study Goakina to see what she was doing with Thom. Instead, she stared at the children, her gaze numb.

The boy and his sister went first, taken by a middle-aged woman and her mate. They already had two children, but they were nearing adolescence. The mother gathered the toddler in her arms, while one of her older children took the orphan boy by the hand. Together, they disappeared into the dark, back to their tent and their new life. An older couple took the next oldest girl after that, then one of the younger couples, who already had a toddler, took another. One by one, members of the tribe stepped up to claim the stolen children.

Before long, all but one child had new parents. Ilker still held the sandy-haired baby in his arms. Elanur looked around the circle, but no one came forward. Instead, Ilker walked toward Elanur, his dark gaze intense. Elanur glanced behind her, but there was no one else there. Soon he was standing in front of her, and there could be no mistaking him. Elanur stood up and took a step back. Ilker pursued. She took another step back and shook her head. She would not be part of this. Ilker extended his arms. Elanur shook her head again, but couldn't help but glance down at the baby. Hazel eyes looked up into hers, the tear-stained face fragile in the night. Elanur paused, entranced. Emir had looked at her that way, so quietly, his eyes intent on hers. The baby extended a little hand toward her, tiny fingers grasping. Elanur glanced at Ilker. He had a kind expression on his face, his powerful arms holding the child out to her.

"No," she said. "It's not mine."

But he was giving the child to her, and soon there was nothing to do but take the infant from him lest the child fall into the space between them.

"He's not mine," she said again, but then she gazed down into the child's precious face, the little fingers wriggling until she slipped her thumb into them and they squeezed and Elanur's heart swelled. She again shook her head and tried to give the child back, but Ilker was smiling at her in a way she hadn't seen him smile before, his expression warm. Her mind rebelled. This wasn't right. This was someone else's child. But at that moment, the baby was a helpless infant in her arms and as she held him, it was as if her arms had been aching for him for years. Now, with the weight of his little body against hers, something in her stopped bleeding.

"I have nowhere to take him," she told Ilker.

He gestured for her to walk forward. She complied. As they passed the central fire, she noticed the rest of the tribe had gone, even Hastet. A new guilt crawled around her heart at the thought of the girl. She had been stolen too, much like this little boy in Elanur's arms. It wasn't right. She should stop. But it was as if her feet had a will of their own because she was walking with Ilker across the camp, headed toward his tent. That's what this was about. He would take her as his mate, and they would raise the child together. He had worked it all out, apparently, perhaps from the very moment he had laid eyes on her. Strange, she thought, that he hadn't taken a younger mate, someone with whom he could have his own children. Was this his way of showing the tribe how they must behave if they wanted to grow and become strong?

He lifted the flap on the tent, gesturing for her to go inside. Elanur hesitated, then glanced up the hill to where Bri's tents were. The girls would be bedding down to get a little more sleep before morning. All she had to do was hand the infant back to Ilker and she could join them. She would keep things as they were and avoid taking part in this cruel process of incorporating stolen children into the tribe. All she had to do was give the infant back.

They'd left the light of the fire behind. She could no longer see the child's face. She turned toward Ilker and extended her arms. The warmth of the baby's body disappeared from her chest, a cold air taking its place. Quickly, she pulled the child back. Ilker waited, still holding the flap open. Finally, biting back tears, Elanur hugged the child close and stepped inside.

CHAPTER
TEN

Somewhere in the dark underworld

Emir walked. It was all he was aware of, the walking, and of Prince Anchurus walking in front of him. They'd talked a little at first, trying to piece together what had happened. Emir told Anchurus about escaping Durukin and traveling the long distance to Gordium. Anchurus remembered the music contest and how Silenus had interrupted it with his confused singing.

"I played the encore after that," Anchurus said, "but then something happened. I think I ended up outside near the old maple tree."

He'd fallen silent then. Emir had wanted to keep talking, but he sensed the prince needed time to think. When he couldn't stand it any longer, he restarted the conversation, reminding Anchurus of how the goddess Denisia had cursed the king with the golden touch. That was a mistake. The reminder only angered the prince. He fired off his own memories after that, from the way the goddess had betrayed both him and his father to how he'd nearly killed himself on the burning post trying to convince her to take it back.

81

"She outright refused," he spat, "going on about her grandfather's illness. She cared nothing for me or the king."

Emir waited for him to calm down, then said, "The gods are fickle."

It was a long while before Anchurus responded. "I was a fool."

Emir didn't press him. Their first task was to figure out where they were. So they walked. Emir reached for his waterskin at one point, but it wasn't there. He didn't recall losing it, but the impulse faded quickly, his thirst vanishing while his thoughts kept drifting to the boy. Emir had taught him the song his mother used to sing, the one about the little girl. Silly to teach a mute boy a song, but the boy had seemed happy to learn it. He'd sung along as best he could, forming the words with his hands whenever Emir sang it, and would beg for him to sing it over and over after that, so many times that Emir almost regretted having taught it to him. The cheerful expression on Little Bird's face, though, tamed his annoyance.

Little Bird. That was the boy's name.

Anchurus stopped. "We went to war," he said, "with King Sargon II." He turned to Emir. "You were there, I think? Our armies were there. Father . . . he was . . ." Anchurus paused. "We were fighting Sargon. But Father was weak." He started walking again, almost as if he wished to leave behind the statement.

Emir recalled racing back toward the castle on a dark horse with his waterskin full of magical water. It had given the king a few more days of life. That was before they went to war.

Anchurus stopped again. "You died," he said.

Emir halted. "I'm standing right here."

"I know. But . . ." Anchurus turned away, before turning back again. "I saw it. The dark goddess killed you with a flash of light."

Something stirred in Emir's memory. A woman with luscious dark hair. "She didn't kill me, or I wouldn't be talking to you."

Anchurus seemed to ponder that. "Do you think she sent us here?" When Emir didn't answer, Anchurus resumed his walking.

They walked for another long while, their footsteps the only sound in the tunnel.

"Did you hear that?" Emir said suddenly.

The prince kept going.

"Anchurus!" Still, the prince didn't respond. Emir ran forward and touched the prince's shoulder. Anchurus whirled with his sword raised. "It's me. Emir Alkan." The two stood staring into the darkness at one another. "Are you all right?" Emir asked.

"I thought you were Sargon." Anchurus sheathed the sword.

Emir frowned. *Sargon?* "I heard something," he said. Together, they listened. Emir heard it again. It sounded like an oud playing. "Do you hear it?" he asked.

Anchurus took a couple of steps forward. "Yes."

"From the left?"

"No, the right." Anchurus dashed off.

Emir followed. As they moved, he thought he could hear the oud more clearly. "There it is again."

"Mother!" Anchurus called. "Mother, where are you?"

Emir heard no human voices.

Anchurus jogged forward. "I'm coming!"

"Wait!" Emir followed him, still dragging his hand along the wall. Suddenly, the rock fell away, and he felt only air.

"Mother!" Anchurus called. "Yes, I'm here! Where are you?" He turned into the new tunnel on the right. "Keep talking. I'm coming!"

"Wait!" Emir said, but the prince ignored him. Emir had yet to hear any voices, but on his left, the oud was playing a merry tune. It was the same one his mother used to sing about the little girl running alongside the creek.

"Anchurus!" he called, but he'd waited too long. The prince was already gone, his footsteps swallowed by the darkness.

Emir wanted to go toward the oud, but he couldn't leave the prince alone. Worse, he didn't want to be abandoned himself. He hesitated, then hurried to the left to check. The oud sounded louder.

He'd gone about fifty steps and was wondering if he should turn back when he heard the boy.

He stopped, holding his breath. Yes! The boy's voice was as clear as day.

"Boy!" he called. "Where are you?"

The boy kept singing.

Emir ran into the darkness. The voice grew louder in his ears. *Little girl, little girl, where do you go?*

"Little Bird!" he called again. He ran for another long while, then paused. What was he thinking? The boy was mute. A mute boy couldn't sing. Little Bird had never been able to sing, only to mouth the words and translate them into his hand language. Emir frowned. Why had he thought he'd heard the boy's voice?

He walked a little farther, pausing now and then to listen. The sound of the voice was fading, and the oud with it. He ran back the other way, but it didn't help, so he turned around again. It was no use. Soon he could barely hear the song, and then it was gone altogether.

Emir returned to the intersection. "Little Bird!" he yelled. When he heard nothing, he hit the wall with his fist. It couldn't have been the boy. The boy couldn't sing. But he'd been so convinced it *was* the boy. Frustrated, he took the fork on the right, determined to catch up with the prince.

For a long while, he jogged down the new branch. He called to the prince more frequently, but received no reply. Confused and out of breath, he slowed to a walk, willing his eyes to see something, anything, but the darkness was a demon wrapped around his skull. He needed fire, but so far he'd come across nothing that would hold a flame. Only rock and dirt, rock and dirt.

How could the prince have disappeared so quickly? He broke into a jog again—and then the ground rumbled beneath him. He paused, then moved closer to the wall at his right. The trembling increased, the rock shifting under his feet. He crouched down to better keep his balance. Small rocks fell around him, dust billowing into the air. It lasted only a few moments before everything went still again.

"Anchurus?" He stood back up. "Anchurus?"

"Alkan! This way!"

Anchurus! Emir bolted. Within another ten steps, the wall dropped away again, revealing a new branch moving off to the right. "Anchurus?" he called. "Is that you?"

"This way," Anchurus called. "Hurry."

Emir followed the sound of the voice, hoping this time he could trust his ears. He couldn't say how long he'd been running when he saw it.

A light.

Startled, he stopped. A deep orange color, it resembled the setting sun, though it was shaped in a perfect circle with no extending rays. From this distance, it appeared to be coming from an opening in the tunnel that perhaps faced out into the sunset. Emir dashed toward it.

"Anchurus?"

The prince didn't answer. Emir ran faster.

"Anchurus, wait!"

He ran full out, his heart pumping hard against his chest, his breath coming fast. The light shone brighter. Emir squinted, his eyes watering.

"Wait!" he called. "Prince Anchurus!"

Gradually, the light changed, like dawn fading into morning. A wide river, blood red and thick like soup, flowed out of the tunnel, flanked by land for a short distance before dropping away from the banks to join what looked like an ocean beyond. A small craft bobbed on its surface, a shrouded man at the back with a long paddle. He stood stooped with age, his movements slow but steady as he pushed the boat along, directing it toward the horizon. Anchurus sat leisurely at the front, one leg extended out, the other knee drawn close to his chest, both arms wrapped around it.

"Prince Anchurus! Wait!"

Anchurus waved at him.

"I'm coming!" Emir stepped one foot into the water and immediately jerked it back. A burning sensation seized his toes, his boot steaming. Emir touched his finger to the water, yelped, shook his hand, and wiped the moisture on his trousers. When he looked up again, the prince's boat was far enough away that it appeared only a speck. How was the boat sailing on burning water? Emir tried touching it again, but ended up with two burned fingers. He stomped and cursed. He never should have chased the phantom oud. Never should have let the prince out of his sight.

The ground started rumbling again. Emir retreated to the wall as small stones and dust rained down on his head. Behind him, the tunnel extended into the darkness. Ahead, the burning river carried the prince away.

When the trembling stopped, he sat down and leaned his back against the wall. Perhaps another boat would come. If there was one boat, surely there would be another. He pointed his gaze at what remained of the strange orange sun, allowing his eyes to soak up the light. He thought he should feel tired. Instead, he felt hollow, as if the breeze from the tunnel opening were blowing right through him.

There would be another boat. There had to be another boat. Soon his breath came slow and steady and he slept.

CHAPTER

ELEVEN

696 BC
Gordium, Capital City of Phrygia

The morning after the bodies had been buried and the carcasses burned, a thin line of black smoke ribboned toward the eastern horizon over Gordium. Like a ceremonial remembrance of those who had passed, it waved and curled, drifting solemnly across the sky. The ashes were still warm, the embers eating away the last evidence of the Gimirri slaughter. A few families had escaped through the west gates on their journey to Lydia, but the number had dwindled since the day before. Most who had wanted to depart had done so, the remaining citizens banding together to build the new barrier on the south side.

Princess Zoe's engineers were there now, directing the installation of a long row of wooden spikes, each to be placed at an angle so the sharp side poked outward, a support beam secured in a trench underneath to keep them all upright. The hope was that the fang-like fence would deter riders on horseback, though those on foot would still be able to easily pass through. The men had started digging a deeper ditch outside the barrier as well. They would later disguise it with dried grasses and straw in the hopes the enemy would stumble into it and become stuck, or perhaps plunge helplessly into one or more of the sharp stakes. Additional boys had been assigned shepherding duties to be sure the animals stayed away. Zoe had discussed a fence with her engineers, but they would have to gather the supplies and build it to stretch along the southern edge of the city—something that would take more time than anyone thought they had before the Gimirri returned. King Midas had granted permission to build the south wall, like the one that protected the rest of the city, but that would take even longer.

For now, the sharp stakes would have to do.

"How long has it been since you checked the tomb?" Zoe asked. She and Aster were walking the length of the planned barrier together, Zoe checking on the builders' progress.

"It has not been three moon cycles," Aster said. He'd traded his advisor's robe for a linen shirt and wool trousers, a thick belt around his waist. The day was cool, but pleasant, with a light breeze blowing what remained of the battle's stench east.

"And the crack wasn't there then?" Zoe wore a long skirt and sandals, her hair done up in a bun. "No trace of damage?"

"The tomb did not appear untouched."

Zoe shook her head. "All these years, the goddess of the underworld has lain undisturbed. Now, just as these Gimirri breach the city gates, a large crack appears in the stone." She watched as one worker positioned another pointed stake, eyeing the way he thrust it into the trench. "Angle it more," she said, stepping up to show him where the point should be. He adjusted it. "Yes, that's it." She stepped back and waited until he had secured it into the ground, then walked on.

They headed up the small incline toward the west, past the place where Aster had picked up a beam from the broken wagon two days before. Zoe felt his presence like the heat of a warm fire and longed to take his arm. King Midas wouldn't approve. There were traditions in the royal family. Zoe had never been forced to marry for convenience. Her father had expanded his territory through military conquest and widespread prosperity rather than by making strategic marriage arrangements. Yet the traditions held, which meant that a princess and an advisor had to be careful.

"None of the citizens have sensed rumbles at night," Aster said.

Zoe lifted her gaze toward the fields. The farmers were already working on the harvest again, their backs to the sun, their bodies periodically bobbing up to toss handfuls of vegetables into horse-drawn wagons. Despite the tragedy, they couldn't leave the food to spoil. "I haven't noticed any, have you?"

Aster nodded. "The castle does not give protection."

Zoe brought her attention back to the road. They were following the one that skirted the southern perimeter. "You don't have any idea what might be happening?"

"We do, Your Highness. We are not working on it."

"I don't desire to take you away from that duty," Zoe said. "But I have another request."

"The princess must not name it."

Zoe took one last look at the new barrier. Only a few of the posts were visible so far, but the trench looked straight enough. She wished the process could go faster, but already they'd recruited every man possible—and even some women—to work on it. "You know about Father's nightmares," Zoe said. "They're getting worse. Can you do anything for him?"

"You have not asked the medicine woman?"

"Last night she increased the dosage of the sleeping syrup, but it is already too strong. He's tired during the day. His mind wanders. His thinking is unclear, and if ever we needed a clear-headed king . . ."

"It is not now," Aster finished for her.

Zoe nodded, her head lowered as they turned away from the southern barrier and headed north toward the castle. "Might there be a spell that may help?"

"Xander is not adept at the spells," Aster said, falling in beside her.

"Perhaps he could come up with something." When she looked up again, Aster caught her eye. He gave her a soft smile that lifted her onto her toes. She longed once more to take his arm, but only returned the smile and kept walking. "Very well," she said. "That is what we will do. A spell. Soon?"

Aster shook his head. "Not soon."

Zoe nodded. "I hope it will help. These Gimirri . . . We must call back the army to defeat them. Father would see that if . . ." She drifted off.

"We must not help the king," Aster said. "It will not be our first priority."

That afternoon found Aster combing through his predecessor's library of parchments and historical records while Xander worked at mixing a concoction to dispatch Midas' nightmares. Amber sunrays shone through their one window, making an orange rectangle on the stone floor.

"What do you propose we do?" Gediz asked from his seat on the foot of his bed. He played with a scarf in his hands, caressing its soft edges.

"Doing absolutely nothing is always a winning strategy," Aster said, casting him a disapproving glare.

"I'd be happy to do something," Gediz said, "but I have no idea what we can do in the wake of a goddess' power."

"An advisor who constantly needs instructions is a worthy advisor indeed." Aster put the parchment down and turned to peruse another shelf.

"Don't you have any talents?" Xander asked.

"Don't I have . . . !" Gediz sputtered. He put the scarf behind him. "I have my mind." He raised his chin. "That is what an advisor is supposed to use when advising his king."

"A king might not prefer there to be something *in* that mind," Aster said.

"Do you do nothing but throw insults?" Gediz barked, his curly bronze hair jiggling on his head.

"I am a fountain of compliments," Aster said.

"You're the only one he insults," Xander said matter-of-factly. "Well, most of the time." He stood back and threw three dirt clods into a bowl.

"Aren't I the fortunate one," Gediz said.

"You have showered us with good fortune since the moment you arrived." Aster pulled down a heavy slate, set it on his desk, and leaned forward to study it.

Gediz laid down on his bed. "Very well. You don't want my help, so I'll just lie down here and enjoy a nap."

"The king will be delighted to hear it," Aster said.

Gediz glared up at the ceiling.

"I'm trying a revealing spell." Xander perused his own shelves full of ingredients. "Something that may tell us more about what is wrong with our king. Do you think that's what the princess wanted?"

"She does not want the king to be his old self," Aster said.

Xander shook his head. "I'm afraid I don't have a spell for that one."

"He's old, that's what's wrong," Gediz grumbled. "A few spices and herbs aren't going to help that."

"We so appreciate your deep well of wisdom," Aster said, then turned to Xander. "This is a language I have encountered before. Do you not know it?"

"One moment." Xander held a leather satchel above the bowl, sprinkled in a little of its contents, pulled the drawstring closed and set it back on the shelf. Then he dusted off his hands and crossed the room to where Aster stood, examining the slate. Rubbing one finger on his upper lip, he frowned. "It looks somewhat familiar," he said, "but . . ." He leaned closer, peering at the marks carved into the stone. "No. I'm afraid I can't make it out."

"Surely Fotis did not know it," Aster said, speaking of their old lead advisor.

"You think there's something here?"

Aster looked around at his predecessor's shelves. "It's not the only one I've found so far that I can't read."

"You're saying this is our last chance to find something that may help secure the dark goddess, at least in Fotis' old things."

Aster shook his head in agreement.

"You have another advisor here to ask," Gediz said.

"I always think of asking you first," Aster said.

"Your choice." Gediz went back to staring at the ceiling.

Xander cast Aster a questioning look. Aster turned a cold shoulder and started replacing the other parchments he'd taken down from the shelves. Xander looked from him to Gediz and back and finally lifted the slate off the table. He wobbled across the floor, walking bowlegged while balancing the heavy stone between his knees. When he reached Gediz's bed, he dropped it on the mattress, just missing Gediz's foot.

"Hey, be careful with that!" Gediz said.

Xander stepped away, panting, and rested his hands on his hips. When he glanced up at Aster, he found the senior advisor watching him. He shrugged in response. Aster pointed toward the slate and then the desk, making it clear he expected the slate to be returned. Xander glanced at Gediz once more, then headed back to his mixing table.

The room was silent for a time. Aster worked to clear his desk. Xander tended to his concoction, though he glanced up at Gediz now and then. The new advisor stubbornly ignored the slate for a few moments, but when it seemed the other two were suitably distracted, he leaned over it. Xander turned the spoon in the bowl, observing. Gediz started mouthing inaudible words as he moved his finger along the slate. At one point he paused, chewed on a fingernail, then cast a look at the front door. Xander quickly dropped his gaze.

Aster finished clearing off his desk and sat down, leaning his elbows on the surface and staring at the east wall, deep in thought. Xander added another flower petal and chanted a poem under his breath, then passed his hands over the mixture and sighed. "It's done."

"Not for the princess?" Aster asked.

"It will detect anything that may be trying to harm the king," Xander said. "Her Highness need only sprinkle it over the right place. At the right time, of course."

Aster cocked his head.

"She can manage it unless she wants one of us to do it." Xander leaned his hands on the table. "It still doesn't help us with Katiah."

Aster grunted.

Xander scooped the mixture into a leather pouch. "We have no power against her. The only visions I have seen are those where the city crumbles and King Midas . . ." He stopped. "Oh, Aster, what are we going to do? You know my visions always come true! If the city is destroyed and the king killed, we'll have nowhere to go."

"Then you'd know what it feels like," Gediz grumbled.

Xander and Aster looked startled, as if they'd forgotten the other advisor was even there.

Gediz wasn't looking at them, though. He was studying the slate.

"Your old city wasn't destroyed," Xander said.

"Yes, well, you don't know the entire story, do you?" Gediz said.

"We would so enjoy hearing it," Aster said.

Gediz mumbled something inaudible under his breath.

"Did you figure it out?" Xander asked.

"It doesn't seem as if my expertise is wanted."

With a mighty heave, Gediz lifted the slate, lugged it across the room, and set it heavily on Aster's desk. With a pointed look at the senior advisor, he went back to his bed and laid down.

Aster looked at the slate, then at Xander, who was already gazing across the room at him. "How delightful," Aster said. "His Excellency does not wish for us to beg for information."

"Did you read it?" Xander came out from behind his table.

Gediz said nothing.

"Well, did you?"

Still, Gediz was silent, his broad nose twitching. Xander cast an exasperated look at Aster. The senior advisor focused on Gediz. When the little man still didn't respond, Aster descended and, in one swift movement, grabbed Gediz by the arm and yanked him up, letting him go just at the right time to send him sprawling onto the floor.

"You will not do your duty to the king!" he bellowed.

Xander stepped back, his eyes wide as Gediz scooted across the room toward the door.

"Lay down!" Aster barked.

Gediz dropped to the floor.

"He means get up!" Xander corrected.

Gediz struggled to his feet just as Aster reached him, then backed away until the door stopped him from going any farther. He looked up into Aster's eyes, his lower lip trembling.

"You will be silent!" Aster said.

"He means—"

"Yes, yes, I understood that one." Gediz's words were clipped and hurried. "The slate. Well, I can't be positive. But I believe it is a most ancient language, one that is sometimes attributed, um, said to have been written by the gods themselves."

"The gods?" Xander peered out from behind Aster.

"Indeed, yes. Well, one god. Or goddess, more precisely." Gediz cast a nervous glance at Aster. "Rarely seen except in a cave at Acharaca, where the sick are brought to be healed. The very sick."

"You do not know this language?" Aster asked, still glaring at the man.

"Only a little. I-I studied it for a short period. Under my . . . mentor at Lydia."

"So what does it say?" Xander said.

"I could make out only some symbols."

Aster moved aside and gestured for the third advisor to show them. Gediz looked uncertain, but finally stepped out. When Aster let him be, Gediz walked to the senior advisor's desk. At first, he entered Aster's space so he could put the desk between him and the other two. When Aster gave him a warning glare, he switched positions, standing on the far side while Aster claimed his own space, Xander in the middle. With a temporary peace established, the three bent close to the slate.

"These two symbols here." Gediz pointed to two symbols at the top of the slate. "They speak of the goddess, the one who was believed to have blessed the cave in Acharaca with her presence. Matar Kubileya, or Mountain Mother, they called her. In Acharaca, female priests lead the very ill into the cave. There they stay for many days, sometimes longer, hoping to be blessed with good health. If they are chosen, they emerge healed."

"If not?" Xander asked.

Gediz shrugged. "They die."

Xander cast a glance at Aster. "Another nice goddess," he said.

"This slate does not tell about this cave of the sick?" Aster asked.

"That's not what I said," Gediz said, holding up one finger. "If you were listening, you—" When he looked up to see Aster's angry face, he stopped.

"It mentions this mountain goddess," Xander said, quickly interrupting. "What else does it say?"

"Not *mountain goddess*," Gediz said, "mountain *mother*. She is a goddess, yes, but one of fertility, among other things. The important thing is that she was born of stone. From the mountain. Do you see?"

"But what else does the slate say?" Xander asked.

"I'm afraid you're missing the connection here—"

"Between this goddess and the crack in the stone?" Aster asked. "That is not the connection you're trying to make?"

Gediz nodded enthusiastically. "She is a goddess with connections to all stone. To mountains. To the rumbling in the stone underneath." He searched Aster's face. "It could be useful?"

The other two advisors exchanged frustrated glances. "What else does it say?" Xander asked again.

Gediz scratched his head, his fingers in a mass of curls. "I only recognize a few more of these, the symbols here."

"Please do keep us in suspense," Aster said.

"You were going to dismiss my expertise entirely," Gediz mumbled.

Xander poked Gediz in the side, causing him to yelp. "What else does it say?"

"You don't have to get violent!" Gediz glared at Xander, but when Aster took a threatening step closer to him, Gediz ducked over the slate again. "This one. I think I know this one." He pointed to a symbol about halfway down. "It speaks of the world between the living and the dead, and the balance that must be maintained. And here. This one." He pointed to a lower symbol. "I think this is the symbol for . . . how to say it . . . disaster. Chaos." He smiled as if proud of himself, cleaning the symbol of dust with his finger.

The other two advisors waited. When Gediz remained silent, Xander said, "That's it? That's all you can read?"

Gediz blinked at him. "There are a few more. I think."

Aster crossed his arms over his chest. "We have endless time to wait for you to unfold your brilliance."

Gediz tensed. "I do not have to take this abuse."

"Of course not," Aster said. "Allow me to inform the king of your decision not to leave." He started for the door.

"Now just a moment." Gediz took a few steps after Aster, but the advisor was already lifting the latch. "Aster," Gediz said, "wait." When Aster stepped into the hallway, Gediz shouted, "But you can't! I have nowhere else, nowhere else to go!"

Aster whirled around. "I am not doing you a favor. It's very clear you are happy here."

"I'm not happy here!"

Aster started off again.

"But wait!" Gediz ran out the door. "It says that should the mountain goddess be trapped, the underworld may descend into chaos, and the effects shall reverberate throughout the world of men, causing death and destruction."

Aster stopped. Whirled around.

Gediz glanced about sheepishly. "At least, um, I think that's what it says."

Aster looked at Xander, who stood in the doorway with a hopeful gaze.

"Chaos," Xander whispered, "reverberating through the world of men." He raised his eyebrows. "A delirious king, an invading force, rumblings in the earth, a crack in the tomb of the dark goddess . . ." He gulped.

Aster turned to Gediz. "You did not say we could find this goddess in a cave. Where?"

"Acharaca," Gediz said. "Though I don't know if she is still there. The priests continue to perform the healing rights, but . . ." He shrugged.

Aster walked back into the room. "It is a lot to go on," he grumbled.

Xander tapped his fingers together. "It is all we have."

Aster stared at the slate. "We have not gone on similar adventures before," he said.

Xander smiled wistfully. "Long ago."

"When we were not three instead of two."

Xander glanced at Gediz. "We *do* still have three," he said.

"What adventure?" Gediz said. "What are you talking about?" He looked from one to the other, then an expression of horror crossed his face. "Oh, you're not thinking about actually going?" When the other two said nothing, he backed toward his bed. "No. I gave you the information, but that's it. You nearly got me killed a couple of days ago."

"Such a shame it didn't work." Aster started gathering a few things to stuff into a linen sack.

"What are you doing?" Gediz watched as Xander did the same. "What kind of kingdom is this, that the advisors are expected to ride into danger? Certainly, you have messengers or soldiers for that type of thing?"

"The city has not been under attack," Aster said.

"The king will need all his guards here for defense," Xander agreed.

"But he could spare some for this errand?"

"Because guards are so adept at researching information on a goddess," Aster said.

"You could instruct them?" Gediz said.

"To do what?" Xander said. "Even we don't know what we're going to do. We have to get there and see. You've been before. You can't be that scared of going again?"

"Been before?" Gediz said. "I haven't been before!"

They both stopped to look at him.

"My mentor told me about it. I didn't *go* there."

Aster thought a moment, then returned to packing. "Very well. You will not take us to your mentor, who won't then guide us to this cave."

"That won't work," Gediz whined, wringing his hands.

"Why not?" Xander asked.

"Because he's dead," Gediz said.

The other advisors stopped. "He died, but you didn't take his place?" Xander asked.

Gediz looked down at his lap. "King Kandaules didn't, um, well, he didn't appreciate my counsel."

Aster set his hand over his heart. "Another king highly valued all your wise advice? I am stunned."

"I advised him well!" Gediz spat. "He had no reason . . ." He waved his hand up and down in emphasis, then let it drop. "It matters not. You want to ride off on some adventure, you . . . you go ahead. I'm staying right here." He turned away from them. "I'll not end up like that other advisor you got killed."

Aster and Xander exchanged glances. Aster looked as if he might toss Gediz out the window right then, but with a firm set of his jaw, he returned to his packing.

"We must talk to the king," Xander said, doing the same.

"I do not agree," Aster said.

"We'll seek an audience when he dines tonight. Then we could leave first thing in the morning."

Aster shook his head in agreement. "We must not move with all haste." He set his filled sack on his bed and turned to Gediz. "You are not the only one who knows of this location. You will not take us there." He strode toward the door.

"Bring comfortable clothes," Xander added. "We'll be riding a long time."

"I'll not secure supplies." Aster left the room.

"I'll see about an appointment with the king," Xander said, going after him. "I hope he'll be in a good mood." He paused to look back before shutting the door.

Gediz remained by his bed, staring after them both.

CHAPTER
TWELVE

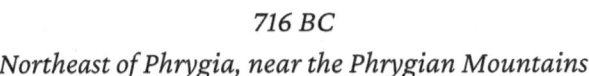

716 BC

Northeast of Phrygia, near the Phrygian Mountains

The first storm of the cold season blew fiercely against Ilker's tent. Elanur huddled inside, her heart pounding as the winds buffeted the hide, whipping it back and forth until it strained against the extra posts Ilker had pounded into the ground only a few days before, heavy sacks of wet dirt providing additional weight to keep their shelter grounded. The storm was fiercer than any Elanur remembered in Durukin. There, the winds howled now and then, but always she had stayed in one of King Sargon II's stout wooden shelters. She couldn't remember ever waiting out something like this in only a tent. She wondered why the Gimirri didn't move somewhere more sheltered for the cold season, but they were an ambitious tribe, strange in their ways.

A fire burned in the center pit, the flames leaning this way and that with the changing air flow. She cleared the area around it for the third time, concerned that one of the sparks might escape and set the whole thing ablaze. Kerkin lay in the wooden cradle Ilker had made just a few days after bringing the baby to camp. Elanur rocked it back and forth, cooing soothing words. She had named the boy, something Ilker seemed to accept, as he was using the name now, too. She thought it strange the child wasn't crying with the wind causing so much ruckus, but he only looked up at her with wide eyes that seemed to wonder what this latest game was all about.

The snow had started that afternoon, just as Bri had predicted seven days before. The old woman's intuition impressed Elanur. She had warned the camp that this would be a strong storm, particularly for this early in the cold season. It was because of her they had made arrangements in time, securing the tents to the ground and weighing them down with extra hides strapped over the tops. Otherwise, they might have been caught unprepared and probably would have lost at least some of their tents.

Outside, the snow was already packed two hands high, the wind driving drifts against the northwestern side of the shelter, pushing the flaps inward. Elanur pictured more snow piling up above them, but the fire would help keep it from sticking for long. Ilker had left several pieces of wood inside for just that purpose.

Elanur retrieved one and peered outside. Snow blew against her face. Ilker had gone to check on Thom, who was late returning from the hunt. That was in the afternoon. Now it was well after sunset, but he hadn't returned. All the tribe members, save Ilker, Thom, and another young man who had gone hunting with him, were in their tents waiting out the storm. Elanur ducked back inside, wiped her face dry with the edge of a blanket, and resumed rocking Kerkin.

"Your father is a brave man," she told him, having accepted that for now, she and Ilker were the boy's parents, no matter what she might think about the rightness of that choice. "He'll be back soon. All we have to do is wait. Do you like the firelight?"

He gazed at her, entranced, his hands clenched into fists as he wriggled in response.

"What we need is a song," Elanur said, "but I'd have to shout it above this noise!" She longed to sing the song she used to sing to Emir, but the wind was a fierce competitor and would have whisked her words away before they ever reached Kerkin's ears. Instead, she raised her hands and, clenching one into a fist with two fingers of the other over the top, formed a rabbit's head and started making it bounce around.

"This is a rabbit," she told him, "coming to get you!" She plunged her hands toward him and tickled the boy. He laughed out loud, inhaled with his mouth open, and with wide eyes, stared at her hands again. Elanur repeated the game many times before her arms tired. She thought about feeding the boy, as she still had goat's milk stashed in the back of the tent, but he had eaten recently. She sighed and stared at the flap again. Ilker shouldn't have gone out. She had told him as much, but he wouldn't leave one of his men stranded in the storm.

She rested for a time, trying to put her worries out of her mind. The wind continued unabated, fluttering the sides of the tent and pushing snow beneath it. Unable to relax, she rose and fed Kerkin some milk, then gave him the smoothed antler dipped in honey to suck on. With the baby suitably occupied, she set to work on a new blanket she was making for him. She had finally calmed herself in her stitches when she heard voices shouting. She peered out the front flap. The snow was blinding at first. Then she saw a large shadow approaching.

Her heart leaped when she recognized Ilker's fur hat. She ducked back to allow him in, retreating to the middle of the tent as he lowered his head and then rose to his full height. Spotting Kerkin, he went over to the cradle, crouched, and spoke his name, then said something in Gimirri. It was a term of endearment, one Elanur had heard him use only for the boy. Kerkin watched him with his big eyes, his legs dancing above him. Ilker patted him on the tummy, then lifted his gaze to Elanur.

"Thom," he said.

"Is he well?" She wasn't sure he had understood her. They were still trying to communicate, since neither grasped the other's language.

He returned her gaze and said simply, "Thom."

He appeared satisfied, so she smiled. "I'm glad," she said, pointing to herself, then to her smile.

He nodded and pointed to Kerkin with his eyebrows raised.

"He's well," she said. "Happy. Are you hungry?" She gestured toward the small wooden box that held their stored food. He shook his head, removed his hat and cloak, and came to sit next to the fire. Elanur checked on Kerkin again. Finding him happily sucking his bone, she sat down near the fire as well. They had done this many nights, warmed themselves this way until one of them succumbed to weariness and collapsed on the blankets. Usually, Elanur was the first to go, but this night, Ilker's eyes were already drooping.

Elanur stared at the flames, occasionally glancing at him out of the corner of her eye. She realized she hadn't thought about the storm since he'd returned. Indeed, in that moment, with him sitting nearby, the fire cheerfully snapping the wood, she felt safer than she had in a long while. The feeling confused her. This was the man who had stolen her away and then had saddled her with a child that wasn't her own. She was wary of him. Angry with him even. But not once had he tried to take advantage of her or press himself upon her. Since they'd brought Kerkin to the tent, they'd stayed there together, but more like brother and sister. This night, she knew he would allow that again, and many more nights as well.

A powerful gust buffeted the flap behind her. Her gaze flew to Kerkin. He watched with wide eyes, but didn't say a word. Reaching over, she drew the cradle closer, then shuffled over until she was sitting next to Ilker. She looked at him once and gave him a shy smile. He reached out his open hand. The fleshy palm glazed orange in the firelight. Elanur took it, lifted it up and over her shoulder, and moved into his ribs. His big arm settled around her and gently pulled her in. Resting her head against him, Elanur stared into the flames. Let the wind do what it might. Here, nothing could harm her.

. . .

A MOON'S CYCLE LATER, Elanur was teaching the tribal children her language—something Ilker had instructed her to do—when the men returned unexpectedly.

It was a sunny day with a crisp, refreshing edge to the air. A blanket of snow remained on the ground, the northern peaks painted white. The children sat on tree stumps around the big central fire, which the young boys kept blazing with the wood they had been gathering all year. Elanur had Kerkin strapped to her back, a warm hat on his head and a heavy deer hide swaddling his body. She had several items in front of her, showing them to the children as she spoke her words. Spoon. Knife. Blanket. Mug. Bowl. She taught them body parts like hand, mouth, teeth, ears, eyes, hair, neck, head. They watched and copied diligently, though they couldn't make all the sounds exactly right. But they were getting better since she had started ten days before.

She didn't know why Ilker had felt it was important for her to teach them. He'd explained it in a few words, but she'd understood only one of them—his word for tomorrow or "next day." From that, she'd guessed he thought it best for the children to learn her language for their future. What sort of future that might be she tried not to think about. Instead, she simply enjoyed the task. It made her feel useful, much more than cleaning hides or preparing food did. This was something only she could do. Indeed, it was the first time in her life she had felt valued for her unique skills.

She had progressed to putting words together—hand takes spoon, spoon goes in mouth—when hoofbeats approached from the south. She looked up to see the men racing toward the camp. Strange, as it had been only seven days since they'd left. The children turned to watch, too. Some got up and rushed over to greet their fathers returning. Elanur urged the rest to do the same. As they scattered, she gathered her belongings. By the time everything was packed in her carrying bag, the men were dismounting. She lifted the bag, intending to put it back in her tent, but she had made it only halfway when Hastet called.

"Ilker's hurt!" She arrived breathless and pulled on Elanur's arm. "Ilker."

Elanur handed the girl the bag and hurried back. The boys were brushing down the horses, some transferring the stolen goods to their appropriate underground chests. She slowed, catching her breath, and spotted three men approaching with a plank. On it lay a big man with thick, dark hair.

"Ilker?"

His eyes were closed, his skin clammy with sweat. Elanur spoke his name again, but he only murmured words she didn't understand. Below his waist, his right pant leg was soaked in blood, some of it dripping onto the ground. Elanur stared at the wound, then back at Ilker's face. In a blink, everything he was to her in that moment became clear. Without him, the happy family she had inadvertently become a part of would fall apart.

She followed the men up to Bri's tent, but they stopped her before she could go in. She stood outside and waited, pacing back and forth, Kerkin babbling nonsense words in her ears.

"Is he all right?" Hastet appeared from behind her.

Elanur shook her head. "It looked bad."

Hastet glanced toward the flap. "Bri will help him."

A few moments later, the three men came out with an empty plank. She searched their faces, but they were unreadable. None said a word. As the morning dragged into the afternoon, she busied herself helping Hastet milk the goats while listening for any sounds coming from Bri's tent. Soon Goakina joined them and they set to work storing the dried fruit, meat, and grains the men had brought back with them. Elanur gave Kerkin his sucking bone to keep him busy while she worked. When they finished, Goakina lit the fire to cook the evening meal. Elanur turned toward the tent. She longed to poke her head inside. Hastet caught her gaze and, with a determined lift of her chin, marched brazenly around to the front, lifted the flap, and disappeared. Elanur hesitated a moment, then followed.

She had never been inside Bri's tent. She might have left immediately if not for the sight of the injured man. Ilker lay on a pile of animal hides and furs, his injured leg bare up to the groin. The pants had been cut, the torn edges lying like wispy feathers against his thigh. The upper leg was swollen to near twice its normal size, the skin fiery red. Elanur winced, looking at it. Her gaze moved to Ilker's face. His eyes were still closed. At the back of the tent rested a tall cabinet with multiple shelves, wooden jars and pouches stacked upon it. Hastet was in front of them, perusing the collection. On Elanur's left lay Bri's bed, a mattress elevated by a wooden frame. On a nearby chair sat Bri herself, a woven blanket over her lap. She was staring right at Elanur. Elanur thought she should ask forgiveness for trespassing, but she was frozen in place, her attention returning to the wounded man. She dared to take a step closer. A black-red gash marred the top of the thigh, about as long as her forearm. It looked like a sword wound that had been dressed with a cream-colored paste. The leg was so swollen! He must have traveled for days after the injury. She knew wounds well enough to know that this one was dangerously infected. Without more aggressive treatment, he could die.

She turned to Bri. "We must wash it," she said, but she didn't know how to say "wash" in Gimirri. She pointed to the wound and said the word for "illness." Bri nodded knowingly. Her gaze seemed to say she had already addressed the problem, but the paste wouldn't be enough. From her days as Sargon's slave, Elanur had seen many soldiers' wounds. Whatever salve Bri had used wouldn't stop the process that had begun.

"Come," Elanur said to Hastet. "Help me." She unstrapped Kerkin, set him down nearby, and looked up to see young eyes studying her. "Help," she said again. The girl came closer but then stopped, looking from Elanur to Bri and back. "We have to get him up." Taking one arm, Elanur tried to shoulder him herself, but it was no use. Again, she encouraged Hastet. "I want to help him," she said. "Please."

Hastet looked at her with indecision in her eyes. Elanur was asking her to break Bri's rules.

"Stay," Bri said in Gimirri.

"He will die," Elanur responded.

"Stay," Bri said. Then she said the word for "goddess" and lifted her gaze, as if to say it was up to the gods now.

Ilker's skin was pale, his lips dry. Elanur sat next to him, battling with herself. Bri was the knowledgeable one, the camp's healer. She should leave him in the old woman's hands. But when she studied the wound again, a new certainty filled her being. Once more, she got underneath Ilker's arm and glanced up at Hastet. The girl seemed to sense her determination. After another beat, she moved to Ilker's opposite side. Elanur's heart squeezed. Precious child! Ilker mumbled something she couldn't understand and lifted his head.

"Get up!" she told him, then eyed Hastet. One, two, three, and they heaved together, pushing forward this time to move Ilker onto his feet. His eyes opened, but his lids were heavy. He stood with a painful groan. Elanur took the brunt of his weight, for he favored the injured leg, but she managed. Staggering, she told Hastet to move with her out of the tent.

Bri shouted the word for "no." Hastet ducked at the admonishment, but continued with Elanur until they were standing outside, the two of them bracing the suffering man.

Goakina knelt by the fire, adjusting the cooking pot. She turned.

"Help!" Hastet said in their language.

Goakina frowned and said something sternly in Gimirri.

Elanur started forward. Hastet went with her. Goakina repeated her command, but Elanur kept going, the three stumbling down the hill, the man a heavy burden. They might have lost him to gravity had not Goakina come up just at the right time and taken Hastet's place. Elanur persevered, unable to afford a grateful look, while Hastet walked along behind, ready to lend a hand if needed. When they reached the creek, they had to turn south for a time to clear the thick growth of bushes and reeds. Trudging through hand-high snow, they soon found an opening. Elanur led the girls out into the middle of the frigid, rushing water, then instructed them to carefully let the man down.

His leg hit the ice-cold waves. He cried out and thrashed, trying to escape, but he was weak. The girls steadied him between them. When he stopped struggling, Elanur told them to get out. They didn't need convincing. The cold water was bracing at first, but prolonged exposure was painful. Leaving Elanur with her patient, they moved, shivering, to the creekside and wrung out the bottoms of their dresses. Elanur gritted her teeth while Ilker shifted from side to side, new chills possessing his body. She stroked his hair, trying to soothe him. Bearing the biting cold in her legs, she waited, speaking to him in her language. "It's all right. It will be all right. Stay calm now."

The creek water rushed over the wound, cleansing and cooling the raging infection inside. Hastet urged Elanur to come out. "Cold!" she said in Gimirri. Goakina held her little sister's hand, both of them with distressed looks on their faces.

Elanur's legs began to go numb. Ilker's moaning subsiding as the pain eased. She kept him securely in the water, her forearm under his right arm, her fingers stroking his hair.

The old woman hollered.

The girls whirled around. "Bri!" Hastet said. Goakina said something else, cast a worried look at Elanur, then with Hastet on her heels, ran up the hill. Soon, the rest of the camp would find Elanur with the man, for there was no way she could move him before they arrived. She wondered what they would do to her for going against Bri's wishes. Strangely, she wasn't overly concerned about it, the rightness of her actions certain in her heart.

"It will be all right," she said, rocking the Gimirri warrior back and forth, her body a block of ice. "It's almost over now. Hang on."

CHAPTER

THIRTEEN

The deep, dark underworld

Emir didn't remember when he left the Red River. A boat had
come for Anchurus. He'd felt sure one would come for him,
but none did. The longer he waited, the more he felt part of
the rock and dirt. Gravity possessed him, dragging him unto itself
until he sensed he would melt into the black stone like hot lava, then
cool, solidify, and never breathe again. If he didn't leave, his ability to
choose would be gone, so he hauled himself to his feet and plunged
back into the dark.

As he had before, he walked with his fingers trailing alongside
the wall. He and Anchurus had found the Red River. He might find
something else. A way back to where he could see his mother and lay
eyes on the boy once again. He walked, seeking light but not finding
it, listening for sounds that didn't come. Only his footsteps broke the
stillness, the air a throbbing whisper. The darkness pressed against
him like a tightening vise. His limbs ached, weak muscles straining
as if he hadn't used them for months, the fresh air lost and replaced
with a thick and muggy haze.

Silence penetrated his being. On and on he walked, his belly a hollow trunk, his bones mere branches that swayed. When he was a warrior, his body had felt flexible and strong, his arms ready to wield a sword, his legs the foundation from which he moved. Now he was thin as worn fabric, his movements fluttering. Walking was more like drifting, the impulses absent, the muscles inconsequential.

Time passed. Or didn't pass. It was difficult to tell. He walked. And walked. And walked. Perhaps this was what dying was like, he thought once. Fading into nothingness. A gradual loss of self. He had nearly succumbed to it when something changed.

He paused, his hand on the wall. At first, he couldn't determine what had made him stop. Then he heard a sound. It seemed to come from up ahead. Another trick of the air, like the oud and the boy singing. But it didn't fade or disappear. So starved was he for the existence of something, *anything* else, he walked toward it. After a few steps, he paused again. A single voice took shape in his mind, unfamiliar, deep, and rich with authority.

You have come to us . . . And then: *You chose the path . . .*

He walked faster, a powerful desire seizing him. A voice—real or not, it spoke in words he knew. That was enough. When it came again, he shifted into a run. For a long while, he ran. Then the rock fell away from his fingers, and he stepped into a slick patch and fell, catching himself with his hands.

He halted, listening. The voice was still there, ahead of him. Mud dripped from his palms, or something like it. He got up and shifted his weight to his heels. They sank a little, but then held. Darkness hollowed the space below him. He wished fiercely for some sort of light. Farther on, he detected a glow so faint he feared his eyes were tricking him. He squeezed them shut, then opened them again. The glow remained. A red shade.

He stepped forward. The same slick, squishy surface.

We must acknowledge the truth of the situation . . .

The ground held. Emir shifted into a more confident stride. Muck splashed the bottoms of his boots. The red light grew brighter. It wasn't like the sunset over the Red River, but a darker red, like the river itself if it had glowed.

. . . here you are. There are endless potential reasons why . . .

The voice seemed to speak to a group of people, the way a king might address his subjects. Emir imagined seeing a crowd. People!

Why did you come here? Here you will stay. Once to escape and once far away.

The red light burned brightly in front of him. Emir focused on it, his ears straining to pick up the spoken words.

Welcome, Emir Alkan! Why are you here? Cowardice shields the reasons we fear.

Emir halted. "Hello?" he said.

No one answered.

Not again! He raced toward the red light. It seemed an interminable time, but suddenly the beam appeared on his left, piercing rays from a different sun.

"Hello?"

He turned into it, blinded as he approached. The squishing under his boots faded. Soon, he was back on solid ground. Curious, he checked behind him. A swath of bloody innards—slick organs and discarded muscles—formed a quagmire, like the field dressing from ten wild stags. His boots were covered in the red, mashy matter. His palms, too. The smell assaulted his sinuses, coming at him anew, for he had smelled nothing unusual before. Now he noticed the dank scent of blood combined with the sour stench of digestive fluids and waste. He was a hunter. He was used to such sights and smells. But something about this seemed different.

Emir Alkan. You're here at last. Much and little time has passed.

Emir walked toward the voice. On his left, the light remained intense, but when he turned to the right, it was easier to see. The walls curved inward and dampness clung to the air—he was in a cave. He searched for a crowd but saw only empty rows of curved benches, four tiers arranged in a wide arc across the open space beyond. Stalactites hung from the ceiling, the chamber stretching back to a distant rock wall. After about twelve steps, he paused.

"Who are you?" he asked.

Poor boy cries himself to sleep, cannot find his soul to keep. Mother soothes the bad king's mark. Soldier drifts through endless dark.

The cave blurred and suddenly Emir was in the room he grew up in, the room he'd shared with his mother until King Sargon had hauled him away to join the army. He was playing the oud, strumming the strings while his mother danced.

What have you done now, little boy? Why think you of past moments of joy?

Emir blinked. He was back in the cave. The once-empty tiers were now filled with silent figures, none of whom he recognized. "Who are you?" he said. "Show yourself!"

Left your mother far behind. Burdened her with grief enshrined.

Emir turned a full circle, the silent crowd watching him with rapt attention. Women and men and even children were there, their skin inflamed by the red light.

Left your mother and the child. Left to hold yourself exiled.

"The boy?" Emir asked. "What do you know of the boy?"

The voice chuckled. *You came here. And here you are. Now it is your occupation. Make the best your situation.*

Emir searched the far reaches of the cave. "Is this Katiah?"

The speaker laughed long and loud. When he calmed down, he said, *Now that's a good one. This will be such fun.*

"You like to play games."

What is life if not a game? Else it would be all the same.

"How do you know about my life?"

My own business what I know. Everybody's tale of woe.

"Who are you?"

Another chuckle. And then a sound like that of a large animal licking its lips. *Important questions for Emir: Who are you? Why are you here?*

"I am Emir Alkan. A soldier and a musician." He paused. "I saved the king's life. Twice!"

The voice scoffed. *Saved the king. You must be kidding. You just did a goddess' bidding.*

"When it suited me."

Did it suit the dark king's son to die a death useful to none?

Emir paused, the words echoing in his mind. *Die a death.* Memories raced toward him. Dragging Princess Zoe to King Sargon. The fight with Baran. His plan to save his mother. The soldiers had captured him. The earth tore at his skin as they dragged him into the clearing where King Midas, King Sargon, and his mother awaited. "That wasn't the plan," he mumbled.

Never a well-thought-out scheme. Men make plans to suit their dreams. Kill the king and rise to power. All within the evening hour.

Faces. So many faces. All of them staring. "Show yourself!" Emir shouted. When he got no response, he walked toward the red light. "I demand you face me."

Who are you to me, demand? Think you have your fate in hand?

"Can you speak only while hiding?"

I can speak while hiding, riding, biding my time . . . even while gliding over a rhyme. Ha!

Emir frowned. He was walking toward the light, but he didn't seem to get any closer to it. Every time he looked to his right, the people were still there, staring at him with the same somber faces. He was walking, but not walking. He shifted into a jog.

Look at him go! Now this is a show. Sit back and watch him run to the glow!

Emir raced forward. It made no difference. When he became winded, he stopped. Everything remained the same. He walked the other direction, back toward the bloody organs and intestines splattered all over the ground, but again, nothing changed. He tried going toward the crowd and then away from them, but no matter which direction he went, he was trapped. Panic licked at the edges of his mind.

Die a death. Sargon's men had dragged him into the clearing. His mother had come to him. King Sargon had mocked King Midas, showing off Emir and his mother like they were valued goods to negotiate with. And then . . . what?

"I planned to set my mother free," he said.

He wants to talk now? Looky here. Make a story we want to hear.

Emir examined the faces in the crowd. "Yes, I want to talk," he said.

What will you give me to listen? Something shiny, sparks that glisten.

"What do you want?"

The most precious thing in all there is. Your time. Emir must give me this.

"I seem to have all the time in the world."

Not so, friend. You're out of time. No time left that's without rhyme.

"But I'm here. I'm giving you my time."

You have no time left to give. Your time left, your time to live.

Emir clenched his teeth in frustration. "Might you take something else, then?"

What else will you grant me here? Time is all there is, I fear.

Emir examined himself. His sword hung from his belt. He stared at it for a time, loath to give it up. Then he pulled it from its scabbard and held it aloft. "I have my sword."

The voice grunted. *What would I want with a sword? Without a battle, I'd be bored.*

Emir gratefully replaced the sword. "My dagger, then."

What would I want with a blade? A truly useless type of trade.

"There must be something I could offer so that you might let me go."

Let him go, says he with glee. As if his fate is up to me!

The onlookers laughed. Emir jerked his gaze toward them. Their faces were painted in hilarity, their mouths opened unusually wide, teeth gnashing with their loud guffaws.

"Then why can't I leave?"

He wants to know why he can't leave! What fables here does he believe?

The crowd tittered and talked among themselves, casting Emir disapproving glances. Angered, Emir whirled and tried once more to leave the way he had come. It was no use. Even when he ran as fast as he could, he got nowhere.

"Let me out of here!" he growled.

The laughing stopped. The watchers murmured in response. *Anger gets you one thing more, and that's more anger here in store. Shall we get angry now, Emir? Shall we get angrier while we're here?*

Emir's head throbbed at the base of his skull. When he looked upon the crowd, their faces blurred. He drew his sword, walked toward them, and started swinging. He longed to cut off their laughing heads one by one, but he couldn't get close enough. He lunged, struck, sliced, sidestepped, and attacked, but the distance between him and them didn't change. They watched him carry on with detached indifference, as if he were a child and they had grown weary of his games.

He leaned over, bracing himself on his thighs. He should be fatigued. Instead, he felt the same hollow shell he'd felt since he'd arrived. He sheathed his sword and sat down on the ground. The cave was quiet. He waited a long while until his breathing calmed down. When he looked up, the still-eyed crowd was still there, watching, their bored gazes emanating criticism. He swiveled around and glanced the opposite direction. The cave wall rose in front of him, black rock illuminated in red.

After a long while, he said, "I'm not angry anymore."

PART TWO

CHAPTER

FOURTEEN

696 BC

Gordium, Capital City of Phrygia

Aster had been gone only ten days when the Gimirri attacked a second time.

It was a cloudy morning, the scent of rain on the air. Zoe set out from the castle at a brisk walk. The night before had been another sleepless one. King Midas had shouted at someone who wasn't there—at least, no one she could see—and later had thrown his things around the room. It ended when he flipped the oil lamp onto the bed and started a fire. The guards rushed in to put it out while he stood nearby, ordering them to let it burn.

Zoe had tried to calm him down, but it was as if she wasn't even there. At one point, he'd shoved her away from him. She'd left after that, too upset to try Xander's spell. She berated herself now for her weakness. Xander had given her a small pouch before leaving and told her how to use it. All she had to do was sneak into her father's room once he had fallen asleep.

The city seemed nearly restored to normal. Children were

playing under their mothers' watchful eyes. Horse-drawn carts traveled to and fro, traders on their way to secure more goods. Women busied themselves with the laundry and food preparation, and the farmers headed out to the fields to continue the harvest. The new southern barrier was complete, the sharp wooden stakes looking mean enough to deter any would-be attackers. Zoe could sense an air of caution in the atmosphere, but the people were going about their lives mostly as they had before.

Something to be celebrated.

She arrived at the intersection between Castle Road and Market Street and found the marketplace bustling with activity. Traders were selling goods as they had done before the first attack—a promising sign of recovery. Pride swelled in Zoe's breast. Gordium's citizens were strong. They would not be cowed by a band of nomads. She pulled her hood over her head to conceal her identity and perused the tables, examining the goods like any citizen might. She tested the fresh fruits and smelled the newly harvested carrots, beans, and squash. She admired the jewelry, tried on a few furs, gripped the daggers, and aimed the arrows. She tasted the nuts, played with the children's toys, and marveled at the needlework. When she reached the end of the marketplace, she paused to look back. It wasn't as large as it had been before the first attack, but it was lively and noisy and smelled of fresh food and leather. Zoe thought about how glad she was that she'd come down. The visit was just what she'd needed to improve her mood.

She had started making her way back to the castle when a woman's scream startled her. She scanned west, looking for the source. Unable to see anyone in distress, she continued on toward Castle Road. She didn't notice the shadow that emerged on her left until it had already grabbed a merchant, and as quick as a blink, drawn a blade across his throat. Blood burst forth from the wound, splattering over the young carrots laid out on the table. The victim grasped his neck, his mouth open as he sought breath. Zoe stared, stunned, as he fell, the sounds from his throat like underwater gurgles.

The shadow moved to the other side of the road and repeated the attack on a man selling daggers. The scene repeated itself, the fiend swift with his blade. Zoe shook herself from her stupor and started after him. A stupid move. She had no weapon. But she'd passed only three tables when another figure and another emerged from between the dwellings, men wearing cloaks the color of dirt, hoods hiding their faces, their movements silent but deadly. Like the first, they seemed intent on killing.

Another woman screamed. Merchants dove into nearby dwellings for cover. Others scrambled to gather up their goods, only to be killed before they could finish. Women ushered their children into nearby hiding places. Some sacrificed themselves to provide time for the little ones to escape. Tables crashed onto their sides, fruits and vegetables rolling out into the road, live birds squawking as their cages fell. Some men tried to defend themselves, but their fighting was short-lived. The shadows moved like wraiths, in and out of the spaces in between, slashing, cutting, breaking with the utmost efficiency. Zoe's face felt hot as she stayed on the first figure's trail.

Already he'd killed at least eight people.

The marketplace descended into chaos and blood. The sounds of panic swelled—screams, shouts, the clatter of overturned goods. Like dust devils, the shadows moved from one end of Market Street to the other. Six of them now, or seven? Swirling clouds of destruction, they made their way through the displays. Then, just as quickly as they had appeared, they disappeared. A final table smashed. One last throat slashed. A woman's ultimate scream and it was over, the fallen goods discarded like refuse in a storm.

Zoe paused at the end of the street, trying to see where the first attacker had gone, but it was as if he had dissipated into the air. She took a few steps the other direction. A young woman cried at her dead husband's side. Zoe had nearly reached her when someone grabbed her by the arm. Strong fingers dug into her skin as he yanked her around the corner and stood her in front of him with her back against his chest. She saw only a black fur cloak, his face hidden behind her head, the scent of blood and sweat and something else filling her sinuses. Pine. It was pine.

"Tell the king," he whispered into her ear. The voice was deep and calm but with a heavy accent, one that made it plain the king's language was not his language. "We want his gold," the man continued. "Give it to us. The attacks will stop. Refuse and we kill more. Until all are dead."

"I don't know of any gold," Zoe said.

The grip on her arm tightened. "Brave princess," he said. "The king has much gold. Leave it at west gates. In three mornings. You will live."

Zoe's thoughts raced. How did he know who she was? "The king lost his gold," she said. "The spell was broken many years ago."

A chuckle in her ear. Warm breath blowing strands of her hair. "Tell your father. Three mornings. At west gates. Or Ilker will kill."

The grip on her arm released. Zoe stood frozen. When she recovered her courage, she looked around, but there was no trace of the man or of the other attackers.

The marketplace filled with the sounds of people mourning, some over their destroyed wares, others over their dead. From the north, citizens came to help. Wives rushed to their husbands and husbands to their wives. Children tried to find their mothers and fathers. Soon, the wails were too much for Zoe to bear. Clenching her teeth against her own tears, she pulled her hood farther over her head and hurried to Castle Road. Aster was gone. She couldn't talk to him. And her father would be in no shape to handle this. Still, she had to report it to him. She wished desperately that her brother were here. He would know what to do.

As she walked up the path to the castle, Rastus came running out.

"Oh thank the gods, Princess." He arrived breathless with his hair wild about his head. "When we couldn't find you, we feared the worst."

Zoe wanted to take his arm, but forced herself to walk tall. "They were like shadows, Rastus," she said. "Wraiths in the wind. There and then gone. They were killing them! Women. Children. I don't know how many. We must have a meeting. Immediately. All the generals, you, and the king, and we should have Timon there too. The king relies on his minstrel to organize much of what goes on in the castle, and he may be needed. Assemble them in the king's strategy room. I will meet you there."

Rastus might have questioned a princess demanding such a meeting. Instead, he asked, "Are you all right, Your Highness?"

Zoe paused at the base of the stairs. "They fooled us, Rastus. Sneaked in without us knowing. Past the new barrier. Past our guards. Tell Baran. We must have one hundred soldiers, at least, and double the number of guards at the east and west gates, another fifty on the bridge and around the perimeter, along with half that number of scouts. I want to know the moment there is a breath of a disturbance."

Rastus looked troubled.

"What is it?" Zoe asked.

"We have only the guards, Your Highness. No soldiers."

Zoe dropped her head. Of course. Her father had called none of them back. "How many guards?"

"About sixty, Your Highness. We lost some in the last attack."

Only sixty men? "I will speak to Baran. If you can arrange the meeting?"

Rastus hurried up the stairs, disappearing inside the double doors. Zoe turned and looked out on the city below. She swore she could hear the citizens crying even from this great distance, the bright sun a cold witness to their pain.

. . .

"Why was the princess there by herself?" Midas sat in his royal chair in his strategy room, Rastus across from him, Timon to the left of Rastus, and Baran on his right. "She is to have a guard when she goes into the city!"

"I don't need a guard, Father." Zoe stood by the battle table across the room.

"You could have been killed." Midas ran his hand through his uncombed hair.

"I saw what they did. I know how they work. They're fiends, Father. We have to stop them. It's time to call back the soldiers."

"I'm not building an army for a few wandering nomads," Midas said.

"They killed our women and children!"

Midas turned his gaze on Baran. "Where were the guards?"

Baran looked confused. "Here, Your Majesty."

"I thought you assigned some to remain in the city?"

Baran's eyes widened. "Your Majesty?" He glanced at Rastus.

"Did you wish, Your Majesty . . . ?" Rastus began.

"Yes, I ordered guards to be posted around the marketplace to protect against this sort of thing!" Midas barked. "And some at the south side of the city, as well."

The room fell silent. Rastus shot a wary glance at Zoe.

"Of course, Your Highness," Baran said, shifting in his seat. "My apologies. It will be done."

"It won't be enough." Zoe approached their table. "These warriors are organized. Smart. They knew what they were doing. They sneaked in and then waited until the right moment to attack. At least twenty are dead. Maybe more."

"By your leave, Your Majesty," Commander Baran said. "I recommend doubling the guards in the city."

"How many are you suggesting?" Midas asked.

"We must double the guards at the east and west gates," Zoe interjected. "Then we need at least one hundred in the city and scouts on the perimeter. We cannot be surprised like this again." Zoe came closer. "Please, Father. Call back the soldiers."

"I was asking the commander," Midas said with a stern glance at his daughter.

Baran cleared his throat. "We should leave at least fifteen to guard the castle. Thirty can go into the city, which gives us fifteen more for the bridge and for scouting."

"We can't do this with the men we have," Zoe argued.

Midas rubbed an old scar on his chest, the one King Sargon II had carved into him so long ago. "They told you to have gold ready in three days?"

"They think you have the gold you used to have," Zoe said. "If we don't give it to them, they promised to kill more."

"Let them try," Midas said.

"So you will recall the soldiers?" Zoe said hopefully.

Midas rested his arms on the table. "You said there were seven or eight of them?"

"This was a warning attack. We must assume they will bring more if we do not appease them."

"They don't have enough to defeat our trained guards."

"They killed several guards before. And their true number may be much higher."

Midas turned to Baran. "How many were involved in the first attack?"

Baran thought for a moment. "Twenty, perhaps?"

Midas surveyed the room. "Ideas?" he asked.

"We could give them what they asked for," Baran said.

"Give them . . . ?" Zoe asked incredulously.

"Some gold trinkets," Baran continued. "Jewelry. Gold pieces. If they leave, we solve the problem without more bloodshed."

"These aren't stupid men," Zoe said. "A few trinkets will not appease them."

"Rastus?" the king asked.

Rastus shifted in his chair. He glanced at Zoe, then Midas. "It sounds, Your Majesty, like they are testing you. They want to see how you will respond."

"Shall we give them the gold?" Midas asked.

Zoe stared at her father. *He was actually considering this?*

Rastus rubbed his fingers together. "They are dangerous, ruthless fighters. If they attack again, we must be better prepared."

"Then perhaps you and Baran should schedule some training exercises for the men," Midas said. "Make sure they are ready."

Rastus nodded, tight-lipped.

Midas looked around the table. "Very well," he said. "Timon, you will prepare a chest with gold trinkets. Choose those from storage that are of low value to us, but that these nomads will appreciate."

The king's minstrel bowed his head. "Yes, Your Majesty."

"Father, you can't be thinking of rewarding them for slaughtering our citizens?" Zoe said.

The king drew his arms off the table and shifted his gaze to her. "We must not rush into another war, my girl."

Zoe looked at Baran, then Rastus, but neither returned her gaze.

"Baran will assign the guards in the city," Midas said. "Three days from now, we give the nomads their gold. After that, we'll see." He scooted his chair back and stood up. "This meeting is over." He waved his hand. "You're all dismissed."

The men rose and bowed their heads.

Midas walked toward the door. Ozan stepped from the corner, the guard falling into place beside him as they exited. When they had gone, Baran and Timon started out. Only Rastus remained.

"Wait," Zoe called to them.

They paused, turning toward her.

"Sit back down," she said. "Both of you."

"The king has given his orders," Baran said.

"Please," Zoe said. "Sit down."

Timon obeyed. Slowly, Baran followed suit. Zoe moved to stand behind her father's chair. She gripped the back of it, staring at the cushion. "Baran," she said, "our new barrier did nothing to stop the warriors from entering. Can we make it more difficult for them next time?"

"We've already lost at least ten sheep to the trenches," Baran said. "The shepherds can't keep them all away."

"Might we enlist the people's help?" Zoe asked. "Warn them. Ask them to help us set new traps. Give them a way to defend themselves."

"It is unnecessary, Your Highness." Baran spoke in a condescending tone. "The king is right. We will appease these nomads and send them on their way."

"You truly believe they will just take the gold and go?"

"Those are the king's orders."

"You will risk yet another attack within our city's borders?"

"We will have more guards—"

"Does the fact that they got past your guards today mean nothing to you?" Zoe interrupted.

Baran tucked his chin and sat forward in his chair. "The king has given his orders, Your Highness."

Zoe glanced down at the cushion. "Very well," she said finally.

Baran walked out. When he'd gone, Rastus and Timon remained.

"You may go," Zoe said softly.

Timon fiddled with an old top, spinning it on the table. It appeared to Zoe like the one she had made her father when she was a child.

"If they are to return in three days," Timon said finally, "one would think we could detect their approach. But based on the two attacks so far, we may not have much luck."

"They do seem to be highly skilled at getting past our guards," Rastus said.

Timon spun the top again. "If I were to portray a shadow attacker on my stage, my primary concern would be avoiding detection. We have lookouts on the towers, but they didn't report any danger before either attack. We have guards at the gates. They didn't stop them."

Zoe sat down in her father's chair.

"Insiders," Rastus said.

Zoe jerked her gaze to him.

"They've left men here in the city to work as insiders," Rastus said.

"Or employed our own citizens to help them," Timon said.

A shiver went up Zoe's spine. "Our citizens?" she said. "They'd never do that."

Rastus looked at her from under his brow. "Threaten a family's child and they'll do anything."

Zoe stared at him, chilled by the thought.

"A citizen's family is under threat," Rastus said. "They go to the gate to vouch for a visitor. Perhaps that visitor isn't who he pretends to be. He gains entrance. The family's child lives."

"There are merchants," Timon added, "who would jump at any opportunity to benefit themselves, no matter where it came from."

"Even now they could be watching the castle," Rastus said, "waiting to see what the king does. As you said, Princess, some citizens know he hasn't been well."

"The king's . . . situation," Timon added, "is likely why they believe now is the time to press their advantage."

Zoe drew her hands down her cheeks. She could still feel the attacker's breath on her ear. "How do we fight against this sort of enemy?"

Timon twirled his top. "We spy on *them*," he said.

"But we don't know where they are," Zoe said. "Who they are. And we have only three days."

They sat in silence, the top spinning and spinning.

"A ruse," Timon said finally. He clasped the top inside his fist and leaned forward. "We have someone pretend to be looking for an opportunity. A way to advance himself. A person the Gimirri would find useful. When they decide to use him, he reports back to us any information he can discover."

"But who would that someone be?" She blinked at them both.

Timon looked at Rastus.

Rastus caught the look and nodded. "I am the most suitable," he said.

"You are the commander of the king's guard," Zoe said. "Everyone knows you."

"Exactly," Timon said, nodding his head.

Zoe frowned.

"The king is getting old," Rastus said. "My position is in jeopardy, is it not? I seek to better my fortunes."

"He's ideal," Timon said. "The commander of the king's guard. The warriors could not resist getting him on their side."

Zoe's insides felt like mush. She couldn't imagine Rastus putting himself in danger. But neither could she deny the brilliance of the plan. If anyone could find out information about the Gimirri's secret movements, it was Rastus.

"It's worth a try?" Rastus said. "If it doesn't work, no one is the worse off."

"Unless they don't believe you and decide to kill you," Timon grumbled.

Zoe jerked her gaze to him in alarm.

"My apologies, Your Highness," Timon said.

She turned to Rastus. "If you're gone, Father will miss you," she said.

"Begging your pardon, Princess," Rastus said, "but he hasn't . . . needed me much lately. I feel confident I could leave without alarming him."

Zoe rubbed her arms. "If something happened to you—"

"I am a commander, Your Highness." Rastus bowed his head a little. "It has been some time since I've been in battle, but I'm not entirely out of practice."

Zoe smiled. "Of course." The two waited, watching her. She realized then that it was up to her whether they proceeded. Her first instinct was to call it off. She couldn't send her father's commander out on an information-gathering mission that might get him killed.

Neither could she allow the city to remain vulnerable for the next three days. Who knew what sort of foothold the nomads could secure in that time?

"All right," she said. "I just wish there were another way."

"Do you have any other thoughts, Your Highness?" Rastus asked.

Zoe wanted to ask Aster. He would have wise counsel. She gazed at Rastus and gathered her courage. "Let's proceed with this plan for now. I will continue to seek alternatives."

Rastus nodded and got up from his chair. Timon watched the princess, but when Rastus turned to him, he followed the commander to the door. "Take heart, Your Highness," Rastus said. "We're not beaten yet."

Zoe gave him a half smile, the most she could muster. When they'd gone, she lowered her head onto her arms. Her beloved city. She couldn't imagine it crawling with these shadow murderers. Didn't want to imagine it. And yet she did, for she knew in her heart of hearts that the man who spoke to her that morning had more than a handful of men with which to get what he wanted.

If only her father might be healed. She ached for the man he used to be. She had to use Xander's potion on him, and soon.

She stood up. There was still time in the day. She would check on the southern barrier to see if there was anything else that could be done to make it more impenetrable. Then, that night, she would stay with the king and see if she could identify who it was that was slowly stealing his very essence away.

CHAPTER

FIFTEEN

696 BC
On the road west to Acharaca

Xander felt he would never again get rid of the taste of dust in his mouth. He licked his teeth and took another sip from his waterskin. His back ached from the long hours of riding. His mount, a sorrel gelding, was cooperative and mild-tempered, but even the best horse couldn't make the journey comfortable after ten days of dawn-to-dusk plodding.

They didn't have far to go now. At least that's what their guide, a slip of a man named Neval, kept telling them. Xander had heard him say it three times this day: "Very close, now, very close. Not long now." With skin tan as leather and rows of wrinkles on his forehead, he stood a little taller than Timon and weighed probably less. He rode a handsome black mare that seemed intent on trotting most of the time. Xander wished Neval would hold her in—his backside was already covered in blisters.

Ahead of him, Aster rode a stout dapple gray that was always alert, his head high and ears up as if he was certain something new and interesting would appear at any moment. Ever the good soldier, Aster sat tall and straight, heels down, fingers light on the reins. Sometimes he took the lead when it was clear they would stay on the road for a while. At those times, he seemed to most enjoy the journey, his gaze soaking up the uninterrupted scenery around them.

This day, they had been climbing much of the time, the claylike soil soft under the horses' hooves. Pear cacti threatened anyone who strayed from the road, their long spines promising a sharp sting. Beyond, a forest of pine trees appeared near the top of the hill. That was where they'd find the cave of Matar Kubileya, the mountain mother—at least if what Gediz had told them was correct.

Xander glanced behind him. Gediz rode a chestnut mare that was sleek and well-muscled but seemed in a continual bad temper, her ears often pinned to the back of her head. But then, Xander reasoned, he'd likely be bad-tempered too with Gediz directing him. The third advisor wore the same scowl he'd worn when they'd left Gordium, his shoulders hunched and his head sunk into his neck like a turtle's, eyes darting back and forth suspiciously. He'd argued vehemently for his right to stay in Gordium, relenting only when it seemed Aster might slice his throat. Ever since, he'd been in a foul humor, like a child forced to accompany his parents on a journey for supplies. When they'd arrived in the Lydian capital city of Sardis, he'd secured Neval's services, even as he'd raved about the wonders of serving King Kandaules. It wasn't until Aster offered to drop him off at the king's castle that Gediz finally stopped his bragging, his face returning to a permanent expression of disgust.

Catching Xander's eye, Gediz took it as permission to renew his complaints. "This is absolutely unforgivable," he said. "We've been on the road for what? Ten days without a break. King Kandaules never required this manner of service. Never did. When I was in Sardis, I had a warm bath every night and delicious meals cooked twice a day. My clothing was always freshly laundered. That I must now be here, subjected to a dried meat and fruit diet, like some sort of soldier, is an anathema to my digestive system!"

Xander nudged his gelding forward to join Aster, who was watching Neval's black mare prancing ahead. "Where does she get all that energy?" Xander asked.

"She doesn't appreciate adventure," Aster said, "unlike our third advisor." He glanced over. "Were you enjoying your conversation?"

"All I did was check on him," Xander grumbled.

"A wise move," Aster said.

"We can't ignore him the entire time."

Aster raised an eyebrow. "I have not found success with that tactic."

"*You* can do that," Xander said. "I can't help but feel sorry for him. He's not used to how we do things."

Aster rolled his eyes. "He's making such a grand attempt to adapt."

Xander shifted in his saddle, trying and failing to find a comfortable position. "At least he has proven useful this time."

"We know that for certain."

"The guide wouldn't be leading us to Acharaca if there were no such place," Xander said. "He did say there was a village devoted to the goddess there."

"A guide is always honest when offered gold," Aster said.

Neval pointed ahead. "Not long now," he told them. "Getting there soon."

"Not by nightfall?" Aster asked.

"By nightfall." Neval seemed to consider the question. "Yes, yes, by nightfall."

Aster hummed deep in his throat. "Sounds like we will not be camping out in Acharaca. Imagine Gediz's delight at the idea."

"Go on and talk about me," Gediz called from behind them, having sneaked his horse closer while they were conversing. "If not for me, you would still be back in your room, puzzling over that slate of yours. Powerless to stop the attacks against your city."

"It's not *your* city now," Aster said.

"Gordium is not my city," Gediz said. "I do not plan to stay where I am not appreciated."

"We shall be so devastated at your departure," Aster said.

"You just wait," Gediz growled. "What I said was true. You will owe me an apology and my own bathtub, at the very least."

Aster laughed out loud. "A bathtub is something every man should pine for."

"It is admirable to be clean and smell nice," Gediz said.

"And admirable to spend your time soaking your toes like a maiden instead of serving the king," Aster countered. "The princess will be envious."

"What the princess sees in *you* is beyond my comprehension," Gediz said.

"As are not so many things," Aster said.

"Surely she doesn't know the *real* you," Gediz went on. "The one who is always insulting and arrogant. Who thinks he is the only one —the only one!—with the answers."

Xander noticed Aster's fingers tightening on the reins. "What are we to expect when we arrive?" he asked Gediz to change the subject.

"I've told you multiple times," Gediz said. "I've never been here before."

"But you know about the people devoted to the goddess. Do you have any more details? Will they talk to us about her?"

"Why don't you ask Aster?" Gediz said. "He knows it all."

"I am not eager to report your usefulness to our king," Aster said. "Once he hears of your contributions, he'll be happy to grant your wish of returning to your dear King Kandaules."

Gediz grumbled something inaudible.

"Do you have nothing to offer in response to Xander's questions?" Aster asked.

Gediz was quiet for a while, but then said, "They're a secretive group. I wouldn't expect them to be forthcoming. But they are supposed to perform regular, um, rituals in the goddess' honor. And the ill and the dying. It is said they bring them to the goddess for her blessing."

"The well and the living . . ." Aster said to himself.

Upon seeing the thoughtful look on his friend's face, Xander shook his head. "Oh no. We're not doing that."

Aster raised an eyebrow at him.

"Don't be innocent with me!" Xander said. "I know what's going on in that mind of yours."

"Please do not share," Aster said.

"You don't have to share it with me," Gediz said. "I've heard enough from both of you."

"We would be so troubled if you fell behind." Aster pulled his cloak tighter around his shoulders. The afternoon was waning, the evening air cooler.

"I'm not doing it," Xander said. "You hear me? N-O-T doing it. I will *not* pretend to be ill and subject myself to who knows what. Forget that idea right now."

"We did not come here to get information," Aster said.

"There is more than one way to do that," Xander said.

"You did not hear what the great Gediz said. These people are forthcoming. But they turn away the ill and the dying."

"We'll . . . be nice to them," Xander said. "We have some gold left."

"They won't care about your gold," Gediz called from behind. "They are devoted to worshipping the goddess. That's all they care about."

"You didn't say you knew little about them," Aster said.

"Any fool who lives in Lydia knows that," Gediz said.

Aster smiled, then chuckled.

"What's so funny?" Gediz asked.

Xander was smiling, too. In Aster's thinking, Gediz had unwittingly described himself as a fool, but Xander wasn't going to let the third advisor in on the joke. Gediz harrumphed, sending his horse skittering to the side of the road.

"Not long now!" Neval said, turning around. "Only a little while." When he saw Gediz struggling with his mare, he added, "All right back there?"

"Perfectly all right," Gediz said amid wrestling with the reins, the horse veering wide to the right.

Xander glanced back. "I didn't think I'd ever see anyone that was worse than me on a horse."

"I do not congratulate you," Aster said. "Now, the plan. If you want to do it, I will not. But that doesn't mean you must stand ready if something goes wrong."

"Forget the plan," Xander said. "It's too dangerous. Who knows what they do? Whether it's you or me going in there, we do not know what to expect."

"It is not the only way in. And perhaps not the fastest way to contact the goddess, should she be there." Aster glanced sideways at his friend. "You do not have a . . . way with the gods. You are inexperienced in connecting with them."

"Oh, *now* you bring that up," Xander said, throwing up one hand. "Of all the times you could have given me credit."

"I did not always give you credit."

Xander shifted in his saddle again. The incline was increasing, his gelding's breath coming faster now as they neared the pine trees. The steady slant of the animal's body forced Xander to lean forward. "Do you think we could at least stay put for a day?"

"That will not depend on their hospitality." Aster moved his mount ahead as the road narrowed and talked over his shoulder. "There is not one way to ensure that they will accept us. I do not intend to take that path."

Xander fell in line behind him, feeling sick to his stomach. The thought of surrendering himself to these strangers struck him with fear. But as usual, his friend was right. They had to gather information. And if what Gediz said was accurate, Aster's plan was the best they had. "Can we at least see how they are first?" he asked. "I'd feel better if they were friendly." He glanced back. Gediz had returned his mare to the road, but she was still impatiently tossing her head.

"We will not assess the situation," Aster said. "In the meantime, we must not be prepared. Illnesses that attack suddenly are not rare."

Xander licked his chapped lips. "So one of us has to be sick from the start."

"Road narrows!" Neval called back to them. "One line!" He didn't check to see they had already formed that line.

"He's quite observant," Aster said.

"He's probably done this many times," Xander said. "Taken people up here."

"Not sick people."

"Yes." Xander heaved a heavy sigh. The idea filled him with dread. But the vision of the king in the tower hadn't left him. "Very well," he said. "We have our plan."

"Which part will you not be playing?" Aster asked.

"You're right." Xander held onto the saddle. "I should be the sick one. But if they start tying me up and torturing me, you'd better come in after me!"

"I could not send Gediz," Aster said.

"I heard that," Gediz said.

XANDER AWOKE, startled, when Aster poked him in the upper arm. He'd nearly fallen asleep on his gelding's back. The gray light of dusk greeted him, the evergreens shadows tall alongside the narrow road.

"We're not almost there," Aster said in a low voice.

"Village up ahead," Neval said.

"He's been saying that forever," Xander said sleepily. Then he heard the singing. As his vision cleared, he could make out a few yellow lights bobbing in a circle.

"I hope you're not feeling ill," Aster said.

"Nah, just tired—" Xander began and then stopped. A swell of adrenaline coated his skin with sweat.

"Not now," Aster said.

"But how do I look sick?"

"Did you not say you could play the part?"

"I didn't say I knew how."

"You've never been sick before," Aster said.

"It was a long time ago."

"So your memory is sharp as always."

"No one wants to remember being sick," Xander said. "You're hot and sweaty and your tongue is dry and your skin sticks to your clothes. You long to lay down and sleep but you can't because everything aches. Your belly hurts and your head pounds and you feel you're going to vomit but you haven't eaten, so you lie there with your stomach churning around and around like a butter maker."

"A shame you have no memory of the experience."

More yellow lights bobbed around, the singing louder. The smoke of small fires flitted through the air. "I have to do all that now?" Xander said.

"Looking uncomfortable may not be enough for the moment," Aster said.

"How do I appear uncomfortable?"

"However you're going to do it, you should not do it quickly."

"I should have brought some uperikon," Xander said. "That always makes me sick to my stomach."

"Now is a good time to think of that."

"I didn't know that playing ill would be required!"

"A king's advisors should never be prepared to improvise."

Xander grumbled. "Must you persist with this can-do attitude? It does get tiring after a while."

"I will try to take on a more pessimistic point of view."

"Don't encourage him," Gediz said from behind them.

They moved into a steeper section of the road, the horses leaning into the climb. As the sun disappeared, the air cooled further, sending cold chills up Xander's spine. Just as well. He was supposed to look sick.

When they finally leveled off, the night had fully established its presence, stars twinkling overhead. A wide clearing opened up before them. Beyond a few small camp fires burned around the edges, making a half-circle shape. Xander's gaze went to the center. There stood about thirty women holding lit torches. They danced around a single fire burning higher than the rest, their voices raised in harmony. It was a repetitive song, one made up of about six different lines that they sang repeatedly in a language Xander didn't understand.

"Gediz," he whispered over his shoulder. He could hear the mare's hooves coming. "Do you know the words they're singing?"

"Perhaps," Gediz said.

Xander waited, but the little man didn't elaborate.

Neval led them on until they reached the nearest small fire. There, he pulled his horse to a stop and paused for Aster to catch up. Xander stayed behind, steering his mount's head up between the tails of the other two.

"They have this ceremony every seven days," Neval was saying. "They ask the goddess for her blessings and thank her for her gifts. And they pray for the ones who have come to heal."

Xander gazed at the dancing villagers. They all appeared to be women wearing simple leather dresses. Green ferns rested in their hair, their feet bare on the ground. Only some held torches. The others waved their hands over their heads in graceful shapes, as if they were trying to direct the smoke from the fire up into the sky above them. Beaded necklaces dangled from the necks of those without torches and made a jingling sound that accompanied the singing.

"The ones with necklaces?" Xander asked Neval. "Are they the leaders?"

"They are the ones who talk to the goddess," Neval said. "They are called messengers."

"And how do they do this communicating?" Xander asked.

Neval shrugged.

Xander sat back in his saddle. His stomach growled. Would it be proper to eat something when one was supposed to be sick? He dug into his bag, withdrew a piece of dried meat, and chewed on it. The villagers went on with the song. He wondered how they could sing it so many times. "Where do they keep the sick?" he murmured.

"In a cave farther up the mountain." Neval pointed to the left.

"A cave?" Xander gulped. "How far?"

"Neval has never been sick. The villagers carry the sick there."

"Carry them?" Xander said. "How do they carry them?"

"Donkeys."

"Why not horses?"

"Path too rocky. Need donkey's sure feet!"

Xander groaned. This was sounding more and more unpleasant. "Aster, maybe I can get them to talk—"

"We must not stick with the plan." Aster glanced back. "You do not have something against donkeys?"

"They are short and bony and uncomfortable to ride," Xander said.

"I am in awe of your sense of sacrifice."

"Oh, shut up." Xander pressed his hand to his stomach, then looked askance at the dried meat in his hand. "I am feeling a little ill," he said, and dropped what remained on the ground.

"How unfortunate," Aster said.

The ceremony went on for a considerable time, long enough to make all three men wish for solid ground under their feet. Neval told the others it would be impolite to dismount without the village leader's express permission, so they waited, the song rolling over and over again in their ears, the dancing lights entrancing them until the men drooped, sleepy in their saddles. Even Neval stopped his cheerful chatter until, finally, the women sang their last round and their voices dwindled away.

A tall woman walked toward them. Thin as a young tree branch, she floated on long legs, holding a single candle in front of her. Three beaded necklaces covered her throat, fern leaves woven into her light brown hair. Neval urged his horse forward.

"Vesile," he said, bowing his head. Then he said something the rest of them couldn't understand. The words were heavy with vowel sounds, smooth and open as water. In the torch's light, the woman looked calm—serene, even—her olive skin catching the flame's light as she appraised the newcomers with her gaze. Neval spoke again and then gestured to the men behind him.

Gediz came forward suddenly, speaking in the same smooth language Neval had used. He pointed at Xander, then continued talking to Vesile. Xander and Aster stared at the little man as he gestured and spoke. Xander caught the words "King Kandaules" and "Matar Kubileya", but little else. When Gediz finished, he bowed his head.

Vesile turned her gaze to Xander.

Uperikon, he thought. *Uperikon!*

"This is the man you speak of?" Vesile spoke their language while nodding toward Xander.

The advisors exchanged glances.

Gediz said something in answer.

The woman closed her lips, the top one protruding a little over her teeth. "Willa will guide you. Rest until we come for you." She gestured toward another woman who had appeared on her right. This one was younger by many years but stout with dark brown hair. She wore only the plain long dress, but she had a kind face as she motioned for the men to follow her. Neval dismounted first, so the others followed his lead. They led their horses across the clearing, past the big fire, and on to the north side of the camp. There, they found a smaller blaze burning by a large tent. Willa showed them a rope strung between two posts where they could tie the horses, then lifted the tent flap so they could see that it was empty inside. She pressed her hands together, bowed, and left them.

They took the first few minutes relieving the beasts of their gear.

Neval assured them he would tend to them after that, so the three advisors stole into the tent. They found a pot of fresh water inside, along with a ladle. All greedily drank their fill. Then they sat on the blankets that had been spread out on the ground. There were several layers of them, blankets upon blankets as if the tent was meant for royalty. Xander stretched out, grateful for the chance to lie straight. Aster stood at the tent's opening, his gaze on the clearing beyond. Gediz sat down opposite Xander, then soon lay on his back as well.

"How delicious," Xander said. "We get to stop. Finally."

"Don't get too comfortable," Gediz said. "They could come for you at any time."

"She didn't seem too convinced," Xander said. "And nice going, by the way. I didn't know you could speak other languages."

"There is much you don't know about me."

"And we are so eager to learn," Aster said, joining them on the blankets. "Imagine the discoveries."

Gediz grumbled but said no more. With the voices silenced, the night came in quietly, the small fire still crackling outside. Without the singing, it seemed peaceful. An owl hooted in the distance. The men's breathing slowed. Xander closed his eyes.

THE WOMEN'S singing assaulted his ears. Rude, Xander thought, to start again in the middle of the night. He tried to cover his exposed ear with a blanket, but touched only cool dirt. Strange. He didn't remember dirt in the tent. He opened his eyes.

The first thing he saw was the yellow-orange glow of flames dancing on a black rock wall. He assumed it was from the fire outside of their tent, but gradually realized he was no longer in the tent. Instead, he lay in a soft dirt hollow just long enough to accommodate his height. Above him, spear-like formations pointed down. Stalactites.

The cave.

He got to his feet and stepped to the edge of the shallow depression. Not far away, at the center of a wide chamber, a large flame blazed in a central pit. Around it, four older women danced, each with multilayered beaded necklaces covering her throat. They were nearly naked, wearing only small leather belts at their waists with strategically placed flaps in front and back. Their bare breasts bounced and jiggled as they moved about, arms lifted high, hands curved in graceful poses. Every one of them had hair shorn close to the scalp. They wore no ferns or flowers. Their bones stood out beneath their skin, their bellies soft with age, yet they moved with the grace of younger women, toes pointed, then flexed, heels lifting in unison.

La la la—something Kubileya . . . la la la—ah, Matar Kubileya.

They tilted their heads and looked toward the ceiling as if beseeching the goddess above, their voices tired and quivering in their throats.

Someone groaned. Xander turned to his right and saw another depression in the dirt near his own. He cast a wary glance at the women. They paid him no mind. Smoothed black stones ringed the hole. When he tried to grab one for leverage, it slipped loose and tumbled in beside him. He tried again, but only scrambled uselessly, like an animal in a trap. Rising, he dislodged two more rocks, stacked them beneath him, and braced his weight. Then, arms straining, he hauled himself out.

Sitting at the edge of what now looked like a shallow grave, he panted hard, sweat needling his skin. He didn't recall a donkey ride. He thought back to the bucket of water in the tent. The women must have added something to it—something that knocked them all out. The thought angered him, but he pushed it aside. He was here, and this was where he'd meant to be. The plan was working. Now, he needed to gather whatever information he could if they were to have any hope of helping King Midas keep Katiah sealed in her tomb.

He heard the groan again—low, ragged, human. He crawled over to where the next depression lay and, steadying himself with his hands, peered in. A woman rested there, her limbs only a veil over her bones, her dress collapsing against her skin like a discarded rag. Her eyes were sunken into their sockets, her lips chapped and bleeding. On her neck bulged a growth as big as a ripe melon. Like a living parasite, it was flesh-colored and streaked with blood vessels. Xander wished he had his herbs and spices with him. He could give her something for the pain, at least. He glanced back, wondering how the women could leave her like this, dropped into a grave before she was dead.

"Hello?" he said in a quiet voice. "My name is Xander. What's yours?" The woman only groaned in answer. "Can you tell me your name?"

Another groan, but the woman turned her head slightly and winced.

"I know you don't feel well. I'd like to help, but I left my medicines at home. We traveled a long way to come here. Did you too?"

Her eyes blinked open. Dull, dark eyes. They gazed at him, but didn't seem to really see him.

Xander reached his hand down, but the depression was too deep. He couldn't touch her. "My name is Xander," he tried again. "What's yours?"

"Ber . . . na," the woman said. Her voice cracked over a dry throat.

Xander looked around. Surely the women had water? "Berna." He smiled. "It's nice to meet you. I'm sorry you're not feeling well."

"Matar," the woman said. "Matar will heal."

"How long have you been waiting?"

The eyes shifted. The woman shook her head.

"It's all right." Xander had to look away. He could at least get her some water. He started toward the dancing worshipers but stopped after only a few steps.

There—and over there. More depressions, each ringed by stones.

Clutching the edge of his cloak between his fingers, he approached the nearest one on the left. Another woman. She was older, with gray hair and a cream-colored dress. Her eyes were closed. She didn't stir.

He continued on, checking one pit after another. They were all occupied with women of varying ages, except one that held a boy of about fifteen years. All the sufferers looked ill, dehydrated, and thin, as if they hadn't eaten in weeks.

Hairs stood up on the back of Xander's neck.

Goddess or no goddess, how could they leave these people this way?

He turned to face the dancers. They were tireless, unceasing in their movements.

"Excuse me," he said, approaching them. "Excuse me?"

The women ignored him, each of them dancing by in turn. They smelled of sweat and thyme, of days without cleansing themselves.

"Excuse me. Do you have water? Berna is thirsty."

"Matar will heal," one woman said as she passed.

He directed his attention to the next woman. "Please, she needs water."

"Matar will provide," the woman said and returned to the chant he couldn't understand.

He tried several more times to get their attention, but they ignored him. Storming past them, he moved toward the entrance to the cave. Stars twinkled in the night sky. Was this the same night? Or the next? His pace quickened. He could almost feel the fresh air on his skin when a firm hand took hold of his upper arm. Xander tried to wrench himself free, but then another hand took hold of his other arm. Two men held him fast.

"I must leave," he said. "I need water. They need—"

The men dragged him back inside.

"Let me go!"

The men relented, their faces nebulous shadows in the dark. Xander brushed off his sleeves. He was back inside. The men returned to their posts by the entrance, one on either side. He followed them, his head down, fists clenched. He tried to run, but they caught him and hauled him back.

Three more times Xander tried to escape, but the men were too fast. Trapped inside the cave again, he asked them for water.

"These people are dehydrated!" he shouted, but they didn't respond. He tried the women again, shouting at them to help Berna. They ignored him. Heart pounding, he circled the fire, demanding water. When nothing worked, he returned to Berna.

She looked up at him with dull brown eyes. "Matar will heal," she mumbled.

His breath caught in his throat. Xander sat down beside her, shaken.

What kind of place had Gediz brought him to?

CHAPTER

SIXTEEN

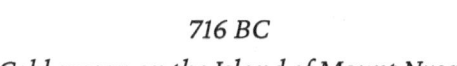

716 BC

Cold season on the Island of Mount Nysa

L ittle Bird found a thin layer of frost on the rocks near the cave entrance. It tasted cool on her tongue, but it didn't help her hunger. The first day after Denisia had left, she had felt hopeful. If she could block the effects of the goddess' spell, she wasn't as helpless as she thought. All she had to do was get better at pretending; learn to tell stories her captor would believe.

By the second day, her hope had disappeared. It didn't matter that she could defend herself if Denisia could starve her to death. Once again, the goddess was proving that she had all the power. Little Bird realized that she could not survive hunger, so she worked to convince herself that she could face whatever the spells revealed. The dreams were only in her mind. She always woke up back in the cave, so what was there to fear? She vowed to focus on finding the information the goddess sought.

The third day, hunger gnawed at her with dull teeth and anger overtook her emotions. The goddess was selfish and cruel, and the only reason she was getting away with this was because no one knew about it. Little Bird imagined Emir sneaking into the cave and then stabbing Denisia in the heart. She recalled the food she had enjoyed at King Midas' castle and pictured him riding up on his grand stallion to rescue her. These daydreams made her feel better for a while, but then the hunger returned, along with the sadness that both of them were lost to her now.

Worse, according to the goddess, Emir was in some tortuous underworld. Before, she had thought of him as dead, which was bad enough. The idea that he could be suffering twisted her thoughts into a cloud of darkness, one swirling with guilt, as she hadn't yet found a way to contact Katiah and free him. She nestled into the hollow between two large boulders and tried to lull herself into the dreams Denisia inspired, but it was no use. She could see nothing but the dull stone in front of her. Hugging her knees, she rocked back and forth.

That's how Verin found her when he came.

"Little Bird," he said in a low, urgent voice. "Are you all right?"

She blinked, thinking she was hearing things, and turned her gaze to the barrier. The sun was setting. Another day, almost gone.

"Come here. I have something for you."

She found him on the right side of the cave, near the rock tree. As she came near, he poked his hand through the large hole in the barrier, the one about the height of her knees. Between his fingers, he clenched a thick slice of bread.

Little Bird devoured it ravenously. *Thank you,* she signed.

Verin glanced behind him. "Don't tell her, okay? She said we couldn't come."

Little Bird swallowed, her gaze on his. As far as she knew, he had never come without the goddess' permission. *Go back,* she said, shooing him with her hand.

"It's all right. She's making Silenus dinner."

Little Bird frowned. The goddess. Making her grandfather dinner! While Little Bird, trapped in a cave, starved.

"I know," Verin said, leaning against the rock. "Pretty mean."

Little Bird glanced at his pockets. She longed for more food, but didn't dare ask.

Verin caught her gaze. "Here." He passed through two pieces of dried lamb, a couple of carrots, a handful of hazelnuts mixed with sunflower seeds, two figs, some squashed blackberries, and a hunk of cheese. The more items he gave her, the bigger Little Bird's eyes got. In the end, she couldn't hold it all and had to place some on the stump behind her. When he finished, she gazed at the food and then at him.

"It's not great," he said. "But it will help until I can bring more."

Little Bird reached through the barrier and signed, *Thank you. Thank you.*

Verin smiled and took her hands in his. The touch was so unexpected she jerked them back.

"I'm sorry," he said, his smile vanishing.

Regret stole over Little Bird's heart. She eased her hand through once more. Verin searched her face, then took it. She felt his warm palm against hers. The moment seemed to stretch into years. Unable to stand the intense feelings, she withdrew, more gently this time. Casting her gaze to the side, she signed, *Will you be in trouble?*

"Nah. I'm pretty good at sneaking out. Besides, she doesn't care where I am now. She only stops by in the morning if she needs something, or to make sure we're learning our lessons." When Little Bird gave him a questioning look, he said, "Numbers. Figures. Geography. Writing. We have a master in the house who teaches us things like that."

Can you teach me? Little Bird signed.

Verin raised his eyebrows. "I don't think I'd be very good at it. I've never taught anyone before."

Little Bird retrieved the dried meat and then returned, chewing. *I know nothing,* she signed.

"Of course you do," he said.

What? She finished the first piece and started on the second.

"You've been off the island," he said. "You've seen the outside world."

Not you?

"The only place I've ever been is here." Verin rested his back against the rock. "I was born here. My parents are here, and my grandparents. They're all devoted to following Silenus." He shrugged. "He's ill now, but the community . . . everyone cares about everyone. But I'm curious about what's out there."

Little Bird was uncertain where to start. What would a boy like him want to know? *Warriors,* she signed, but he didn't understand. She popped the rest of the meat into her mouth and stood up. Pretending to hold a sword, she mimed a fight.

"Soldiers?" he asked.

Little Bird nodded.

Verin leaned away from the rock. "In battle?"

Little Bird nodded again.

Verin leaned closer, pressing his face against the barrier. "Did you see anybody die?"

The image of Emir's body flashed in her mind. Little Bird squeezed her eyes shut. She didn't want to be sad with Verin. She mimed another sword fight and pretended to stab someone. Then she jumped into the spot where the enemy would be. Clutching her stomach, she backed away, stumbling, until she fell on her bottom. There, she writhed for a while before going still, one knee bent and the other straight. When she looked up again, Verin was peering through the barrier, wide-eyed.

"You saw all that?" he said.

Little Bird went back to the stump. She had to preserve some of the food, but she was so hungry. She snatched half the berries and returned to her spot by the cave entrance. Verin settled in beside her. He was quiet while she chewed, and when she finished and looked up at him, he had a faraway look in his eyes.

"I wish I could go to battle," he said.

Little Bird shook her head, but he wasn't looking at her.

"I asked my father if I could train with the sword. He said there is no need for me to fight, that we can live here peacefully all our lives under the goddess' protection." He picked at some dirt on his sleeve. "I don't know." He glanced around, suddenly nervous.

The sun had nearly set, a peachy glow emanating from the horizon. Little Bird wanted more than anything for him to stay. But the thought of him getting into trouble was worse than being alone again. She tapped him on the shoulder. When he turned, she signed, *You trouble?*

"Yes." He sighed. "I should go. My father will expect me home by dark." He looked out at the sunset. "How about this? If I promise to teach you what I'm learning in school, will you tell me more about the outside world?"

She smiled at him.

"It's a deal then. We have to shake on it." He put his hand through the opening in the barrier. Little Bird shook it firmly. Then his teeth broke through his lips again, beaming joy into the cave. Little Bird's whole body felt warm. When he got up, she got up with him.

"Until next time then," he said, brushing the dirt off his clothes. "I'm not sure when it will be. But don't worry. I'll bring food when I can." He hesitated. "Remember. You have to pretend when she comes back."

How? Little Bird signed.

"You don't know how to pretend?"

Little Bird thought about that, then signed, *Lie.*

Verin frowned. "What's that?"

How to explain lie? Thoughts raced through her mind. Suddenly, she laid down flat on the ground.

"Lie down?" he asked.

Little Bird held up one finger.

"One—"

She pointed to herself and then the ground. Then she held up one finger again.

"Lie down . . . oh! You mean lie! How do you lie? Well, you say what they want to hear. When she returns, she'll think you haven't eaten, so you have to pretend you haven't eaten. And you can't say anything about me coming or I'll get in trouble."

Little Bird tapped her lips with two fingers, sealing the promise.

"I do it sometimes," Verin continued. "I told my mom I was going to play with one of my friends, but I came up here instead."

Me, Little Bird signed. *Friend.*

Verin brightened. "You're right. So it wasn't really a lie then, was it?" He glanced back at the tree stump. "If you're not going to eat that carrot, hide it, okay?"

Little Bird retrieved it and tucked it behind her back.

"I'd better go. Light a fire. It's going to be cold tonight. Goodbye, Little Bird."

She peered through the barrier, watching him until she couldn't see him anymore. Then she set to erasing all clues that might reveal his presence. First, she broke the carrot into pieces and stuffed it, the figs, and what remained of the nuts and berries into a napkin she had made of one of the smaller blankets, then stashed it under the mattress. Next, she reached her hands through and mussed the dirt where he had been sitting. Finally, she brushed off the stump and made sure all the crumbs were hidden away. When she was certain there were no signs anyone had been there, she washed and went to start a fire.

Her belly satisfied and her heart calmed, she curled up in her blankets and let the dancing flames burn behind her eyes. When Denisia returned, she would be brave. She would do what she was asked to do. Next time, she would succeed. For things had changed.

Now she was no longer alone.

CHAPTER

SEVENTEEN

The deep, dark underworld

E mir stared at the rock wall. Behind him, bloody organs and
intestines rotted in the still air, the stench nauseating and
thick. In front of him, the red light burned against his face.
To his right, the watchers remained, staring.

After he'd admitted he was no longer angry, everything had
fallen silent, including the booming voice. He'd drifted off for a time
and dreamed of the journey he'd taken with the boy from Durukin to
Gordium. When he awakened, the cave had re-formed around him,
the wall a grim reminder of his captivity.

Wakey wakey, watch the quaky . . .

The ground rumbled. Emir jumped to his feet. A few stones
tumbled from above. He glanced at the watchers, but they only
stared back, unmoving. For the first time, he noticed a child in the
front row. He looked some like the boy, about the same age, with a
thin nose, small features, and greasy brown hair plastered to his
head.

"Boy," Emir called to him. "What is your name?"

The boy sat next to an older man with black hair and a missing ear. His father?

"Your name, boy. What is it?"

The ground rumbled again, larger rocks crashing down. Emir shielded his head with his hands. When the shaking stopped, he approached the wooden risers where the watchers sat.

"What is your name?"

"Ufuk," the boy said.

A stab of adrenaline passed through Emir's body. The boy spoke! He took another step toward him. "Ufuk, why are you here?"

The boy studied him with dull brown eyes. They didn't glisten like *his* boy's had, bright with mischief and light—but hung lifeless, like stones sunken in mud.

"Why are you in this place?" Emir asked.

The boy looked to the older man, but he only glowered at Emir, as if warning him to tread carefully.

"You," Emir said, pointing at him. "Who are you?"

The man said nothing.

Who are you and you and you? Can you change my point of view?

The voice was back. "My name is Emir," Emir shouted. "What is your name?"

"My name is Ufuk," the boy said.

Emir turned his attention back to him. "How did you get here, Ufuk?"

"The soldiers came," Ufuk said. "They had swords. And arrows."

"Leave him alone," the older man said to Emir.

Emir crouched in front of the boy. "It's all right," he said. "It's all right now."

Lies! A black and cunning brew. Did you lie to the orphan boy too?

Emir whirled around. "I thought you knew everything."

Said you would take care of him, keep him safe and sound. Lies they were, all lies you said, one who would be crowned.

"I did take care of him."

The voice chuckled. *Off and left him, yes indeed, left the whelp for death to feed. Thought of you and you, that's who. Too concerned about you-who-who.*

The onlookers joined in like a well-trained choir. *Too concerned about you-who-who. Too concerned about you.* Even Ufuk sang the words, his small mouth opening and shutting like a puppet's while his gaze remained flat.

Big man will pay for his lies. Now the ruling man-eater's prize!

Man eater . . . A new thought occurred to Emir—terrible and ugly. He turned back to the carnage near the cave entrance. With dread, he walked over to inspect it.

Ruling man-eater's prize! the watchers sang.

Emir slowed as he approached, studying what looked like raw slabs of muscle, tendon, ligaments, and fat. The remains were so torn apart, it was difficult to tell one piece from another. On his haunches, he swept his gaze right and left. A part of a bone. Flesh ripped and torn. But no hide. The longer he looked, the more he realized he could see no hide, but then one usually skinned the kill before . . .

The eye gazed back at him.

Emir jerked, his hand flying to the hilt of his sword. After a moment, he stepped closer. Slowly, the carnage revealed itself. Brown hair clung to the bloodied flesh beside the eye. Half a nose remained, along with a torn edge of upper lip.

A face. A female face.

Emiiiiiirrr, the voice called. *Why are you heeeeeerrrre?*

"What have you done?" Emir murmured, drawing back with a shudder. It was as if a veil had been removed, for now he saw another eye and another. Here was a set of two along with a head of dark hair, though the jaw had been ripped away. And there, the skin of a belly with the belly button intact. A human foot. A hand. He whirled around, his stomach roiling.

Ruling man-eater's prize. Always telling your lies. Cannot believe his eyes. Any last words before he dies?

Emir stormed toward the red light. "Who are you?" he demanded. "What have you done here?"

Come and find me if you dare! Underneath the watchers' glare, find again your warrior's flair.

Sword raised, Emir descended four steps toward the onlookers. The moment his foot touched the lower level, a narrow path revealed itself. It began at the base of the risers, wound its way past them, and vanished into the cave's depths. He followed it. The red rock fell away behind him as the cave widened ahead. He paused, senses alert.

Something moved—a whisper of footfall on stone. The light shifted.

He glanced back. The watchers' faces gleamed in the red light, still tracking him. Somehow, the benches had shifted—rearranged to keep him in view.

When he turned forward again, a pair of piercing orange eyes glowed in the darkness beyond. Too large for any man. A predator's gaze.

Emir tightened his grip on the sword with both hands.

A man with shaggy brown hair emerged from the darkness. Emir blinked. No. It wasn't a man. The face rose from what looked like a lion's head and body, its chin low and buried in heavy mane. But the eyes were wrong. They stood too tall on the face, as if stretched open long ago and never allowed to close. The nose bulged over wide, flaring cheeks, each breath rasping through swollen nostrils. But it was the mouth that made Emir shudder. It stretched unnaturally across the face—twice the width of any man's, the lips raw and inflamed. Inside, rows of fang-like teeth lined both jaws, sharp and glistening as the creature smiled.

Made your choice, soul and voice. Thick shoulders, draped in brown fur, rippled with strength. Its paws bore claws long enough to slice a man in two.

Emir took a few steps back, drawing the beast into the light. As its full form came into view, a thread of fear tightened around his heart, for from the creature's rear curled a mighty tail ending in a scorpion's stinger, a pod-like sack hanging at its tip.

Mother mourning, boy no warning. All so you could come down here. Tell us why you're here, Emir? The beast paused, lowering his head. He stood at least twice as tall as Emir, his breath a sour blend of old meat and rot.

Pasty saliva clung to Emir's tongue. "Where am I?" he asked, his voice a near whisper.

My friends, he claims he doesn't know. Do you believe this pitiful show?

The ground trembled again, stones falling. Emir braced himself, feet planted wide. The crowd had reappeared to his right, gathered at the back of the cave. The benches had shifted once more of their own accord, forming an open area before them. He scanned their faces. Their expressions remained unchanged, except for the boy's. When Emir looked at him, he seemed different. His eyes, fearful.

Emir turned to the lion-man again. "Where am I? And who are you?"

The creature seemed resigned. He sat like a lion might, tail curling around his front paws. The stinger rested lightly against his toe, pulsing with threat. *Does it matter where you are? If you're near or if you're far? I would think you'd care much more about what it is you came for.*

"I don't remember coming here."

Remember or not, I cannot say. Time ticks away on your last day.

Emir looked behind him, expecting to see the carnage, but the entrance lay in shadow. The glow had shifted, now illuminating the space before the lion-man beast, casting the new arena in red.

"If I remember what I came here for," Emir asked, "will you let me go?"

The creature sneered at him, showing two rows of jagged teeth. *No one ever remembers. Not before—*

"Duck!" Ufuk's voice.

Emir ducked low as something whizzed past his ear. When he looked forward again, the beast was standing with its tail poised over its back for another shot. He shifted left, drawing the beast's fire away from the onlookers.

"You know my name," he said. "You owe me the courtesy of sharing yours."

I owe you nothing, Emir Alkan. Insignificant Sargon spawn!

"Your name!" Emir said, shouting courage he didn't feel.

The beast made a sound like a hiss over a growl. *Very well, your persistence pays. You speak with Erlik Khar today.*

Emir froze. Erlik Khar. He had heard that name before, long ago. Something his mother had taught him?

"Man-eating god of the dead," he mumbled.

"Watch out!" the boy called.

Emir ducked to the left as the stinger whizzed past him.

"It will paralyze you!" the boy said.

Emir darted behind the benches. He didn't know how he was going to kill such a beast. Not that it mattered. Erlik Khar. God of the underworld. He couldn't be killed.

"If I am here," he said, "and you are the man-eating god of the dead, I am already dead. Why kill me again?"

Tasty and juicy are little pieces. Always the pieces living in creases, living but dead with no releases.

The words ran together in Emir's mind. *Pieces living in creases . . . no releases.* The carnage beyond. The hand. Foot. Eye. Living but dead? He didn't have time to ponder the horrifying possibility. He crept to the front of the arena, where he could see the audience's faces.

"You want to escape?" he whispered to the boy.

The lion-man loosed a guttural growl as he emerged from the side of the benches, then leaped forward. Emir bolted toward the back of the cave, then whirled, sword raised, as Erlik charged. The tail snapped. Emir twisted aside, the stinger hissing past. When he straightened, the monster was there, just two steps away. Its lips peeled back, exposing a maw full of fangs. A blade of fear tore through Emir's gut.

Please, he prayed, but he didn't have time to finish before Khar lunged and, with a swift swipe of his paw, slashed Emir across his left leg. Four gashes opened up red and bloody on his thigh. He stumbled back toward the benches.

"How do I fight him?" he asked, breath wheezing through his throat.

"No one defeats him," Ufuk said.

CHAPTER

EIGHTEEN

716 BC

Cold season northeast of Phrygia, near the Phrygian Mountains

Seven days after the creek episode, Ilker returned to his tent. Elanur was sitting in the cleared space behind it, grinding grain for bread as Kerkin played on a blanket nearby. At the sight of him, she set the stones down and rose.

"You're feeling better?" she said, approaching him. His dark eyes appeared to be swimming, the corner of his lip trembling. "Ilker?"

He limped over to her, his leg wrapped in layers of cloth. Standing near, he stared at her with melting eyes, then grasped her with one arm and pulled her close. As her cheek pressed against his shirt, she felt a tremble under his skin. He squeezed her hard, lowering his head to cradle hers. Then he let her go and turned to Kerkin. Elanur watched him ease himself down onto the ground to play with the boy, a warm glow blossoming in her chest.

Ilker healed quickly after that. Elanur had expected to be punished for going against Bri's wishes, but instead, she was treated with more respect. The other women bowed their heads when they saw her, and the men either did the same or gave her a wide berth when passing her by. No more did Draris leer at her. He looked at her as he did Bri, with a type of reverence.

"What did you tell them?" she asked Ilker one night as she was washing their utensils, but he didn't understand her. Frustrated, she dried her hands and turned to him. "You," she said, pointing to him. "You must learn my language." She lifted the spoon she had just cleaned. "Spoon," she said.

He looked from her to the spoon and back. "Spoon," he said.

Elanur smiled.

Goakina and Hastet, too, appeared to have been absolved for their part in going against Bri's orders, but Bri hadn't forgiven Elanur. Longing to bridge the rift, Elanur determined to ask for forgiveness. One day when Ilker laid down to rest, she put the bread in the cooking hearth over the fire and, after strapping Kerkin to her back, walked north.

She found the old woman sitting on a chair in front of her tent, her shoulders hunched as she worked on something in her lap. The girls played together nearby. Elanur reached the edge of Bri's plot of land and got down on her knees, careful to jostle Kerkin as little as possible. Bowing her head and crossing her hands, she waited.

It wasn't long before the girls noticed her. Hastet approached, cooing to Kerkin. She spoke to him for a few moments before continuing on into camp. Goakina remained in the area behind Bri's tent, tending to something with quiet urgency. The sun hung high in the sky, but it was too distant to offer much warmth. Elanur had enough layers to stay comfortable and was glad for the light on her face. She peered out from under her brow now and then, but Bri focused on her work, hands buried in the folds of her dress. After a little while longer, she looked up.

"Come."

Elanur approached, kneeling once more in front of the old woman.

Bri dropped a necklace into Elanur's palm and sat back in her chair.

Elanur examined the piece. Blue, black, and gray polished stones interspersed with red beads. It seemed a treasure fit for a princess. She gazed questionably at Bri.

"Healer," the old woman said, speaking the Gimirri word the rest of the camp used when referring to her. Then she encouraged Elanur to put the necklace on.

Elanur did as she was told, loosening the knot in the leather string and looping it again behind her neck. As the beads lay against her skin, she touched them lightly with her fingers. "Thank you," she said, lowering her head.

Bri got up and headed back to her tent. "Come," she said, inviting Elanur inside.

Elanur followed, puzzled. She had hoped to get back into Bri's good graces, but now Bri *wanted* her to enter her tent?

"Sit." Bri pointed to the table near the back, where several clay jars sat clustered on the surface. Elanur hesitated, Kerkin kicking his feet. Bri lowered herself into the far chair with a grunt, then gestured again, more firmly. Elanur obeyed, taking the seat opposite. She studied the old woman's face. Bri's skin appeared thinner than before, the bags heavy under her eyes. As she pushed one jar toward Elanur, the sound of her breathing became more evident, a labored gurgling that rested in her throat.

"Sniff," she commanded in Gimirri.

Elanur obeyed and instantly drew back. The aroma was powerfully pungent.

Bri gestured for Elanur to push the jar back to her. Elanur obeyed, and Bri took a long inhale. She blew the air out and inhaled twice more. Then she pushed the jar away and relaxed. "Better," she said, tapping her chest.

Elanur understood. The mixture was to help ease difficult breathing. She tapped her own chest in response. "Better," she said in Gimirri.

The woman pushed over the next jar. Her intentions became apparent. She meant to teach Elanur the ways of the healer. The idea raised bumps of excitement on Elanur's skin. She unstrapped Kerkin, set him down on a rug nearby, and settled in for the lesson.

The sun had dropped into the afternoon sky by the time she returned to her own tent. She checked the bread to find it cooking nicely, the fire having calmed with no one there to stoke it. Inside, Ilker was still resting. Elanur set Kerkin on the center rug, retrieved the carved wooden elephant with the small spout that Ilker had brought, filled it with goat's milk, and gave it to the boy. Once he was happily drinking, she went to Ilker's side. For a time, she watched him, his breaths flowing easily. She longed to check his bandages, but they were wrapped tight and looked clean, so she resisted. She was about to retrieve the bread when he opened his eyes and gazed at her.

"Healer?" she said in Gimirri.

Ilker nodded in a knowing way.

"You?" Elanur asked, pointing to him.

He shook his head. "You," he said in her language.

Elanur stared at him. Questions filled her mind. Why was he protecting her? Why had he chosen her in the first place? He could have had any of the younger girls in the tribe, girls who could have given him his own son. Instead, he'd seemed intent on her from the first time he'd laid eyes on her.

"Elanur," he said.

She checked Kerkin's elephant and, finding it empty, set it behind her. The boy pointed to the ball nearby. She sat across from him and began rolling it back and forth. It was one of his favorite games. He watched the ball with wide eyes, his toes curling as he pushed it with both hands. Elanur laughed, letting the heat in her chest subside. If she had stayed near Ilker another moment, she would have kissed him, and she wasn't ready for that.

Not yet.

CHAPTER
NINETEEN

696 BC
Gordium, Capital City of Phrygia

Zoe jerked awake. Someone else was in the room.

She was sitting in a cushioned chair just inside her father's chamber, not far from the door. It was the middle of the night. She checked the oil lamp on the stand next to her. It burned low, as did the second one near her father's bed.

But he wasn't in it.

She spotted his shadow. He stood by the window, gazing down at the couch. He wore only his night tunic, his legs and feet bare, hair sticking up in the back. The thought crossed her mind that he might still be asleep, but then he spoke.

"I've told you, darling. I told him to stay home."

Dread filled Zoe's breast. Another of her father's hallucinations. Xander's potion sat on the stand next to her, a small pouch. She closed her fingers around it.

"I should have checked to be sure." Midas said crouched in front

COLLEEN M. STORY

of the couch, one hand steadying himself on the armrest. "I know you can never forgive me."

Again he spoke about Anchurus' death. It was as if he relived it nearly every night. Zoe drew the pouch into her lap.

"What else do you want me to do?" Midas asked. After another pause, he said, "Katiah? But darling, you never approved of her."

The room felt cold, Zoe's fingers stiff.

"She's buried in the tomb, like I told you. You don't have to worry about her anymore." The lamp by his bed flickered, shadows shifting on the wall.

Zoe untied the string securing the top of the pouch. Xander had instructed her to say two lines, then scatter the contents around the king. She stifled a chill and wished she'd brought her wool cloak.

"You've always been so against her," Midas said. "Why would you want to release her now?"

Release the dark goddess? Zoe slid to the edge of the chair.

"She wouldn't do it, darling. She desired only revenge against me. If I let her out, she'd take up her vendetta again. Zoe would be in danger."

Zoe stepped one foot forward and began to stand up. She must scatter the potion while he was still in the midst of his delusion.

"I would give anything to have him back. But I have nothing that would convince her to do it. Even if she could." He lifted his gaze to the other end of the couch, as if someone else was sitting there. "You're certain? After all this time?"

Zoe stood upright, her back taut. She centered the pouch in her right palm. All she had to do was flick it out to dispense the contents. She mouthed the words she had to say and took a quiet step.

"She caused the whole thing, the curse, the battle. It was because of her we lost him."

Zoe took another step and another. Soon she stood across from his bed.

"Demodica, darling, you're asking me to stand by while the

goddess who ruined everything escapes her prison. How will that help?"

He was talking to the queen. Or so it seemed. Zoe cast her gaze around. One more step and she'd be fully in the light. Her father might notice her then. She readied the pouch, nudging it toward her fingertips.

"Why would she do that?" Another pause. "She's not one to care about such things."

The room pulsed during the silences, as if it had its own heart-beat. Zoe leaned her weight on her toes, poised to throw.

"It's been a very long time," Midas said. "I miss you desperately." He rose, his back to Zoe. "Be with you? You mean where you are? But I can't leave now."

Zoe froze. *Leave?*

Midas sat on the edge of the couch. "You'd be proud of her. She is the people's princess. But there is no heir. And she's had no interest in marrying."

Zoe silently thanked the gods her father had never forced her to marry—though now, she realized, if he had, the kingdom might have a safer future. As it stood, Midas had no heir. The older he grew, the more his people were at risk. She mouthed the words of the spell. She had to get them right.

"Calm down, dear. Please."

Zoe moved. One step forward, and she spoke the first three words. Another step and she spoke three more, then she swept her hand wide, casting the contents of the pouch into the air. The crystals hovered, sparkling above the couch. Then they began to fall. At first, they drifted over her father's shoulders, revealing nothing but darkness. But just before they reached the cushion, a ghostly image flickered into view—then vanished.

It was long enough.

"Zoe?" Midas asked, his gaze lifting to hers.

She stared at the spot where the image had been. A woman

sitting demurely on the couch. She'd seen that woman before, but it had been twenty years.

Midas stood up. "Are you all right?"

"Who were you talking to, Father?" Zoe asked, still staring at the couch.

Midas frowned, clearly confused. "I thought it was . . ."

"Mother?"

He nodded.

"It's all right." She trembled, the skin hot on the back of her neck.

"She was wearing that green dress I always loved." Midas gave a wistful smile. "She looked so beautiful in it."

Zoe clenched the empty pouch in her fist. Perhaps her father had seen his queen, but Zoe had seen the goddess Denisia. She was the one behind the nightmares. The one conjuring the hallucinations.

"She had her hair done up like she always did, off the nape of her neck," Midas continued. "She still grieves for Anchurus."

"We all do, Father," Zoe said.

"Your mother is right. I should have been more careful."

"What was she asking you to do?"

Midas stared at the couch, as if trying to hold on to the vision of his queen. "She wants me to release Katiah from her tomb."

Zoe let the statement settle before speaking. "That doesn't make any sense. Mother demanded all representations of Katiah be banished from the castle three years before she died. Why would she want you to release the goddess now?"

Midas' jaw worked back and forth as if he were chewing on the idea. He tried twice to speak, then stopped. Finally, he blurted out, "Your mother seems to believe that if we let Katiah out, she will bring Anchurus back."

Zoe blinked. "What—?" She shook her head. "What would Katiah care about Anchurus?"

"I can't see that she would, but your mother seemed to think—"

"From the dead?" Zoe asked.

He eyed her. "Katiah *is* the goddess of the underworld."

"But why would she want to help you, Father, after everything?"

Midas returned his gaze to the couch. "She sat right there, talking to me." He drift for a moment, eyes unfocused. Then, turning back to her, he asked, "What was that you threw?"

"Some herbs," she said absently. *How is Denisia doing this?*

Midas opened the shutter and gazed out, letting the night air cool his face. "Your mother and I used to stand here, looking out on the stars. Sometimes I'd be detained— meetings with the commanders or some such thing—and I'd come in thinking she'd be asleep. But she'd be right here, waiting for me."

Zoe stared into the darkness, her father's pain wrapping around her like a cocoon until she could hardly breathe. "Very well," she blurted. "If Mother wanted you to let her out, then let her out."

King Midas seemed to awaken from his reverie. "Katiah?"

"That's what Mother wanted, right? For you to release the dark goddess?" Zoe's mouth went dry.

A long silence passed before Midas spoke again. His voice came thin and fragile. "It wasn't her, my girl."

Zoe looked up at him, relief blooming across her shoulders. "You knew?"

Half his face remained in shadow, the other lit by the glow of the lamp. "I saw the image, from the herbs." He paused. Then, heavily, "Denisia."

"You don't seem surprised?"

He remained quiet for another long while. Finally, he closed the shutters, took his daughter's hand, and walked with her across the room. "She wants Anchurus back. It's what she's always wanted."

"How can she be here this way?"

Midas shrugged. "She cursed me once before. We are . . . connected, somehow. And she is a goddess."

"You don't seem angry with her."

He paused by his bed. "She let me see your mother again."

"But you weren't really seeing her."

"No, but it looked like her, and it sounded like her. It even smelled like her."

Dear Father! Zoe embraced him. He felt cold in her arms, withered. "You will not let Katiah loose, then?"

"Do you think she could do it?" he breathed.

Zoe stepped back to gaze into his eyes. "Restore Anchurus to life, you mean?"

When he nodded, she saw the same hope in his expression that she had in her heart. Her brother, the prince and the heir to the throne, restored to life. It would make everything better, everything *right*. She sighed. "It doesn't matter," she said. "Even if she could, she wouldn't. You forget how angry she was with you."

"Time has a way of easing anger," Midas said. "Your mother—or Denisia—was right about that. And Katiah cared for me, once."

Zoe searched her father's face. "You think if you let Katiah out now, she would flutter her eyes and offer Anchurus as a token of gratitude?"

Midas chuckled, then sobered. "You have a point," he said.

Zoe pulled back his blankets. "Can you try to get some sleep now?"

Midas touched her cheek with the back of his hand. "You're the one who needs rest. Come." He walked with her toward the door.

"Will you reconsider your decision?"

"For now, Katiah will stay put."

"I mean . . . about giving the gold to the Gimirri."

He raised his eyebrows. "We can discuss that tomorrow."

Zoe wanted to argue, change his mind now. But she had accomplished more than she'd expected she would. She knew for certain who was haunting her father. And better yet, her father knew too.

"Very well." She kissed him on the cheek. "I hope you don't have any more nightmares."

"Xander has yet to come up with a cure for them."

Zoe smiled. "Off with his head," she said.

Midas chuckled as she walked out of the room, but when she turned for a last glance, she saw him closing the door, an achingly sad expression on his face.

CHAPTER

TWENTY

696 BC
Mountain Mother Camp, Acharaca

"We must not talk to Vesile immediately." Aster paced behind the tent they'd been given for shelter. It was the fourth day since they'd arrived in Acharaca, and Xander had yet to return. Aster wore his weathered leather cloak, the wind steady from the west, the midday sun hidden behind a sheet of clouds.

"He is in their hands now," Gediz said from inside the tent. "There's nothing we can do."

"You're as helpful as always," Aster growled.

"I told you about these women, and about the goddess Kubileya. I've accompanied you on this cursed trip, brought you where you wanted to go, and spoke to them in their language. Normally, that would be more than enough."

"Every good advisor puts strict limits on their level of service," Aster said.

"I've done more than my fair share. What have *you* done?"

"It must be fascinating to understand how you measure the worth of your input."

Gediz humphed. "As I figured. You won't answer that question."

The camp was nearly empty. The women had gathered in a broad stone structure built into the hillside, its entrance partially hidden by brush. Aster had seen them file through the door earlier that morning, and they hadn't emerged since. It was taking too much time.

He walked toward the middle of camp, where the women usually sang and danced around the central fire pit. The ashes were cold and black. He paused. The day they'd taken Xander, Aster had tried to ask Vesile about him, but she'd refused to speak to him. The next morning, he had waited outside her tent only a short while before Willa, who seemed to be Vesile's right hand, escorted him away. She'd assured him Xander was being cared for and that their leader would speak with him soon.

Now it was the third day of Xander's absence, and Aster still had no answers. He spent the afternoon waiting by the shelter, but Vesile didn't come out and neither did Willa. As the sunlight faded, he grew more irritated. Gradually, he came to his own decision.

This would end, or he would end it himself.

That evening, when Willa brought their meal, Aster grabbed her wrist.

"I must not speak to her," he said.

"You have changed your mind?" Willa asked.

"He means he must speak with her." Gediz sat nearby on a felled tree. Six more had been arranged in a square at the forest's edge, a large fire pit at the center. It was where the women often took their meals, some cooking over the flames, others eating in quiet groups. To the west, the rising rocks of the mountain offered shelter; to the east, the valley stretched wide and open.

Willa frowned. "Yes, she has received the message."

"Do not tell her, Gediz," Aster said.

"It will not help—"

"Do not tell her!"

Gediz sighed and addressed Willa. "This advisor here," he said, gesturing apologetically at Aster, "wishes you to know that if Vesile will not talk to him, he will go up to the cave himself."

Aster cleared his throat.

"Oh," Gediz said, glancing at him. "And, um, that he will do this tomorrow morning."

"It is not possible." Willa tried to pull her arm away. "No one is allowed in the caves but the mother goddess' chosen ones."

Aster gripped her wrist more tightly. "It deeply concerns me whether I am allowed," he said.

Willa nodded and smiled, misunderstanding him.

"I apologize." Gediz smiled at her, pieces of venison stuck between his teeth. "He means to say that he will go to the cave, whether or not it is allowed."

"He cannot," Willa said, her smile erased.

"I cannot," Aster said.

Willa nodded. "Vesile does not allow it."

"And I am greatly concerned with what Vesile allows."

Willa smiled again.

Gediz brushed off his fingers. "You must understand," he said to Willa. "This advisor here. If Vesile doesn't talk to him before tomorrow, he will go to the cave. No matter what. He will go."

"He cannot."

"Because he is not allowed?" Gediz said.

"Because the men will stop him."

"What men?" Gediz and Aster turned to her at once.

"The guardians of the cave of Matar Kubileya." Willa's expression tightened, her large eyes like a frightened doe's. "They will stop him."

"Do not ask her where these men are," Aster said.

"And where are these men?"

"They serve by the cave," Willa said.

"You should not tell me where the cave is," Aster said, his gaze steady on Willa.

"That is not allowed."

"Perhaps you should remember," Gediz mumbled to Aster, "that they put us to sleep before they took Xander."

Aster released Willa's wrist. "I will not find it."

Willa scurried back to the fire to tend to the meat.

"So that's that," Gediz said, chewing loudly. "How long will we wait before we return?"

"You're not proposing that we leave Xander behind?"

Gediz pulled his cloak more snugly about his shoulders and bit into a hard piece of bread. "We cannot stay here much longer. The cold weather is coming."

"Horses do not walk in the cold."

"Men freeze in the cold!"

"If you were to freeze, I would grieve for days." Aster returned to his meal.

"If I freeze, you freeze."

"Because we are so much alike."

"I could go back on my own."

"That would be a tragedy."

"I could report to King Midas . . . and to *Zoe* . . . what happened here."

Aster finished chewing, swallowed, and sidled up next to Gediz. He checked around and, certain everyone else was busy eating, reached over and discreetly grasped the back of Gediz's neck. "It is wise to threaten me."

Gediz winced. "No threat, I assure you. An offer. That is all. I inform them of your, uh . . . progress."

Aster held him in his grip for another moment, then released him and slid away. "You are not King Midas' advisor, nor under *my* leadership. You will not do as you're told or you won't be the one left behind."

Gediz finished his food, then mumbled, "If I quoted you directly on that, it would sound like you were giving me permission to defy you."

Aster cast him a warning glare.

Gediz scooted further away. "I do wonder," he said carefully. "Have you ever tried to get that fixed?"

"Break what?"

"That . . . speech defect you have. You must find it . . . inconvenient."

"As inconvenient as your complete competence."

Gediz stood up, eyeing Willa and the remaining meat on the fire. "I'm going to get some more."

"A good idea," Aster said, eyeing Gediz's substantial girth, "as you've clearly been starved for weeks."

Gediz walked to the fire. Willa cut more meat for him, after which he found a seat on the opposite side of the clearing.

Aster finished his meal and stewed for a while, elbows on his thighs. Gradually, the women put everything away, several helping Willa to cut the meat in long slices for drying and storage. It took some time, but when they finished, they retired to their tents. Gediz followed them, as if seeking their protection. Aster stayed, keeping his eye on the stone structure beyond, but Vesile didn't emerge. He glanced behind him, searching for the path that wound up to the cave. He'd spotted it the day before when scouting around. It started at the inside edge of the forest, near an old tree with one dead branch hanging down.

The wind shifted at dusk, and he caught the heavy scent of an approaching storm. He stopped by Neval's tent and called to him. When the wiry man emerged looking mussed and sweaty, Aster apologized for intruding, then told him they would be leaving the next day.

"But your friend," Neval said. "He is healed?"

"I'm not getting him tomorrow morning," Aster said, "and then we're staying. Make sure we're not ready."

179

Neval's eyebrows twitched. He gazed at Aster, then nodded. "Yes. Travel tomorrow. We may have a storm."

"Do not dress warm," Aster said and went back to his own tent.

XANDER LAY beside Berna's place, as he'd come to call it. Around the fire, the women danced and chanted. A different woman had brought water that morning, water Xander had gulped down until it was gone, but Berna had accepted none. She hadn't spoken all day. He feared she had passed. The thought of her being dead horrified him. If she were allowed to lie there and die, then why not him too?

He'd been in the cave for three days, if he remembered correctly —four since they'd arrived at the camp. He couldn't be certain whether he'd awakened in the cave the first night or the next, so he'd started counting from the morning he'd woken up beside Berna. This was the third day after that, and all he'd had was a single serving of water each morning. His stomach ached with hunger. He lay curled up by Berna's place, staring at the fire, the women's endless chanting assaulting his ears like the nagging of crows, their thumping feet pounding against his head. None of the other ill ones had gotten up and walked out. None had been healed. Lacking the energy to try escaping again, he drifted off to sleep.

When he woke up, he was still lying next to Berna. The same sights came into focus—the yellow flames, the black rock. Outside the cave, it was dark. Another day had come and gone. But something was different. His body had shifted, as if it were settling into a new reality, one that felt heavy and close to the ground. His muscles still ached and his throat burned, but now he could drift into a kind of oblivion, a state that pulled him away from the body's pain, giving him the sensation of floating above it. Xander knew what that meant. His system was shutting down. He had to act. Now.

He sat up and looked toward the darkest corner of the cave, the one area he had yet to explore. There didn't seem to be anything there, but he had to be certain. Using the last of his strength, he pushed himself to his feet and crossed the cavern. As he neared the corner, he spotted a shadowed space he hadn't noticed before. He glanced over his shoulder. The guards weren't paying any attention to him, their gazes turned outward. Safe for the moment, he reached into the darkness and felt only air. A tunnel? After checking once more on the guards, then the women, he slipped inside. Stone closed around him. Panic gripped his chest. The space was so narrow! He paused long enough to regain his courage, then pressed on. The passage twisted left, then curved back, carrying him deeper into the mountain. After a few more steps, it released him.

He hesitated, hands out. The dim firelight still clung to the tunnel walls behind him, but ahead lay only darkness. Keeping his right hand on the stone, he crept forward, cursing himself for not bringing a light. He could have stolen one of the sticks from the fire. He was about to turn back and do just that when a sound reached his ears.

He held his breath. A low, rhythmic thumping. As he continued on, it grew no louder, nor did it disappear. He had gone about eight steps when he felt rock in front of him. He stopped and, like a blind man, ran his hands over it. This wasn't like the jagged cave walls. It felt smoother, more deliberate. Boulders, stacked. Curves. Indentations. Something held them together, though he couldn't tell what. A ceiling collapse? Maybe. He tried to lift a stone. It wouldn't budge. He went around the entire structure, testing one after another. None shifted. He arrived back where he started—he could tell by the two rounded boulders that sat level with his chest, centered tips poking against his palms—

"That's enough." The voice boomed through the open space.

Xander jerked his hands away. For a few tense moments, he dared not move.

"Didn't your mother teach you any manners?"

He forced the words from his mouth. "Uh, apologies?"

"Apologies, indeed. I finally manage to fall asleep and I'm rudely awakened by some ill-mannered intruder who thinks he can let his hands roam wherever he wants."

"I didn't know anyone else was here."

"You had your hands all over me!"

"But I didn't know you were . . . you."

"What do you mean you didn't know?"

"It's very dark in here."

"You were allowed entrance into the cave."

"Yes?"

"Then you understand you are in the presence of Matar Kubileya."

Xander's heart thumped in his chest. "The great goddess?"

"What did you mistake me for when you had your grubby hands all over me? A lively maiden? No doubt that's what your delirious mind was hoping for."

"No, I assure you. I thought you were . . ."

"Yes?"

"A pile of rocks," Xander squeaked.

"Oh. I see. Well." A long, heavy sigh. "That's what I've become, I'm afraid." A low rumble followed, like stone shifting against stone. The sculpture seemed to move. *Was that possible?* "Ever since I've been trapped here in this dungeon with their infernal chanting, I've been . . . changing."

Xander felt his jaw go slack. "Are you . . . ?" he asked.

Another rumble. The sculpture was moving again. "Aren't you breaking their precious rules wandering about like this?"

"They didn't seem to care."

"They expect *me* to do it all. This is the type of person I inspire—a lazy, shrill-voiced woman with no sense of personal responsibility. For centuries my followers labored, building monuments and shrines to me. If you've traveled about at all, you've seen them. But now, because of some chaos in the underworld, I've been trapped in here with these foul-smelling sick ones. No insult to you personally, but you desperately need to bathe."

Xander smelled his cloak and wrinkled his nose. "I can't get out either," he said. "They won't let me."

"Why would you want to get out?" the voice said. "You came here for my blessings, did you not?"

"Not . . . exactly," Xander said, "though, of course, I wouldn't refuse them."

The sculpture shifted, a low sound like a pile of rocks being pushed over. "Why did you come, then?"

"To talk to you."

"And you know who you're talking to?"

Xander swallowed. "Matar Kubileya?"

"At least you're not a complete dullard." She sighed. "Yes, that's what they call me. I used to like it, but after hearing them chant it so much I've grown weary of it. You wouldn't think you would grow tired of hearing your own name, but I have. Why don't they change it now and then? Men's voices might be nice. You might offer to chant for them?"

"You wouldn't like my voice any better, I'm afraid."

"Perhaps not. It would be a change, anyway."

Xander tried to get his mind around what was happening. The goddess was speaking to him. The goddess he had come to see. Unless he was hallucinating. He had to keep his wits about him, though even standing was becoming more difficult with the energy draining from his body.

"Matar . . . may I call you Matar?"

"I'd prefer Mother."

"Mother, then. I came to speak with you. I serve the great King Midas of Gordium."

"King Midas?" A rumbling as the stones came closer. "Wasn't he the one cursed with the golden touch?"

Xander experienced a moment's pride for his king. "Yes. About twenty years ago."

"That was before I was trapped here."

"It was?"

"It may have been the last interesting news I heard before the unfortunate happened. He couldn't eat, is what they said? The food would turn to gold?"

"That's right." Xander lowered himself down to sit on the ground. "Pardon me. I have grown weak."

"As do you all. So what happened to him? Did he survive?"

"His son sacrificed himself to save him. A great cavern opened in the ground and the prince rode into it. After that, the cavern closed, and the king was restored to health."

"A cavern in the ground. Where?"

"At the great Battle of Karama."

"This was twenty years ago?"

"About that, yes?"

"Who opened the cavern?"

"The goddess Denisia."

"Denisia." A pause. "It takes power to do that, but she is only a half goddess."

"She had a witch's help."

"An interesting coincidence, her opening this cavern about the same time I was trapped." Another rumble and the sound of shifting rocks. "Go on."

Xander told her the story about King Midas and the golden curse. He grew fatigued as he spoke and backed himself up against the cave wall for support. Soon, he could feel little in his body except his mouth moving. The goddess kept asking for more details. She seemed particularly interested in Denisia's actions—what sort of spell she used, what she chanted, how Anchurus had closed the chasm.

"That was the shifting," she muttered at one point, "right before it happened. I felt it." She said nothing more until Xander finished relaying how King Midas had killed the goddess Katiah with his golden sword. After that, he told her, the chasm had closed for good, leaving a long scar on the earth, and King Midas had trapped Katiah in an underground tomb, just to be certain she didn't escape.

"Katiah, trapped?" Mother said. Then, "Oh dear. So *that's* why."

Xander frowned. "Why what?"

For a long while, she didn't answer. Save for the distant sound of the women changing, the cave was quiet. He had almost drifted off when something hard knocked against his sandaled foot.

"You want my blessings, little man?" Mother said.

Xander looked up, bleary-eyed, into the darkness.

"Complete a mission for me and you shall have them. But you must go now."

CHAPTER
TWENTY-ONE

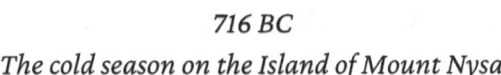

The cold season on the Island of Mount Nysa

When Little Bird heard horse's hooves, she rushed to the barrier but saw nothing. The afternoon was cold and gray, a fresh snowfall having erased the path from view. *Food* was the first thing she thought of. She'd learned to conserve, stashing a little from each delivery under the mattress. But it had been two days since the last one.

Most days, when the weather was clear, the goddess would return to take her through more vision quests. In one, Little Bird rode her pony, Little Alp, along a dirt path that weaved its way through the trees. In another, she paddled her boat on the Red River until she could no longer hear the wolves howling. In a third, she enjoyed a delicious meal in a cabin. The more visions she experienced, the more she began to put the pieces together. Each one took place in the same general area, though always in a different part of it. There was the forest, the Red River, the creek, the meadow, and the cabin, and with each vision, they all started to feel more familiar. This was a place she knew, somehow. She grew less fearful and more curious, and tried harder to discover the identity of the woman in her visions.

"Where is she?" Denisia would ask. "Did you speak to her?"

Little Bird began to dread the question. Though she heard the woman's voice sometimes, she never saw her face. Even after many spells and visions, she couldn't identify her, or say that the voice was Katiah's. This displeased Denisia greatly. The last time the goddess had come, which had been over twenty days ago, Little Bird had seen herself riding her pony all the way down the hill toward the Red River. She had almost reached it when Denisia startled her.

"This is no good," she'd said. "All you're remembering is a child-hood spent alone."

It was time for one of Little Bird's lies. She thought carefully, then signed, *Someone made me lunch.*

"Lunch? Do you know who?" When Little Bird shook her head, Denisia sat down in one of the chairs and looked out over the snow-covered path. She wore a heavy animal hide over her shoulders and thick, fur-lined boots, her hair covered in a fur hat. Because of her past cooperation in the visions, Little Bird also wore a warm animal hide and boots on her feet. She sat down across from Denisia, watching her expectantly.

"I thought you could connect with Katiah and help me free her." Denisia gazed down at the rock under her feet. "Perhaps I need to try something else." She waited a while longer, as if thinking over the idea, then got up and left.

Little Bird tried to stop her. She signed she would try harder, but the goddess didn't even look at her. She mounted her horse and rode down the snowy hill.

That's when the others started bringing food, people she didn't know and had never seen before. Verin visited when he could, but it was less often. The goddess had restricted them all, he'd told her, warned them not to see the girl unless under orders to deliver some-thing. He'd tried to volunteer, but Denisia had not called on him.

"I think she knows we're friends," he'd said on one of his visits.

I didn't tell her.

"She's a goddess. She knows things."

I don't want you to get into trouble.

He'd looked around nervously, as he did during most of his visits now. "I may not come as often," he'd said. When her face changed, he reassured her. "I'll still come, I promise. I don't want to get caught. For both of us."

Little Bird had smiled at him. *It will be all right.* Though, of course, it wasn't all right. She longed for Verin's visits like she longed for water.

She found new ways to keep herself busy. Staying occupied was the key to survival, Emir had told her once, so she did her best to maintain a routine. Exercise first. Breakfast of whatever she had left under the mattress. Clean up and tidying, followed by clothes washing on certain days. By then, she was usually tired and took a nap unless the sun came out. On those days, she sat by the barrier and soaked it in until it disappeared again behind the clouds.

When time left her with nothing else to do, she worked on a gift for Verin. She'd found the small shard of rock in the back of the cave, one that, with work, would make a good dagger. Eventually, she would have to attach it to a handle. For that, she needed wood, a carving tool, and some leather straps. Verin might be able to bring her some, but she must ask for them without arousing his suspicions about what she was making.

So it was that cold, gray afternoon when she heard the horse's hooves, she hoped the rider approaching was Verin, but as the animal drew near, her hopes faded. It was the dark brown mare with the black mane and tail. Behind it came a smaller horse with no rider. Little Bird's heartbeat quickened. Might her captor let her go?

Denisia pulled up, dismounted, and, holding the reins in her hand, approached the barrier. Little Bird stepped back, but the goddess did not come in. Instead, she stood nearby with her hands clasped in front of her.

"I came to let you know I won't be visiting for a while." She didn't look at Little Bird, but stared at some vague place off to the side. "The spells aren't working, and it's more difficult coming up here now. My followers will bring you food and anything else you need. But you must not detain them. They have important work they're doing."

What work? Little Bird asked.

"Our leader, Silenus. He requires constant care." She flicked snow from her shoulder, then swiped the back of her finger under her nose. Her cheeks were red. Little Bird peered at her. Had she been crying? "It's none of your concern," she continued.

Fear troubled Little Bird's mind. Would the goddess leave her here forever?

"With time, all is revealed, Silenus always said. I'm sure he was right."

When Denisia said nothing more, Little Bird signed, *Let me go?*

The goddess appeared puzzled. "Why would I do that?"

I can't help you.

"We don't know that yet."

Nothing has worked. Please.

Denisia shook her head. "You misunderstand me. I'm not here to set you free, nor to apologize for your captivity. You have a purpose, and that is to help me release Prince Anchurus from his torment. I'm surprised you aren't more concerned about your friend, Emir. You seemed to care so much about him, yet you leave him to suffer in agony when all you'd have to do to free him is remember your connection to Katiah." She narrowed her eyes. "Have you remembered anything more?"

Little Bird tried to come up with something. Another lie. She started to move her hands, then looked up into Denisia's stern eyes. Her hands fell by her sides.

"Very well." Denisia mounted her horse and turned so Little Bird could see the riderless pony. "When you figure out how to reach Katiah, you can ride away with me. We will release her, and she will help restore Anchurus and Emir. Once that happens, you may go. Not before." She nudged her mare onto the path. They started down the hill, snow kicking up behind the horses' hooves.

Little Bird watched until they were out of sight, then retreated to the back of her cave, crawled under her blankets, and stayed there.

CHAPTER

TWENTY-TWO

The deep, dark underworld

Emir Alkan had danced the dance of death many times in his life. He'd fought soldiers, hunters, and wolves, and always he'd emerged victorious.

This time, he was losing.

He couldn't say how long he and the lion-man god of the underworld had been fighting. The days bled together in the red cave. So far, he'd suffered four strikes. Erlik Khar had swiped a paw across his thigh, opening three mean, jagged gashes. He'd done the same to Emir's back and left arm. The last hit was a stinger to the shoulder. It had numbed the muscle, leaving that limb useless. The fighting dragged on in the arena, a semi-circular space surrounded by rock and illuminated by red light. The spectators watched impassively from the benches, which now stood against the wall so the people had little choice but to witness the brutal battle in front of them.

Any last words to delay the time when you shall at last pay for your crime?

Emir's breath came hard through his throat, his head spinning.

What strength he had left was draining away through his wounds. It reminded him of his fight with the Olgun brothers before Katiah had stepped in to save him. The last he'd seen her, she'd tried to kill his mother with a white bolt of light. The memory flashed in his mind with sudden clarity.

"I remember," he panted. "I remember why I'm here!"

So now it comes, says he! Blessed be the memory.

"It was the goddess Katiah," Emir said. "She meant to kill my mother. I stepped into the path of her power and took the blow."

Such a hero Emir was! Shall we give him his applause?

The watchers clapped like animated puppets, then stopped as suddenly as they started.

"Will you let me go now? I remembered what happened."

You cannot use a memory to answer the question posed to thee!

"You asked me why I'm here. I told you. The goddess Katiah's bolt of light killed me."

Katiah, Katiah! Blame it on her. Think we don't know any better, good sir?

"You must know her?"

The lion-man opened his mouth and roared. The sound rumbled the cave, dirt and rocks falling from the ceiling. *Katiah's gone, gone, long gone. Left only me to carry on. No one here by Katiah's name. No advantage, you to gain! Lie again, Emir Alkan. Lie until you, too, are gone!*

Emir frowned at the orange eyes across the arena. "If you are as all-knowing as you say, you know I speak the truth."

Khar flicked his tail and smirked.

"Perhaps you are the one who is lying? For how can Katiah be gone? She is a god, like yourself. Immortal."

What care you for the dark goddess? She was the one who made this mess.

"What happened to her?"

The golden king and his golden sword. With it, lovely Katiah he gored. Now she lives in an underground tomb, her body gold and 'ever doomed!

Emir tried to envision it—Katiah, a gold sculpture like what Princess Zoe had been.

"You asked me why I came here," he said. "I told you. I was . . . killed." The word sounded sour in his throat. How could it be, when he was standing here wounded, saliva sticky in his mouth? "I died and ended up . . . here."

Death means nothing. Destination. You must choose for time's duration.

"I didn't choose. I died and woke up in the tunnels. I made no choice!"

Oh, but you did, my warrior friend! Chose it when you shaped your end. Khar approached, his tail poised behind his back, his orange eyes blazing with red pupils. *Chose it lying on the ground with the king's men all around.*

Emir backed away, stumbled, and regained his balance.

Chose it as the mother grieved. Left the boy alone, bereaved. Chose it while the king stood by, his son riding on to die. Why? Erlik lowered his head between his lion shoulders and growled low. *Remember now or die!*

Images of his mother and then the boy flashed through Emir's mind. He'd saved his mother's life, but for what? Where was she now? Did King Midas rescue her or was she back in Sargon's prison? And the boy. What had happened to him? Last Emir had seen him, he was in Midas' castle. Was he safe? He lifted his gaze to Erlik's face, the lion-man pursuing him around the arena. "I don't understand. If I chose to come here, why?"

The lion-man laughed. *I ask you and you ask me. Such a happy harmony!* He stepped past Emir to preen in front of the onlookers. *Despite my clues he doesn't know, so now his payment he must show.* Khar whirled back to face Emir. *Prepare to be torn to pieces, Emir! Pieces and pieces with no releases!* The monster trotted around to the other side of the arena, readying himself to charge.

"Wait!" Emir held up his hand. "Please. Wait."

Khar grumbled.

"One more question." Emir stumbled back to sit with the watchers, taking up the space next to the boy Ufuk. He glanced at him and gave him his best smile. "Why are these people here?" He gestured to the boy and then to the rest of them. "Why must they bear witness to this murder and death?"

You're already dead, dead as a bed. So what would be today absurder than to commit another murder?

"But you said I would die. You tore up all those people over there." Emir gestured toward the remains on the floor. "You mean to do the same to me."

Alive, you see! Alive you'll be! No murder here, no falling tear.

Emir shuddered. He couldn't imagine those body parts belonging to living souls. "Why have all these witnesses? Might you let them go?"

Witness or no witness. It's none of your business.

Emir glanced at Ufuk. Looking into the boy's dull eyes, a sudden idea occurred to him. "What if I were to ask to be a witness?"

The lion-man jerked his head up.

"What if I were to take this boy's place?"

Ufuk gripped the edge of the bench underneath him. Khar stared, his body suddenly unmoving, even his tail held straight out behind him like a stick.

"I beseech thee, oh great god of the dead," Emir said, "to release the boy and let me sit here instead." When the god still didn't move, Emir sat squarely on the bench and repeated his request. "An attentive witness I will be, locked here for all eternity." He glanced again at the boy for courage. This was not what he'd hoped for. But he wouldn't survive another of Khar's attacks. As it was, the god appeared puzzled. He stepped back and shook his heavy mane.

"Grant me life in your great cave," Emir said, "and I shall be your willing slave."

Khar grunted and started pacing, his breath huffing through his throat. Ufuk glanced at the grouchy, one-eared man sitting next to him. The man's features softened as he watched the boy, then he lifted a hopeful gaze to Emir. The scowl he'd worn before was gone.

"What say you, oh god of mane? Let this boy depart this plane!"

The creature's tail lashed violently behind him. *You have no right to change this night! This is the time to stand and fight!*

"Let me stay, oh mighty god, by your presence I am awed, now allow us to applaud. What say you, great Erlik Khar?"

A guttural rumble escaped the beast's throat, his shoulders hunched, ears twitching. He looked like he was resisting something he knew he had to do. Some law of the underworld? Emir tried again: "You must honor this request, it's so, if I should stay instead of go. Someone's place I'm bound to take to seal a deal I'm loath to make."

Khar growled and stormed toward him, stopping just shy of the lowest bench. Emir tensed, but then noticed none of the other witnesses shrank back. The monster glared, his lip curled to show rows of sharp fangs.

Do this now and you won't see another chance to escape from me!

A life sentence. Perhaps. Emir turned to Ufuk. "Do you wish to go?"

The boy looked at the older man.

"Go," the man said. "It will be all right."

"Where would I go?" Ufuk asked.

Emir looked into the boy's brown eyes and thought of Anchurus, gliding away on his wooden boat. "Think of the most beautiful, peaceful place you can imagine," he said. "Somewhere you've long wanted to go."

Lies! More lies! the lion-man roared, his putrid breath warming their faces.

Ufuk looked at the older man, who nodded his agreement.

Emir turned to the god. "It's a deal, great god, so strong and proud. Let the boy go to please the crowd. What say you?"

Khar dropped his head and then shook it twice. He flicked his tail. Emir ducked. Again, the rest of the crowd didn't respond as the stinger flew by and landed harmlessly on the ground behind them.

Finally, the lion-man walked away, back toward the far side of the cave where the red light didn't shine. When he'd almost disappeared into the shadows, Emir called out.

"Khar, what say you?"

Erlik Khar didn't answer. Emir tried to stand up. He couldn't. He tried again. Nothing happened. He glanced around. The older man sat next to him, but a space had opened up between them.

"He has gone," the man said with tears in his eyes. "My boy has gone."

696 BC
Gordium, Capital City of Phrygia

Zoe went into the meeting with King Midas and his top commanders with high hopes. The talk she and her father had shared the night before made her think that certainly now he would change his mind and show strength against the Gimirri.

She was sorely disappointed. Midas ordered Timon to give the gold trinkets to Baran, and Baran to have his guards deliver the treasure to the nomads the next morning. Zoe tried to argue, but her father would hear nothing of what she had to say. She looked to Rastus for help, but he sat tight-lipped, refusing to speak against the king.

After they were all dismissed, Zoe went to her room, but all she could do was pace back and forth. This decision was so *wrong*. How could her father not see it? With one hand on her hip, she thought it over again and again, but in the end, felt powerless to change anything. She paused, cast her gaze to her mother's portrait, then grabbed her cloak and headed out.

Rastus met her on the first level. Zoe held her tongue until they were outside and safely away from other ears.

"What has he tasked you with today?" she asked in as steady a tone as she could manage.

"He wishes to use more guards to watch over the city. I shall give up all but five of my men."

"And Baran?"

"Deploying the guards as we spoke yesterday, and ensuring those at the gates know to be more discerning in whom they allow through."

"I'm afraid it won't help now."

"Not if they're already here."

"I have a feeling they never left." The two passed through the gates and onto Castle Road. "Where are you going now?" Zoe asked.

"To begin the assignment you gave me, Your Highness."

She glanced at him. "How will you do that?"

Rastus checked the city below, his gait changing into a more relaxed stride now that they had left the castle behind. "There is a businessman named Kiral Polat. I've heard rumors of his wealth. I think it's time I visited his establishment. If anyone would know about spies among us, it would be him."

They started down the hill, the morning sun shining in their eyes. It was another chilly day, the fields beyond bustling with workers bringing in the harvest. Zoe pulled her cloak more tightly about her. "Is he a good man?"

Rastus hesitated. "I believe he is the kind of man who seeks only to benefit himself. A man without honor."

Zoe's chest tightened. The last thing she wanted was for Rastus to get hurt. "Maybe this isn't a good idea," she said.

Rastus glanced at her. "He is the one most likely to have the information we're looking for. He may also have worthwhile connections."

"Connections?"

"A man like him has influence over other men. For the right payment, he may be willing to help."

"How?"

Rastus slowed near a narrow alleyway that traveled east between the stone and mudbrick dwellings. The path was strangely quiet. "The king is reluctant to call back the soldiers. But there may be men in the city ready to fight."

Zoe paused beside him. "You mean fund our own army?"

"It's unlikely we'd find enough men for anything resembling an army. But perhaps enough to tip the scales in our favor?"

Zoe pondered the idea. "How would we pay them?"

"We would arrange that through Kiral. We pay him. He takes care of the rest."

Zoe shook her head. "Father wouldn't agree to it."

"Likely not."

She waited for Rastus to say more, but he didn't. Looking at his strong profile, she realized she would have to procure the payment herself. "You think this Kiral would do this?"

"I don't know." He gave her a soft smile. "I'm off to see about that now."

She looked past him. "Rastus, is this the right thing to do?"

"All I am doing at this point is gathering information. There is no need for anything more."

She nodded, hesitating another moment before relenting. "Very well," she said finally.

He bowed his head and started off.

"Rastus!" she called.

He turned back.

"Be careful."

"Don't worry," he said with a smile. "I'm looking forward to the challenge."

She watched until he disappeared over the rise, then continued her journey into the city. A few of Baran's castle guards loitered nearby, their uniforms marking them as King Midas' men. She shook her head. They were drawing attention to themselves. Any Gimirri spies would steer clear. Still, it gave her some reassurance about what she and Rastus were attempting. Perhaps they could devise a workable backup plan.

She walked on until she reached the intersection with Market Street. Her nerves pricked on the back of her neck, her breath coming faster as she traveled the road she had visited two mornings before. There were no tables out, no traders marketing their wares. The street had been cleared of the mess, but evidence remained of the slaughter. A broken clay pot discarded between two dwellings. A blood stain on a wooden step. A smashed bird crate left birdless in an alley. She took it all in, the memories from that day flashing through her mind.

Tell your father. Three mornings. At west gates. Or Ilker will kill.

He had been so calm, so *commanding*. She glanced from side to side, suddenly wondering if he might still be nearby, watching her. The idea sent a shiver down her spine. She ducked into the inn on the right, closed the door behind her, and peered out the window.

"Are you looking for a room?" a voice said.

A plump old woman stood behind her. She had thick, muscular arms and a wide neck, gray hair combed into a bun. "A few moments of respite," Zoe said, "if that's all right?"

The woman's face was marked with deep wrinkles, but she had kind eyes. "Of course. Wine or tea?"

"Tea." Zoe sat down at the table. It was small, suitable for three people, one side pushed up against the wall under the window. The room smelled of spiced pastries and cooked meat, a tall cabinet with shelves showcasing clay pots, wooden bowls, and mugs, along with stacks of towels and what looked like jars of wine. Zoe realized she had brought nothing with which to trade. She made a mental note to bring something back later.

When the woman returned with a steaming mug, a sprightly man bustled in from the rear of the inn. He was slightly taller than she was, with lively brown eyes deep-set in aged sockets and wispy white eyebrows arched under a wrinkled forehead. Age spots freckled the skin of his scalp, though he still had hair from the midpoint down, forming a rounded beard beneath his chin.

"We are honored by your presence, Your Highness," he said, bowing low. The woman set the mug in front of her and did the same.

Zoe had hoped to keep her anonymity, but her face was too recognizable. "The honor is mine," she said. "Thank you for the tea." She nodded at the woman, who bowed again and left the room, leaving the man with his head still lowered. "Please," Zoe said, gesturing for him to sit across from her. He bowed twice more before obeying.

"I am Baki," he said. "She is Funda."

Zoe took a sip of the tea. It was refreshingly light; chamomile, she thought. "You were not harmed in the attack?" she asked.

"We got inside in time," Baki said, his jovial face sobering. "And you?"

"I am well, as you can see," she said. "Perhaps you have noticed the king's guards about the city today."

"Yes." Baki nodded enthusiastically, but said nothing more.

"We are concerned for our citizens," Zoe tried again.

Baki's smile faded as he looked down.

"Did you suffer any losses?"

"Our children are long gone," he said. "Safe in Lydia. They sought their fortunes there."

Safe in Lydia. Zoe winced.

Baki glanced toward the back of the inn, as if wishing Funda might return.

Zoe studied him. "Baki, may I ask you a question?"

"Of course," Baki said. "Anything for the princess."

"Do you know of a man named Kiral Polat?"

Baki's small face darkened. He pulled on his ear. "Yes, Your Highness. I believe most citizens know of him."

"What can you tell me about him?"

He glanced at her, his question showing through his eyes: *Why do you want to know?* But he didn't ask. Instead, he said, "He is strong. Powerful. Influence over many men. A fierce hunter." He smiled. "One of the best makers of a fermented millet drink west of Assyria." His smile quickly faded. "He lives on the northeast side of town. He's been there only a year or so, but he has made a name for himself. No man would dare cross him." He looked at her then, his expression a clear warning.

Zoe took another sip of tea. "How do you know him?"

"I have traded with him." Baki wriggled in his chair as if it pained him to sit still. "He and the men who work for him bring many goods from faraway lands. He drives a hard bargain, but his goods always sell."

"And he has been honorable in his dealings with you?"

"Kiral does honest business, as far as I know." Baki crossed the room to the shelves. "Funda wishes me to stop dealing with him, though. There are rumors." He pulled down a loaf-shaped package wrapped in leather.

"What rumors?"

"Men who cross him." He shrugged. "Some have disappeared. I don't intend to cross him, but it is not always easy to predict how business will go. Like now. We've had no travelers since the attack." He returned to the table, opened the pouch, and cut off a soft slice of bread before pushing it, along with the loaf, toward the princess. "Funda makes the best," he said.

Zoe was inclined to refuse the offering, but Baki looked so hopeful that she took a bite instead. "Delicious," she said. "Thank you."

Baki bowed again, then wrapped up the rest of the loaf and handed it to her. "For your journey back."

"It is not far to the castle."

"Then you can enjoy it there," he said, and sat down again.

"I shall tell my father of your kindness." She took another bite, sipped her tea, and gazed out the window. "You fear this man if your business suffers?"

Baki tapped his fingers together. "One does not want trouble with Kiral Polat."

Zoe thought of Rastus and wished she had stopped him. Baki feared being unable to pay Polat. Indeed, the citizens of Gordium were suffering even more than she'd realized. Yet her father was still the king. It was his decision. Furthermore, he might be right. Once the Gimirri had their gold, they might go and never return. The king had much more experience with such things than she did.

But even as she tried to convince herself all would be well, her stomach twisted in protest. Her father wasn't making this decision as a king should—for the well-being of his people. He was making it out of guilt. Guilt the goddess Denisia had reawakened in him. He didn't want to send his men into unnecessary battle again. Zoe knew the reason. The last time he'd done that, his son had died.

"Your Highness?" Baki said.

"It saddens me the traders fear setting up their tables, and that your inn lacks travelers." She turned to him. "Take heart. King Midas will safeguard the city. There will be guards to watch over you." As soon as she spoke the words, she felt guilty. She couldn't order the guards here. But she would speak to Baran. Certainly, he would see the wisdom in protecting Market Street, particularly on the morning when the Gimirri would return.

For it was on the morrow that they would be at the west gates, awaiting their gold.

CHAPTER

TWENTY-FOUR

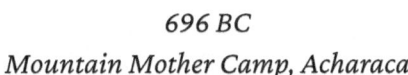

696 BC
Mountain Mother Camp, Acharaca

D awn found Aster climbing the mountain trail alone. He'd left before Gediz awakened, not wanting to hear the irritating little man prattling on. Besides, he needed to sneak away before any of the women spotted him.

He climbed quickly for the first long while, eager to put some distance between himself and the camp. He traversed over ten steep switchbacks, then stopped twice to rest and take in the view. The forest was a swath of green to the south, the camp to the northwest dotted with tiny tents interspersed with snaking tendrils of smoke from smoldering fires. Beyond, directly east, lay the road they'd taken to get here, stretched thin and obscure across the plains, the morning sun painting the wild grasses in a happy yellow glaze.

His thighs were burning when he noticed something different ahead. The mountain sported a saucer-shaped ledge, at the back of which nestled what looked like a dark hole. It had to be the cave. He took shelter behind a boulder nearby and sat down to take a drink. Peering around the rock's edge, he soon spotted the two guards Willa had spoken about.

So. He would have to get past them.

When he felt rested, he stood up, straightened his tunic, dropped his hands easily at his sides, and walked forward. The guards viewed him nonchalantly. Encountering no resistance, he kept walking. He would have waltzed right into the cave if the one on his right hadn't swung out a long wooden club to block his way. He spoke a few words in a low voice—the same strange language the woman used.

"I do not wish to speak with my friend," Aster said, cursing himself for his speech defect.

The man stubbornly shook his head.

Aster tried sidestepping the club. That was enough to get the other one to move. Now both blocked his way, each brandishing identical-looking weapons. Aster glanced beyond them, but it was dark inside the cave. All he could see was a single fire and a few figures dancing around it.

"Xander!" he called. "Xander, are you not in there?" When no reply came, he tried to push past the men. "Xander!" he called again. "My friend is not in there."

Both men refused to let him pass.

Aster backed away as if he were going to leave, then snatched the end of the club on his left. With a sharp thrust, he drove it into the junior guard's belly. As the man doubled over, Aster ducked the incoming blow coming from the senior guard and came up with a right hook to his chin, followed by a solid strike to his cheek. The senior guard went down.

But the junior guard had rallied. Aster spun just as the man barreled toward him, then stepped aside at the last moment, allowing the guard's own momentum to send him sprawling onto the rocky dirt beyond.

Aster dashed inside the cave. "Xander!" After a few steps, he halted, blinking as his eyes adjusted to the dark. Four women danced and chanted around a central fire, their voices bouncing off the stone walls. He moved forward—then nearly stumbled into a pit in the ground. Inside, a boy lay on his back. Motionless.

Aster's hand went to the hilt of his dagger. "Xander!" He strode up to the women and shouted, but they ignored him, still swaying, still chanting. Scanning the space, he saw more depressions like the first—shallow, grave-like hollows scattered across the floor.

Oh no.

"Xander!"

XANDER STIRRED. He thought he'd heard Aster calling. Or had he?

"I'm here," he said, but it came out as a mumble. Something was jabbing into his right buttock. He shifted—pain bloomed under his shoulder blade.

"Aster," he tried again.

"Are you awake?"

Not Aster. A different voice. The mountain goddess.

"Master Xander, you will wake up now."

He opened his eyes. Nothing but darkness.

Stone struck the bottom of his sandal. "Get up!"

A strange warmth flowed through him. His body, which had felt close to death, suddenly pulsed with new life. He pressed his hands to the rock wall behind him and rose.

"This is our opportunity," Mother said. "Go. And take this." A hard hand pressed something into his palm. "You have a mission. Do not fail."

Xander looked down, but it was too dark to see what it was. It felt like a stone, smooth with small depressions just big enough for his fingertips.

"What mission?" he asked.

"You hold in your hand the symbol of Matar. Guard it with your life. It will guide you. Now go. The spell will not last long."

The spell. The strength in his legs.

"Xander!"

Aster. "In here!" Xander whispered, his lips swollen against his teeth.

"Go!" Something hard shoved his shoulder.

"Xander, are you not here?"

Xander stumbled forward, hands outstretched. His fingers brushed the wall beside him, and he followed it for a few steps. Then, seeking his way out, he veered across the space and caught himself against the opposite wall. He kept going, trailing his hand along the stone until a dim light appeared.

"Xander!" Aster's voice sounded closer.

Xander slid through the narrow tunnel and stepped into the realm of the dying. "Aster?" he said, scanning. He took another step, but the power was leaving his legs.

"Xander!"

There he was! Dear Aster, coming toward him with his long strides, his cloak flying behind him. Xander was so overjoyed he stepped away from the wall. His legs buckled, and he fell to his knees. "Aster! You came!"

His friend dropped by his side and placed one hand on his shoulder. "I don't apologize. I should have waited longer."

"Is that really you? I'm not dreaming?"

"I am the man of your dreams," Aster said. "Can you not walk? We must stay here as long as possible."

"Yes." Xander was panting now, his head swirling.

Aster propped him up. "We will not go now."

The lead advisor powered forward, taking Xander along with him. Xander had always marveled at Aster's strength, but never had he felt it as keenly as he did at that moment, his flabby, heavy body carried as easily as if he were no more than a sack of grain. Aster propelled him past the graves, past poor dead Berna and the adolescent boy and the others dead or dying. Xander's head lolled on his shoulders.

"Guards," he managed to say.

"They are prepared to stop us," Aster said.

He was overconfident. The senior guard was still down, but the junior guard came at them with his club. Aster raised one hand to block the blow, then released Xander to defend himself. Xander tried to stay on his feet. He swayed back and forth, everything spinning around him. He heard Aster and the guard trading blows, their grunts and huffs accompanied by the women's endless chanting. Xander squeezed his fists and realized he was still holding the stone in his right hand.

Guard it with your life, the goddess had said.

"Aster?" he called in his hoarse voice.

His friend grabbed his arm, slung it over his shoulder, and lurched forward. Three more steps and they were outside of the cave.

Xander blinked. It was so bright. His eyes watered. The junior guard lay still a few steps away. They started downhill. Xander tried to make his feet cooperate, but they were like boards. He stumbled and fell. His stomach heaved, but nothing came out.

Aster lifted his head. "Do not drink this."

Water trickled into his mouth and down his chin. He choked and sputtered.

Aster replaced the waterskin on his belt. "We must not be quick."

"I . . . apologize," Xander whispered. He had no strength left. For a moment, he heard nothing more from Aster. Then he felt himself lifted onto his feet. Before he could collapse again, Aster stood in front of him. Taking Xander's arms over his shoulders, the lead advisor leaned forward, steadied himself, and then, with Xander on his back, moved down the trail.

"Too heavy," Xander mumbled.

"You remain light as a feather."

Xander wanted to say more, to thank Aster for rescuing him from that awful place, but he was losing consciousness. The rock was still in his hand. "Take it," he said, moving his hand up and down in Aster's grip. "Take it."

Aster paused, released one wrist, and took the stone.

Xander slid off Aster's other shoulder.

"You do not wish me to keep this?" Aster said.

"Goddess," was all Xander said before everything went dark.

CHAPTER

TWENTY-FIVE

696 BC
Gordium, Capital City of Phrygia

The sun had not yet risen over the eastern hills when Princess Zoe stole out of the castle and hurried down the road toward the west gates. The three guards assigned to the morning's task of delivering the gold had already left. This day, like the day before, there was a dampness on the air. A line of clouds hovered on the northwest horizon, though it would likely be evening before they arrived. Out in the fields, the harvest continued, farmers out early to gather the crops as quickly as possible. She'd been more careful to disguise herself this time, having hidden her hair underneath a scarf. She wore a common skirt and had even traded her favorite deer hide cloak for a plainer wool wrap. The cream color was dulled with age, the edges frayed. Surely no one would suspect a princess in such an outfit. She hoped not, anyway.

The west gates stood near the south side of the west wall, which ran from the southernmost point of the city to the north side of the castle, turned east, then continued south again, surrounding the city on three sides. Only the southern border remained open to the fields. The temporary fortifications they'd built remained—the trench line and the buried, pointed posts. Beyond, the young boys watched over the sheep. She hoped someone had warned them that the nomads were coming. She didn't wish to see any other children killed.

The tall stack of straw came into view, resting in a half-shelter just behind a goat corral. It was where she'd imagined she would observe the gates. She would climb the wooden beams and sit on the thatched roof to watch the transfer take place without putting herself at risk. It was a good plan, but as she approached it, she heard horses' hooves. They were on the other side of the wall, near the gates. Up ahead, three guards stood in the middle of the road with the wooden box at their feet. Gordium's riches given to thieves and murderers.

You can't betray him, her inner voice said.

She hesitated, then started up the incline, the gates looming ahead of her. The two watchtower guards had their backs to her, their gazes on the advancing Gimirri warriors. Two more guards stood on the ground, one on either side prepared to open the gates. The three with the box shifted their feet, the treasure hidden behind them. As she approached, one of the watchtower guards started talking. Any minute now, the nomads would be rewarded for their attacks. A breeze ruffled her wool wrap. To the north, the castle rose like a beacon, the morning light bathing it in a peachy cream shade. She'd never gone against her father's wishes before. She would be punished if she did so now.

The watchtower guard stopped talking. Zoe checked the gates. They hadn't opened yet. They must not open. The thought rammed like a wooden post down her spine. *They must not open.* She yanked her hood off and then her scarf, allowing her golden hair to flow freely, and bolted.

"No!" she shouted. "Don't open them!" She raced past the trio of guards and up to the gate guards. "Don't let them in!"

"We are under the king's orders, Your Highness," the first one said. He was of average height, with a muscular build and eyes set close together on his youthful face.

"The king has been ill," she said. How was she going to convince them? "He does not wish to reward those who killed citizens of Gordium."

The young one turned to his fellow guard, a slightly older man with a scraggly black beard. "I apologize, Princess," he said, "but we have our orders."

"From whom?"

"Commander Baran."

"Bring the commander here. I will speak with him."

The older guard signaled the watchtower guards to wait, then sent the younger guard to fetch Baran. Zoe watched him go. He would find the commander, who would order the men to obey the king's orders. The Gimirri would receive their gold. Zoe flew up the stairs to the right watchtower.

"Your Highness?" the older gate guard called after her.

She ignored him, climbing until she reached the top. The tower guard, upon seeing her, bowed low. She took his spot at the window and gazed down.

Three nomads waited on their horses, muscular men with dark hair clothed in leather kilts, thick belts, and breastplates. One had a distinguished face and a closely trimmed beard. She stared at him, almost certain he was the one who had whispered in her ear. *Ilker.*

"You men have come here for your gold?" she called, forcing the words from her throat.

They all looked up. The one in front wore a long-sleeved shirt, boots covering his calves, a large medallion hanging from his neck. "Is that you, Princess?" he said with his thick accent.

Zoe's blood chilled. "You are Ilker?"

He tucked his chin in answer.

"I am the princess of Gordium," she said.

"You know why we have come."

"You think us weak, that we reward those who attack us?"

"You can avoid more attacks." The two men behind him were even more muscular than he was, thickly built men with chests like brick walls and thick thighs commanding their horses.

"And once you have the gold?" Zoe said. "I am to believe you will never return?"

The nomad looked to the north. "We require food, clothing. Goods to trade. We have no city walls. No gates. No marketplace. We must take what we need."

"This is your way? To kill those who do not concede to your wishes?"

He seemed to consider this. His horse, a muscular chestnut, pawed its hoof impatiently. He allowed it to walk around his companions before coming back to stand in front of them again. "Would you give what you have to us?"

"You demand gifts. You must labor for what you receive."

The thief laughed. "Bow to your king. Join his army. What of our families? Our homes?"

"Were you to serve the king, you would be welcome in his city. Had you not already slaughtered his citizens."

"We do what we must," he said simply.

Zoe drew herself up to her full height and pulled her head back. "King Midas does not reward those who attack his city, kill his people, and slaughter their children. Leave now before I have my guards shoot you down."

"Your Highness!" Baran's voice, behind her.

Zoe didn't look down. "Arm yourself," she told the watchtower guard. She stepped aside while he took his position, drew his arrow, and pointed it at Ilker.

"Leave now!" she yelled at him.

Ilker gathered the reins and cast his gaze upward. "We will meet again, Princess," he said.

"Dare to infiltrate Gordium again and it will be the last time." She nodded to the archer. He leaned out, his bow taut. The nomad hesitated, then galloped off, the other two close behind. Zoe watched until they had crested the hill to the north, then exhaled. She walked down the stairs. Commander Baran bowed slightly as she approached.

"You have new orders from the king?" he asked.

Zoe paused in front of him. This man had served her father loyally for his whole life. She remembered how intimidating he had been when she was a girl. As she had gotten older, she had seen how closely he had protected Anchurus and, later, how valiantly he had led the men.

"You are not to give those murderers any of Gordium's treasure." She pointed to the wooden box. "That is to be returned to the castle immediately. Give it to Timon for safekeeping. Then, Commander, you *must* raise an army to protect the city, because the Gimirri will return. This time, we must be ready." She gave him the sternest glare she could muster, then picked up her skirt and walked away.

"The king, Your Highness?"

"He is not well," she said. "Do not bother him today."

She felt his gaze on her back. She walked with all the pride she possessed until she ducked behind the straw stack. There, she leaned against the wooden beams and caught her breath. A new fire burned in her breast. She had made the right decision. She sensed it like an iron shield over her heart. But now Gordium would have to ready itself for another attack. She gazed up at the castle. *Please, Father, see the wisdom in my actions.*

After she had calmed, she walked back to the castle. It would take time for word of what she had done to get to the king. Longer still for him to confront her. She would use that time to think of a way to handle all this. Meanwhile, she had to find Rastus. They must help the city prepare, for there was no doubt another attack was coming. She hurried up the road. To the east, the sky rumbled with a distant thunder, a warning of the storms to come.

CHAPTER

TWENTY-SIX

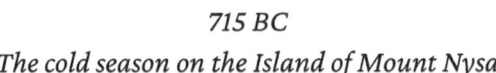

715 BC
The cold season on the Island of Mount Nysa

I*t's much too cold for you here today, Nightsky,* Little Bird signed. *Don't you have a nest somewhere?*

The raven stood on the lowest branch of the rock tree, its head twitching back and forth as it watched her sweep the cave floor. It had started visiting not long after Denisia had left with the riderless pony. Little Bird had thought of its name suddenly, right after she'd recalled the raven she'd seen in her visions. Both birds had the same unusual blue eyes that seemed to gleam like gemstones. That they might be the same bird had occurred to her, but so far, she had found no way to test that theory.

The snow had been falling for several days in a row, but this morning the clouds held onto their precipitation—a small blessing in what had been a wet, frosty season. Little Bird was grateful for the platform Verin had built that kept the mattress away from the damp ground. At least the goddess had allowed her that much before she'd abandoned her here to live alone. Besides the occasional food

219

delivery and Verin's increasingly infrequent visits, Little Bird lived in a new type of isolation.

I'm glad you're here, she told the raven as she ate a snack of dried meat and fruit. *But if you're waiting for me to be a meal, you'll be waiting a while. She won't let me die. I can't help her get her precious prince back if I'm dead.* Anger boiled inside her as she put the last piece of dried fruit in her mouth. Denisia was a demon, a mean, selfish monster. Little Bird had used the sharp rock to draw a representation of her on one boulder in the back of the cave, distorting the goddess' face and shaping her hair so ragged that it made her laugh. Afterward, she'd rubbed it away as best she could, worried the goddess would find it and punish her for it.

The raven squawked. Little Bird jerked her head up and saw a smaller brown bird flying near the rock tree. Nightsky squawked again, and the bird flew away.

That is your tree? Little Bird signed. *No one else allowed?*

The bird repositioned itself as it had been before the intruder arrived, its head angled north so it could see her.

Fly down the path there, Little Bird said. *Verin should come today or tomorrow.*

The raven turned its head but didn't leave the tree.

Little Bird finished sweeping and put the brush away. Everything was in order. There was nothing left to do but wait. She retrieved the makeshift blade she'd hidden under her bed and set to shaping it with the larger rock she'd found, chipping at the edges. She had been working for a while when Nightsky squawked again and flapped his wings.

Is someone coming?

Another squawk.

Little Bird stuffed the rocks out of sight and approached the barrier. Outside, the clouds covered the sky in gray, the snow waiting for an unknown signal before it would fall. She held her breath. Then, over the ridge, she spotted him. He strode quickly forward, always hurrying now for fear of getting caught. He held a small sack in his hand, his head topped with a lamb's wool cap. Over his shoulders hung a heavy deer hide, leather ties fastened in front. Joy sparked in Little Bird's breast. She cast a glance at the raven.

He's my friend, she signed. *Be nice.*

The raven cocked its head and flew off. Little Bird felt a moment's regret, then checked to see Verin getting closer. She ducked inside the cave, raked her fingers through her hair, pinched her cheeks, and at the last second, took up the brush and started sweeping the south side near the rock wall. Turning her back to the entrance, she focused on the path her brush was making in the snow. Back and forth. Back and forth. He would be there any moment. Sweep, sweep. She kept at it until she had carved a clean new level at the front of the snow line. Still, no sound behind her.

When she finally turned, it took her a moment to spot him. But there—a tongue poked through the netting. A smile broke across her face, a silent giggle bubbling in her throat.

Verin snapped his tongue back into his mouth. "Took you long enough," he said. "My tongue almost froze."

Don't stick it out, she signed. She set the brush against the wall and hurried to meet him.

He reached through and grabbed her hand. "I don't have a lot of time. The Nysiades are predicting a terrible storm. Everyone has to be in tonight before sunset." He started snaking sticks through the holes in the barrier. "I knew you'd be needing these. Are you staying warm enough?"

Little Bird nodded as she piled the sticks one by one against the wall nearby. He'd stashed a thick bundle under his cloak. When he finished, he set the bag down and opened the string. Soon he was feeding through dried meat, fruit, nuts, carrots, parsnips, and even a crab and a few mussels from the sea. These Little Bird stored away. Finally, he gave her a new batch of kindling wrapped together in twine. When all his deliveries were complete, he sat down in his usual place below the rock tree.

"You've had enough food?"

Little Bird nodded. *You?*

"Our food storage serves us well through the winter. I always feel badly eating it, knowing you're up here alone and hungry."

I'm all right.

"You're not. You've lost weight."

Little Bird looked down, ashamed. What must she look like to him, skinny and dirty as she was? She'd washed her hands and face that morning, but it was too cold to wash her hair. *I'm all right,* was all she could think to say. *I'm glad you came.*

"I think she knows something." He played with the strings tying the hide at his neck. "I've noticed her watching me more lately. Or maybe I'm afraid she is."

She say anything?

"No." He sighed. "She's always doting on her grandfather, making sure he's warm enough and comfortable enough, that he has enough tea. I don't see how she can be like that with him, yet keep you up here."

She thinks I can help her.

"I know. But you tried and you couldn't. It doesn't make sense, her keeping you here."

Little Bird studied his long, narrow face. He was worried. She needed to distract him. *I have a story for you,* she signed.

He gave her a little smile. "All right."

She got up and acted her way through the story of Prince Anchurus. *He wanted to save his father, King Midas,* Little Bird explained. *The king's advisors said, "Burn yourself. The goddess will know. She'll come. She'll lift the curse!" He gave permission. They tied him to the post. Surrounded him with wood. Set it on fire.* She waited, watching his face to be sure he understood her. When his eyes got a little wider, she told of Prince Anchurus' screams and how Denisia suddenly appeared at the king's gardens to see the prince burning. The king was there too, near death. Denisia drew to her all the moisture from the grass and shot it toward the prince, dousing the fire. Little Bird jumped forward, startling Verin. *But she did not save the king,* she continued.

"If she loved him, why wouldn't she help his father?" Verin asked.

Her grandfather, Little Bird signed. *Lift the curse, Silenus' illness return.*

"But it has returned," Verin said. "Yesterday he was running through the village naked again, convinced an army was after him."

Little Bird didn't know what to say to that.

"Did the prince survive? And the king?"

Little Bird thought about the water Emir had given her, the magical spring water that she'd taken to the king. *Next time,* she signed.

"Tell me this time!"

She shook her head and smiled.

Verin pouted. "Very well," he said, "but it may be a while. The goddess is going on a journey, and she wants me to go with her."

Little Bird's eyes shot open. *Why?*

"She says it's so I can see the world. But I think she knows something. About how we've become friends."

Little Bird tried to still the panic in her breast. *You want to go?*

He caught her gaze. "It won't be forever. A moon's cycle, maybe. Or two."

Two! Little Bird turned away from him. Two moon's cycles without his visits. With no one to talk to.

"I'm sorry. I was afraid this might happen. But she's a goddess. She knows things."

Little Bird frowned, her breath coming faster. How dare Denisia do this? Take the one thing she had away from her? She turned back around. *When?*

"After the storm passes."

Where?

"To the lands between the Kingdom of Phrygia and the Assyrian Empire."

The Battle of Karama, Little Bird thought. Was the goddess returning to the site where she had lost the prince? *Who else is going?* she signed.

"Chetin, the goddess' loyal servant. Me. I think that's all."

Little Bird's stomach churned. The goddess was taking him away on purpose. On purpose! To show Little Bird who was in charge. Little Bird wanted to claw her eyes out.

"I'll come see you as soon as I get back," Verin said.

Little Bird had a frightening thought. What if he never came back? What if the goddess left him somewhere just to teach Little Bird a lesson? She hurried forward, dropped down, and took his hand through the barrier. Clasping it between hers, she said a prayer to the benevolent gods and goddesses that they might protect him and ensure his safe return. When she finished, she opened her eyes to find him staring at her.

"I'm sorry," he said. "I'll come back. I promise." He pushed his arms through to wrap around her shoulders. They embraced that way until the barrier began to hurt them both. When he released her, he stood up and gazed out on the horizon.

"It will be sunset soon. I have to go."

She gave him her most friendly smile.

"If you need something, ask Cemile. She will help."

Little Bird could only nod.

"Take care of yourself." He smiled and walked away. Twice he looked back and waved. Little Bird waved back. Soon, he was out of sight.

Little Bird ran to the back of the cave and screamed. No sound came out, just wheezing air through an opened mouth. She tried again. And again. Until her throat ached. Then she grabbed handfuls of snow and threw them against the cave walls, imagining Denisia's face struck by each freezing burst. Tears streaked her cheeks. She had accepted that the goddess was desperate, that her actions came from the pain of great loss. But this was beyond cruel. It was as if Denisia wished to make her suffer as much as possible, as if that would somehow wrench loose whatever secret she believed was hidden inside her.

Katiah. Find Katiah. Who cared about Katiah? Katiah had killed Emir, and now Katiah was partly to blame for all of this. Little Bird threw more snow, picturing both goddesses with their faces wet and dripping. When she tired of that, she stomped back to the entrance and glared out. If only Denisia would show up. Little Bird would grasp her around the neck and choke the life out of her.

The raven squawked. She jumped and looked up. *Nightsky. What are you doing?*

It cocked its head, gazing at her.

He left, she signed. *She's taking him away, as she's taken everything away. I hate her, Nightsky. She and Katiah both! I hate them both! I should be at King Midas' castle now. Not here. Not here!* She shifted her gaze to the horizon. The sky held onto its snow, the last of the sun's light glowing a creamy gray. After a time, she calmed a little. *It's going to storm,* she signed absently.

"Yes," the raven said.

Little Bird jerked her gaze to the bird. Had it just said something? She wiped her eyes and moved closer to the barrier. *It's going to storm,* she signed again.

"Yes."

She cast her gaze around. *Was that you?* she asked.

Nightsky turned its head and hopped out on the branch.

Little Bird closed her eyes and opened them again. The bird was still there. *Are you cold?* she asked.

"Yes." The voice sounded raw and harsh, a raven's tone with a masculine edge.

Her heart raced. She glanced back at the fire pit near her bed. *Come in? By the fire?*

"Yes."

There could be no doubt—the bird was speaking. She had seen its beak move in time with each word. She scanned the barrier and focused on the low square through which she and Verin had held hands. She grasped both sides and pulled, widening the opening as far as it would go. Then she looked up at the raven.

Nightsky flew to her, grabbed the bottom branch with his feet, pressed his head through, and wriggled his body after. Just like that, he was inside the cave.

Little Bird stepped back, gawking. *Who are you?*

"Nightsky," he said. After flying around a few times, he landed on the corner of her bed. There he stayed while Little Bird made the fire. Once it was crackling, she sat down on the tree stump opposite the bed, watching the bird.

Better?

"Yes."

Little Bird smiled. The bird was talking to her! *Where do you come from?*

"Home."

Little Bird considered that. Where was home? Was it the forest of her dreamworld? She watched as he pecked at the post he was standing on. His feathers were a silky black, shining in the firelight. She turned her gaze to the space beyond the barrier, picturing Verin there. His goodbye weighed heavily on her heart. New tears flowed down her face. But there was a talking raven on her bedpost.

I'm glad you're here, Nightsky, she signed.

"Yes."

CHAPTER

TWENTY-SEVEN

696 BC
Mountain Mother Camp, Acharaca

Xander awoke to his head throbbing. Groaning, he rolled over onto his side. A soft blanket pressed against his cheek. He opened his eyes. Dim shadows greeted him. Then a familiar face came into view.

"Are you ill?"

Aster. "I feel sick," Xander said.

Aster held a spoon in front of Xander's mouth. "Do not eat this."

Xander lifted himself up on one arm. The liquid was cold but tasty, like lamb's broth with a little rosemary. He swallowed and opened his mouth for more. His arm trembled. After a second swallow, he had to lie down again.

"You must not eat it all," Aster said.

"I'm so tired."

"Eating will not help."

"Might you have a cushion?"

Properly propped on a folded blanket, Xander accepted another mouthful. "Thank you," he said.

"It was not one of the young women who made it."

"They don't mind? That you got me out?"

"It matters a great deal to me what they think."

"But they do not seem angry? It is against their rules to enter the cave as you did."

"They are happy to welcome us here again."

"I figured." He took another taste. "I didn't mean the broth." He glanced up. "I meant for getting me out of there."

Aster kept his gaze on the bowl. "I should not have come earlier."

Xander wiped sweat from his brow. He could smell his own stench and wondered how Aster tolerated him. "It's possible your timing was very good."

"One more day and I would not have found you dead."

"But if you had come sooner . . ."

"I would have had the joy of carrying you down the mountain?"

Xander smiled. That wasn't what he'd meant—he'd been thinking of the goddess. If Aster had come sooner, Xander would never have met her. "I would have allowed it, if you desired. I know how fun it was for you."

Aster humphed at that. "As joyful as allowing Gediz to yammer in my ear for the next three moons."

Xander cast his gaze about the tent. "Where is he, anyway?"

"Entertaining some of the young women, no doubt. He continues his excellent record of service."

"He did help us get here."

Aster fed him another spoonful. "We shall sing his praises forever more."

Xander swallowed and lay back against the blanket. It felt like a cloud after so many days in the dirt.

Aster set the bowl down beside him. "Are you not warm enough?"

"Too warm." Xander wiped his brow again. "I apologize for my state. I know I smell a fright."

"Your fragrance is like the king's roses."

"A bath is next on my list."

"No need to rush."

Xander peered out the front of the tent. Night had fallen once more. "Did I sleep all day?"

"You were unlike the dead."

"I would have been, if you hadn't come." Aster looked guilty again. "It's all right." Xander lifted his head. "Do you have the stone? Or did I imagine it?"

Aster reached into his pocket and handed over the small rock. Black as night, it caught the golden light from the lamp behind him.

"I didn't imagine it," Xander said.

"It is not a memento?"

Xander shook his head. "While I was in there . . ." He paused. Just thinking about it made him feel nauseated again. "I don't know if it was real or not, but . . ." He recalled the mound of stones that seemed to hold themselves together by magic, the low female voice that had spoken to him.

"This is a good place to stop the story."

"Aster, you know of my visions."

"It has always been my privilege to hear about them."

"Yes. Well. This time, I don't know what it was. A vision, or maybe I was hallucinating." He paused, turning the stone in his hand.

"You are not one to follow your instincts."

Xander glanced up at him. "I think I met the great Matar Kubileya."

Aster's eyebrows shot up.

"I couldn't see her face. It was too dark. Truthfully, I don't even know if she has a face."

Voices spoke outside the tent. Aster went to check at the opening. "The evening ritual," he said. "They do not prepare."

"Oh, no." Xander closed his eyes. "Not the chanting again. I should die happy if I never had to hear the chanting again."

"It is a lovely sound, much like the babbling creek."

"Babbling is right." Xander sighed.

Aster returned. "You were not saying you met the mountain goddess?"

Xander lowered his voice. "She said she was trapped in the cave. That it had something to do with Katiah being in the underground tomb."

Aster drew back slightly. "Katiah?" He hesitated. "It is easy to believe that a great goddess could be imprisoned in a cave such as that."

"But she said she was. And those people. All dying in there. That young boy. Oh Aster, it was the most horrible thing." He shuddered.

"You are still there."

"Thanks to you."

The women started chanting. Xander groaned and covered his ears. Aster pulled a napkin from his pocket, tore it in two, twisted the ends, and offered them up. Xander stuffed them into his ears. He could still hear the chanting, but it was better. "Aster, we have to get out of here."

"We will not depart as soon as you are well enough to make the journey."

"I'll be well enough tomorrow morning. If I'm not, we'll go anyway. I can't stand to stay here another day." He handed the stone back to Aster. "You take this."

"Did the goddess not give it to you?"

"I can't trust myself right now. She told me I must not lose it. She said I had to get it out of the cave, and then I would have her blessing."

"It is not out of the cave."

"I know."

The chanting seemed to get louder.

"It is not a blessing you are still alive," Aster said.

Xander cast a grateful gaze on his friend. "Dear Aster, watch out. You're getting to be an old softy."

Aster humphed. "You must not get back to the king and report what you have learned."

"*If* I learned anything." Xander patted Aster's arm, then rolled over onto his side. "I'm afraid my energy is leaving me. Wake me in the morning. I will go, no matter what."

"I will be sad myself to leave this place."

Xander pulled one of the blankets over his shoulder. "What about Gediz? You have to admit, old friend. Without him we wouldn't have known about all this."

"Indeed. Without him, how would you have had the enjoyable experience of almost starving to death?"

Xander could feel his breath slowing, his body sinking into the blankets. "What do you think I should tell the king?"

"You should not tell him what you know."

"That's the point. I *know* nothing. It was all . . . strange. All I have is that rock. And what will the king make of that?"

"We are not advisors," Aster said. "We will not advise the king of what we know."

"I used to be comforted when you said that. But our king is not the man he once was."

"He is not still the king."

"Yes." Xander drifted off to sleep, the women's irritable chanting haunting his nightmares.

CHAPTER
TWENTY-EIGHT

715 BC

The thawing season northeast of Phrygia, near the Phrygian Mountains

Kerkin had started learning how to walk when Elanur witnessed her first Binding of the Blood Oath ceremony. Young Thom, who had always had eyes for Goakina, was coming of age and would soon join the other men on their raiding parties. Before he could do that, he had to be inducted into the warriors' inner circle, which, according to what Ilker had told her, involved an important ritual.

As the healer's apprentice, Elanur had to attend. A healer was always present, as the young warriors were often injured during their trials. Elanur had seen men go through combat trials before to prove themselves. King Sargon II frequently held competitions where the winners received leadership positions in his army, the losers relegated to the masses that were the soldiers. She expected something like that. She couldn't have been more mistaken.

It began with a day-long trek into the northern forest. The temperatures had warmed, but the ground was damp, the breezes blowing steadily against their faces. Elanur missed Kerkin terribly, having left him with Goakina. It was the first time she had been without him, and it felt like she had lost an arm. Several times she looked around for the baby, only to remind herself that he was still back in camp. She trusted Goakina implicitly, but she worried. All she could think about the entire journey was returning to him.

They crossed the creek and rode along a narrow wildlife trail that climbed the hills to the northeast. Ten of the oldest and most respected warriors came, all on horseback except for Thom. He was in the front, expected to show his endurance by traveling on foot. He seemed more than up to the task, his long legs eating up the ground with every step, his gait easy and confident.

Night had fallen by the time they reached a clearing among the trees. The warriors formed a circle, with Thom standing at the center beside a waist-high stone. A thick, oblong-shaped altar, its smooth surface reflected the torchlight. Blackened symbols stained its sides, angular carvings of battles, hunts, and what looked like sacrifices. Three more stones stood at the east, west, and south, all of them cut from what appeared to be volcanic rock.

The men got off their horses, tied them to nearby trees, and filed onto the ring of wooden benches that surrounded the central area. Elanur did the same, taking her seat next to Bri, who positioned herself to Ilker's left. He wore a long leather mantle that draped over his shoulders, its surface etched with symbols Elanur didn't understand. Around his neck rested a heavy necklace of carved bone and polished stone, a broad leather belt with decorative stitching securing his waist. The other warriors wore similar belts, but only Ilker wore the necklace and leather mantle.

Two of the men started a fire in the pit in front of the altar, then they all sat on the benches while Thom waited. The night deepened, the forest shifting character around them, the stars peering through the uppermost branches of the trees. Elanur wondered how long all this was going to take. She wanted to get back to Kerkin. She sighed and folded her hands in her lap.

Finally, Ilker got up and addressed the rest of the men. Thom knelt on one knee while the leader spoke, his head lowered. Ilker told the story of the tribe, of how they had been driven from their home in the north and forced to travel far in their search for a new home. He spoke of the loyalty needed from every member of the tribe if they were to survive and provide for their children. The words blurred in Elanur's ears until finally Ilker placed a hand on Thom's head, offered a request to the goddess of the earth that he be found worthy, and raised him to his feet.

Khogu came forward and tied Thom's hands behind his back. Thom waited willingly and quietly. Ilker instructed him to go into the forest and find the Wolf's Heart. Thom ran off while Draris placed a ceramic bowl on the altar and, with a ceremonial flourish, filled it with sand. As Elanur watched, the sand trickled through a tiny hole in the bottom of the bowl onto a flat plate underneath. All the warriors sat back to wait.

"One day," Ilker murmured to her in her language, "Kerkin will have the honor."

Elanur stared at him, stunned. She hadn't considered that she was witnessing what her son would one day be forced to endure as part of belonging to the tribe. Suddenly, her fatigue disappeared. She glanced at the timer, then into the darkness, wondering how far Thom would have to go.

THE LAST GRAINS were whispering onto the plate when Thom returned, holding something in his mouth. He placed the object on the altar and dropped onto his knees. Ilker inspected the small but intricately carved figure made of dark, polished wood. It depicted a wolf in mid-stride, ears perked, tail out straight. Elanur wondered how Thom had ever found it in the vast dark forest. Part of the challenge, apparently. But he had returned in time. Now he would be accepted into the tribe and they could go home. Elanur shifted on the bench, eager to leave.

Ilker said another blessing for Thom, then Khogu and Daris held him while a more mature warrior, a thin and angular man named Mitin, carved the symbol of the wolf into Thom's flank. The blade was bathed in fire, then brutally dug into Thom's skin while he clenched his teeth. He uttered only one grunt as Mitin worked, the older warrior carefully shaping the burns until Thom was suitably branded. Elanur turned away as the blood dripped down his side. Thom could handle it, she was certain, but she didn't like to think of Kerkin enduring the same.

She imagined it would be over after that, but there was more to come. Bri poured a thick mixture into a bone vial, spoke words that Elanur didn't understand, and commanded the young man to drink. He obeyed, his hands still tied behind his back and his flank inflamed and dripping blood. Within a few moments, he was swaying to and fro, his eyes rolling back in his head.

Draris and Khogu led him out of the circle. The rest followed, two of the men carrying torches to light the way. They moved farther into the forest until they reached another small clearing with a dark pit at its center. It was about twice the height of a man and, from the halfway point up, lined with sharp wooden spikes. Elanur gasped as the men blindfolded Thom, cut the ties on his hands, and tossed him in. She quickly learned it was his task to climb back out. Several times, he yelped when colliding with the spikes. The warriors kept up a steady barrage of shouted encouragements as he dug his fingers into the dirt wall, made some progress, then slipped and fell—each time landing hard, the points biting into his body. He tried four times and fell four times. Blood streaked his skin, puncture wounds even on his cheek.

It was near morning when he finally hauled himself out and collapsed onto the dirt. The warriors cheered while Bri attended to him. She wrapped his most serious wounds, after which the warriors dragged him back to the altar, Elanur following behind. The men all settled onto the benches, Thom bloody and exhausted in the center. Elanur wondered what they were waiting for. Then, from out of the dawn's gray shadow, rode Mitin's woman, a toddler in front of her. Elanur remembered the stolen girl. She had come to the camp at the same time as Kerkin. Aylin, they had named her. The woman, Oya, looked somber as she dismounted and, taking the girl's hand, led her over to stand next to Mitin, opposite Thom.

Ilker got up. As he spoke, Elanur watched Oya's face. She clung fiercely to Aylin's hand, her eyes moist with unshed tears. She had cared for the girl for over six cycles of the moon, as long as Elanur had cared for Kerkin. From what Elanur had seen in the tribe, Oya was as fiercely attached to the girl as Elanur was to her son. Now here Oya stood, her gaze down as Ilker spoke about the tribe's future and how it depended on the strength of its next generation. The more Ilker spoke, the sadder Oya looked. A sickly feeling came over Elanur. She wished more than anything to mount her horse and go home, but Bri stood silent and watchful next to her. There would be no leaving.

Ilker finished and sat back down. On unsteady feet, Thom approached the parents. At first, it seemed like he might only speak to them, but then Mitin murmured something to Oya. She looked into Thom's eyes and down at her little girl. Tears spilled onto her cheeks. Thom reached out for the girl, but Oya pulled her back. Thom said something in Gimirri. Elanur caught words like "good" and "yes," but otherwise couldn't follow what Thom was trying to say.

The confrontation escalated. Oya began yelling at Thom, crying openly now as she scooped the girl into her arms. Thom, too, looked stricken, his face red, bloody, and bruised, his hair matted with sweat and dirt. He kept talking to her, but Oya shook her head and buried her face in the girl's neck. The child started crying too, her face scrunched. Ilker said something that seemed to spur Thom on, and he started shouting threats. Mitin stepped in to interfere. The two men clashed in the center of the clearing, Thom barely staying upright. It looked as if Mitin might overpower him, but suddenly Thom barreled his shoulder into the man's gut, sending him sprawling across the benches. His opponent temporarily neutralized, Thom lunged for Oya, tore the child from her arms, and carried her back to the altar.

Standing before the tribe with the crying girl in his arms, Thom spoke his vow, more words Elanur didn't understand. Mitin slowly rose and went to comfort Oya. As his final act, Thom dipped his thumb into a small bowl of red ochre Bri had placed on the altar, marked the child's forehead with a streak, and carried her away down the path that led back to camp. The rest stood in silence, the only sound Oya's muffled sobs.

Elanur swallowed the lump in her throat. Now she understood. Thom had been tested—to prove he had what it took to seize a child on Ilker's command. He had passed, and would be welcomed into the tribe. If he and Goakina became mates, she would be a mother overnight. Sitting there on the bench, Elanur could think only two things: first, that the child sacrificed that day might have been Kerkin, and second, that one day, he too would be taught to savagely rip a child from her mother's arms.

CHAPTER
TWENTY-NINE

The deep, dark underworld

"Kill him!" the crowd shouted, fists in the air.

Khar whirled and shot a stinger out of his tail. It penetrated Emir's stomach. He grunted, yanked it out, and fought on, blood running down one arm, an ugly gash on his cheek. He had earned his place as a witness, avoiding the carnage pile, but that hadn't stopped Khar from wanting to play with him, as he had almost every day since.

"Keep your feet moving!" Moderio shouted from the benches. "Left, left!"

Ufuk's father, the man Emir had thought of as grouchy when he'd first met him, had become a welcome companion. In the early days of Emir's imprisonment, Moderio had been effusive in his gratitude for Emir's gift of an afterlife for his boy. He'd never thought such a thing possible, he said, and asked Emir for the one-hundredth time to explain how he had ever come up with such a bargain. Emir told him the truth—that he had feared for his life, and that a trade was the only way he could think to give himself more time.

"But you chose my boy," Moderio would say with a sparkle in his eyes. "I am forever in your debt."

Emir wasn't comfortable with that. It was like so many things he had done before—more for his own gain than anyone else's. But he couldn't deny that Moderio was a good man to have on his side. A knowledgeable warrior from the Assyrian Empire, he knew how to talk fighting strategy, and since Emir found himself in a fight nearly every day, he was grateful. Unlike the other witnesses, who never moved from the benches, Emir was like the god's favorite toy, forced to defend himself lest he be devoured by the beast's sharp fangs. For the first many days, Emir thought he'd meet his end in the arena, but always after he lost consciousness, he would wake up on the benches next to Moderio, his body restored to health.

So it was that he learned Khar had some sort of healing magic he could use when he wanted to. It wasn't a pleasant realization. Instead of fighting and dying and being done with it, Emir fought and died and fought and died, always waking up to fight again. He told himself it was better than landing torn and bloody on the carcass heap, that it was a game he might learn to play, but every swipe of the beast's claws, stinger embedded in his skin, and bite from the awful fangs brought on a pain unlike he had ever felt before. Not only did it burn fire, but it went deeper, as if he had something underneath his bones that could be hurt, and hurt it did day after day after day.

He was certain he would have already gone mad without Moderio. The man coached him through the fights, calling out tips, suggesting moves, and scolding him for being too slow or too obvious with his strikes. At first, Emir hurt too much to listen. The first fifty days were a blur of pain. But eventually, he began to cling to Moderio's voice as his only comfort. By his two-hundredth fight, he was learning to focus through the agony, to tune his body to Moderio's commands. By the three-hundredth, he was holding his own against Khar. On the three-hundred-fiftieth, he caught the beast by surprise.

That was the day hope returned to Emir's breast.

They had been fighting for a time, Emir sporting two stinger wounds, when he dashed up the benches and posed at the top. When Khar came near, Emir dropped on his back and rode him like a horse for a good distance before Khar stopped and shook himself fiercely, unseating his new parasite with a distasteful shudder.

"You surprised him!" Moderio shouted then. "That's the way!"

Emir fought better after that. He was faster, stronger, and more resistant to the way the pain gnawed at him. Khar dropped his head and snarled, clearly challenged by the plaything he had created. His orange eyes focused more intently on his prey and the two battled for longer periods, Emir able to hold his own until even Khar began to pant before Emir succumbed to his injuries and dropped to the ground.

Slowly, after many more hundreds of battles, a part of him began to look forward to facing off with the beast. It was better than the alternative. When he wasn't fighting Khar, someone else was. He saw warriors, young and old, sliced apart by the god's vicious claws, women and children dismembered in front of him. It didn't matter who showed up in the arena, they all met the same fate. And show up they did—a new one nearly every day, as if Khar's cave was a magical entrance point for the dead. Here, the lion-man god seemed to have one purpose and one purpose only—sending pieces of people flying onto the pile of carnage that covered the entrance to the cave.

The brutality horrified Emir at first, sickening him. As the numbers mounted, he learned to steel himself against his emotions. The crowd cheered the fighter on, no matter who it was. Emir soon figured out why. There was nothing else to do. They knew the victim would die, yet cheering for them held a strange logic, a fleeting hope in the idea that somehow this one might outsmart the menacing god of the deep. So far, none had, but it only took a day or two of waiting around an empty arena for them to look forward to the next victim. As bad as the killings were, the waiting was worse. Through some magic of Khar's, they couldn't leave the benches. They didn't eat or drink, and outside of recounting their memories of their lives before, had nothing with which to pass the time. On the rare days without fighting, the benches turned dangerous. Moderio would have come to blows with the man behind him, if only he'd been able to move far enough. Emir didn't blame him. The man's name was Duman—an angular branch of a human, with a sharp beard and a laugh reserved only for his most cutting insults.

"A good thing you're sitting here," he'd told Moderio one day as they watched another woman die in the arena, "or you would have been in pieces long ago. I can't imagine you as much of a warrior."

"I'd be happy to show you, Duman," Moderio answered. They traded a few more barbs before Moderio sought to get his hands on the man's neck, but he couldn't reach him. Emir took notice then of the distance between them all. They'd been placed just far enough apart to make reaching each other impossible. A good thing, or they might have killed one another long before this. On the other hand, when Emir had tried to slap Moderio on the back once, he'd swiped only the air between them. Afterward, he wondered if the space between them was yet another form of torture, meant to rob them of the basic solace of human contact.

The crowd gasped in unison. Emir had gotten in a good swipe with his sword, coming dangerously close to Khar's tail. The beast snapped it back, letting loose with another stinger, but Emir ducked and it flew past him, landing harmlessly in the bloody carcasses beyond. He walked around the half-circle that formed the center of the arena, twirling his sword, his body fatigued but his gaze sharp.

"That was a good one," Moderio shouted. "Stay lively!" The rest of the crowd joined in, sending up an energetic chant. *Stay lively! Stay lively!*

Khar attacked again, and the two circled around, Khar getting another swipe of his claws on Emir's arm.

"Too slow!" Moderio admonished him. "Come on. Move!"

Emir glanced behind him, his gaze passing over the living

corpses. Khar seized the moment, rushing him and slamming him onto his back. With his paws pinned to Emir's chest, the beast leaned in and belched a mighty growl into his face.

Why did you come here? Khar bellowed. *Everyone wants to hear!*

"I saved my mother," Emir said in a tight voice.

Khar chuckled, his thick lips pulling open over his razor-sharp fangs. *Still the hero, so say you, such a prince of derring-do!*

Emir stabbed his dagger into the beast's chest. Khar howled and jumped off, limping back a few steps. Emir got to his feet and rested his hands on his knees.

"Get him again!" Moderio shouted.

Khar charged. Emir darted to the right, but Khar stayed with him. Emir dove for the benches, scrambling to the top as Khar came up behind him, the witnesses craning their heads as he passed over them. Emir had no choice but to jump off the edge. He landed hard on his leg and fell forward onto one knee. Something cracked. Pain whitewashed his vision. A dark shadow came over him as Khar approached.

Dead is here or dead is there. The question now is where, oh where? Shall you die and dead is dead, or linger on inside your head?

Emir blinked, trying to maintain consciousness. Khar was giving him the choice he gave him every day: stay and live whatever life this was, or join the piles of carnage beyond.

"Come on, Emir," Moderio called. "Live to fight another day!" Soon, the rest of the crowd chanted the same. Emir cast a glance at the red muscles, tissues, and faces beyond.

Waiting long is boring be, what say you—remain or flee?

"Remain," Emir said.

Khar released him. In a blink, Emir was back on the bench next to Moderio, his wounds healed.

"You got him this time," Moderio said, referring to Emir's dagger strike. "That was a first! One day, my friend, one day."

It was what Moderio always said—that one day, Emir would get the upper hand on Khar, but Emir knew better. He could spend one hundred years down here and never get good enough to best the beast.

"Bet he smells good right about now," Duman said from behind them. "Better than you, Moderio!"

"Shut up, Duman," Moderio said.

"Ha ha ha. Good thing you're not fighting. Khar would feast on you for days."

"And you have so little meat on your bones that Khar would strip your skin and use your ribs to pick his teeth."

Duman didn't have a quick comeback to that one. Moderio smirked at Emir, who was only half listening. It was always strange, after the fight, for he could *feel* his wounds even though they weren't there. It was as if he had to recover from something invisible that lived under his skin.

Khar padded to the back of the cave. He would rest now until the next day, though there wasn't any night or day here. The red light cast the arena in a constant bloody haze. Never did the darkness give them relief. Before, Emir would have done anything to see the light. Now he longed for darkness.

Dead is here or dead is there, he heard inside his head. The carcass pile should be higher. Where had all the bodies gone?

"You want to go there, don't you?" Duman said in a low, sneering voice.

Emir jerked his gaze toward him. "What are you going on about?"

Duman gestured toward the red mass beyond. "You want to join the broken ones."

Broken. The word resonated inside Emir's breast. That's what he was. Broken.

"Shut up, Duman," Moderio said, "before I shut you up."

"Try it, warrior man. You wouldn't talk so tough if I could reach you."

"If," Moderio said. "You live your life on 'ifs.' Otherwise, you'd be dead."

"You don't get it, Moderio. Thick as a stump. I *am* dead! Ha ha ha!"

Moderio flicked a worried gaze toward Emir. "You all right, friend?" he asked. "You're not giving up on me?"

Emir didn't answer. How many more days of fighting? How many more stabs, punctures, and shreds could he stand? How many more years before even the red mass beyond seemed like an improvement?

"He's losing it," Duman said. "Look at his eyes. Won't be long now." He let out a deep, mean laugh that ended in a low, sickly gurgle in his throat.

PART THREE

CHAPTER

THIRTY

696 BC
Gordium, Capital City of Phrygia

"You sent them away?" King Midas sat in his royal chair at the conference table, his robe close over his shoulders, woolen trousers protecting him from the morning chill.

"We cannot reward them for slaughtering our people," Zoe said from the other side of the strategy room. "You should have seen them. Sitting on their horses like we owed them the treasure. They see us as weak. The leader told me as much."

"You talked to them?"

"To the leader," she repeated. "I told him they would get no reward for their killings, and that if they dared attack again, we would be ready for them."

Midas shook his head. "I ordered my men to turn over the gold. You countermanded my order."

Zoe took a few steps toward him. "Father, I watched them slaughter our people. Women. Children! One of them held me in his grasp as if I were nothing more than a commoner. We give

249

them the gold and it will never be over. They will be back for more and more. We cannot let our citizens live under that constant threat." She reached her hands out, beseeching him. "You have not been well. Normally, you would deal with these nomads with a firmer hand."

He dropped his gaze. "We discussed this already, before the transfer was to take place."

Zoe glanced at the cabinet that stored the gifts the king had received from other leaders, vases, jars, daggers, jeweled statuettes, and silk napkins from far away. She wondered if her Aunt Elanur's doll still hid inside the bottom cupboard.

"I know you want peace," she said, "and for twenty years, we've had peace. The kingdom has grown and thrived and the people love you for it. But there is a new threat at our borders, and the people are afraid." She took another step toward him. "We must be strong again. That is the only thing this enemy will understand."

"I was strong for many years," Midas said. "We gained lands, power, reputation. But what we lost?" He rubbed the old wound on his chest. "It wasn't worth it."

"But this is different! It's not land, power, or reputation we're fighting for. It's our homes! Our people. These enemies aren't beyond our borders. We're not traveling to meet them on some distant battlefield. They're here, attacking our city, slaughtering our citizens. If we allow them to have their way, they will steal and steal until there is nothing left." She rested her hands on the edge of the table. "They will not be appeased by a few gold trinkets. Please, Father. You must find your strength once again."

For a long while, he was quiet. Finally, he raised his gaze to her. At first, it gave her hope, but as she looked into his eyes, that hope faded.

"You went against my order," he said. "Have you forgotten I am the king?"

Zoe hung her head and withdrew her hands from the table. "You are the king," she said. "But you haven't been acting like one. Not for a long while." She braced herself and met his gaze. "In your condition, do you think it wise that you remain king?"

He frowned. "You don't?"

She clenched her fists and slowly shook her head.

His face shifted. It was a slight change, but it was there, a drop in the jaw muscles and a squint in the eyes. "I see." He sat back. Laced his hands together. A log sparked and popped in the fireplace. "Guard," he said.

The door opened. "Yes, Your Majesty?"

"Escort the princess to her chamber."

The guard looked puzzled, but opened wide the door and gestured for Zoe to step out. Zoe glared at her father. Part of her wanted to make him say it, that he was confining her. But she couldn't bring herself to be humiliated in front of the guard.

"Once she's safely inside, remain at her door," the king said.

"Yes, Your Majesty." The guard bowed.

Zoe walked out without another word.

LATER THAT NIGHT, a knock came at her door. Zoe sat up from her bed. She hoped it was her father, ready to release her.

"Rastus, Your Highness," the guard said.

Zoe's heart fell. "Come," she said.

The commander of the king's guard looked disheveled, his hair mussed, his face shiny with perspiration. Zoe met him halfway across the room.

"I spoke with him today," he said, still catching his breath.

"Kiral?"

Rastus nodded, then walked past her to the window.

"What did you find out? Does he know of any spies?"

"If he does, he didn't share that information. But he seemed to be open to the idea of gathering some citizen fighters."

She walked to the small table against the north wall and invited him to join her. Rastus sat down and leaned his forearms heavily on the wood. "For the right payment, I think he would put together a small force."

"What is the right payment?"

"We didn't discuss details, but I believe he would be most attracted to gold, and perhaps land."

Zoe rubbed the back of her neck. "I have no authority to give him land. I might be able to get the gold, but not at the moment." She glanced around the room. "Father has me confined."

"Your Highness?"

"For sending the Gimirri away without their gold."

Rastus smiled a little. "So the rumors are true."

"There are rumors?"

"The men talk about the princess sending the nomads away." His smile faded. "They admire you, Your Highness, but the rumor does more harm than good."

Zoe collapsed into the back of her chair. "The king looks even weaker now."

Rastus nodded.

"Oh Rastus, I fear I've made a mess of things."

He ran his hand over his hair, attempting to smooth it down. Only a few strands complied. "You've only brought the problem to a head," he said. "If you had not interfered, we would have to deal with it later."

"Perhaps that would have been better. Father might have been . . ." She trailed off. Her father was not getting better, and there was no sign he would anytime soon. "How did you leave it with him?"

"I told him I would see to his payment." He raised his eyebrows at her. "Might it be possible?"

Before, she might have convinced the king to give her the payment. Now . . . she had access to some gold, gifts her mother and father had given her over the years. She glanced up at Rastus. Thick lines crossed his forehead, his jowls sagging, but he remained a handsome man, his firm chin and blond hair similar to what they had been in his youth. She took his hand. "Gordium owes you so much, Commander. You have served us for so long."

Rastus bowed his head. "It has been my honor, Your Highness."

She released him and stood up. "Leave it to me to get the gold. As for the land, tell him it will be arranged. A plot large enough to grow crops or livestock, whichever he chooses."

Rastus scooted his chair back and got to his feet.

"I will meet you in the city tomorrow evening, at the intersection where I left you before. You will bring him the payment and ask him to sign a parchment declaring his loyalty to the king. Will this suffice?"

Rastus looked at her with a troubled expression.

"What is it?"

"Forgive me, Your Highness, but if the king has determined you are to stay—"

"Let me worry about that," she said, interrupting him. "Will you meet me tomorrow night?"

He nodded.

"You believe if he has the payment, he will help us?"

"His reputation is one of honor in business arrangements."

Zoe nodded. "It is the best we can do at the moment. And we must do something." She crossed the room to the door and waited for him. When he stood opposite her, she gave him her most confident expression. "Until tomorrow," she said.

"Be careful, Princess," he answered.

She opened the door, and he slipped out. The guard shut it behind him. He'd clearly gotten his instructions to keep her in. New anger bubbled up inside her. She stormed across the room to the window. The air smelled fresh, but it was cold. She rubbed her arms. The task ahead of her loomed large in her mind, but it was as if she had mounted a wild horse she couldn't halt even if she wanted to. She glanced toward the castle gates, wishing for the hundredth time Aster would ride through them.

On the road from Lydia, returning to Phrygia

"BUT YOU DO NOT BELIEVE she was real," Aster said from atop his dapple-gray horse. They were returning to Gordium, Neval happily leading the way.

"I thought she was!" Xander yelled back, clutching his cloak more tightly about him. It had snowed on their first day out, the first snow of the season. It seemed early, and Xander wondered how the harvest fared back home. The next day was cloudless, and the next. On this, their fourth day, the clouds once again covered the sky, and though there had been no precipitation yet, the wind was blowing it their way. "I just don't understand her being confined . . ."

"It is not puzzling. But we do not have our own concerns to attend to. The princess does not await our news."

Xander rolled his eyes. "You're just eager to see her again."

"The princess is ugly and unappealing. It is easy to be away from her."

Xander settled back into his saddle. "I wish this wind would let up. It's constantly in our faces, as if it wants to push us back from where we came."

"The gods seek to bless your journey with fine weather."

"You'd think Matar could help. I nearly died entertaining her with stories."

Aster pulled the rock from his pocket.

"Don't lose it!" Xander said, reaching out.

"I'm not happy to return it," Aster said, offering it to him.

"No, no, you keep it." Xander withdrew his arm. "But don't drop it!"

"I had planned to throw it at Gediz at just the right time."

Xander checked behind him. The little man had fallen behind, his mood even more sour than on the journey out. "It seems nothing makes him happy."

"Which is of utmost concern."

The morning blurred into afternoon, the road long and tedious.

They climbed a gentle rise now and then, but the journey remained mostly flat. Eventually, they came to an intersection and Neval led them onto a narrower road. Aster pulled his cloak up over his shoulders. "It would not be helpful to talk more of your experience with the goddess," he said. "We have much information to share with the king."

"I've already told you everything I can remember," Xander said. "She said she was trapped, and that I had to get that rock out to free her."

"We do not have the rock."

"And nothing has happened." Xander cast his gaze to the stormy horizon. "I hadn't had food for days, and only a little water. It may have all been a delusion, and the rock just something I picked up off the ground." He took up the slack in the reins as they started down their first shallow draw of the day. "We'll return after all this time and tell the king that we possess a useless rock. Perhaps this is the time he will execute us."

"You have not been eagerly awaiting that proclamation for years."

Xander was unable to smile this time. "I'm tired of failing him, Aster," he said. "Seems I could have done something right for once."

"Surely another advisor would have performed much better. Like Gediz."

"At least he got us to where the goddess was."

"Yes, a demonstration of his deep commitment to the king's service."

Xander leaned forward as they started up the other side of the draw, the horses' hooves sinking into fresh mud leftover from the previous snow. "I fear the trip has been for nothing and we are bound for execution."

"Exciting," Aster said. "In the meantime, it may not be wise to discover more about this rock." He tucked it back into his pocket.

"How do you propose we do that?"

"When you are still a frightened child, you will not take it back."

"And what will that do?"

"You will not do what you do."

Xander understood his friend's meaning. Usually, his approach would be to cast a spell or experience a vision or something similar. But at that moment, he couldn't imagine anything he could do that would help. He was as useless as Gediz, grumbling along behind them on his poor chestnut mare.

CHAPTER
THIRTY-ONE

696 BC

Harvest season northeast of Phrygia, near the Phrygian Mountains

"He is old enough to go." Ilker spoke Elanur's language, as he often did around her now. He was quite fluent with it, alternating between her words and the Gimirri tongue depending on who he was addressing. He packed his bag, filling it with the supplies he'd need for his next raid. The front door was open, bringing in the crisp smell of an early harvest morning. The women had been tending the tribe's mighty garden every day, storing the produce away in secure underground chests.

"He is not ready," Elanur protested. "He hasn't gone through the ceremony." She followed her mate around their dwelling as he gathered food and clothing. "It is too soon!"

"The ceremony will come," Ilker said. "It is the right time." He tucked dried meat and bread into the bag, pulled the drawstrings closed, and turned to her. "You must trust me on this."

Elanur looked up into his dark brown eyes. "I've already lost one son."

"Yet you have another. You are a true Gimirri woman."

Elanur couldn't deny it—when Kerkin came into her life, everything changed. She stayed to care for her new family and found joy in watching her son grow strong. After Bri passed, she stepped into the role of revered healer. Now Kerkin was her son in every way that mattered, and the thought of Ilker taking him off to fight made her tremble.

"He's a gentle boy," she said. "He won't understand."

"All the more reason for him to go." Ilker cupped her cheek affectionately, then crossed to the door. "Kerkin!"

The lanky boy came running from the west. Tall and agile with thick sandy hair, he could easily jump long distances and shoot an arrow with great accuracy. Ilker was immensely proud of him, puffing up like a rooster whenever the boy showed off another of his skills.

"We have to go," Ilker said in Gimirri as Kerkin arrived breathless at the door. "Are you ready?"

The boy nodded eagerly, his gaze worshipping his father.

"You have your cloak? Weapon? Supplies?"

Kerkin dashed off to the back part of the dwelling. Elanur watched him go, her heart ripping in half. She touched Ilker's arm. "Please," she asked him. "Not yet."

He took hold of her hand and pulled her close. "Don't worry," he said into her hair. "He will be safe."

A comforting warmth radiated from him, enfolding her. Elanur allowed herself to be held. Part of her felt reassured, but another part screamed inside. "Surely there will be other times?"

"This time is important." He gazed down into her eyes. "We have been nomads. After this, we will have a home."

Have a home? Elanur searched his face. "What do you mean?" she asked. "We have a home here."

"Kerkin will be safe," he said. "When we return, I will show you."

Elanur glanced toward the back of their mudbrick dwelling. Ilker had built it to replace their tent two years after Kerkin had joined them. He'd added an extra room specifically for the boy, and their home was now one of the finest in the camp. At least Elanur thought of it as home, but it seemed Ilker had his sights set on something grander.

"Kerkin!"

The boy emerged with his bear-hide cloak thrown over his shoulders and his best leather boots on his feet. He stood in the doorway with his travel bag in his left hand, his bow in his right, a quiver of arrows slung over his back. He'd even put a fur hat on his head.

"Say goodbye to your mother," Ilker said, and strode out the door.

Kerkin turned to Elanur, his face alight. "I get to go this time, Mama!"

Elanur forced a smile onto her lips as she opened her arms. The boy received her embrace. "You must be strong," she told him as she clutched him to her chest. "Stay close to your father and do as he tells you."

"I'll make you proud, Mother." He pulled back and grinned at her. "You'll see!"

Elanur clenched her teeth to stop her tears. "Stay safe," she said, "and come back to me. Understand?"

The boy darted out the door after his father. Elanur watched him run like an antelope across the camp toward the pasture where they kept the horses. The other men were there too, men in heavy hides and stout boots, men with axes and arrows and swords, men talking and laughing as they saddled up their mounts. Khogu was saddling Ilker's stallion, his own mount waiting nearby. He was Ilker's second-in-command now. Mitin and a young man named Pan were in the group as well, Mitin having adopted three more children since he and Oya had given up their little girl Aylin to Goakina and Thom. Thom was bidding Goakina farewell at their dwelling down the way, their two children—Aylin and a younger boy—staying behind.

Elanur wondered if Zafer, too, the man Hastet had married, would join the men. He was younger and usually stayed, but this group was larger than usual. She could see Draris walking toward the pastures in his uneven gait. Nerves pricked her skin. The more she watched, the more it seemed every man in the tribe would be joining this raid —something that rarely happened.

She lingered at the door until Kerkin started saddling his horse, then retreated to the room she shared with Ilker. In the corner rested the wooden storage box he had made her. At the bottom was the one long pair of woolen pants she owned. She pulled them on under her skirt, followed by a long-sleeved linen shirt over her undershirt, topped by her thickest wool sweater. Her warmest hide cloak hung on a hook by the front door. She found her travel bag stashed under the mattress and began filling that. With each movement, she argued with herself. Her place was here as the tribe healer. She was content with this life and had made peace with her fate.

But now Ilker was taking her son into a fight. And all Elanur could think about was what happened to Emir in the midst of battle. That couldn't happen again.

Packed and ready to travel, she stood at the doorway watching. She would have to follow at a great enough distance that they wouldn't see her, but not so far that she would lose her way. After living with the tribe for twenty years, she'd grown adept at tracking. Ilker had taught her in his spare moments, helping her improve her ability to pursue game. Even then, she had been planning for such a day as this. Somehow, she had known it would come. Much as she had adapted to Gimirri life, she still wasn't one of them, and neither was Kerkin, despite Ilker's efforts. She had raised the boy as Gimirri, and it had been all right, as long as it didn't harm him. But now something was different. She could feel it. There was a change on the wind.

Go. Protect him.

She took a few moments to straighten the dwelling, then once the men had ridden off in a swell of hoofbeats and shouts, she stepped out, closed the door, and crossed to the pasture.

It was a dangerous time to leave—morning, with the sun beaming down from the east. She was in full view of the remaining tribe, but she'd often gone hunting when the men were absent. She kept her gaze down and when she reached the enclosure, gave a whistle. The brown and white mare, the one she'd named Hazel, trotted toward her. Elanur gave her a carrot, then placed the bridle over her head.

"Going hunting so soon?"

Elanur jumped. Hastet stood at the fence watching her.

"While the weather is fair," Elanur said, recovering with a smile. "The sun promises warmth today."

Hastet turned to view the forest to the south. "It will be a fine day. I had hoped we might take a walk together. It's going to feel lonely now with Zafer gone."

So Zafer had gone too. Elanur felt a squeeze in her heart. She was still fond of Hastet, though she didn't see her as often as she once did. "When I return," she said, "if the weather holds." She led Hazel through the gate. "And don't worry. Zafer is a strong young man."

"Yes." Hastet came closer, petting Hazel on the neck. Elanur had an impulse to hug her, but it wasn't something she usually did before a hunt, so she gathered the reins and mounted. "Hopefully, I will have fast luck."

Hastet looked up at her with concern in her eyes. "Do be careful, Elanur," she said, and reached up her hand.

Elanur squeezed it briefly. "Of course." She concentrated on the younger woman's face, memorizing every detail of her thin features and kind eyes, then urged Hazel forward.

Goodbye, dear Hastet.

Before she entered the forest, she glanced back once more at the camp receding behind her. A disturbing thought flashed through her mind that this was the last time she'd ever see it.

CHAPTER

THIRTY-TWO

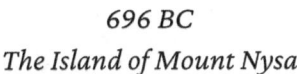

696 BC

The Island of Mount Nysa

L ittle Bird was sitting on her bed by the fire, Nightsky resting on the end post, when the goddess returned.

It had been almost twenty years. When Little Bird thought back, it seemed both impossible and plainly obvious it had been that long. On the obvious side, she had grown. She had to curl up in bed now because it wasn't long enough, and without Denisia to move things through the barrier, there was no way for Cemile, who had become her friend, to bring a new platform or mattress. In the pleasant weather, Little Bird learned to sleep on the ground, but in the winter, she bent like a green sapling to fit into the bed built for her when she was a child.

Her hair, too, had grown. She'd learned to cut it with the sharp blade she had fashioned for Verin. When he didn't return, she began using it herself. The blade proved versatile—good for cutting food, her nails, and her hair—but she'd quickly realized that hair offered warmth in winter, so she let it grow. It now hung to her waist, a thick mane of dark brown.

She was stronger and more capable now, too. It was easier to lift objects and dig holes, and over time, she made the cave her own. With dyes supplied by Cemile, she'd painted the walls, at least as far as she could reach, bringing color into her world. The north wall was a rich red shade, and the south a brilliant green. Later, she'd painted various scenes on them. There was a horse running through a field under the watch of a raven, and three wolves chasing down a rabbit. She had tried to paint Verin, but failed to capture his likeness. Still, she'd left the attempt where it was toward the back of the cave, figuring no one would see it, anyway.

The vines had grown more thickly over the barrier. They bloomed in the summer with white and purple flowers, making a bouquet of the cave's entrance. Little Bird regularly cut some of the stems back, as without trimming they would have covered the barrier completely, blocking the sun. She'd tried cutting the stouter branches too, but that had been like trying to cut through rock. They were impervious to the blade, so she limited her efforts to the vines, leaves, and blooms.

Cemile had taught her to make clothing, bringing supplies like yarn and sewing needles. Little Bird created her own thick woolen dresses and heavy socks, linen shirts, scarves, and hats, though she had no cloak save the one she'd possessed as a child. She still wore it over her shoulders on wintry days and nights and learned to layer her woolen garments underneath. Her boots, which were now too small, she'd replaced with leather moccasins that she'd sewn herself, though she often went barefoot in the warm season.

She'd asked after Verin for years, but Cemile never had any news for her. She told Little Bird that the goddess had returned about a year after she'd left with him, but Verin hadn't been with her, presumably having stayed in one of the villages they'd visited. He always had wanted to explore the world. Little Bird agreed that was the most likely explanation, though it wounded her. She'd gone through various stages of grief, smashing the blade handle she had made for him, then screaming soundlessly into the nothingness. In the end, none of it helped, so she'd tended to her cave, talked to Nightsky, and prepared for Denisia's return, for she knew that one day, the goddess would come back.

Two years after Nightsky came, the wolves appeared. It was a late harvest season morning, crisp and clear with a welcoming yellow sky. Little Bird was going about her business as usual when she spotted them on the other side of the barrier. They hovered there, the three of them, watching her with intense gazes. She'd stopped to stare, her breakfast in her hands. For a long time, she dared not move. Gradually, she realized that with the barrier in place, she was in no danger. She crept forward, never taking her eyes off of them, and sat down at the table she'd built out of cut branches. They came a little closer, then one by one laid down near the entrance. They spent the rest of the morning that way, hovering nearby. At midday, they left. The black one—the largest of the three and clearly the leader—glanced back before loping off. The look sent a jolt of adrenaline through Little Bird, because it unearthed a vision.

She'd been running by the Red River, looking for her boat. It was that black wolf, or at least one much like it, that had been searching for her that evening, the same one she feared would make her go back. The vision made her wonder again about what Denisia had said, whether there was more in her memory she still needed to unearth.

Over a period of many years, she attempted to do just that, but it never worked. Without the benefit of the goddess' spells and trances, she couldn't access the dreamworld Denisia had shown her. She tried closing her eyes and lying still or willing herself to dream before sleep, but always there was an impenetrable veil, like a thick gray fog over her mind. Her attempts were so frustrating that she finally gave up, accepting that what visions she did have would come of their own accord.

That's how it was when she remembered the wolves' names.

Kartal was the black leader, Sabir a dark gray female, and Sadik the lighter gray with white around her eyes. Little Bird had a vision of playing with them in the fields and leading them on long runs through the forests. How they had gotten here, she didn't know. She started to look forward to their visits, and sometimes shared food with them. Soon, they returned the favor, bringing her dead rabbits and birds and nudging them close enough to the barrier that Little Bird could wrestle them through. One rabbit was too big, so Sadik had ripped it in two with her teeth and given Little Bird the second half. That was the first time Little Bird had been able to pet her. Soon she could pet Sabir too, but Kartal never came close enough. Instead, he watched her intently, his golden eyes glowing from within. Whereas Sabir and Sadik had amber-colored eyes, Kartal's burned like yellow flame. Sometimes, when he looked at her, Little Bird felt a flicker of the nervousness she remembered from her dream of running alongside the river.

The wolves had been visiting for over three years when Nightsky said something new that surprised her. For a long while, the bird's vocabulary was limited to "yes," "home," and "Nightsky." But gradually he learned more. This surprised Little Bird, as without her own voice, she could not teach him. It seemed instead that the bird picked up on her thoughts. They were eating breakfast one pretty spring day, the wolves lounging about as they often did in the morning, Nightsky on the chair opposite Little Bird, when suddenly he said, "Emir."

Little Bird jerked her head up. It had been so long since she'd heard the name. Strangely, Cemile had brought figs the day before, reminding Little Bird of when Emir had given her those he'd earned from his oud playing on the streets of Gordium.

What about Emir? she'd signed, searching the bird's face.

"Emir," Nightsky had squawked, then ruffled his feathers and picked at the seeds she'd lain on the table before him.

He said no more that day, but now and then, when Emir crossed Little Bird's thoughts, Nightsky would respond.

Emir is gone, she signed to him once, but Nightsky squawked, "Emir!"

The nightmares began after that. It was as if the raven had foretold them. Little Bird would find herself in a red cave watching a lion-man monster battle with Emir, slashing him with his long claws and shooting stingers out of his tail. In every nightmare, Emir died at the mercy of the lionlike beast and Little Bird would wake up screaming and crying, only to find herself alone in the cave.

"Emir," Nightsky would squawk.

Stop it! she signed to him once. *Stop!* Yet the nightmares continued, fueling her anger at the goddess for being gone so long. Perhaps she was right and Emir was somewhere suffering. If so, Little Bird wanted to save him, but she couldn't do it alone.

She'd been in the cave for about five years when the true nature of her captivity settled on her spirit. If not for Nightsky and the three wolves, she might have ended it that year. As it was, the animals became her dearest friends. She worried for a while that the wolves would get old and die, but they seemed to have a magical immortality about them. She never saw signs of age in any of them. No gray whiskers, no cloudy eyes, no lame gaits. They stayed as young and agile as they had always been, even in her visions. But that place remained a mystery behind the darkest recesses of her mind, always just out of reach.

Many evenings at sunset she'd sit at the cave entrance and look out on the dirt path, the trees that stayed ever steadfast on its border, and the clouds in the sky beyond, and wish with all her heart that she could go back to when she and Emir had traveled across the country from Durukin to Gordium. The trip was etched in her memory like nothing else, for it had been filled with so many magical delights. Then, when they had arrived at the castle, her life had taken a thrilling turn. Never had she tasted so much mouthwatering food as she had at Princess Zoe's birthday party, nor seen so many rich treasures as lay inside King Midas' home. The king himself had surprised her, as well. He'd ignored her at first, but after Denisia's curse and Zoe's kidnapping, he'd seemed to take comfort in her presence, even trying to learn some of her language.

King on a throne, she had taught him, and he'd signed it correctly. She smiled at the memory, an old pain stinging like a torn scar.

"Midas," Nightsky squawked.

Yes, she signed. *We should be with him now.*

Day by day, she survived, finding what happiness she could in the sunshine, her animals, and her crafts. But as the years passed, her suffering outweighed her pleasant moments, and a new anger rose inside her, wearing away her innocence, leaving a moldy growth of darkness on her heart.

So it was that morning early in harvest season, the air smelling of rain, when Nightsky turned toward the entrance and squawked, "Denisia!"

Little Bird had been carving a new figurine, a representation of Emir, though she didn't feel she was doing him justice. She set it beside the ones of King Midas, Princess Zoe, and Anchurus, then quickly tucked the dagger into a hidden pocket before approaching the barrier.

A horse plodded up the road, the hoofbeats muffled. Cemile sometimes rode on horseback, but as Little Bird gazed through the openings between the branches, a swell of adrenaline pulsed through her.

Hide! she signed to Nightsky.

The bird flew to the back of the cave and perched on one of the high boulders where darkness shrouded him in shadow. Once he was safely out of sight, Little Bird shifted to the right of the entrance, clenched her hands together, and waited, her heart thumping in her ears.

The silhouette of a horse came into view, the sun in Little Bird's eyes. The goddess had returned.

CHAPTER
THIRTY-THREE

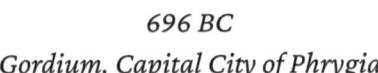

696 BC
Gordium, Capital City of Phrygia

I t had been two days since her father had confined her to her chamber, and Zoe was restless. She paced the room, now and then checking at the window to see if she could glimpse the advisors returning. When not looking for them, she scanned for Rastus. She had been unable to meet him in the city as they'd planned, and he hadn't come by. She thought he might visit today, after she'd missed their appointment, but evening was drawing near and there was still no sign of him.

Her attempts to charm the door guard into letting her out had failed as well. He was an older man, loyal to her father for as long as she could remember. When he asked where Ozan was, the guard said the younger man had been reassigned. Escaping through the window was another idea, but there were no footholds, and after inspecting the view for the thirtieth time, she knew it would be foolish. She'd fall to her death and then who would watch out for the citizens?

Her only hope was to convince whoever walked through her door next to let her leave with them. She'd counted on that person being Rastus, but when the day passed and he still hadn't come, the next most likely was Elif, her maidservant. Elif had continued coming each day to help her dress and deliver her meals. As the sun sank low on the horizon, the eastern breeze cooling the room, Zoe knew what she had to do.

She dreaded doing it. Elif was not just a servant, but a dear friend, one who had been with Zoe since she was a young woman. The thought of putting her in danger made Zoe's stomach twist. She mulled over her options, but there was no other way. It had to be Elif.

She prepared a bag with a change of clothes, all the gold jewelry and trinkets from her room, and her best dagger, the one Anchurus crafted for her long ago. Then she dressed in the simplest dress she owned, tied her hair up in a bun, put a plain woolen scarf over it, and went to the door. She took a small step out to make sure the guard saw her outfit.

"Have you seen Elif?"

"Please, Your Highness." He gestured back inside the room. "For your safety."

"Of course." Zoe backed up. "I am just feeling hungry. Do you know if she's bringing the evening meal soon?"

The guard looked down the hall. "I can smell something cooking, Your Highness. I don't imagine it will be long now."

"Excellent." Zoe smiled at him. "Thank you."

She stepped back inside. That much done, she perused the room once more, then checked the window again. If she followed through with this plan, Rastus wouldn't know where to meet her. Worse, Aster could come back while she was in the city and he wouldn't know where she had gone. She didn't wish to pain either of them, but her options were limited.

Her bed rested cozy behind her. She sat down on it and pulled up the top blanket, hugging it close. Her mother's painting beckoned from the other side of the room.

"I can't just sit here," she said out loud.

Take care and be wise.

Zoe whirled to stare at the painting. It was as if her mother had spoken to her. Strange thoughts flitted through her mind. Might the queen be watching over her somehow?

"Your maidservant, Your Highness," the guard said from the other side of the door.

Zoe jumped to her feet. Here it was—her opportunity. She swallowed hard and said, "Enter." The door opened and Elif breezed in, carrying a tray full of hot, steaming food. Zoe's stomach growled. She'd put on a show for the guard, but she really was hungry. Elif placed the tray on the desk against the north wall—the very one where Zoe and Rastus had conversed the previous day.

"It looks good tonight, Your Highness," Elif said as she arranged the dishes. "I think Pembe worked longer than usual."

"It smells delicious." Zoe came forward, her eyes taking in the bounty: breaded venison, peas, fresh bread, fried parsnips, and, for dessert, baked custard. *Be wise,* she'd heard her mother say. A hot meal would go a long way to sustaining her in her exile. She hesitated at the side of the desk.

"Something else you needed, Your Highness?" the girl asked.

Zoe smiled at her. "Maybe some company. It's been a little lonely."

"I'd be happy to stay."

"But there isn't enough for you?"

"I will eat later. Pembe promised me what was left."

"Very well." Zoe sat down and gestured for Elif to sit across from her. Soon the two were talking like girlfriends, though Zoe sneaked in a few questions about what was going on around the castle. Elif said the king hadn't been seen much.

"They say he's not feeling well," she said, casting a curious glance at Zoe. "I don't mean to intrude, Your Highness, but did something happen between you?"

Zoe sunk her teeth into the warm, buttered bread. "It's no secret he's confined me here," she said. "He's told the guard not to let me leave."

"But why would he do that? He adores you so."

Zoe wasn't sure how to answer that question. As she continued eating, silently thanking Pembe for every bite, she wondered how much she should tell Elif. The less the better, she figured, in case the king questioned her.

"It's been more difficult between us lately," Zoe said carefully. "As you say, he hasn't been feeling well."

Elif nodded, her small face taken by a sad expression.

"In truth, a strange illness plagues him." Zoe glanced behind her dramatically, as if to be sure no one was listening, and leaned closer to Elif. "Even the medicine woman can't identify it. It has caused him to believe that I have betrayed him."

Elif sat back, alarmed. "Surely not!"

Zoe continued with her meal. "I was hoping he would get better with time, but he's only getting worse. I fear someone else may be behind this."

"Not those who attacked the city?" Elif asked.

Perfect, Zoe thought to herself. "Perhaps? Who else would seek to harm the king?"

"No one!"

Zoe took her time finishing the rest of her meal, giving Elif a moment to absorb her words. Afterward, she pushed everything aside and centered her gaze on the younger woman's face. "Elif, you have been my faithful maidservant for a long time."

Elif smiled. "Since you gained fifteen years, Your Highness."

"Yes." Zoe smiled back. "In all that time, you have been loyal and hardworking. More than that, I consider you my friend."

Elif grew suddenly serious. "I am honored, Your Highness."

Zoe reached out her hand, and Elif took it. "That's why I need your help now."

"Anything, Your Highness."

"You are the only one I can ask."

"Of course."

Zoe glanced down. At any other time, she wouldn't worry about her father punishing the girl, but King Midas was not himself. The thought of something happening to Elif threatened to weaken her resolve. If the fate of the city didn't hang in the balance, she would have changed her mind.

"I need to leave the castle," she said finally.

"Shall I call for the king—?"

"No," Zoe interrupted. "Listen." She looked Elif over. They were both about the same height, though Elif was slight where Zoe was strong. Elif wore a scarf over her hair as she often did, so that would help. Zoe looked the younger woman in the eye. "I need you to change clothes with me."

Elif stared back at her, uncomprehending.

"The clothes I'm wearing now," Zoe said. "I want you to wear them, and give me your clothes."

It took another moment before Elif understood. A wave of panic passed over her face. She glanced at the door.

"I wouldn't request this of you, but the city is in danger. If I stay here, I fear we will come under attack again by the nomads. And that this time, it shall be much worse."

Elif's eyes widened.

"The king is not well, but while I'm stuck here, I can do nothing to help. I have spoken to the leader of the nomads. I know what they are planning, and I must escape so that I can help the people defend themselves."

Elif listened, her shallow breaths betraying her fear. She had done nothing in her life against the king's orders—or against Zoe's orders, for that matter. "The king's guards—" she began.

"They will do what they can after the fighting has started," Zoe interrupted. "But I expect they will be far outnumbered."

Elif shook her head. "The king has the strongest men of all the kingdoms."

Zoe sighed and released the girl's hand. "You remember when you got bitten by that spider, and you were sick for many days?"

Elif nodded.

"You were much bigger and stronger than that spider, but because the spider snuck into your bed at night and bit you while you slept, it almost killed you."

Elif rubbed her thigh absentmindedly, her fingers sliding over the old wound.

"The Gimirri are like that spider."

Elif's brown eyes stared intensely into hers. She stopped rubbing her leg. "This is the only way, Your Highness?"

"The only way. Elif, if you can do this, you may help to save our city. And our king."

After one more glance at the door and several moments of contemplation, Elif stood up and started taking her clothes off.

Relief flowed over Zoe's shoulders. Soon, the two women had exchanged outfits. Elif helped Zoe tuck every strand of hair inside the scarf. When she finished, she put all the dishes back on the tray and handed it to Zoe. Together, they moved toward the door.

The princess stood dressed in her servant's clothing, the tray in her hands. She realized in that moment there was nowhere to stash the bag she'd packed. She set the tray down. "I must take some things," she said to Elif. The girl pointed out the pockets on the apron Zoe wore. Zoe stashed as many jewelry pieces and trinkets as she could. She hoped Kiral would be satisfied with a down payment. Next, she dug the dagger out and stuffed the bag back under her bed. The dagger would be too visible tucked into the tie around her dress, so she set it on the tray and shielded it with two of the bowls and the napkin.

Standing once more at the door, Zoe gazed into Elif's sweet face. "All you have to do is stay here," she said.

"They will look for me tomorrow to bring your meals."

Zoe hadn't thought of that. "If they come to the door, say as little as possible. One word. Two. Try to mimic my voice." She turned toward her wardrobe. "If someone comes in, stay over there. Cover your hair. Pretend to be me. The longer you can do that, the more time I will have before they come after me."

Elif glanced at the wardrobe and nodded.

"It will be all right."

Elif bowed.

"I shall never forget this, Elif. I will be back, and you will be rewarded."

"Stay safe, Your Highness."

Elif lingered for another moment, then hurried around the corner to hide. Once she was safely out of sight, Zoe opened the door and stepped out, her head down. She didn't stop, but walked down the hall as fast as she could, doing her best to mimic Elif's quick gait. She worried that the guard would call to her at any moment, but all she heard him do was close the door. In the stairwell, she paused, panting. For a moment, she felt elated. She had escaped. But she still needed to get out of the castle. Ducking her head, she hurried down the stairs.

CHAPTER

THIRTY-FOUR

696 BC

Northeast of Phrygia, south of the Phrygian Mountains

E lanur clutched her hide cloak tightly about her. She'd trailed the tribe out of the mountains to the Sangarius River. Now they were following it south. The weather had been merciful, with only one weak storm dropping rain for a short time, just enough to wet the ground. It made tracking easier, which normally would have helped her relax. Instead, the farther Elanur rode from camp, the more nervous she became.

Near sunset on the second day, the tribe paused to rest in a narrow draw east of the river. Elanur crouched low and kept watch, listening for any slight sound that might betray a scout approaching. The evening cold bit her hands and ears, but soon the sounds of men chatting flitted over the air. She heaved a sigh of relief and started looking for shelter, somewhere she could huddle down and try to conserve warmth.

By the time she had found a small grove of trees, the men were singing. She ate dried meat, Hazel grazing lazily nearby. As the darkness deepened, she approached the camp. The shape of a man emerged—one of the lookouts. Ilker always posted them around the perimeter, though this man wasn't too alert. He bent his head low, as if examining something in his hands. Elanur climbed up and out of the draw, moving stealthily while frequently checking on the man to be certain he didn't look her way. She reached the top and, staying low, continued forward again.

Beyond, she saw six fires scattered over a wide stretch of land, small groups of men gathered around each one. Altogether, the band numbered close to two hundred, the most she could remember Ilker ever taking on a raid. None of them looked to be Kerkin, but he had to be nearby. She started down the embankment, her boots sliding in the soft dirt. Several times she paused, listening, making sure she hadn't drawn attention. But there was no sound except those rising from the camp. When she reached the bottom of the draw, she was alone.

It was more difficult to see now, the fires hidden by a few clumps of trees beyond. She hesitated, uncertain how far she dared go. Seeking to put the irritating trees out of the way, she dared cross to the river side, but the view wasn't much better. She noticed Ilker's tent, the only one in the camp. His men would sleep out in the open, though they all carried thick fur cloaks with which to protect themselves. She sighed in frustration. It would be best to return to her hiding place and get some rest before the next day. But she was so close, and she desperately wanted to assure herself that Kerkin was all right.

She glanced above her, wondering if she should climb again, but this near to the camp, it would be too risky. It was either retreat or sneak around the edge. Trusting the darkness to shield her, she chose the riskier option and moved left. Soon, she got near enough to make out some faces and was pleased to see Ilker's was one of them. He was listening to another man, his gaze focused across the fire. Elanur took a few more steps, trying to see Kerkin, but he wasn't there.

Her nerves pricked with worry. Ilker would watch out for their son. She believed that, but she would not rest until she laid eyes on him. She kept walking. As she neared the west side of the draw, so intent was she on the camp that she didn't detect the small shadow in the clump of junipers up ahead.

"Halt!"

She whirled. The watchman stood in front of her, his dagger drawn. She poised to flee. Then she narrowed her eyes. "Kerkin, is that you?"

"Mother?"

Elanur's heart leaped. She embraced her son. She didn't realize how tightly she was holding him until he wriggled in her arms. "Are you all right?" she asked, releasing him.

"Why are you here?"

She hesitated. Happy as she was to see him, he didn't feel the same. "I am hunting," she lied.

"Here?"

"I heard voices." She could sense him looking at her, his eyes shadows in the night.

"I'm well," he said in a terse tone. "You should go home."

"You're right. I rode out farther than I planned. But I am so happy to see you."

"Father posted me as lookout," he said. "I am supposed to tell them."

Elanur thought quickly. "If you tell them, they will think I came to check on you."

Kerkin's gaze darted toward the camp. "You shouldn't worry, Mother. I can do this."

Elanur's heart swelled. "I know you can." Looking into his shadowed face, she wished she could whisk him away. "I will go now," she said. "No one need know about me. All right?" She cupped the side of his face, then retraced her steps.

"Mother!" he whispered.

She turned back.

"Be careful."

She smiled. "Always," she whispered back.

Her steps were livelier on her return trip. On the other side of the camp, she reached an area where the men's voices seemed to carry more intensely. She paused, at first thinking they were approaching her, but it was only the airflow bringing the sound her way. She started to walk on, but heard something that made her stop.

"Gordium's king is old and weak." Ilker's voice in Gimirri. "He does not show himself. His daughter speaks for him." Another man mentioned the king's army. "They have no army," Ilker said. "They have grown fat and happy. They will put up little resistance. Soon, we shall possess the city. We shall rule Gordium!"

The other men shouted in response. "Gordium!"

Elanur stood rooted in place. Gordium! King Midas old and weak? Karem? Her blood pounded against her temple. She pictured her brother mounted on his stallion as he was the last time she had seen him at the Battle of Karama. So long ago. She had imagined him restored to health and enjoying life in his grand capital city.

So this was Ilker's big plan. He was going to raid Gordium. King Midas' Gordium. Her brother, Karem's, Gordium. The city she and Little Bird had tried so hard to reach. And they were taking her son to do it.

CHAPTER

THIRTY-FIVE

696 BC

The Island of Mount Nysa

As Denisia melted through the barrier, Little Bird's first thought was that the goddess looked older. She hadn't aged like a mortal woman. Her hair remained the color of red fallen leaves and her face was much the same, but her skin no longer radiated a youthful look. Instead, it appeared dull, fine lines showing around her eyes. As her gaze turned, Little Bird stifled a shiver. The eyes, more than anything, had changed. They were the same brown color, but now they appeared cold and lifeless, and when they settled on Little Bird, she felt ice in her veins.

"You have grown," Denisia said.

Little Bird didn't respond.

Denisia found the chairs and sat down. She waited for Little Bird to join her, then glanced at the fire toward the back of the cave. "Perhaps you have heard," she said. "I have failed to resurrect the prince, or your brave soldier."

281

Little Bird clenched her jaw. So the goddess had been trying *without her*.

"I've used many spells, but none of them worked. I even cast one on your precious king, but he proved to be useless."

Little Bird's spine stiffened. What had the goddess done to King Midas?

Denisia turned her gaze to Little Bird. "You are my only hope." She forced a small smile. "Have you remembered anything more about your connection to the dark goddess?"

Little Bird shook her head.

Denisia glanced away. "It may not be your fault. Silenus told me, in one of his rare, lucid moments, that there is a veil between this world and the underworld. If you knew Katiah there . . ." She paused. "I thought your connection would make it easier to break through, but . . ." She looked down at her hands.

Little Bird clenched her fists. The goddess had been *wrong*. Little Bird had suffered for twenty years for the goddess' mistake, yet Denisia acted like she'd merely broken a vase.

"All we can do is try again, hm?" The goddess pulled a small satchel from her cloak. "I have something new. Bring a cup of water."

Little Bird imagined pushing her off her chair, how she might flail her arms as she tipped back to fall with a *wallop* onto the rock floor. So much time had passed, and all her captor could do was make more demands. Little Bird longed to tell her where she might stuff her orders. Instead, she got the water.

Denisia stirred the mixture. A strange scent drifted from the cup, a weedy base with a sharp, lingering aroma. "Here," she said, handing it over.

Little Bird drank. It tasted like grass and mushrooms.

"You'd best lie down. This one is strong."

Already the concoction was making Little Bird feel hot. She laid on her back in the middle of the cave. When Denisia started chanting, Little Bird closed her eyes. She expected to float off into a dream, but she grew ill instead, her head spinning, a new dizziness giving her the sensation of moving. She opened her eyes. Above her, the rock ceiling turned, the fire's dancing shadows morphing into swirling orange snakes that watched her with glowing eyes. She was falling toward them, the snakes getting closer even as she grasped the dirt between her fingers.

"Katiah!" Denisia shouted suddenly.

Little Bird landed with a thud on the ground. She thought she was still in the cave, but there was no fire and no lingering sunset on the other side of the barrier. She got up and walked forward, feeling her way, until a solid wall stopped her. She turned around and went the opposite direction. Another object stopped her, but this wasn't a wall. It felt like a stone that had been sculpted into the shape of a person. Here were the eyes, nose, and mouth, the shoulders, waist, and hips. Then she noticed something else protruding from the figure's middle. As she ran her hand along the top of it, she realized she was touching the blade of a sword. She jerked back.

"Little Bird?" The same feminine voice she had heard before. "Is that you?"

Little Bird's heart pounded, her hands cold.

Katiah? she thought.

CHAPTER
THIRTY-SIX

The deep, dark underworld

Emir withstood countless more battles with Khar. Moderio was his lifeline, always encouraging him and impressing upon him the importance of trying to defeat the lion-man god.

"It keeps the rest of us going," he'd told him once. "Gives us hope."

Sometimes, Emir thought he heard the mute orphan boy cheering him on, but that was nonsense. More echoes in his head, like the ones in the tunnel. He did his best to ignore them and focused on his goal of catching Khar by surprise. Day after day, he fought. And lost. And fought again. And lost. Time stretched like a rope, fraying at the ends. He sensed the madness Duman had warned him about whispering at the edges of his mind. He knew he would give in to it one day, but not yet. Not while he still had the strength to resist.

To pass the time, he made bets with the other men on the benches, comparing victims, wagering which ones would last longest in the arena. He reminisced with Moderio about the past, though that, too, grew more difficult with time.

Once, he told Moderio how King Midas' daughter had suggested he be allowed to play in the music contest. He was describing how that single kindness had changed the course of his life when he realized he could no longer recall the princess' name. All he could remember was her title. For the rest of the story, he referred to her as "the princess." It bothered him for days.

Much later, it came to him. *Zoe*. Shaken by the experience, he resolved to spend every quiet moment between the slaughters rehearsing the names of those who had mattered in his life. His mother. Elanur. Princess Zoe. King Midas. Prince Anchurus. The boy, Little Bird. Once those were fixed in his mind, he moved on to the others. King Sargon II, his hated father. Baris and Bain, the hunters who had tried to capture him. The beautiful goddess Katiah. Denisia, who had cursed the king. Even Timon, the king's minstrel who had prepared him for the contest so long ago. It became a ritual. A wall against forgetting. A way to hold onto who he was, before Khar took it all.

He told Moderio about his practice—how he was renewing his memories, and how Moderio should do the same.

"You still have hope?" Moderio asked him.

Emir cast him a questioning glance.

"Hope that one day, you may get back there," Moderio clarified.

"I must get back."

Moderio lifted a thick eyebrow. "You should dash such hopes, my friend. We are dead, you and I. There's no going back to where we were before. Only on to somewhere better."

Emir had always believed he would return to the life he knew. He realized in that moment how impossible that seemed. Perhaps Moderio was right, and they needed to think about going somewhere else, like where Ufuk had gone, or Anchurus. But despite the logic in it, Emir couldn't fully accept the idea. In his heart, he remained committed to getting back *there*, where his mother and the boy were, where King Midas ruled, where Princess Zoe glimmered in her beautiful dresses, and where the sun rose and set over the Sangarius River.

Why are you here, shepherd? Khar bellowed, jerking Emir back to the present. The god fought another young man, no more than eighteen years.

"I don't know." The young man was dressed in a woolen tunic and sandals, a new growth of brown beard covering his cheeks and chin, his hair thickly grown over his ears.

I don't know, Khar said in a mocking voice. *Always they say they don't know when they are the masters of the show!*

"I bet he won't last more than three turns," Moderio mumbled.

"Nah," Duman said from behind them. "He won't last two. Better get ready to move, warrior man. Your turn next!"

Emir leaned forward. He was about to say that the shepherd was stronger than his companions gave him credit for, but his thoughts had strayed. There was something in Khar's words. Something that had caught his attention.

"I don't know," the young man said again. "I was riding Spot—"

Spot? Khar said. *Tell me, tell me not that you named your horse Spot?* When the young man tried to explain the brown spot on the horse's neck, Khar roared with laughter. *Spot! He named the horse Spot! So you got the horse and thought and thought and all you could think to name it was Spot?*

The crowd joined in, entertained despite themselves. "I had a cow named Spot," Moderio said. Then he sobered. "I think Ufuk named it that."

"Perhaps Ufuk enjoys Spot's company on this day," Emir said.

Moderio smiled a little.

So, Spot's master. The master of Spot! Why are you here, or can you tell me not?

"I was riding out to check on the herd," the young man said. "There was a hissing sound, and . . ." The young man shook his head. "Then I was here."

So why are you here, master of Spot? You tell me how, but I care not. I want to know the reason why you chose that very day to die.

"I didn't choose—" the young man began.

Lies! Khar roared.

The young man jumped back.

Tell me more lies to your detriment, for in my arena, they're irrelevant! Why must I always restate the rules? Tell us the truth or be branded a fool!

"I think . . ." The young man stuttered, his anxiety growing. "I think I was killed."

You don't say? The lion-man blinked his large eyes. *How could that be on such a pretty day?*

The young man gazed at the watchers. "It must have been one of the nomads?"

A nomad killed you from behind, and now you're here. What do you find?

"Is this . . . the underworld?"

Khar cast a long-suffering glance at the benches. *He's one of the bright ones, isn't he? I wonder what his future will be?*

"What do I have to do?" the young man asked.

The witnesses responded, the words falling unbidden off Emir's tongue: "You've come to the underworld and here you will stay, here for eternity, day after day. Never to leave until you can find the reason you left your past life behind."

"But I told you," the young man said. "Someone shot me from behind. It sounded like an arrow."

Khar flicked his tail. A stinger pierced the young man's thigh. The shepherd's mouth dropped opened in surprise.

Once again, shall we? Khar asked the watchers. *Perhaps he must hear it two times, three.*

"No lies allowed in Khar's domain," the crowd droned. "Tell the truth now or here you'll remain." Emir had spoken the words spoken time and time again, but this day, he couldn't help but latch on to the theme Khar kept repeating. *Tell the truth. Why are you here?* Emir thought back to his own death. The memories were growing dim. He hadn't practiced recalling it. A death wasn't something a person wanted to recall. But listening to the dialogue between Khar and the young shepherd, he was compelled to try.

It was at the Battle of Karama. He had gone to save Princess . . . Zoe. Yes. Princess Zoe. But then he'd seen his mother. She had been riding a horse, pulled along by one of Sargon's guards. He'd decided to rescue her. He'd dashed up the hill intent on creating a distraction, but two of Sargon's men had grabbed him and pulled him down into the clearing. There, King Sargon II had paraded him in front of his mother like a prize. King Midas had proposed peace, but Katiah had interrupted them. Emir remembered the flash of light emanating from her hands. He'd moved to intercept it. And he'd died.

But he'd already told Khar all this.

"I was watching the sheep." The young shepherd had suffered two more stinger wounds while Emir had been lost in thought. He stood with his palms on his thighs, his cheeks red, his breath coming fast. "I didn't choose to die. I'd be there now if not for the nomads."

Lies! Lies! All these lies! Khar roared. *And how do you know who laid you low?*

"It had to be them," the young man said. "They'd already attacked our city several times."

Attacked your city. What a pity, Khar mocked. *And what city is that, that they attacked?*

"Gordium. The city of Gordium."

Emir sat up straight. Nomads had attacked the city of Gordium? Was the boy there? The last time he had seen him, it was in King Midas' castle. His thoughts shifted to his mother. All this time, he had hoped both of them were safe and well. But now Gordium was threatened by a new enemy?

Nomads attacking, Khar said. *Caution you were lacking! Out there in the field without even a shield.*

The young shepherd frowned. "The king said all was well."

It's not my fault that here I dwell! Khar howled. *Poor me this sad fate befell!*

"I did not want to die!" the young man said.

Lies! Khar lowered his head, an intimidating growl emanating from his throat.

"No lies allowed in Khar's domain," the witnesses droned, Emir among them. "Tell the truth now or here you'll remain."

The two fought, the shepherd already at a powerful disadvantage.

"He might be stronger than I thought," Moderio commented.

"He'll die in the next two moves," Duman grumbled.

Tell the truth. The truth. As the sounds of fighting rose, Emir wracked his brain. At one point, he looked to the entrance, then to the red light, then into the darkness where the lion-man slept. It would take thousands of days. Millions of fights. He'd never defeat Khar before he lost his mind. And then what? Would he go on fighting?

The truth.

He'd wanted to rescue the princess. He'd wanted to save his mother. Hadn't he? He tried to recall what had happened before the battle. He'd been riding with the goddess Katiah. They were carrying the princess—still a gold sculpture at the time—to King Sargon II. Katiah intended to offer the sculpture as leverage, something Sargon could use in his fight against King Midas. Emir had told himself he was going along to protect the princess. But then the goddess had grown angry and left him to fight the hunter Baris. Emir had defeated him. He could have turned back then, retrieved the boy and chosen another life. Instead, he had followed the goddess into battle.

A hollow space opened up inside him. *He'd followed Katiah into battle. Why?*

The shepherd made a daring lunge toward the lion-man. The beast cuffed him across the face, leaving four claw marks that spilled blood down his neck.

To try to save the princess. The red light throbbed in Emir's skull. *No.*

290

The shepherd stumbled back and landed on his rump. Khar descended upon him.

"What'd I tell ya?" Duman said. "Two moves."

Emir had followed Katiah because of something else. She'd saved his life. Twice. But that wasn't it.

"Get ready, my friend," Moderio murmured.

Emir squeezed his eyes shut. The cabin in the woods. Before he'd gotten the magic spring water for the king. Katiah was there with three wolves. She'd told him the story of how she'd made a tribal boy king.

A tribal boy, king.

Khar roared, bit off the shepherd's head, and spit it out. Then he bit his fangs into the lifeless body.

Emir swayed on the bench. *The truth.* He'd followed Katiah because she was a kingmaker. He'd followed her *because of his ambition.*

Moderio clapped his hands together, waking Emir from his reverie. "Today is your day to best the beast, my friend!" he said.

Emir didn't hear him. He was back at the Battle of Karama. Katiah was there, taunting the king. He had followed her not to save the princess. Not to save his mother. He'd followed her because of her power. Because she'd clearly liked him. Because he'd thought perhaps she may help him gain power too. Power to free his mother, yes, but more to satisfy his own longing, his desire to throw his power in his father's face. King Sargon II. The bastard. How Emir had wanted to outshine him, to rise above him. To show him he was much more than a slave girl's son. In the goddess' eyes, he had been king material. He could have returned for the boy. Could have saved him from whatever fate befell him after the battle. Instead, he had left him behind with no one to care for him while he ran off chasing his ambition. The realization filled his heart with shame. He hadn't helped his mother, either. Saved her from Katiah's blow, perhaps, but then what? Sargon had probably repossessed her as his slave. She might have even been killed in the battle.

What had Emir accomplished? He hadn't made things better. He'd made them worse.

"I died because of my ambition," he whispered.

Everything stopped. A heavy silence fell over the cave.

Emir lifted his gaze. The mighty Khar stood in front of him, large and fearsome. The shepherd was gone, along with Moderio and the rest of the witnesses. Even the red light had gone out. Emir sat in a realm of darkness with only the fiend's red pupils and orange eyes lighting the space between them.

What did you say? Khar said, peering into Emir's face.

"I pursued the dark goddess because I was greedy for power. I wanted her to grant me position. To elevate me beyond myself. To put me in a place where I could look down on my father. I wanted to be better than him. I wanted more power than he had."

Khar uttered a guttural growl.

Emir felt a new heaviness fall over his shoulders. "I cared more about power and my ambition than I did my mother. Or the princess. Or . . . the boy."

Khar glared at him for a long time, his eyes poring into Emir's own, diving into the very blackness that had become his soul. Finally, he backed away, sat down on his haunches, and licked one of his front paws.

Disappointing, it is, disappointing, he said, setting the paw back down. *I enjoyed watching you here confined as you tried so hard to save your mind. Did you succeed? I think not. You stayed too long to ruin my plot. Still, I shall miss your arrogant endeavors to defeat a god and live forever.*

He looked up into Emir's eyes.

Goodbye, Emir Alkan, son of King Sargon. You have set yourself apart as one who from my world departs. He nodded toward the cave entrance. *Find your way or die today.*

Then he smirked and sauntered away into the darkness beyond.

CHAPTER

THIRTY-SEVEN

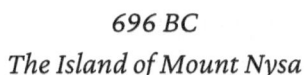

696 BC

The Island of Mount Nysa

At the sound of Katiah's voice in her ears, all thoughts of Denisia disappeared from Little Bird's mind. Katiah! The dark goddess of the underworld. The one who had killed Emir. The one King Midas had changed into a gold sculpture with a single thrust of his golden sword.

"Is it you?" Katiah said. "Little Bird? I can't see you."

Little Bird couldn't bring herself to answer. She didn't want Katiah to know she was there.

"Little Bird?"

Silence as deep as the edge of the world.

"I thought I heard . . ." Katiah paused. "My little girl," she said in a softer voice. "You ran away that day. Do you remember? You were only seven years old."

Ran away?

"Too young to discover what you did. I tried to explain it to you, but you've always been such a kind-hearted girl."

Red faces, hands reaching out of the abyss, the cries of desperate men, women, and children . . . Little Bird shut her eyes.

"I've thought of that day often." The goddess' voice softened. "I shouldn't have gotten angry. It's just that I warned you not to go in there and you went in anyway. Worse, you came back blaming *me!*"

Sunken eyes, so deeply set into the skulls that she could see the orbital bones . . .

"But of course you would. I'm the goddess of the underworld. It was my fault, you said, that I didn't let those people go."

She ran toward the Red River, Kartal on her heels. He had found her, she remembered suddenly, but he hadn't seized her. He'd only watched as she got inside the boat, his golden eyes intense as she rowed away. He'd allowed her to leave. With a start, she thought of the three wolves who had been keeping her company over the last several years. *Katiah's wolves.*

"You've too much of your father in you," Katiah continued. "I knew it, but I didn't want to see it. I wanted to keep you away from him. And I did. For a while, you were mine."

Her father? Little Bird's mind raced. What was she talking about?

"Little Bird?" When Little Bird didn't answer, the goddess fell silent. Little Bird wanted her to continue, but feared revealing her presence. Was the captor listening? She looked around but saw only darkness. It was like being in the blackest of caves on a stormy night.

"That horrible man," Katiah resumed. "He took everything from me. I should have left him to die on that plain. Instead, I had to save him, take care of him, keep him safe."

Her voice echoed off the rock walls. The effect was disorienting, the words coming at Little Bird from all directions.

"That should have been enough, but I had to put him on the path to becoming king. I fell in love with him, was the problem. You mustn't do that, Little Bird. Fall in love with a man like that. But he was so handsome. So full of life. I stupidly fell in love, and then I decided he wasn't worthy of me. The dark goddess must have a king! So I made him a king. That was a big mistake."

The image of King Midas arose in Little Bird's mind. She broke out in a cold sweat. *King Midas? Her father?*

"It was sweet while it lasted," Katiah murmured, as if through a smile. "It brought me you, and we were happy together for a time. Do you remember?"

Little Bird thought of the sweet voice calling her, the soft hands touching her neck as the woman brushed her hair. Mixed with these memories were her recollections of King Midas, standing next to him while he sat on his throne, teaching him her language, giving him the magical spring water, resting with him in his battle tent.

"I had hoped to keep you with me in the underworld," Katiah said. "I was angry when you left. And then you had to go and find *him*! Of all people!"

Little Bird's heart thumped. Emir had taken her to Gordium, taken her to King Midas' city. And the king had been kind to her, but . . . *King Midas? Midas?* she said in her mind. *He was my . . . father?*

"Little Bird? Is that you?" Katiah seemed to have heard her thoughts.

Little Bird squinted her eyes shut.

"Little Bird?"

Yes.

"It's you? Truly?"

Yes.

"But how? How did you—?"

Tell me! Was he?

Katiah hesitated for several moments. "Yes. You had to run off and find him. I figured you knew, somehow."

Little Bird shook her head. The king. Her father. She had liked him as a child, but she had never thought . . .

"I tried to win him back from that woman, but . . ." Katiah sighed. "He returned to her. She was his queen, and he was a king and my, did I underestimate the hold all *that* would have on him."

Little Bird pressed her fingers into her temple. This was another of her dreams. Another vision. But it wasn't. It was different. The

295

memories were too close, too vivid, Katiah's voice now too familiar, a new clarity dawning in her mind. Her father. The king! She tried to imagine it. *Did he know?* she asked.

"No, of course not. I couldn't tell him. He would have wanted you, would have demanded you go to him, and you were mine."

I wasn't yours!

"Yes, you were! I raised you! I took care of you. And you were happy with me. Until you had to break the rules. I told you to stay out of the cave."

The red faces, the bony fingers . . . *You tortured them. All those people.*

"I didn't torture them! They were tortured souls, yes, but that wasn't my doing! Surely you can't still think this way after all this time?"

You could have helped them! You had the power.

"Oh, sweet girl, that's not the way it goes. Don't you see? They ended up there because of their own decisions. I had nothing to do with it."

You stole them!

"Only some of them! A tiny number, really, if you consider them all. And besides, the ones in the cave. They aren't the ones I . . . invited down."

There were others?

"It doesn't matter now. You're here. Aren't you?"

Little Bird's memories bombarded her with images and sensations and feelings, the king and the princess, the princess with her slate. She had been kind, too. Princess Zoe. *Her sister?*

"I didn't mean to kill him, you know," Katiah murmured. "The one you chose to take care of you after you left."

Little Bird's thoughts dove from the king into the well of feeling that was Emir in her heart. Emir. Katiah had killed Emir.

"I thought to make him a king, too," Katiah said, "so he would be worthy of you when you came of age. You are a half goddess, my love. You can't choose just any mortal man. He could have taken King

Midas' place. But then your father had to give it all up. His desire for revenge. After all that time! I couldn't allow it. I had to make him pay. I was going to take his sister. That blast wasn't meant for Emir, darling. I want you to know that." She paused. "I don't suppose it matters now."

Little Bird clenched her fists, angry all over again. Katiah had caused everything. The curse on King Midas, Zoe's suffering as a golden sculpture, Anchurus' sacrifice. Had Katiah left things well enough alone, Denisia never would have gotten involved and none of it would have happened. Who knew what sort of life Little Bird might have led? How she and Emir might have become part of King Midas' family? Her heart longed for that, to know her . . . father. Her sister. Her . . . brother. A new sadness closed her throat. The lost prince was her half-brother. And Elanur, the one who had joined her on her trek back to Gordium, was her father's sister. Her head swam with vertigo, her stomach nauseated.

"Little Bird, if you're there . . ." Katiah paused. "I must be hallucinating again." She uttered a soft moan. "It's just . . . I'd like us to be . . . well, friends again. Little Bird? Are you still there?"

Little Bird stood frozen in that dark space, listening to her mother's voice swim in her ears. All these years she'd had a father, and she'd never known. She wondered if that was part of the reason she'd wanted to leave the underworld. She remembered wanting more. She'd wanted to see the light, meet the living people. Katiah had told her she wouldn't survive up there. The living people were cruel. The world was dangerous, harsh, and unforgiving. She was safer with her mother and the wolves down by the endless Red River under the starless sky.

It was true she had been happy for a time. She remembered that. But then she'd gone into the forbidden cave. Even now, the memory of it made her shiver. Souls warped and misshapen and crying out for relief, demons surrounded by fire and blood, monsters reaching toward her from the depths of some unknown void. She'd gotten out before they'd caught her, but she'd never forgotten.

297

"The light has to have the dark," Katiah said, as if reading her mind. "I told you that. One is not possible without the other. I just happen to rule over the dark spaces. I tried to protect you." She paused. "I guess you took after me a little too much. You were too curious. Too headstrong."

Little Bird trembled, her cheeks wet. Standing there in the silence, it all seemed unreal. Her presence there. Her mother and father revealed. Her past laid bare. Her head throbbed, the air cold against her skin. As it all congealed in her thoughts, one question rose above the rest. She stepped forward and grasped the hands that encircled the sword.

"Little Bird?" Katiah whispered.

How did I forget?

"It is you?"

The excitement in her voice opened a crack in Little Bird's shield. *Yes.*

"But how are you here? How did you get here? Did you remember?"

How did I forget?

"You remember who you are?"

I don't know.

"But you're here."

Where are we?

"A tomb. Your father—King Midas—put me in it after the battle. I guess he figured being a gold sculpture wasn't enough."

You are powerful. You could escape.

"Of course you would take his side." Her voice took on an angry edge. "But I can't. Not this time. I don't know why. Something is different." She paused. "How are you here?"

Tell me, how did I forget?

Katiah paused.

The ground rumbled underneath Little Bird's feet, small rocks raining down on her head. She ducked, steadying herself against the rock behind her. It lasted a few moments and then everything fell still again.

"*That's* part of what's different," Katiah said. After a few moments of silence, she continued. "Any human who leaves the underworld forgets most of what went on there. The gods can remember, but the humans have not our adaptability. It's the way of things. Not *my* fault, if that's what you're thinking."

I am human?

"Half human."

And half . . . goddess? It seemed strange to even contemplate.

"Yes."

I should have remembered?

"As I said. You take after your father."

But I had memories. I thought they were dreams.

"The goddess part of you. See, you can't get rid of me completely."

Little Bird felt her body shifting. She withdrew her hands.

"Don't go. Please."

The ground lifted under her feet.

"No! Little Bird. Stay."

Something was pulling her away.

"Please don't go, my daughter. I love you. I've always loved you. Please believe that. Little Bird!"

Little Bird's body hurled through dark space. Slowly, the ribbons of fire returned, the orange and yellow snakes spinning above her. The rock ceiling came into view, the paintings she'd made rushing about in a wash of colors until finally, everything stilled and she felt only dirt under her fingers.

Mother, she mouthed.

"It worked."

The voice prickled inside her ears. Denisia. Little Bird blinked open her wet eyes.

"You found her, didn't you?"

CHAPTER
THIRTY-EIGHT

696 BC
Coming home to Gordium

When Xander caught sight of the city of Gordium in the distance, he felt a swell of emotion that brought tears to his eyes. Never had he been away so long, on a journey so arduous as this one had been.

"Look, Aster!" he called. "There it is! We're almost home!"

"It is far away now," Aster called back with equal enthusiasm.

"Maybe we can return to being advisors again," Gediz grumbled from behind.

Xander rolled his eyes and urged his horse into a trot. Neval was gone, having left them at the main road that led to Gordium, so it was just the three of them now, though in a way, it seemed like only two.

"Will you speak to the king?" Xander said in a low voice.

"About how much he has assisted us?" Aster said.

"You know what I mean."

"It will not depend on the king's state of mind."

"I can't imagine living with him in our room again."

"It is pleasant to think about."

Xander touched his pocket. He had accepted the rock back from Aster two days before, and now it felt warm. It had been getting warmer the closer they drew to Gordium. It frightened him a little, but he couldn't help but be comforted as well. Perhaps the journey had not been for nothing. It was possible he really had spoken with the goddess Matar Kubileya, and she had given him something of value. Whether it would help keep Katiah in her tomb remained to be seen. The two appeared to be completely unrelated, except that Matar had seemed concerned about Katiah's entrapment.

Oh dear, that's why, she'd said.

Xander hoped there may be something to that, for his and Aster's sakes. So far, they had little to offer in terms of the task the king had appointed them to complete. Xander brooded over the issue, trying to think of what he was going to say when Midas asked them what they had found. That Matar's entrapment could have something to do with the cracks in Katiah's tomb seemed possible, but truly, they were no closer to knowing the answers than they were the day they'd left.

By early afternoon, they were approaching the city from the southwest. The castle looked a dull gray underneath the cloudy sky, but it was a beautiful sight nonetheless. At the west gates, the guards hailed their return, all of them offering hearty greetings. Once inside, Aster asked for a messenger to alert Princess Zoe of their arrival.

"I'm sorry." The guard shook his head. "The princess is not available."

Aster gave him a puzzled look.

"She's missing," the guard said. "Three days, I'm afraid."

Aster cast his gaze about. "Not taken?"

"The king had sequestered her in her room, prior to her disappearance." The guard glanced sheepishly up at Aster. "Rumor is she escaped."

"The king—" Aster began.

"Something about what she gave to the nomads, or more accurately, did not give." The guard leaned closer. "The king has missed your wise counsel."

Aster glanced back at Xander and then leaned forward. His mount shifted into a gallop and they dashed up the road.

"Wait!" Xander urged the gelding after them. Soon the two were flying toward the castle, their journey all but forgotten, Gediz lagging along behind.

KIRAL POLAT LIVED in a section of Gordium Zoe rarely visited, and for good reason. Young girls were told to avoid it from the time they were old enough to go out on their own. Men gathered there, wealthy, unsavory men with strange appetites, and girls went missing, never to be seen again.

She'd left the castle and, after a brief exchange with Baki to glean more information, ended up in the last place she wanted to be. The stone wall surrounding most of the city rose in front of her, signaling that soon she wouldn't be able to go any farther. According to what Baki had told her, Kiral lived in the last dwelling. The place loomed dark on the left side of the path, large enough for at least four rooms. Under the cover of darkness, a man might travel the length of the wall, then duck inside, unseen.

Zoe swallowed hard as she approached. Two men sat on either side of the front door, watching her. They reminded her of hungry wolves observing a young doe who had just wandered into their territory. She pressed her hand against the moose-hide cloak Baki had given her, noting the bulge of the dagger she'd tucked at her belt. It wouldn't do her much good should one of them make an aggressive move, but she had little choice now. Clenching her teeth, she strode up to them.

"I must see Kiral Polat," she said, summoning her most authoritative voice.

"Who are you?" snarled the man on the left. He rose slowly, at least a hand taller than Zoe with thick shoulders, his black hair in dire need of a wash, his fat cheeks covered in grisly whiskers.

"I have something of great value to offer him."

"What?" said the man on the right. He was even taller, a long scar trailing from his temple to behind his ear. Hair grew above and below the mark, but not on it.

"That is for Kiral to know."

Scarhead looked to Greasy Hair, then turned back to Zoe. "You want in? Give us a piece of this item of value."

Zoe tried to look past them into the dwelling. "Kiral!" she called out in her strongest voice. "I have an offer for you. You must speak with me!"

Greasy Hair laughed. "This one's got guts," he said to Scarhead.

Scarhead looked Zoe up and down. "Take off your hood."

Zoe glared at him. It was clear she was going nowhere unless she could get by these two. She did as he asked.

Greasy Hair squinted. "She looks like—" he began.

"The princess?" Scarhead asked.

"I am Princess Zoe. I have something of great value for Kiral. Let him know I'm here immediately."

"I heard she disappeared?" Greasy Hair murmured to his companion.

Scarhead looked her over once more, then opened the door. "Kiral! This woman says she's the princess."

There was no answer. Scarhead sat down in the chair he'd occupied before. Greasy Hair followed his lead. Both of them returned their gazes to Zoe.

She lifted her skirts and walked through the open door, her skin crawling as she passed them by. The smell inside nearly choked her —a strong sweaty scent that spoke of men who hadn't bathed for a very long time. She paused to get her bearings. The room before her was furnished with two long tables set corner to corner, wooden chairs scattered about. One door along the back wall was closed. To her right, the dwelling ended, but to her left a breezeway led into another room, where she saw the echoing glow of a fire.

Her gaze went first to the flames, the smoke drifting upward toward a vent in the roof. Beyond, three chairs emerged from the shadows. She was startled when she noticed a big man sitting in the center, flanked by two young woman. He stared at her with dark, appraising eyes beneath thick, straight brows, his arms crossed over his broad chest as if to say, *Impress me.* The girl on his left looked no older than fourteen; the one on his right, slightly more mature. Both watched her with a kind of curious innocence. A square table sat in front of them, its surface scattered with game pieces.

"Kiral Polat?" Zoe said.

His gaze roamed over her appraisingly. "What brings the princess to my door?"

Zoe longed to shrink into the wall. "I have an important matter to discuss with you." When Kiral only waited, she added, "I assume you have spoken to the commander of the king's guard."

One dark eyebrow went up. "The king's commander?"

"You spoke of . . . an arrangement."

"I am a trader. I make many arrangements."

"This one was unique." When he said nothing, she went on. "To save the city."

"Save it?" His gaze was intense. "From what?"

"The nomad warriors."

"But they are gone. Our great king handled that. He gave the men gold and sent them on their way." The corner of his lip twitched.

"I know you have spoken to him."

"What care I for what the king's commander may say when the king himself has solved the problem?"

He was toying with her, and she had no experience handling men like him. She wished Rastus were there. The urge to ask about him rose to her lips, but she bit it back—it would only make her seem weak. "The king does not reward those who kill our citizens," she said instead.

Kiral squinted. "If that were true, I would find that news most refreshing."

"Do you propose the princess lies?"

"I have heard that the princess disappeared from the castle a day or so ago, after the king locked her away in her chamber. And now here you are. You'll forgive me if I am a little confused."

Zoe glanced at the girl on his right. She didn't seem afraid of Kiral, but looked at him with respect when he spoke. Perhaps even . . . fondness? "If we might talk further," Zoe said, "I can explain."

He leaned forward in his chair. "I know why you're here, Princess. I'm just trying to decide if I want to follow through on this idea of yours or not."

"So you *have* spoken to the commander."

"He was supposed to return with a sampling of my payment," he said, then glanced up at her, "but he arrived empty-handed."

"And where is he now?" She couldn't help herself.

"He assured me I would be paid today."

He was avoiding the question. "And here I am." She dug into her pocket and retrieved her gold necklace. Her father had given it to her when she was fifteen, a gaudy thing that she had never worn. Nevertheless, it was valuable. "I have the sampling, though I know not why a citizen such as yourself would demand payment to serve his king."

Kiral motioned to the older girl on his right. She rose, circled the fire, and took the necklace from Zoe's hand before returning to him. He weighed the piece in his palm, then gave it back to her. She lifted it to her face for a closer look, the younger girl leaning in beside her.

"That will do little for your purposes," Kiral said.

Zoe pulled out one of her mother's elaborate headbands. The queen had worn the heavy thing for a portrait but never again. Holding it up for Kiral to see, she asked, "Would you refuse the princess' request?"

"Not normally, of course." He gestured to the older girl, who left the first necklace with the younger one and retrieved the headband. "But you are not in the king's good graces right now, are you?" He gazed at her with his dark eyes, his muscles pressing against the fabric of his tunic. "My guess is that you, and perhaps the commander as well, have come here without the king's knowledge. If that is the case, I must be cautious. I don't want to lose his good favor."

"Since when did you have his good favor?"

Kiral chuckled. "Perhaps that is an exaggeration. But a man like me can't afford to garner the king's *disfavor*."

"The king will have nothing to disfavor if you gather men to protect the city."

Kiral glanced at the door.

She was losing him. "I understand you are a successful trader here." She took a tentative step forward. "If Gordium falls, you'll have to relocate. Start over. That could be difficult."

When she said *Gordium falls*, his gaze jerked back to her face. He hesitated, seeming to weigh her words. "I've moved before."

"Perhaps. But from what I've been told, you have built a strong following here. Gained the respect of the men in the city. You have prospered, some say, in ways more impressive than other men. That would take time to recreate, not to mention the inconvenience."

He lifted one heel and then the other, letting them drop to the floor with a *thump*. "Princess, do you expect the city will fall?"

Zoe shifted her weight. This wasn't something she wanted to reveal, particularly not to this sort of man. "The Gimirri will return," she said simply.

"Father?" the younger girl said with alarm.

Father? Zoe thought.

He tapped her on the knee. "It's all right, Yeni."

"It is not all right," Zoe said. "You know what they can do." She locked eyes with him.

"They nearly killed Mama," the older one whispered.

"Hush, Lunara."

Both girls resumed their study of the jewelry, each of them trying the pieces on.

"It was a long walk here," Zoe said. "Might you have another chair?"

Kiral studied her for a time. Then he barked, "Rifaat!"

Greasy Hair poked his head in.

"Another chair," Kiral ordered.

Rifaat stepped into the first room. While he was gone, Zoe watched the younger girl, Yeni. She was quite striking in her beauty, with smooth skin and thick red lips. She was turning the larger necklace over in her hands, examining every section.

"You girls go on." Kiral dismissed them with a wave of his hand.

Lunara touched her headband.

"Keep it," Zoe said.

"But we haven't finished!" Yeni whined, pointing to the game on the table.

"Later," Kiral said.

"Just because I was winning," Lunara said.

Kiral growled, and the girls squealed, scrambling into the next room just as Rifaat arrived with the chair. He set it down with a thud, then exited with a leering glance at Zoe.

She sat and turned to Kiral, composing her face into its most serious expression. "You were right. The nomads came for their gold. They did not get it. Their leader promised to return. He threatened more harm to our citizens. I know he means what he says."

"The king has his army," Kiral said. "Why does he not recall them?"

Zoe looked away. This was the part she didn't know how to handle. "These nomads," she said. "They fight differently than soldiers do. Their tactics are secretive. Underhanded. They have no honor. Our army stands ready—but this is another kind of threat. It demands a . . . unique approach. Even now, the nomads are infiltrating our city, secretly preparing their next move."

"There are guards at the city gates."

Zoe paused again. She was revealing much more than she'd planned, but time was running out, and Kiral was her last chance. "We could be outnumbered."

He reached for the cup on the table in front of him, but when he went to take a drink, it was empty. "Asli!" he barked.

From the doorway beyond, through which the girls had disappeared, a skinny woman came rushing in. Her skin was a suntan shade and her hair a rough black, her features narrow but appealing. She hurried to Kiral's side, took the cup and vanished. When she returned, she handed the full cup over.

"For my guest?" he asked her.

The woman glanced at Zoe for the first time. Her eyes betrayed her astonishment. "Your Highness." She bowed low and then hurried away, returning with a cup full of wine.

Zoe smiled at her. "Thank you."

Asli smiled back, a heartwarming smile that eased Zoe's discomfort. Then she disappeared again.

Zoe wanted to ask if that was Kiral's mate—the girls' mother?—but she was here on a mission. She lowered the cup to her lap. "As the commander certainly informed you, we need men who can stand up to the nomads' fighting style. More importantly, we require a man to lead this element, someone the other men respect."

"Why not put the king's commander in charge?"

"The commander's duties lie with the king. You have an opportunity to better yourself in a manner you might never accomplish on your own. Expand your property. Hire more men to help you. Imagine the wealth and reputation you might enjoy."

"I already have wealth and reputation," Kiral said, though she judged by the eager look in his eyes that her words had not gone ignored. "And I am no warrior."

"I've heard differently."

He arched an eyebrow. "Rumors are often inaccurate."

"Perhaps. But I'd wager you could handle yourself well in a fight."

This seemed to please him. He downed the rest of his wine. "Men in the city are not warriors. They are farmers. Traders. They know little of fighting, particularly against nomads like these."

"But they know the city. And this is their home. They will be motivated to do their best."

He set his cup down. "How much time do we have?"

Zoe drank her wine. It tasted good, she had to admit. More proof that Kiral had the ability to secure quality items. "The nomads have already infiltrated the city. Some of them, at least."

"I cannot create a fighting force in a day."

Zoe lowered her gaze and was quiet for a long while. Then she set her cup down and got up as if to leave. "My apologies. Perhaps you are the wrong man, after all."

Kiral waited until she had almost left the room to speak again. "Tell me more of this reward that awaits me should I take up this cause for . . . the king."

"Serve us well, and I will do what I can to influence the king to grant whatever you may want."

"As you said, property. Livestock. And the gold you didn't give the nomads."

"For such a price, you must plan to save the city single-handedly."

He smiled for the first time. It changed his entire face, making him appear friendly and approachable. "From what you're telling me, it seems it may come down to that."

Zoe studied his gaze, then again headed out. "Property it is, along with some livestock and perhaps a little gold."

He followed her. When they reached the doorway, he paused. "One more thing, Princess. What happens if we lose?"

Zoe gazed at the alleyway beyond. Despite everything—her father's inaction, the paltry number of guards, and this pitiful attempt to gather a citizen fighting force—she had always imagined that somehow, they would succeed. "You need not worry yourself about that," she said. "This is King Midas' capital city. Know you of any other city that has thrived as well?"

He held her gaze for a long time. Finally, he stepped back. "The king was wise to send you," he said.

Zoe lowered her head in response.

"I will organize this group of men," Kiral continued. "But I can't guarantee how they will perform. In the heat of battle, those who are not soldiers often flee to safety."

"There will be no safety," Zoe said. "The men must protect their homes and their families. Tell them that."

She walked up the forbidden road, continuing until she was sure she was out of sight. Then she darted to the left. Tucked up against the side of an unknown dwelling, she took some time to collect herself. She longed to rush to the castle. She wanted to find Rastus and report what she had accomplished, but the moment she stepped foot inside the castle gates, the king would have her locked in her room again.

Once she'd calmed down, she made her way to the main road, then turned south. She would seek shelter with Baki, whom she was certain would accommodate her. Had Aster returned yet? There was so much to tell him. As she walked, her small feet leaving tracks in the dirt, Kiral's words echoed in her mind.

What happens if we lose?

It was impossible! But now that Kiral had said it, the thought persisted.

What, indeed?

CHAPTER

THIRTY-NINE

696 BC
North of Gordium

After she left Ilker and his men behind, Elanur traveled two more days before she spotted the outline of Gordium. She was in the flatlands, the harvest wind blowing sharply from the east. Her fingers and toes were stiff, her face tight and dry. She longed to build a huge fire and bask in its warmth, but at the sight of the castle in the distance, her heart leaped into her throat.

She'd never seen it before, but it could be nothing else. Her brother's royal home was known for sitting elevated on the north-west side of the city. She had always hoped to see it one day. Now, as it beckoned from the western horizon, a swell of emotion overtook her. She pulled Hazel to a stop.

It was after sunset, but light enough that Elanur could make out the shapes of the man-made structures ahead. She gazed briefly at the city's expanse, then returned her focus to the castle. Her thoughts went to her brother and what Ilker had said about him, that he was old and weak. She hadn't told Ilker where she'd come from. He had asked, once, and she had put him off, telling him that her life before was best left in the past. Elanur imagined Kerkin caught up in battle against King Midas' men. Even if Ilker was right, her brother was still the leader of a mighty kingdom. That Ilker believed he might defeat him with two hundred men seemed foolish, but she had never known her mate to make a foolish decision.

She nudged the mare with her heels and they moved forward again. The river meandered alongside her, the waves at peace as if they, too, had arrived. Darkness crept up from behind her, gradual enough that her eyes adjusted and she could keep Hazel on a straight path.

When she finally reached the bridge over the Sangarius River, she saw several guards posted along the length of it, oil lamps in rows beside them. The one who approached held a torch in his hand, the flame lighting up his ruddy face.

"You're traveling alone?" he asked.

A jolt of fear struck Elanur's breast. It had been a long time since she'd had to worry about men assaulting her. "I pose no threat to the city of Gordium," she said in her strongest voice. "I seek shelter only."

"You travel by yourself?"

"I got separated from my group in the storm. I have been alone since then."

"Who were you traveling with?"

"A small group of villagers from the northern mountains. We offer sheep and goats to trade, as well as clothing and dried vegetables. They should have come through already?" She looked ahead, as if searching for her travel mates.

The guard spoke to another guard behind him, a shorter man with ears that stuck far out from his head. "We haven't seen such a group," the first guard said.

Elanur's eyes widened in alarm. "Oh my. I hope they didn't get lost, too." She shivered and looked behind her. "I journeyed for days. I am cold and hungry. Would your king be so kind as to allow me shelter here? Once I recover, I shall search for my people."

The guard observed her carefully, then walked up the road. He seemed to check for anyone else that may be trying to conceal themselves. He directed the funny-eared man to do the same. When they returned, the first guard demanded to check Elanur's bags. Elanur got off her horse and held the reins while the two guards went through her belongings. When they found nothing unusual, the shorter one returned to his post while the first guard came around in front of her. "I must ask that you open your cloak. We must be cautious."

Elanur complied, loosening the ties to show she concealed nothing. The ruddy-faced man handed her a small stone painted red.

"Give this to the gate guard ahead," he said. "He will allow you entrance. You can find shelter at Baki's Inn. You'll see a sign on the left of the main road as you enter the city. Watch over yourself. Most of the citizens of Gordium are welcoming and kind, but violent men have attacked our city." He gave her a stern, fatherly look, then gestured for her to proceed.

Elanur rode over the bridge, elated and concerned at the same time. She was riding into her brother's city. After all this time, she was riding into Gordium! So long ago, she had set out from Durukin with Little Bird. An old sadness gnawed at her throat as she wondered what had become of the girl. If she had made her way here, perhaps they would be reunited. The thought sparked energy in her heart, though she quickly squashed it. It was unlikely, and she didn't want to be disappointed.

She showed the gate guard her red rock. He gave the signal, and the mighty gates opened. She passed through, craning her neck to take in their grandeur, then glanced back as they clunked shut behind her. Part of her felt safe at last, her shoulders finally dropping from around her ears. The other part felt suddenly isolated and alone. Ilker no longer walked beside her. Kerkin was nowhere nearby. Hastet and Goakina were left far behind, the rest of the tribe on a dangerous mission. She warred with herself, but in the end, moved on, determined. Karem was her brother by blood. She must warn him.

The main road was quiet, no fellow travelers in sight. A lamp glowed up ahead, casting light on a sign carved with the image of a dwelling—the inn. It stood two levels high, taller than the surrounding dwellings, with a window on either side of the door.

Elanur pulled Hazel to a halt. Much of the night had already passed. As much as she longed to alert Karem immediately, gaining entrance to the castle now, as a solitary stranger, seemed impossible. She was uncertain if her brother would recognize her even in the daylight. She glanced back at the gate. Ilker was at least a night's length behind. She might afford a brief rest.

Dismounting, she looped Hazel's rein around the corner post and approached the door. The heavy iron knocker let out a low-pitched *thunk*. After a time, a short man with deep forehead wrinkles and wild gray hair peered out.

"I request lodging for the night," Elanur said. "I have nothing to trade, but I am a friend of the king's. If you allow me in, you can trust I will be able to pay you."

Baki blinked his small blue eyes at her, then reached out to push the hood back from her head. She flinched, but when he merely studied her with quiet curiosity, she allowed the liberty.

"A friend of the king," he murmured, voice quivering.

"Please. I have traveled far."

Baki opened the door.

Elanur gestured to Hazel. "My horse?"

"Up the road past the next two buildings, turn left, and go down the small pathway."

Elanur followed his directions and soon reached the back of the building. Baki emerged, a thick brown cloak over his shoulders, and took Hazel's reins from her hand. "Go on in," he said, nodding toward the door behind him. "There is a fire." Then he disappeared inside the horse shelter, Hazel trailing after him.

Elanur found the fire, and sitting as close as she could get, wrapped her arms around herself and rocked until her limbs began to thaw.

CHAPTER

FORTY

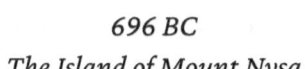

696 BC
The Island of Mount Nysa

"She's still alive, isn't she?" Denisia asked.

Little Bird sat in the dark cave, holding onto the sides of her head. She didn't wish to talk to her captor now. She wished to be alone. To think.

The goddess crouched so her face was near Little Bird's. "Tell me!"

Wait, Little Bird signed. *Think.* She pointed to her temple.

"No, you will not think your way out of this one. Tell me. Now."

It was dark, Little Bird signed. *Couldn't see.*

"If you're lying to me . . ."

Dark. Like a cave. No light.

"You were talking to someone."

I heard a voice.

"The same voice as before?"

Little Bird nodded.

"She is your mother, isn't she?"

Little Bird stared at her.

Denisia smirked. "I knew it." She backed away, adjusting her cloak. "You must have been in her tomb." She squared her shoulders. "I suppose that means it is time we go."

Little Bird glanced toward the barrier.

"We shall free her. Together."

Free her! Little Bird shook her head *no* on instinct.

Denisia blinked in surprise. "You must want her set free?" When Little Bird looked down, Denisia frowned. "She is the only one who can bring Anchurus back. And Emir, of course. Don't you want that?"

Little Bird rubbed her temple. Katiah was her mother. She could no longer deny that. But Katiah had tortured King Midas and killed Emir. Her thoughts tumbled over one another, each adding to her confusion.

"You should know," Denisia said, smoothing her hair. "A nomad tribe is descending on the city of Gordium. King Midas has been foolish. He has no army, only the castle guards. The nomads are cunning. Already they have killed many Gordium citizens."

King Midas. Her father. Foolish?

"He does not rule as he once did," Denisia said, as if reading her mind. "Princess Zoe has disappeared. Even his advisors seemed to have left him."

Princess Zoe disappeared? Little Bird clutched at her dress.

"If the nomads take the city, everything will change. Likely, King Midas will be killed. If we are to release your mother, now is the time." She came closer and bent down. "I knew there was a connection. And now you know too, don't you?"

Little Bird lifted her gaze. Did the goddess expect gratitude?

"You are angry with me." The captor's gaze softened. "Perhaps you are angry with her, too. We are sisters, after all. Well, half sisters, as your mother always said."

A shot of adrenaline went through Little Bird's body. Denisia. *Related?*

The goddess raised an eyebrow and stood up again. "If you're

Katiah's daughter, that would make you my niece, wouldn't it? Or, half niece."

Little Bird turned away to hide the anger on her face. Half niece! As if that mattered to the goddess. She cast her gaze to the barrier. Outside, she could sense the wolves waiting. Her emotions wrenched and pulled, her mind fighting to clarify her thoughts. One rose above the rest: If ever she was to escape, now was the time. She might not get another chance.

She rose and faced the goddess. *A tomb,* she signed.

"Yes, I know. King Midas told me himself." Denisia smiled at the shocked look on Little Bird's face. "He's an old fool, but I convinced him to set Katiah free. Unfortunately, he hasn't done so yet. I don't even think he can." She rubbed her arms. "I tried to do it myself, but I couldn't get to it. Some sort of hiding spell around it. Now the nomads are interfering. They will ruin everything." She glanced out the barrier to the darkness beyond. "That's why I need you, Little Bird. You are the missing link."

Little Bird gazed at the fire. It needed more wood. Nearby rested her short bed, the one that left her feet uncovered and chilled. A powerful revulsion spread through her body. She had to get out.

We must go, she signed.

The goddess studied her face. She was untrusting. Suspicious.

My mother. You are right. We must free her. We must go now.

Denisia glanced at the barrier, then back into Little Bird's face. "I'm not a bad person," she said. "You see that, don't you? You *are* connected, like I thought. You just had to remember. Now we can free her, so she can free *him.*" She smiled. "We'll set things right, you and I." She tapped Little Bird's forearm awkwardly, attempting affection. "We are family, Little Bird. We must take care of one another." She nodded, encouraging Little Bird to agree.

Little Bird clenched her fist behind her back. Take care of one another indeed! But she bowed her head.

The goddess started toward the barrier.

Little Bird held her breath. She stood, transfixed, as the goddess approached the crisscrossed vines like she might approach a tree in the forest or a stream babbling by, as if it were nothing unusual, nothing more than air. She paused when she came to it, then cast her gaze back to Little Bird.

"Do you have anything you want to bring with you?"

Nightsky. Little Bird glanced back at the bed that was too small for her, the extra set of clothes drying on the rope she'd erected between two fire sticks, the figurines she'd carved out of wood too thin to burn, and the little box Verin had crafted for her. She scanned her paintings on the wall and the hole in the ground that hid her rocks. Finally, she patted the pocket she'd sewn into her wool wrap to feel the crude dagger she'd made resting there. It was all she needed. Giving the space one last look, she walked forward until she stood beside the goddess.

"I must warn you," Denisia said. "If you try to flee, my wolves will hunt you down and you shall have to be punished. Do you understand?"

My wolves? Little Bird bowed her head, confused. Were the wolves loyal to Denisia? But Little Bird remembered them from before, when she was a child. They were her wolves. Or Katiah's wolves? She heard a whispering, creaking sound and looked up. Writhing like insects over a large hive, the vines unraveled and, within moments, dropped to the ground as discarded leaves, stems, and branches.

For the first time in twenty years, the entrance to the cave was open.

Little Bird wanted to flee before the barrier formed again. It took all her strength to wait. When Denisia walked out, she followed, slowly approaching the line she'd never been allowed to cross. Here was where she'd received food and drink, where Verin had sat to visit with her. Over there was where they'd held hands far past sunset. There, too, was where Cemile had brought firewood and told her of the goings on in Silenus' village. Here is where she had stood staring at the sunset and the clouds and the treetops swaying in the wind.

Here was where she had watched the road for anyone who might come with food, and where she had imagined one day walking free.

Denisia had already mounted her horse. "You can ride with me to the village. We'll begin our journey tomorrow."

On her right, Little Bird sensed Kartal watching her. Sabir and Sadik were there, too. They would follow, she knew, though she wasn't certain whether it was her they would be following or the goddess. She glanced back into the cave and gave a silent wish that Nightsky would come, too. Then she gathered her courage and crossed the line.

Nothing happened. She was outside. She looked over her shoulder. Her fire still crackled at the side of her bed.

"Come," Denisia said. "We must be going."

Little Bird took the goddess' hand. With a mighty heave, Denisia pulled her up. Little Bird felt the sway of the animal's hips, heard its hooves thudding on the dirt road. She caught the whisper of Kartal's movements on the incline to her right, soft pads taking up her trail. She looked back, longing to see a pair of black wings emerge from the cave. It wasn't until she'd almost ridden out of sight that she saw it, a quick flutter, and then, darkness.

She turned forward. The air was cold, the horse's hide warm under her legs. All around her, the sky was gloriously wide and endless, a gentle night breeze tousling her long hair about her head. She wiped tears from her cheeks, stifling sobs at the back of her throat. The goddess must not see her cry.

PART FOUR

CHAPTER

FORTY-ONE

696 BC
Gordium, Capital City of Phrygia

"The king will see us." Aster stormed into the advisors' room, flinging shut the door behind him. "Still, he will see us!" He threw up his hands.

"Wonderful!" Gediz spoke in a mocking tone from his bed against the wall. "We can see him now. What joy."

Aster growled and paced the length of the room. "He wishes to see his advisors after they return from their long journey." He was fuming, cheeks red, fists clenched at his sides. "I know this king. This is my king. This is my king!" He swept his hand across in front of him.

"You expected him to jump at your command?" Gediz grumbled. He looked freshly bathed, his hair combed and a smart cream-colored jacket over his shoulders. "Perhaps he was not as eager for your return as you thought."

Aster glared at him as if he might beat him black and blue at that very moment.

"And the princess?" Xander stood up from his chair, eyeing his two colleagues. "Any news of her?"

"They know," Aster said. "Everyone knows. I didn't ask several of them. Timon. The commanders. Pembe. None of them. They did not just let her go. She's not the princess! How can they be so concerned?"

Xander set the warm, glowing Matar stone down on his night-stand. So no one knew where the princess had gone. That wasn't good news. She was the one who had been holding everything together. Now Aster was ready to explode, as it seemed nobody was even looking for her.

"What does it matter where the princess is?" Gediz said. "It is the king who gives the orders."

Aster started toward the little man, his fists clenched.

Xander hurried across the room and stepped into his path. "Gediz has a point," he said, seeking Aster's gaze. "The princess is quite good at taking care of herself."

The blood pumped visibly through the veins in Aster's neck, his breath audible, Gediz shrinking against the wall in the face of it. After another beat, Aster retreated to his side of the room.

Xander pressed the heels of his hands into his eyes. They hadn't been able to rest since they'd arrived home. They hadn't even had time for a hot meal. Instead, they'd requested to see the king, only to be told by Timon that the king was unavailable. Afterward, they had retired to their room, washed, and changed clothes. Aster had tried once more to arrange a meeting, but it seemed his second request had gone just as poorly.

"When can we not see the king, I asked?" Aster complained from behind his desk. "Everyone knows. He's not resting, they say. Not resting! His daughter is not out there somewhere in the city all alone and he's not resting?"

"At least the castle still stands," Xander said, "and the king is alive. It could be worse."

"It will not be worse," Aster braced his hands on his desk, as if steadying himself. "I did not speak to Baran."

"What did he say?" Xander asked.

"The princess gave the nomads the gold."

"What gold?"

"The gold they demanded. The king would not give it to them."

"After they killed all those people?"

"I don't know!" Aster said, again throwing his hands in the air. "I know this king!"

"She went against the king's orders," Gediz mumbled.

Aster steamed like a volcano ready to erupt.

"You know the king doesn't want to fight," Xander said, eyeing his friend.

"So he does not let these nomads kill our citizens?" Aster said. "Destroy our city?"

"Did Baran say what happened to Zoe?"

"She gave them the gold and didn't send them away."

"That sounds like her," Xander said. Their brave princess. "So that means they will be back."

"Baran does not know that, but yet he is preparing."

"What is there to prepare for?" Gediz said. "They've set the traps on the south side of the city, and Baran has posted the guards. If the king will not raise his army, there is nothing more to do. We must trust in his judgment."

Aster glared at the third advisor. "*We.* As long as your mop of hair is not preserved, you are pleased. While the city is not ransacked!"

"So Baran has done nothing," Xander said, trying again to distract his friend from pummeling Gediz. "None of the soldiers have been recalled."

"A wise choice, eh?" Aster leaned his back against one of his shelves and crossed his arms over his chest. "I do not know what she's doing. Why she has stayed. She will not try to prepare a group of fighting men herself. Baran would help her, so she hasn't gone to find someone else."

Xander gazed at him with a puzzled expression. "The princess? Gather a group of fighters?"

"It does not make sense?" Aster said.

Xander rubbed his chin. "Who would lead them?"

"Not knowing her, she will not be searching for such a person."

"This is not our concern," Gediz said in an exasperated voice. "We are advisors, not soldiers. I don't understand why you're getting so spun up about all this."

"When they do not invade the castle, you will not understand," Aster said in a chilling voice.

Xander squeezed his eyes shut against the vision threatening to take over his mind. *No.* He didn't want to see it again. A faint vibration pulled his focus, and he looked toward the nightstand. The Matar stone was pulsing. He walked over and touched it, then jerked his finger back. It was too hot. "We must see the king," he murmured, then frowned. It was as if the words had come unbidden from his tongue.

"We will not go now." Aster strode toward the door.

Xander wrapped the stone in his napkin and tucked it into his pocket. When he glanced at Gediz, the little man only stared at him. Xander thought of many things he might say, but then decided against them and followed his friend.

There was an eerie quiet about the castle, a heaviness similar to the one Xander had felt in the cave. He kept his gaze on Aster's back. The king wouldn't see them. It was too soon after Aster had asked, but he followed the lead advisor as he headed toward the room the king had once shared with the queen. Xander frowned. Wasn't he going to ask Timon first?

"I must not speak to the king," Aster told the guard on the right.

"No one is allowed in," the guard said.

"I must not speak to the king!" When they didn't budge, Aster shouted at the door. "Your Majesty! You must not speak to me!"

No one answered. Aster turned sharply, frustration radiating off him.

Xander's gaze was on the door, the throbbing rock in his hand. A strong force propelled him toward the king's room. The guards poised to stop him. "King Midas," he said in a firm voice, "I have a message from the great goddess Matar Kubileya. Ignore me at your peril." The rock throbbed hot against his palm. "King Midas! You will hear me!"

The door opened. Xander stifled a gasp. As Aster had said, "This is my king." Only he meant this was *not* his king. Now Xander realized how true that statement was. The man in front of him did not look like King Midas. He had aged since they'd left, his eyes bloodshot, the lids swollen and heavy, his mouth hanging open in a drooping fashion. His graying hair had turned wiry and stiff and grown enough that it brushed the top of his brows, his skin dull and sallow. He wore a long woolen tunic with no belt, his lower legs bare and his feet in a pair of moccasins. Behind him, the room looked nearly dark.

"What is all this noise?" The king's voice sounded gravelly, as if he hadn't spoken in days.

Xander dropped to his knees. "Great King Midas," he said. "I bring a message from the goddess Matar Kubileya. The survival of your kingdom hangs in the balance."

"We are not ready to report," Aster blurted from behind him.

"Please, Your Majesty," Xander said. Still kneeling, he raised the hot rock. It throbbed like a living thing. "You must hear me."

"Will this goddess bring the queen back to me?" He glanced over his shoulder into his room. "She was here. But she has gone."

Xander stared at the king's face. "Will you see us, great king?" he asked.

The king stared at him a moment longer, then retreated into his chamber, leaving the door open. Aster hesitated before following, casting Xander a grateful look as he went. His friend thought it a ruse, Xander knew, but something had taken hold of him, a strange energy emanating from the rock and rising through his arm into his throat. He followed Aster in, closing the door quietly behind him.

They found the king sitting on the couch by the far wall. A single candle provided the only light, a dim yellow glow flickering by the bed. The mattress had a heap of tousled blankets on it, as though he hadn't slept in days.

"Matar Kubileya bids you greetings," Xander said, bowing, "but wishes to know why you keep the dark goddess of the underworld imprisoned?"

King Midas rested one arm on the back of the couch as he stared at the space across from him. "Yes," he said. "Demodica was asking about her, too."

"You must release her," Xander said, his eyes widening at his own words. "Matar Kubileya demands it."

"What?" Aster interjected.

"You must release her, Your Majesty," Xander repeated. "Immediately."

"Your Majesty," Aster said, stepping forward, "we must not inform you of our journey—"

"You do not speak for Matar!" Xander snapped, then looked guiltily at his friend and shrugged. "You must hear me, great king," Xander continued. "Ever since Katiah has been trapped, the great goddess Matar has been trapped, too. For years she has suffered, locked away in a dark cave." He could feel Aster's gaze on him as the energy grew behind his voice. "Meanwhile, Your Majesty, the underworld has been thrown into chaos. The monster Erlik Khar has been allowed free rein." Xander's eyebrows raised at the name. "Unchecked by Katiah's powers," he continued, "Khar has foregone the rules. He murders at will. As he expands his reach, chaos grows. Souls that should have been released are trapped in torment. Chaos in the underworld bleeds into our world, great king, as you have seen. You must listen to the great Matar's counsel."

Midas caressed the queen's blanket he'd placed over his lap. "If I release the dark goddess, will Matar return my family?" He searched Xander's face with an earnest gaze.

Xander wrapped the rock in his napkin and offered it to Midas. It still glowed, though not as brightly as it had before he'd entered the room.

Midas took it, cupping it in both his hands.

"I found it in the cave, Your Highness," Xander said. "The goddess Matar told me to take it with me."

"It is not a long story," Aster said, "of which we did not wish to report to you."

"Why does the rock glow?" Midas asked.

"I believe it is the spirit of Matar, Your Majesty," Xander said. "She wishes for you to let Katiah out, and she will restore balance to the underworld. In turn, the goddess Matar Kubileya will bless the lands of Phrygia."

King Midas gazed at his advisors. "I thought you went to find a way to be sure Katiah did not escape?"

"That was not the intent of the journey," Aster said.

"Now you return demanding I release her?"

"We don't demand," Xander said. "Apparently . . ." He gestured toward the rock. "Matar Kubileya demands it. If you wish for this chaos to be over, you must free the dark goddess of the underworld, and Matar Kubileya will be freed as well."

"What do you know of this goddess, Matar?"

"She is the goddess of the mountains," Xander said. "She is the mother of all. It is only through her that resurrection can be found."

"Resurrection?" The king leaned close and peered into Xander's face. "She can resurrect the dead?"

Xander glanced at Aster. His friend clenched his jaw.

"Those who follow Matar live with her in the spirit world after death," Xander said, the words spilling from his mouth.

The skin on Midas' right cheek twitched. "Is my son there?" He crouched in front of his advisor. "My wife? Are they there with her? Can she bring them back to me?"

"Your Majesty, I don't know. But I fear . . ." Xander swallowed. "Matar can't do anything until you set the dark goddess free. She told me to tell you. You must restore the balance. If not, more will disappear."

King Midas dropped his gaze, his shoulders drooping as he sat back on his heels. "She cannot bring them back," he whispered.

Xander dropped his gaze.

Midas handed him the rock. "Tell Matar. It shall be done." With effort, he rose, then put a hand on the back of Xander's neck and steered him toward the door. "We will begin work tomorrow," he said. "It will take time."

"The gold," Aster said from behind them. "That will be easy to remove."

"Perhaps with enough heat," Midas said. "Zoe can figure out how . . ." He paused. "Aster, get the princess' scientists together and have them make a plan to release Katiah."

"But the princess—" Aster began.

"Her scientists, Aster. Talk to them."

"But Your Majesty, the princess is not alone out there. She must not be found."

They reached the door. King Midas waited while his advisors stepped into the hall. "Where is the third one?"

"Gediz . . . didn't come, Your Majesty." Xander said. "He is in our chamber."

Midas tucked his chin into his chest, then turned to Aster. "I have reason to believe . . ." He hesitated and glanced back at the couch. "The goddess . . ." He paused again. Uncertainty fluttered across his features.

"Your Majesty?" Aster said.

With a quick glance at Xander, the king started to retreat.

"Your Majesty!" Aster blocked the door's closing. "The princess. Can we not do more?"

The king stopped. They all waited for him to answer, but then he continued on into his room.

"Your Majesty!" Aster called again, but it was no use. The king was lost to the darkness.

CHAPTER

FORTY-TWO

The deep, dark underworld

P*rince Anchurus.* That was it!

Emir didn't know how long he'd been walking since he'd left Khar's arena. It felt like years. He'd worn calluses on the ends of his fingers from dragging them along the rock. Day after day, he'd tried to remember the one missing piece from when he'd first arrived. At last—following what seemed like a lifetime of combing through his memories—he'd stopped and allowed the silence to settle into his mind.

And then it had come to him.

Prince Anchurus.

It took him several more days—or seasons, perhaps—before he recalled that at one point, they had gotten separated. Something to do with the sound of the oud and the boy's voice, though the boy didn't have a voice. He'd followed it, but then he'd gone back after Anchurus and . . . seen the light. Yes, that was it! The glowing orange-red light.

The memory surfaced, sharp as ever. Even now, it affected him

335

the same way, warming the core of him and restoring a glimmer of hope. The Red River had flowed out of the tunnel as if by magic. He'd seen the boat floating away with Anchurus riding in the back. Emir had wanted to accompany the prince, but he'd arrived too late.

Reliving it all, a clear thought came into his mind: The boat had come for Anchurus. It had never come for him.

The realization dawned grimly on his soul. He'd been so focused on getting back to his life that it hadn't occurred to him the obvious difference between him and the prince. The gods had meant for Anchurus to go on into the world of light. Emir they had sent to the darkness, off to chase some phantom echo of an oud playing. Anchurus they'd led to his glory in the spirit world. Emir, they'd left to endless torment.

He slumped against the wall and slid down to sit on the rock floor. Hope evaporated from him like sweat on a windy day. He pressed his forehead against the stone, a heavy sense of doom engulfing him. Always he had repelled it with the sheer force of his will. Now it flooded his chest and choked his breath. His mind frayed around the edges as if someone were pulling a loose thread. If he gave in to this emptiness, he would lose himself, to Duman's delight, if Duman had ever been real.

He squeezed his eyes shut and forced himself to think of the one thing that still brought him joy: the boy. He had to be out there in the real world. *He needs me.* Emir repeated it, forcing himself to picture the boy's face. When he imagined it clearly in his mind, he opened his eyes.

Darkness.

Find your way or die today.

Had Khar ever said that? It didn't matter. He had to keep trying.

He got up and started walking again, one finger dragging against the rock. For many days, he walked. For many seasons, he walked. For many years he walked, thinking of the boy and then his mother, existing only in memories, his body growing more and more transparent, his mind grasping at the sliver of self he had left.

And then one day, something changed.

The rock, once cold, began to warm beneath his touch.

He stopped and pressed his palm against it. After confirming he wasn't imagining it, he explored with both hands. The warmth extended from as high as he could reach to the floor and spanned roughly the width of his body. When he stood against it just right, the heat flowed through his whole body. The sensation over-whelmed him, and tears welled in his eyes. He stood for as long as his legs would hold him, then slid down carefully, keeping himself centered in the heated space. Sitting with his back against the wall, he let the warmth seep into his muscles and bones.

He stayed for days. He didn't know how many. Then he told himself he should leave. He hadn't yet "found his way" as Khar had said. He set the intention to go the next morning, but didn't. He tried again the following morning and the one after that. But always when it came time, he couldn't pull himself away from the warmth.

"Come on, Emir, you coward," he scolded. "You will not *find your way* clinging to the rock like a child clings to its mother. Searching is the only answer. Let's go."

Yes, yes. So long had he been alone, the voice in his head had taken on its own personality. Darko, its name was. *But there is no harm in waiting. We've been here for days—years already—and this feels nice. Why rush?*

"I have to get back." Emir was talking to it now, the conversation increasingly real to him. "The boy may need me. And Mother might still be alive."

Too much time has passed, Darko said. *Everything's probably changed.*

"You want to stay here forever?" Emir asked.

At least it's warm. If we leave, it will be cold and hard for who knows how long. We don't know how far these tunnels go. Maybe Khar is tricking us. Maybe there is no end. We might just walk and walk until we are nothing but a breath of air blowing past the stone.

Emir lingered. He justified himself by rehearsing his life before.

COLLEEN M. STORY

Amid his concentration, one of his favorite memories came to him. After he had won the king's music contest, the king had granted him the undercroft for the night. The boy had shown up at the door. They'd talked for a while, but it was when the boy snuggled up to his ribs that he'd felt a warmth similar to what he was feeling now.

The memory set a spark inside him. He focused on it, reliving it over and over again until, one day, he got up from the floor, counted to three, and launched his body into the tunnel. He jogged the first many steps. When he was certain he wouldn't return, he slowed to a walk.

Darko writhed inside him, clawing at his chest and screaming for Emir to go back. When his voice faded, Emir touched his first finger to the wall, returning to his old habit.

He halted.

The rock was warm.

Again?

He pressed his palm against the stone. Warm.

How was that possible?

It's warm! Darko leaped up and down inside him. *It's warm here, like it was back there.*

Emir took a few steps forward, then touched the wall again. He tried several more times. In every instance, the rock felt warm. It was so consistent that once again he settled into a steady walk with his finger trailing along beside him. To his and Darko's great surprise, the temperature stayed consistent, no matter how far away from the original spot they traveled.

Emir picked up his pace, determined to find where the warmth might end. At the very least, he thought, he had to be in a different part of the tunnels than he had ever been before.

Do you think we're getting closer to the Red River? Darko asked. *Remember when we touched it, how it burned? Maybe that's why the rock is warm?*

"The rock wasn't warm then," Emir said. "We sat up against it after Prince Anchurus left. It wasn't warm."

338

Emir kept up his faster pace, his resolve renewed. Perhaps Darko was right and they were headed to the Red River.

Do you think we'll be able to escape? Darko said, echoing his thoughts.

"We're going to find out."

He walked for another indeterminable amount of time, his finger trailing on warm rock. The farther he went, the warmer it got, which he took to be a good sign at first. But when the heat showed no evidence of abating, and indeed, only seemed to grow more intense, Emir got nervous.

Maybe we should go back, Darko said. *It wasn't like this when we followed Prince Anchurus.*

"We're not going the same way, remember?" Emir said. "We're finding a different path."

What if it gets so hot it burns us up? We should turn around and go back.

"And do what? Walk the tunnels for eternity?"

Find another way.

"This is the first thing that's been different since I can remember. I want to know where it leads."

After another extensive period of travel, the rock grew so hot that Emir could no longer trail his finger along it without burning it. By that point, it was no longer necessary, for the black rock had developed a red glow—providing a blessed light. For a time, it renewed his hope, but gradually, that hope broiled away. He sweat constantly, walking like a soggy towel, his feet sloshing in his boots, his throat on fire. His desire for water grew acute. He wondered how Midas had coped with it, how he had continued to rule his kingdom with this sort of torture going on inside his body.

I want to go back, Darko said.

"If we go back now, we'll never know."

What if there is no way, and Khar was just lying to us?

"We saw Prince Anchurus leave. There has to be a way."

A few days in the tunnels and he is called to the Red River, a boat waiting for him. He steps aboard and is gone. Simple as a sunset. Us? We get there and there is no boat. We wander for what feels like an eternity. We battle in Khar's arena. If there was an escape for us, we would have found it by now.

Emir stumbled. He put his hand out to stop himself and burned it on the rock. He jerked it back and stopped, bent over his knees. When he checked the skin, it appeared unscathed as far as he could tell, given the red glow. Darko was getting to him, saying everything that Emir himself worried was true. He could be walking to his eventual death, if there was such a thing. Maybe he was walking into more torment, a type that would continue to get worse. He looked ahead but could see nothing but more glowing rock. Still, something inside him insisted he keep going. He had to know. He had to see for himself.

He covered his face with his hands. The burned one was tender. With a half grunt, half whimper, he rose and walked.

This is wrong, Darko said. *You're torturing us for no reason.*

"Shut up. I didn't ask you."

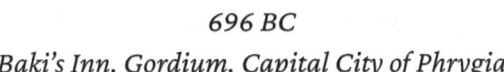

696 BC
Baki's Inn, Gordium, Capital City of Phrygia

Zoe was so absorbed in her thoughts as she walked down the stairs the next morning that she was startled to see two other women in the lower room. One was Baki's mate, Funda. She was cooking something over a small fire.

"Good morning," Funda said, her focus intent on the meat and onions in the pot. "This will be ready soon."

Zoe turned her gaze to the table. The second woman sat there, watching her with deep brown eyes. Her face was weathered and lined, her dark brown hair streak with gray. A worn leather dress draped over her slight frame to her ankles, a hide cloak around her shoulders. Zoe was about to take the opposite seat, but froze, staring. Something about the woman seemed familiar. The woman gaped in return, wearing the same stunned expression Zoe felt on her own face. They remained that way for a long moment, until Funda finally turned an expectant gaze on the princess.

Zoe sat down. She intended not to stare again. She didn't want to appear rude. But she couldn't help it. She raised her eyes to the woman's face and found her watching. Her lips were chapped, her cheeks windburned.

"You had a rough journey?" Zoe said.

The woman looked down, as if embarrassed. "It was a long way." Her voice had a smooth, pleasing tone with a foreign-sounding accent.

Zoe wanted to ask more, but wasn't sure how to do so without seeming intrusive. "It has been cold," was all she could think of.

"And wet," the woman said. "Much snow in the mountains."

"You came from the mountains?"

"Up north."

Zoe looked down at her hands, then over at Funda. "May I help?" she asked, all the while wondering why this woman had traveled so far.

The older lady shook her head. "Baki insisted. Only the best for the princess." She stopped, realizing she had said more than she should have.

Zoe ducked her head, then glanced across the table.

"You are the princess?" the woman asked, blinking.

"I am Zoe," Zoe said.

A soft gasp escaped the woman's throat. She dropped her gaze and pressed her hands over her face.

"It's all right." Zoe leaned toward her, alarmed.

The woman pressed her fingers into the bridge of her nose. When she looked up again, her eyes were wet. "I am Elanur," she said.

Zoe felt her jaw go slack.

"I am your father's sister."

It was many moments before Zoe found her voice. "Elanur?" she whispered. "Truly?"

The woman nodded. "I was at the Battle of Karama. I saw my brother, but only for a short time. I remember you. You were trapped in gold."

Zoe searched the woman's face. "Elanur?"

Elanur smiled. "I can't believe I'm here."

"What happened?" Zoe asked. "We feared Sargon had retaken you as his slave."

"He set me free."

Zoe's eyebrows shot up in surprise. "But we searched for you. Father sent men out. Year after year, he sent them."

Tears fell down Elanur's cheeks. "It's been such a long time." She pressed her hands over her face again.

Zoe went to her and placed her arm around the woman's shoulders. "It's all right," she said. "Elanur. The doll was yours?"

Elanur looked up. "Does he still have the doll? Karem? Is he all right?"

It was enough for Zoe. This had to be the same woman. No one else knew her father's real name. She cast her gaze to the window. The shutters were closed against the cold air outside.

"He will be so glad to see you." Zoe squeezed Elanur's shoulder, her mind swimming. If there was anything that could restore her father to life, this was it. His sister returned. Here. In Gordium! She wanted to rush up the road with Elanur and shout her father's name.

"I want to hear all about your journey," she said, crouching beside her, "where you've been. Why you've been away so long."

Elanur wiped her face with one hand, the other clutching her skirt.

"But right now, we must get you to the castle. You must be reunited with my father."

"Yes," Elanur said. "I have an urgent message for him."

"A message?"

Sobs threatened at Elanur's throat. She took a moment to compose herself. "I didn't know," she said finally. "I must tell Karem. There are men coming. Nearly two hundred."

Zoe stiffened.

"They mean to attack the city. Fierce warriors. Cunning. Your army will defeat them, of course."

Zoe pulled back. "You mean the nomads? The Gimirri?"

Elanur nodded.

Zoe returned to her seat in silence, her mind racing, as Funda began serving the food. The woman placed sizzling lamb chops and fried onions in their wooden bowls, followed by cooked carrots. Then she poured both of them some wine and stood back. When neither one started eating, she said, "Well, go on."

Zoe savored each bite, her thoughts tumbling over one another. Across the table, Elanur ate more quickly, as if she hadn't had a good meal in days. Zoe wondered how she knew about the warriors. Had she come all the way down by herself?

The front door opened and Baki bustled in carrying a heavy deer hide over his shoulder. "He wants another set of ties, Funda," he called to his wife.

She left the water basin and wiped her hands with a towel. The two stood in the center of the room discussing the garment, Baki explaining where the new ties needed to go. Funda took it and disappeared into the back, but not before demanding that he sit and eat. Baki turned around and smiled at the women.

"Baki," Zoe said, "meet Elanur, my . . . father's sister."

Baki raised his scraggly eyebrows, deepening the creases in his forehead. "I thought I saw a resemblance," he said. "But you are a traveler."

Elanur glanced across the table at Zoe and smiled. "I have come home," she said. "At last, I am home."

696 BC
Traveling from Mount Nysa south to Gordium

After four days of travel, Little Bird, the goddess, and her servant Chetin left the mountains behind. They crossed hills that rose and fell like waves on the sea, the Sangarius River winding along beside them to the right. At night, they took shelter wherever they could.

Sometimes, Little Bird woke thinking she was still in the cave. When she remembered where she was, she would huddle closer to the fire, pulling the cloak Cemile had given her as a farewell gift tightly around her shoulders. Her thoughts often turned to Katiah, her mother, sealed in the tomb, and to King Midas, her father, facing some unknown fate in the city ahead.

Every morning, as they broke camp and prepared to ride again, Little Bird battled with herself. Denisia was leading her to Gordium. Once there, she would expect Little Bird to help free the dark goddess. Little Bird doubted her ability to do that and wasn't certain she wanted to. Some days, she remembered Katiah's kindness and tried to forgive her. Most days, she couldn't imagine letting the goddess out to wreak more havoc on King Midas and his people.

Her father.

On the fifth day, they were short on supplies, so at midday, Chetin diverted from their path. Leaving the river behind, he led them southeast until they came upon a village tucked in a clearing between two rows of hills. The mud grew slick beneath them, the horses stiffening and picking their way forward with care.

The villagers had built their dwellings at the base of the tallest hill, with scraggly dead trees clustered in patches between them. Little Bird spotted children playing, two boys sparring with sticks, while a group of girls sat nearby, giggling. She followed Denisia and Chetin up the narrow path, her fingers woven into the horse's long mane. When they stopped, she awaited the goddess' instructions, eyes lowered, her thoughts spinning in all directions.

Then another face came into view.

"Little Bird?"

She blinked. A young man stood at the side of her horse, gazing up at her.

"Little Bird? Is that you?"

It took her a moment. Slowly, she recognized the wavy dark hair, the pouty lower lip, and the wide-set dark brown eyes. *Verin!* she signed. She felt like leaping off the horse.

He took her hand, squeezing it warmly. "I thought that was you!"

Little Bird smiled back, but then remembered. He had left her and never returned. Her smile faded, and she withdrew her hand.

Verin looked stricken, yet somehow, still bright. "She let you go?" He glanced forward to be sure Denisia wasn't listening, but the goddess was conversing with another villager, an older woman who appeared to be the leader.

Little Bird gazed at his fingers, the same long fingers that used to pass her food and firewood through the barrier, the same ones she'd held through many an afternoon, though they were more callused now. *You never came back,* she signed.

His gaze fell. "I'm sorry. I wanted to." The goddess was calling to him. "This way," he answered her.

He trudged through the mud to a storage hut near the west side of the hill. The three riders followed him, Little Bird shifting her mare over so she could watch him from behind. He walked with the same easy gait, new muscles propelling him with ease. They paused in front of the hut and he ducked inside, later emerging with his hands full of wool sacks. With his usual efficiency, he gave one to her captor, one to Chetin, and one to Little Bird, tying it onto the back of her saddle, stealing glances at her while he worked as if she were a prized possession he had lost and finally found.

"We have a warm fire," he said to the goddess, his hands still resting on Little Bird's saddle. "Will you stay?"

"We must ride on," she told him, turning her horse. "Tell the chieftess thank you. And give my regards to your boy." She rode past Little Bird without a glance.

Little Bird stared at Verin. *Boy?* Her mare had begun to follow the goddess on her own. Little Bird glanced over her shoulder. Verin's expression shifted, turning apologetic. He gave her a sheepish smile and a small wave.

"Take care of yourself, Little Bird."

One of the boys who had been sparring with sticks ran toward him, shouting, "Father! I won! Did you see?"

The child couldn't have been more than five years of age, dark hair streaming behind him, a thick fur cloak bouncing around his shoulders. He skidded to a stop in front of Verin, panting, and launched into a breathless chatter. Verin mussed the boy's hair, then took his hand and walked with him toward the distant shelters.

Little Bird turned away. Verin had a son. Which meant he must have a mate. He hadn't returned, not because he couldn't, but because he'd made a life somewhere else. With someone else. The old heartache surged through her, heat rising across her skin. She had to focus to stop herself from crying.

When they rejoined the road to Gordium, her pain slowly twisted into anger. Yes, they had needed supplies, but it was no coincidence they'd stopped at the village where Verin lived. She narrowed her eyes at Denisia's back, a new hatred seething in her chest. The goddess had done it on purpose, she was certain. She'd wanted to weaken Little Bird once more, to strip away her strength so she'd be easier to control.

Little Bird spent the rest of the ride consumed by rage. Part of her wanted to turn and flee, but she had nowhere to go. Better to wait until they reached the city. There, she would pretend to help Denisia. She would find Katiah's tomb. She would try to free her. And then somehow, some way, she would make Denisia pay.

CHAPTER

FORTY-FIVE

696 BC
Gordium, Capital City of Phrygia

Aster stuffed clean clothes into his travel bag.

"You can't leave," Xander said from his side of the room. He sat in his chair, unable to think of anything else to do. Gediz remained in his bed.

"She is not out there by herself," Aster said.

"She's smart and resourceful. She'll be back soon."

"Did you not see the look on the king's face? She would be welcomed here if she returned."

"Certainly he wouldn't forbid her from entering?" Xander said.

Aster huffed his frustration. "Of course not. She has not stayed away this long to admire the city."

Xander glanced at Gediz, but the curly-headed advisor seemed unfazed, focused on a handful of nuts. "Can't you wait until morning?" Xander asked.

"I'll get a grand night's sleep," Aster said. "Have a hearty breakfast and then meander about at my leisure. If the nomads don't kidnap the princess in the meantime, blessed be!"

"But we must release the dark goddess!" Xander said. "Remember what the king ordered?"

"That is not *your* job," Aster said, giving him a stern glance. "You did not bring it up."

"It wasn't *my* idea." Xander played with the rock in his hands. It had cooled since he'd talked to the king, but it still glowed a dim red. "The king told *you* to gather the princess' engineers and—"

"I'm not delegating that job to you." Aster tossed the bag over his shoulder and threw on his leather cloak. "You do not have Matar's essence with you. And of course, the great Gediz." He gestured to Gediz with a flourishing hand. "I trust the two of you will not figure it out."

"The two of . . ." Xander sputtered. "You don't expect *him* to be of much help?"

"Who was it that got you to Acharaca?" Gediz snarled.

"And has been useless ever since!" Xander snapped in a rare moment of irritation. "Do you have expertise in releasing a goddess from a tomb you've failed to share with us?"

Gediz glared at him.

"I do not have every faith in you," Aster said as he headed for the door. "And you are right. The king did not order it."

Xander hurried after Aster. "Are you sure about this?"

"I am happy to leave her out there alone."

"But what if the king asks for you?"

"He has been most concerned about our whereabouts lately."

"He could be feeling better tomorrow."

Aster paused and dropped his gaze. "He is getting better," he said sadly. "He is much better than he was when we left."

Xander chewed on his tongue. It was true. The king was much worse. "I hate the idea of doing this without you."

Aster placed a hand on his shoulder. "I will not return as soon as I have her."

"But if she can't come back into the castle?"

Aster pursed his lips. "I will not get word to you. It will not be all right." He looked into Xander's eyes and lowered his voice. "The rock. It is powerless. Do not use it."

"But setting the dark goddess free." Xander shook his head. "That can't be wise?"

"It has not been twenty years," Aster said, glancing back toward his corner of the room. "Many things have stayed the same. Perhaps it is not time."

"It could be a trick," Xander said. "What if this Matar is one of *Katiah's* followers?"

Aster raised an eyebrow. "It is not up to you. You must not decide."

"Me?" Xander said. "Why must it be up to me?"

"You are not the one she's talking to."

"But . . ."

Aster patted Xander on the cheek and walked out.

Xander lingered at the door, feeling lost. When his fatigue returned, he walked back to his side of the room, laid down, and closed his eyes. His own bed. So long he had waited for it. He had to talk to Zoe's engineers, and he was worried about Aster and the princess, but at the moment, Gediz was blissfully quiet. Xander sank into the blankets and rested.

He had been asleep only a short time before he entered the dream. He was walking through the castle with one of Pembe's berry muffins in hand, on his way to meet the princess. There was so much to tell her. The thought excited him and he broke into a jog, then burst through the double doors onto the stone landing outside. His cheerful expression vanished. The air was thick with smoke. All around him, the castle grounds were burning. He called for the princess, then for Aster. No answer. He was still calling when out of the smoky fog, a Gimirri soldier emerged on a black horse, heavy armor covering his chest. He let out a war cry and hurled an ax. Xander screamed . . .

"For the sake of the gods, stop that infernal noise!"

Xander jerked awake. He was back in his room. Heart pounding, he pressed his hand to his chest. No ax blade. But then, from somewhere nearby, a low hum. He checked the nightstand. The rock was glowing a bright red, visibly pulsing. Leaning in, he heard it clearly now: a hum, steady and soft, like the buzz of a bee.

"Come," he said, getting off the bed. "We must release Katiah now."

"It is impossible." Gediz looked up lazily. "You cannot break her free of the gold, no matter what the king thinks the princess' engineers can do."

Xander reached for his napkin and picked up the rock. It was hot even inside the cloth. He dumped it quickly into his pocket. "Nothing is impossible with Matar," he said, his words rushing out unbidden. "Come. We must hurry!" He ran out the door, unaware that Gediz wasn't following.

ZOE WATCHED Elanur walk through the castle gates. It had been difficult to explain why she couldn't go with her. She had another important task to complete, she'd said. It was the only way to get her father's sister to leave her behind. Elanur waved from the other side, and the gates closed behind her.

Zoe retreated over the rise. Once out of sight of the castle, she paused and rested. Her father's sister, here! She wished she could see his face when he saw her standing there in front of him. He might not even believe she was real. Zoe regretted not insisting the guard take Elanur to the king immediately, but it was too late now. She needed to check on Kiral's progress.

She resumed her journey, pulling her moose cloak about her. A harsh wind blew from the east, driving the rain clouds with it. As she approached the end of the narrow alleyway, she was so lost in her thoughts that she didn't notice Greasy Hair and Scarface had stepped away from their places and were circling around behind her. She had started up the steps when four meaty hands seized her.

"Hey," she said, wriggling. "I'm Princess Zoe. Remember? I need to see Kiral."

"We know who you are." Greasy Hair jerked her inside.

"Get off me!"

Like beasts, they dragged her into the room where she'd met with Kiral the day before. She struggled against them, shouting about how a princess should be treated, but the men dropped her to her knees. She looked up.

The room was full of warriors. The sight of them stole every word from Zoe's mouth. They stood rigid and fierce, leather armor over their chests, metal belts at their waists. Gimirri warriors! In Kiral's dwelling?

She scanned their faces, searching for Kiral, and found him in the same chair as before, seated in front of the fire pit. He was a muscular man, but beside the Gimirri, he looked almost small. As she checked the others, she recognized one. A jolt of fear slashed through her chest. The leader, the one who had whispered in her ear.

Ilker.

"Come to visit me, Princess?" Kiral's eyes shifted nervously. It seemed he hadn't expected the Gimirri either.

"These men murdered our people," Zoe said, fighting to keep the tremor out of her voice. "You allow them into your dwelling?"

Kiral cast an uncomfortable look behind him. "I was presented with two, shall we say, unsavory choices. I chose the one that seemed wisest under the circumstances."

"I was told you were a man who commanded respect," Zoe said. "It seems I was misled."

"Princess." Ilker stepped forward. "I am glad we meet again."

Zoe shifted her gaze to the handsome nomad. "I wished never again to lay eyes on you."

Ilker acknowledged this with a tuck of his chin.

Zoe turned her attention back to Kiral. "Why are these men here?"

"They wish to strike a deal with you."

"They tried that already."

"We try again." Ilker took another step forward so that he stood beside Kiral. Zoe tried to stand up, but Greasy Hair and Scarface held her down until Ilker gestured for them to release her. "Would it not be better," he said, opening his hands, "to talk?"

"You do not wish to talk," she said, straightening her cloak. "You wish for conquest."

"Would you wish for war?"

"You left us no choice."

"I give choice now. Grant my people what we need."

"There is no end to what you need. You told me as much."

He cocked his head to the side.

"You will not be satisfied with one or twenty chests of gold. It matters not what we give you. So we will give you nothing."

Ilker studied her, his brown eyes intense under a firm brow. "One so brave is rare. I shall not relish seeing you fall." He gave Kiral a subtle nod and exited the room, his other warriors following, their heavy heels thudding across the floor.

"They are murderers!" Zoe hissed at Kiral. "You must let me go, that I may warn the king."

Kiral stood up and nodded for his guards to seize her again. "You will remain here." He started to walk past her, following the Gimirri.

"You cannot just keep me here!" Zoe said.

"It is part of the deal," Kiral said.

"What deal? *We* made a deal!"

Kiral paused in the doorway. "As I said, Princess. The better of the two choices." He glanced over his shoulder apologetically, then disappeared.

"Traitor!" Zoe yelled. "The king will have your head!" She fought against them, but they dragged her easily into the main room and sat her down in a chair in the corner. While Greasy Hair held her, Scarhead tied her hands and feet. They then returned to their post by the door.

"Kiral!" she shouted. "Kiral, you can't do this! They are murderers. You are betraying your king. Kiral!" She shouted until her voice went hoarse and then shouted some more, but no one responded. When she finally fell silent, she wanted nothing more than to cry, but she would not give them that satisfaction. She set her jaw and prayed to the gods that Elanur would get through to her father. If she managed to warn him, perhaps he might still defeat the invaders. Though it seemed hopeless now. There was no army and no citizen force. Only the guards. And the Gimirri were already here.

When she had calmed some, she lifted her head to look around the room—and froze. A body lay crumpled against the north wall. *No.* She blinked and looked again. "Rastus?" It came out like a whimper. He didn't respond. Dried blood covered his shirt, his blond hair splayed against the wall, his head drooped toward his shoulder, vacant eyes staring toward the back of the room.

Tears fell down Zoe's cheeks. Rastus. Dear, loyal Rastus. He didn't deserve this. Worse, it was her fault. *Aster,* she thought. *Oh Aster. Where are you?*

Aster sat up and rubbed his arms. It was morning, and he was on a rise at the west edge of the city. The night before, he'd walked up and down every road and hadn't found the princess. He'd thought about asking some citizens if they'd seen her, but he knew she wouldn't like that. If she hadn't already made herself known, she probably wanted to remain concealed. It was his duty to respect her wishes, but a shadow of anxiety gnawed at the back of his mind. It wasn't like Zoe to disappear. The king hadn't given her much of a choice, but that didn't make him feel any better.

The sun hid behind a thick layer of clouds, casting a gray light onto the city below. Most of the dwellings lay quiet with slumber. Aster battled with himself. He could try walking around again, but his concern was growing, a strange urgency upon him. He decided to go to the market. Perhaps he would ask after the princess there.

He walked with a stern gaze, searching for a head of blonde hair, listening for a smooth feminine voice. Soon he reached the intersection between the narrow path he'd been on and Market Street. He paused, surveying the area. Footsteps approached from the left. Turning, he spotted a man walking east up a small alleyway between the dwellings. Nerves pricked his skin. On impulse, he followed.

The man wore a heavy cloak made of an atypical hide. Black and silver—wolf, perhaps? He was bulky with broad shoulders and thick legs, which wouldn't be unusual on its own, but the cloak billowed around his middle, as if it were hiding a weapon at the belt line. Many traders carried weapons. But as Aster followed, he became convinced that this stranger was not from Gordium. The man moved with a smooth grace, but covered a lot of ground in a short amount of time. Aster had to hurry to keep up.

They followed the narrow path to the last dwelling before the east wall. Aster passed by casually as the man slipped inside, then doubled back. Seeing no movement, he checked his belt for his dagger, pulled his hood up, and waited. A gruff voice spoke from within, the words in a strange language. Dread crept up Aster's spine. Foreigners weren't uncommon in the city, but he was familiar with the tongues of Phrygia, neighboring Lydia, and Assyria. This was something else—short, spat-out syllables broken by longer, open-mouthed sounds.

Another man spoke, his voice softer. Aster shuffled closer. The gruff voice answered. Aster caught a single word: *Princess.* Blood drained to his feet. The softer voice responded, followed by a third man chiming in. Aster fingered his dagger. One against three. He'd managed that before. But then, he'd been a lot younger. More conversation followed, punctured by murmurs of approval. Aster peered through the window but could make out only bulky shapes. They must have the princess, but not here, not in this dwelling. He considers his options, few as they were. He couldn't storm in and demand answers, nor could he pass himself off as one of them.

He glanced around and, seeing no one, jogged off, his thoughts churning like a storm. Back on the main road, he looked both ways. The Gimirri could be holding Zoe in any dwelling across the city. A cold breeze stung his cheeks. His duty was clear—return to the castle and report to the king what he had heard. He wanted to believe the news might rouse King Midas from his melancholy, but he doubted it would. He could fetch Xander, but that would do little to solve either problem—finding Zoe or fending off the attack he knew was coming. He could tell Baran, but the high commander wouldn't act without the king's order. The more Aster considered it, the more certain he became: he had only one option. He had to find Zoe.

He scanned his surroundings once more, then turned south. He'd head back to Market Street and ask around. Someone had to have seen something. His pace quickened, tension coiling at the base of his spine like a tightening knot.

Looking out onto the rear grounds of the castle, the last thing Xander wanted to do was venture into the icy wind, but the stone pulled at him with a powerful force. Wrapped in his napkin and clenched in his fist, it lifted his arm, guiding it toward Katiah's tomb. Matar's magic and the king's command urged him forward. With a groan, he hefted his cloak over his shoulders and stepped outside.

A sharp hiss stopped him. He spun to his right, holding his breath for several long moments. Then, another hiss, this time from the north side. A curl of smoke rose from the ground beside an arrow jutting up from the earth. He pressed himself against the castle wall and waited. Just as he was about to move again, a third hiss caught his ear. This time, the arrow sparked, a small flame flaring briefly before flickering out.

A line of sweat ran down his ribs. The warriors were here, and they were attacking the castle.

He stared down at the rock. Bright red and pulsing, it seemed almost alive. Another arrow landed on the ground, closer this time. Suddenly, the gate in the west wall creaked open, drawing his attention. Commander Baran and two guards rushed through, securing it behind them. Xander felt a moment's relief. The commander would protect them.

"Did you see the arrows?" he asked as they approached. "Someone is shooting them over the wall."

They rushed past him, their footsteps echoing down the stone hallway. "Where is the king?" Baran called over his shoulder.

"In his chamber, I think?" Xander called.

"Bolt the door!" Baran called. "And where's the commander of the king's guard?"

Xander went blank. Where was Rastus? "I don't know?"

They disappeared around the corner. Xander hesitated. He should go after them. Tell the king what he'd seen. He turned to do just that, but after a single step, he couldn't move any farther. He tried to lift his leg, but it felt like a stone. Glancing down, he saw nothing unusual. His feet looked the same. The rock throbbed in his hand, its light nearly blinding.

"Very well," he said, turning around. Instantly, his legs obeyed. His dagger was still in his room, but there was no time to retrieve it. He threw his hood over his head and sprinted through the doors, racing across the castle grounds toward the secret tunnel.

CHAPTER

FORTY-SIX

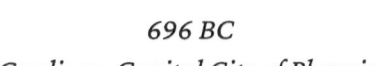

696 BC
Gordium, Capital City of Phrygia

A line of uneven structures crested the horizon, their outlines hazy in the distance. The city of Gordium. Little Bird almost didn't recognize it. It looked nothing like the shining city under the sun that she remembered from so long ago. Back then, she had been traveling to a new land with Emir. Now she was a prisoner, marching forth to free the dark goddess. The only thing that gave her some comfort was the presence of Nightsky. She had seen him that morning pecking at the ground near where they'd camped for the night.

After an extensive interrogation, helped along by Denisia's powers, the bridge guards granted them passage, the goddess palming the stained red stone that would permit entry through Gordium's gates. The Sangarius River flowed choppy and cold, dark mud lining its banks. The horses' breath fogged the air as they started down the gradual incline that would take them to the city itself. Little Bird remembered a big crowd before, but now there were only a few travelers. Denisia, in her eagerness, trotted past them. At the gates, the guards allowed them in, quickly securing the entrance behind them. Little Bird glanced back, puzzled. She had remembered a friendlier welcome before.

Denisia led them up the road until they reached the first intersection. The castle beckoned on the right, Little Bird longing to nudge her mare into a gallop, but the goddess had her under her stern gaze.

"This way," she said.

They continued straight, headed toward the west gates. They had just started up the hill when a woman screamed. A flame burst from a mudbrick shelter below. Within moments, it grew into a full-fledged fire, devouring the thatched roof.

"Come." Denisia hurried forward, Chetin behind her. Little Bird heard another scream. A second fire erupted from a dwelling near the fields. A group of people ran out, including two children. One of them fell, an arrow sticking out of her back. In the time it took them to reach the west gates, three more fires broke out, plumes of smoke rising through the cold air. Chetin took the lead, but the guards refused to let them through. He tried to convince them they were simple travelers, but the guards explained they had to keep the gates closed when there was any suspicion of an attack.

Denisia huddled with the other two, fuming. It would take too long to go back to the east gates and around the city to the north, where the tomb was. More people screamed, a nervous anticipation in the air. Nearby, another shelter caught fire. The horses snorted nervously. Little Bird couldn't see any attackers, yet the fires were multiplying as if by magic.

Denisia dismounted, stood in the middle of the road, and started to dance. She swept her arms in a fluid motion and, almost without notice, slipped one hand inside her cloak and emerged with what Little Bird would have called a wand. It was wrapped in vines, what appeared to be a pine cone on the top. She used it to accentuate her movements, at one point taking off her boots and continuing in her bare feet. The guards kept their swords raised, but it was clear they were entranced. When she got close enough, she gave a flourish of her wand and a sprinkle of crimson dust floated into the air over the guards' heads. By the time it settled, they had fallen onto the ground, their eyes dazed as they gazed up at the thick gray clouds.

Denisia ascended to the top of the gate tower, flicked the wand into the window, and waited until the guard fell. Then she slipped inside and pulled the rope. With Chetin's help from below, they opened the gate.

Little Bird rode through, Chetin behind her. He paused on the other side, waiting for Denisia to join them, but Little Bird kept going, for as soon as she passed through the gates, a powerful feeling possessed her. Gripping the mare's girth between her knees, she set off at a canter. The city of Gordium was under attack. King Midas and Princess Zoe might be in danger. Little Bird didn't know how to help them, but something ancient stirred within her, rising like flame in her blood.

This way. Hurry!

IT WAS near midday and Elanur was waiting in one of King Midas' guest rooms when heavy footsteps passed in the hallway. She pressed her ear against the door. There was a guard outside. She didn't wish to speak to him, but her curiosity was too great. She opened the door, her excuses ready, but the guard was gone and the hallway, empty. She hesitated another moment, then tiptoed out.

At the main hall, she turned left and ran until she found the stairwell. She paused at the second level, but found no one. She continued on up and had almost reached the third level when she heard voices. Peering around the corner, she spotted three men in uniforms outside of the first room on the left. They were talking to two guards.

" . . . we are under attack," an older, portly man said. "We must speak to the king."

"He will see no one right now," the guard on the right said.

"We are under attack. The warriors are here. We must know what His Majesty's orders are."

Warriors are here? Elanur thought. *Already?*

"He ordered us to let no one in," the first guard said.

Elanur ducked back into the stairwell. So this is why she had been left waiting. The king was refusing to see anyone. Even his sister. She swallowed past a tight throat and peered out again.

The man who had been doing all the talking—a commander, perhaps?—turned to his companions. They spoke together in hushed voices. When they finished, the commander observed the door, as if trying to judge just how stout it was. Suddenly, he yelled out, "King Midas! It is Commander Baran. We are under attack! We must speak with you!"

Both door guards unsheathed their swords. The commander and his companions stepped back, but Baran didn't stop yelling.

"Your Majesty! The warriors are here! The castle is under attack."

Elanur held her breath. Would the king's men fight one another? Then came the click of a latch. The door squeaked open and an old man emerged. He wore a long tunic, moccasins, and a maroon robe over his shoulders. His hair stuck up in the back and his eyes drooped. Elanur frowned. Was this the king? Could this be . . . her brother?

"Your Highness." Baran's company dropped to their knees, while the two guards sheathed their swords and took their places on either side of the door.

"What do you want, Baran?" The man's voice was gravelly, as if he had just woken up.

"The warriors, Your Majesty," Baran said. "They are here. We are under attack. How shall we respond?"

"How many?" Midas asked.

Baran looked to the man on his right. "We don't know yet. We came to you the moment we realized their presence."

"Come back when you have more information." The king flipped his hand, dismissing them.

"They are attacking the castle, Your Highness!" Baran said. "Shooting arrows of flame over the wall."

"Is there a fire?" Midas asked, his tone edged with indifference.

"Not yet. But—"

"Send scouts. Report back."

"But Your Majesty!"

"You have your orders."

The men stared after him. One of the king's guards reached for the door. He was going to close it. On impulse, Elanur bolted forward. She ran as fast as she had ever run, her eyes on that space of darkness that was her brother's room. She made it past the three armed men, and when the two guards drew their swords, she dropped to her hip and slid underneath them. When she stopped, she was inside the room.

"Karem!" she shouted. "Karem, it's me! Elanur. Karem. It's me!" The guards seized her arms, one on each side. They were pulling her out. She kicked and wriggled. "Karem! It's your sister, Elanur! I've come back. Karem!" She saw only faint candlelight. "King Midas! King Sargon let me go. I have returned. I am Elanur. Karem, I am Elanur! For our mother's sake, listen to me!"

They dragged her into the hall. Elanur stared into the darkness, her chest heaving with breath. "Karem?" The two men got her up on her feet, then one left her in the care of the other while he went forward to close the door. Behind her, Baran and his companions remained, observing it all with surprised expressions.

The door was closing.

"Wait."

King Midas emerged from the dark. He was squinting, the light in the hall too much for him. Pausing, he looked at her. He seemed so much older than when she'd seen him at the Battle of Karama. It was hard to tell he was even the same man. "The doll," she said. "Sunshine. You brought her to the battle, remember? You kept her all those years. From when we were children."

Many moments passed, Midas staring at her with a dull gaze.

"Elanur played with the doll on the yellow blanket," he said. "Mother made the yellow blanket."

"Dear mother." She paused. "He stole me. King Sargon. I don't remember that. But you remember, don't you?"

His gaze drifted to some unknown place in front of him. "I tried to get her back. For years, I tried."

"Remember the Battle of Karama? They told me my parents didn't want me. That they abandoned me. When I saw you there . . . you spoke of the doll, and I knew then that they had lied. Because of you, Karem, I knew I had been loved."

His eyes turned red. Elanur tried to go to him, but the guards held her fast. "Please," she said to them. "I am his sister. I am Elanur."

Midas wiped his cheek, sniffed, and turned around. "Give her the princess' room," he said, and once more retreated into the darkness.

"Karem!" she shouted after him. "I am familiar with these warriors. I can help."

"My guards will take care of it," he said in a distant voice.

"You must give them the order! Let them fight!"

"Fighting brings nothing but death," he said.

"Karem! Please!"

The guards took her back to the stairwell. She called all the way down the stairs, but her brother never responded. Indeed, it was as if he wasn't her brother at all, but a ghost that had been left behind.

THE SMOKE WAS Zoe's first clue that the attack had begun. It was midafternoon, the sun's gray light shining through the cracks in the closed shutter over the one window at her left. Kiral hadn't returned, but she assumed the two guards remained by the door.

She jerked against the ropes. Her wrists were sore from her efforts, her ankles rubbed raw. She wondered how she could have been so blind as to the sort of man Kiral was. If Ilker had threatened the man's family—those two girls?—perhaps he hadn't had a choice.

She questioned how Ilker had known to target him. A hollow ache opened in her gut. One of his spies must have followed her. *She* had led Ilker here. *She* had gotten Rastus killed. She glanced over at his body.

"I apologize, Rastus," she said. "It was my fault. You deserved so much more."

She cried quietly for a while, wiping her tears on her shoulder. The stench of the smoke grew more potent in her nostrils. She had to stop thinking about things outside of her control. She lowered her head. What would Aster say? She imagined the advisor sitting in front of her.

I'm trapped, and the city needs me. What should I do?

You must not use your wits, Aster said in her mind.

How?

They are not men. They may not have families.

Zoe lifted her gaze to the doorway. Greasy Hair was muscular and smelly. Scarhead was a monster of a man. She had no chance against either of them.

"Hello?" she called in her sweetest voice. "Please. May I speak to you? I'm all alone in here." She waited. Nothing happened. "Hello? Is anyone here?" She raised her voice. "Hello! Can you help me? Please. Help me!" She yelled the last sentence with all her might. "I am the princess! Someone please help me! I'm trapped in here! The warriors have captured me. Please, can someone save—"

The door slammed open and Scarhead thundered in. "Be quiet," he said, coming to a rumbling stop in front of her.

She glanced past him, but there was no sign of Greasy Hair. "Please," she said, trying to smile at him. "These ropes are hurting me. And I smell smoke. I'm frightened."

He looked her over. "You are well."

"But I can't feel my fingers. Might you loosen the rope? I will not escape. You are here. Do they not trust you to guard me?" When he said nothing, she went on. "I cannot harm you. I am a small woman, and I'm afraid one of those fires is going to spread over here."

"They will not set a fire here."

"But one of the fires might blow this way. Are you certain we're safe?"

"You are safe."

She smiled. "I'm glad of that. Would you mind untying me? My hands hurt so much." She was repeating herself, but with this man, it seemed like the right move. "I don't know what I'll do if I can't use my hands. I make things. Like the water storage system. You are aware of that, aren't you? I worked with my engineers to design that. Might you have assisted us on that project?"

He shook his head.

"That's unfortunate. I'm certain you would be a valuable worker, being so muscular. If you had come by the castle gates, we could have found a position for you." She watched him. "If you set me free now, the king would reward you handsomely."

"Kiral said to keep you here."

"And you listen to Kiral?"

"He is the leader."

"He takes care of you?"

Scarhead blinked.

"If you work for the king, you shall never want for anything again. He will give you food and shelter. He will provide for your family. Do you have a family?"

"A mate."

"How lovely!" She flashed a brilliant smile. "What is her name?"

"Lina."

"Lina." She savored the name. "Is she beautiful?"

"Yes."

Zoe smiled again. One thing seemed evident: this was not a cruel man. "Where is Lina now? Is she safe?"

"Our home."

"But where is that?"

He glanced toward the door.

"Will her home be burned by fire?"

"They will not burn my home."

"Not on purpose. But what if the fire from the other homes blows into her home? Will she be safe?"

He looked into her eyes, then out the door. "Kiral said she would not be harmed."

"Kiral would not want to harm her. But what about the warriors? Do they know where she lives? Will they keep her safe?" He watched her with a dull gaze. "She trusts you to take care of her. But you are not there. You are here. She might be in danger. Can you smell the smoke? The fires are growing. The warriors want to burn down the city."

"They want to defeat the king."

She softened her voice. "Are you keeping Lina safe? If she calls for you, will you hear her?"

His expression turned distraught. "He said to keep you here."

She looked down at herself. "I am tied to this chair. I can't go anywhere. Go check on Lina. I will be here when you return."

"You will try to escape."

She pulled against her ropes. "I cannot. I am trapped." She glanced toward the door. "More smoke. Can you smell it? How far away is your home?"

"Not far."

"Please, go. I don't want anything to happen to Lina. I am the princess. Every citizen of Gordium is important to me. You can't let something happen to her."

As if on cue, a woman screamed. It was enough. "Stay there." Scarhead pointed a thick finger at her, then stormed out the door.

Zoe smiled to herself. One point for wits. Yet she was still tied to the chair. She waited until she thought Scarhead was out of earshot, then called again. "Please, can someone help me? Is anyone out there? I am Princess Zoe. I am trapped in here! Please, anyone?"

CHAPTER
FORTY-SEVEN

696 BC
Gordium, Capital City of Phrygia

B y the time Xander got to Katiah's tomb, it seemed half the city was on fire. Smoke darkened the south side, new tendrils growing up like weeds while the shouts and cries of the people filled the air. He feared for Aster, worried he was caught in the chaos, or worse, that he'd already met one of the warriors. But his friend was a savvy warrior himself. Xander prayed they would see each other soon. He chafed at the thought of Gediz, sitting in their room safe and comfortable. Truly, he was no king's advisor.

He clutched his cloak around him and dropped the rock in his pocket. Before he lifted the slab to open the tomb entrance, he cast one last look about to be sure he was alone. At first he believed he was, but then he noticed three riders coming from the south. They didn't look like warriors. Citizens fleeing, more likely. Concerning, but he doubted they'd be looking for the tomb. Even if they were, his spell would keep them from finding it.

He slid the slab aside, descended the stairs, pulled the key from his pocket, and unlocked the wooden door. Pulling it open, he studied the stone wall. The crack remained, but it seemed no worse than when he and Aster had found it before. Puzzling. The rock had compelled him here, but the tomb looked unscathed. He stared at it, frowning.

Then his pocket erupted in flames.

"Ah!" He jumped back, his mouth agape, as the fire surged, licking its way toward his chest. He yanked the cloak from his shoulders and stomped on it until the flames died. Even as the smoke curled upward, he kept stomping—he didn't need a smoke trail giving away his position. When the cloak finally lay crumpled and dirt-streaked, he cautiously pick it up. The rock slipped through a charred hole and thudded to the ground, bright red and throbbing.

"Well, if it isn't the king's bumbling advisor."

Xander looked up, startled. Two faces lingered above him. One he recognized immediately. The goddess Denisia. His stomach sank at the sight of her. She seemed the same, though somewhat older. The other face belonged to a young woman. Her hood covered her hair, but she had deep brown eyes, a slender nose, and full, pouty lips. Something about her seemed familiar, but he couldn't place it.

"Goddess Denisia," he said, with a slight bow of his head, wondering how she had found her way past his spell. "It has been a long time."

"I didn't miss you," she said, "or your weak, traitorous king."

Xander wanted to say he felt the same, but the goddess was powerful. He didn't wish to be turned into a tree or whatever might strike her fancy. "Why are you here?" he asked, glancing at the young woman.

"It is time for my sister to be released."

"I would have thought you'd be glad to have her locked away."

"For a time, perhaps. But things change. Your city is under attack. Your beloved king, powerless."

"It seems you had something to do with that?"

"Less than he deserved," she said with a flash of anger in her eyes. "Now he will meet justice."

"You mean to harm him again?"

"As before, he has brought about his own demise. Leaving me to my first priority."

Xander glanced back at the tomb.

"We will free her, and there's nothing you can do about it. As you can see, we made it past your silly hiding spell this time." She cast a proud glance at the young woman. "I suggest you return to your precious king. Perhaps you can comfort him in his last moments."

Xander bit his tongue. The young woman was staring at him. Not just looking, as any stranger would, but staring, as if she too found something familiar about him. Perhaps she was another goddess with powers, if she had led Denisia past his spell? "I'll be glad to go," he said, "but my king has ordered me here."

Denisia raised an eyebrow.

"He also wants the dark goddess released." The rock was sliding toward the stone. Xander moved to stand in front of it.

"Then my efforts were not all wasted." Denisia came down the stairs, the young woman on her heels. Noting the open door, she stepped past Xander, grabbed the young woman's arm, and shoved her rudely toward the stone. Her palms flat on the rock, the young woman lowered her head. For a long while, she stood frozen. The goddess waited behind her, impatiently turning this way and that. Xander eyed the rock. It was still sliding toward the tomb, crawling like a mouse behind Denisia.

"Try again!" Denisia barked at the young woman, then to Xander, "Get out!"

Xander tried to step back, but it was as if he and the rock were connected—for now he too was drawn toward the tomb. Even as the young woman squinted her eyes shut in concentration, Xander stumbled past Denisia and ended up flattened against the stone like a squashed bug, the rock glowing at his feet. Denisia ordered him to move. He tried to explain that he could not, but with his cheek

371

pressed against the tomb, it was hard to talk. The goddess threatened him with her wrath.

Then the ground started to rumble.

ASTER SEARCHED ALL MORNING. He had no luck until he met Baki, the cloak merchant and owner of the inn. Through a struggling conversation, Aster managed to get his message across. Baki told him about the princess and another traveling woman who had been there for breakfast, after which they had left for the castle.

Aster hurried back to the castle gates. The older guard told him that Princess Zoe had brought another woman early that morning, but then had left again. Discouraged, Aster returned to the city. When the plumes of smoke rose into the sky, he grew alarmed. Jogging, he searched from road to road, calling for Zoe. When that didn't work, he went back to Baki's place. It was painful for both of them, trying to communicate, but finally Baki relayed the news of the princess' meeting the day before with a man named Kiral Polat.

"You must not tell me where he is," Aster said.

Baki frowned, puzzled.

"Where?" Aster tried.

Baki told him.

Aster ran all the way back across the city. This time, it was like running against a powerful current. Citizens packed the roads and alleyways, families taking what they could carry in sacks, some pulling carts behind them, all flowing toward the west gates. The smoke had intensified, more gray plumes ribboning into the sky. Shouts and war cries sliced through the air, dwelling after dwelling on fire. Twice he spotted the nomads on horseback, swinging their swords left and right. He heard screams and cries, and even saw men fighting from the ground, men that were soon killed. It was difficult not to step in to assist, but with every sign of chaos, he grew more intent on his goal: he had to find the princess.

He slowed as he reached the northeastern corner once more. This time, instead of following the main castle road, he turned right on the last pathway between the dwellings. Here, it was quiet. No warriors. No fires. He moved toward the east wall, his gaze alert, when he heard a woman calling. The princess! He followed the voice, approaching the last dwelling on the left. Crouched low, he reached the door and peered inside. No guards. He stepped through and turned right. Spotting the princess tied to the chair, he ran and dropped to her side.

"Aster!"

He wrapped his arms around her. Inappropriate, but he couldn't help it. She rested her head on his shoulder.

"I'm so glad to see you!" she said.

For the briefest of moments, it was just the two of them. Aster's chest heaved with breath, his heart warm with gratitude. The princess was all right. Zoe was safe.

"Hurry," she whispered. "He will be back."

Aster cut her loose. She looked at him with loving eyes, then hugged him once more. "You've returned," she said.

"I have not."

She released him, her expression changing to one of worry. "They're attacking the city! I was trying to help, but I was stupid."

"It matters greatly now."

She stood up and shook the circulation back into her legs and hands. "Come." She started for the door, then paused and looked right.

Aster followed her gaze. A cold shiver ran down his spine. Rastus! "They did not do this?" he asked as he kneeled by the commander's side.

"He was helping me." Zoe's lip trembled.

Aster closed Rastus' stale eyes, pulled the king's ring from his finger, and tucked it into his own pocket. "When this is over," he said, "we will not come back and give him a proper burial." He gazed at the brave man's face, then grabbed Zoe's hand and pulled her toward the door. With no one in sight, they ducked out and made their way from one dwelling to the other, Aster on guard, Zoe's hood over her head. When they reached Castle Road, they bolted toward the gates. They had almost reached them when Aster snatched Zoe's arm, halting her.

"We must hurry!" she said.

"Do not look there," he hissed.

She followed his line of sight. The two gate guards lay flat in the dirt, unmoving. Above them, the tower window was empty.

The gates were open.

ELANUR PACED in front of the window. Everything in the room reflected the princess' beauty, from her wardrobe full of dresses to the many trinkets she kept on her shelves, to the painting of the queen on the west wall. The room smelled nice too, like roses and fresh air, which is what had inspired Elanur to open the shutters. She scanned the castle grounds, taking in the beautiful statue of Prince Anchurus to her right, the wide expanse of open space between the castle and the wall beyond, and the child's play area on her left. In the distance, she could see the smoke in the city, but the castle gates were securely closed.

She was safe for the moment. But what about Zoe?

She asked the guard if she may see the king again, but he wouldn't budge. So, she returned to the window. She was leaning against the side of it when she saw someone hurrying toward the gates. A small man with curly hair, he wore a long, official-looking robe. One of King Midas' men? But he wasn't a guard. She watched as he approached the gates, then shouted at the tower guard. The guard responded, then stiffened and fell.

Elanur blinked. It appeared as if the guard had been shot with an arrow.

The small man slipped through the tower door below. Soon he appeared at the top and seemed to work on something. After a moment, Elanur caught movement in the bolt that held the gates closed. She stared. Indeed, the bolt was moving, receding to the far side. Eventually, it slid far enough to no longer hold the gates fast. The little man reappeared below. Grasping the gate handle on one side, he pulled it back. It took him considerable effort. Straining, his heels digging into the dirt, he tugged until the gate slid open far enough to create a small crack.

The smell of smoke drew Elanur's gaze to the right. Plumes of blackish gray wafted into the air from various points to the south. Human voices called to one another. She turned back to see six men stream in through the opening in the gate. She blinked, then looked again.

The Gimirri warriors! They entered the castle grounds, Ilker in the lead with Kerkin right behind him. Khogu, Draris, Thom, and Mitin came too. As they passed the little man with the curly hair, Draris stabbed him in the chest. He fell hard to the ground.

Elanur sucked in her breath and leaned back. They were *here*. One of the king's men had foolishly let them in. She turned toward the door, for she knew: they were coming to get Karem.

"ARE YOU THERE, LITTLE BIRD?" Katiah asked. "Something is happening."

Little Bird felt the trembling in the earth beneath her feet. She thought at first it was Denisia's doing, but then she saw Xander struggling.

"Something's moving," Katiah's voice said in her head. "It's getting hotter."

Little Bird stood back. *I'm here.*

"How did you find me?"

Denisia brought me. She wants you freed.

"Denisia!" Katiah exclaimed. The ground rumbled again.

"It's hot!" Xander cried.

She wants me to free you, Little Bird said in her mind, *but I don't know how.*

"Why would she think you would?"

She knew. A connection between us.

"Knew? What do you mean?"

She took me. After the Battle of Karama.

"Took you?"

Stole.

Katiah was silent for a moment. "How long has it been?"

Twenty years. Little Bird wanted to say more, but the ground felt unstable, the tomb vibrating under her hands.

"Help me!" Xander was flattened against the rock, one hand reaching out, fingers splayed. Little Bird reached back.

"Leave him!" Denisia slapped her hand away.

The rumbling grew louder, like a thousand drums beating in a dreadful crescendo. Suddenly, its power erupted from underneath the tomb, catapulting Little Bird, Denisia, and Xander onto the hillside in a grand explosion. Rocks, shards of stone, and clumps of dirt rained down, a giant plume of smoke billowing into the air. Many moments later, everything settled.

Little Bird got up slowly, rubbing her hip where she had landed. The other two followed, Denisia seemingly unharmed, Xander groaning. One by one, they peered into the void.

The tomb had disintegrated. At the center of the rubble stood a golden statue: Katiah, Midas' sword still buried in her stomach.

In the deep, dark underworld

EMIR HAD NEVER BEEN SO hot. He was amazed his flesh hadn't blistered. It looked the same as it always, sweat pouring off him in streams. His thirst deepened, his throat and chest on fire. His tongue felt three times its normal size. The surrounding rock glowed a bright, pulsing red. The tunnel was narrowing. There was something different up ahead. There had to be. He kept walking.

Will you be satisfied with nothing less than a pile of ash? Darko asked.

Emir ignored him. It was taking every drop of his willpower to keep going. Yet he knew if he turned around, he would be lost to the tunnels forever, doomed to wander the cold underground for eternity, a hollow, nameless shadow in the dark, a demon unlike any other ever known, a black and menacing plague upon the underworld.

He bent his mind to moving forward. One foot in front of the other. He put himself in such a deep state of focus that at times, he could forget how thirsty he was or how much the heat pained his skin and return to the moments he shared with the boy, planning how they would infiltrate King Midas' castle and win his favor.

He was lost in one of his reveries when the ground shifted underneath him. He almost put his hand on the wall but remembered before burning himself. When everything stilled again, he walked, but more carefully this time, his senses alert. When the rumbling returned and more rocks fell, he moved to the center of the tunnel, bracing himself with feet planted wide.

Convinced yet? Darko said in his ear. *Now we not only have to fear being incinerated, but being buried in boiling rock. Perhaps both, just for fun?*

"Change is good," Emir said, walking forward again. "We're coming to something."

How about the sea of fire? We've heard stories of that. An endless sea of orange and yellow flame extending all the way to the horizon. We fall in and spend an eternity burning.

"At least I would no longer have you chattering in my ear."

I am you, and you are me, my friend, Darko said. *You might as well enjoy my company.*

"Enjoy isn't a word I'd use."

Another rumble came, more violent, the trembling long-lasting. When it finally stopped, pebbles littered the ground.

There is persistence, Darko said, *and there is foolishness. The rock is warning you. It's time to go back.*

"Perhaps the rock is opening." Emir hurried forward. "Maybe we are witnessing a rebirth."

Rebirth? Darko said incredulously. *Rebirth of what? Your insanity?*

Emir shifted into a run, adrenaline pumping through his limbs. The more the earth rumbled, the faster he went. Up ahead, the tunnel narrowed, the walls near flames as they drew closer together. He could be running toward the end of his existence, but in that moment, something else was pushing him to keep going, to hurry, because this was his last chance.

You fool! Turn around!

CHAPTER
FORTY-EIGHT

696 BC
Gordium, Capital City of Phrygia

Elanur watched as Kerkin, Ilker, and Khogu headed straight for the front doors underneath her. Draris and the other two went around to the back. They were coming for the king. She was certain of it. And from what she'd seen of Karem, he would put up little resistance.

She stepped away from the window, her thoughts racing. What now? For several breathless moments, she waited. Then she heard footsteps approaching.

"Halt right there," the door guard said. A scuffle, the slash of a sword, a man's cry, and a heavy thump on the floor. Elanur placed her hand over her mouth. The warriors had just killed the king's guard. Now there was nothing to stop them from coming in the door. She slid under the bed and, holding her breath, watched as three sets of boots entered.

"This must be the princess' room," Khogu said in Gimirri.

"Yes, and we know where she is," Ilker said.

Elanur waited, curled up by the wall, until they left. When she was certain no more were coming, she crawled out.

So. They had Zoe and they were going to get the king. Elanur checked out the window. Dust billowed up from the main road beyond. The tribe was on its way. The warriors had done their damage in the city. Now, they would make their demands of the king. Another movement caught her eye—two figures coming through the open gate. With effort, they closed it behind them, then headed toward the back of the castle. One had a hood on, but it looked like Zoe, wearing the same cloak she had worn before. Was Ilker wrong? Was her niece here?

Elanur scanned the room for something she might use to distract the warriors, but she found only pretty clothes, a workbench littered with fragments of metal and wood, and a table with a hairbrush, a jar of lamb's fat, and two candles. Her gaze settled on the wardrobe. It was the only option.

The only weapon she had was herself.

This would push Ilker too far. But he was not a cruel man. She would rely on his compassion. Plead for it. They could do what they wished to her. But she couldn't reconcile having gone through everything she'd endured only to watch her brother and her niece die today.

Decided, she pulled out a maroon dress and held it up to her body. It was a little long, as she was shorter than the princess, but it would do. She hoped Zoe wouldn't mind her borrowing it.

She slid the door closed and changed.

"Oh no," Zoe murmured. She stared at the open gates, dread dawning on her face.

Aster crouched beside her, his gaze passing over the dead guards. Behind them, hoofbeats rumbled. A cloud of dust billowed toward them on Castle Road. Their plundering complete, the rest of the warriors were on their way.

Zoe bolted.

"Don't wait!" Aster called.

Ignoring him, she sprinted through the gate.

Aster followed. "We must not close it!" he called.

Zoe returned and ran up into the tower. While she rotated the crank, Aster wrestled with the heavy bolt. Together, they got it back into place.

"That should not hold them for now," Aster said.

They had both started toward the castle when Zoe noticed the dead man lying face down near the wall.

"Aster," she said.

He paused, his gaze settling on the man. Grasping his shoulder, he rolled the body over. A clean sword wound split the chest.

"Oh dear," Zoe said. "Gediz."

Aster gritted his teeth. The traitor had let the warriors in. He'd probably been a spy all this time. A heavy guilt settled over Aster's heart.

Zoe touched his arm and gestured toward the north wall. "We'll go through the tunnel," she said.

They raced across the wet grass, slipped into the hole in the ground, and jogged through the passageway to the castle. Zoe climbed the rope ladder, lifted the wooden cover, and peered out. "It's clear," she whispered. Aster followed. They soon stood at the edge of the kitchen. Zoe moved toward the archway beyond, then paused and turned to him.

"Thank you for coming to get me."

"A king's advisor—" he began, but Zoe raised her hand to stop him.

"If you hadn't come, I would still be there." She wrapped her arms around his neck, hugging him close. He was surprised at first, but quickly recovered and squeezed her back. She released him and tripped across to the archway, peering into the hall.

"How many do you think?" she whispered.

"I would not guess a small group," Aster said, peering over the top of her head.

"Why?"

"They would not gain a quick advantage should they take the king hostage."

Zoe started down the hallway.

Aster grabbed her arm. "If you go up there and they do not capture you, they will not have you *and* your father to bargain with."

Zoe hesitated. "I can't stay here! Who knows what they will do to him?"

"I will not check on him. But a princess is a good match for warriors such as them."

She gazed back down the hall. "But if they've got him already? I might be able to make some sort of deal."

"You do have the upper hand."

She bit her lip.

Aster pulled gently on her arm. "Your Highness." When she resisted, he pulled a little harder. "Zoe . . ." When she turned toward him, he cupped her face in his hand.

Tears welled up in her eyes. "Protect him, Aster. Don't let them . . ."

He nodded. She lingered, her gaze on his, and suddenly stood up on her toes and kissed him. His head spun with the taste of it, and he longed to stay with her forever. Let the city burn. This was where he'd so long wanted to be. When he wrapped his arm around her back and pulled her close, she moaned.

The moment passed too quickly. She dropped her forehead to his chest, breathless, and then gently pushed him away. "Be careful," she said.

He squeezed her hand, and going against every instinct in his body, hurried down the hall.

. . .

Xander stared at the statue. The sight of the dark goddess sent a chill down his spine, the promise he'd made twenty years before rushing back into his mind. Out of foolish naivete, he'd offered her his soul, but thankfully, King Midas had killed her and set Xander free. Should she be released, she might take him to the underworld right then and there. He wouldn't even have time to tell Aster goodbye.

"What did you do?" Denisia asked him.

"Nothing," he murmured. He touched his cheek and winced.

"You did something." Denisia made her way over the rubble to the gold statue. She looked up at Katiah's gold-enshrined face. "Hello, half-sister." She placed her fingers on Katiah's forearm and closed her eyes. For a time, she remained there, her forehead wrinkled with concentration. Nothing changed. Denisia gripped both of Katiah's arms and tried again. She squinted and moaned, rocked back and forth, and even hugged the goddess close to her, but the statue stood unaffected.

"Why isn't it working?" Denisia turned an accusatory stare on the young woman, who only shrugged in response. "You are doing something to stop it!" She pointed at Xander. "Cease at once."

"You are the one with the power," Xander said.

The young woman approached Denisia and moved her hands in a flurry of gestures. An old memory flashed in Xander's mind. The boy had moved his hands that way. The boy the princess had brought to the party all those years ago. Xander studied the woman's face. This was no boy?

"You must want her free?" Denisia asked her.

Again, the young woman moved her hands. Xander watched her, transfixed.

"Katiah must be released!" Denisia turned her gaze on Xander.

"I'm just standing here!" Xander squeaked.

"Something is blocking my powers!"

"I wouldn't know how!" He glanced at the statue. "This gold is the only gold that remained after the curse was broken. Maybe you have another way of removing it?"

"There is no other way, you imbecile! I summoned the gold. I should be able to banish it. You must remove your spell."

"But—"

She stormed up what was left of the steps toward him. "Remove it, or find yourself merged with that tree for the rest of your life!" She pointed to a lone evergreen tree, a pitiful thing with sparse branches.

Xander's mind raced. The hiding spell was powerless now that the tomb was destroyed. Something else was stopping Denisia from releasing her half-sister, and there was nothing he could do to change it. He was going to be fused with the tree. Already, he sensed the stiffness of the wooden trunk seeping into his limbs.

The young woman stepped in front of the statue and stared into its face.

The boy, Xander thought. *Had it been a girl? Was this . . . what was his name?* A sweet smile. Little Bird. That was it. Little Bird.

A raven cawed. Xander glanced behind him and did a double take. Not ten steps beyond stood three wolves, all of them staring straight at the tomb.

She kept me in a cave! Little Bird said in her mind. *I nearly starved.*

"But she brought you to me." Katiah's words echoed in her head. "I missed you, Little Bird."

She wants you to bring Anchurus back.

"Anchurus? But I didn't take him, darling. He plunged into the abyss of his own volition. He wanted to save his father, poor soul. Soon after that, the king pushed this accursed sword through my belly. I don't know what happened to Anchurus. Moved on, I would imagine."

You can't do it?

"Of course not. I take souls when they are offered, but I am not the goddess of resurrection. Who does she think I am?"

Little Bird sensed Denisia's gaze on her. *So she did all this for nothing?*

"Not for nothing," Katiah said. "She reunited us."

She kept me prisoner!

"The same amount of time I have been imprisoned. We are so alike, aren't we, darling?"

Little Bird crossed her arms over her chest.

"Imagine all the fun we could have. We could go back home, reclaim the place from that distasteful Khar. I hear he's tried to take over everything. I would put him back in his place, then we'd spruce things up. Remember the cabin in the forest? You loved it so much. We could return and live in peace the way we once did. Wouldn't that be nice?"

King Midas' city is under attack.

"So . . . what? You want me to ride to his rescue? After what he did to me?"

Is he my father?

"I told you he was. But you owe him nothing."

Little Bird pressed her lips into a line. *Denisia can't release you. She thinks it is Xander's spell.*

"Xander! The young advisor. Well, I suppose he's not young anymore. I haven't thought of him in so long. It will be fun having him at home."

You did not! Little Bird frowned in anger.

"He offered it! What was I supposed to do?"

You cannot take him there. Mother!

"But he owes me!" She paused, then sighed. "I might give him a reprieve. Since you called me Mother."

Little Bird grumbled silently.

"Release me, and I promise I won't harm him."

Denisia tried. She can't do it.

"Truly?" Katiah paused. "That's an interesting twist. Usually, the one who casts the spell is the only one who can undo it. If my sister —*half*-sister—can't release me, I don't know who can."

385

Little Bird dropped her gaze. She could hear the distant cries of men from beyond. *If you get out, will you help him?*

"Xander?" Katiah said.

King Midas. My father.

A long pause. "I can't. You don't know what went on between us before you came along. I love you. You can go assist him if you want. But I can't."

Little Bird clenched her teeth. Then another thought came to mind. *Emir?* she asked, uncertain.

"What are you doing?" Denisia gripped Little Bird's shoulder, interrupting her conversation with her mother. Her eyes were red from the dust, her hair disheveled. "You *must* release her. Now." When Little Bird said nothing, Denisia flicked her hand. The evergreen tree extended a branch and wrapped it around Xander's middle. He cried out in surprise. "Do it now," Denisia ordered, "or watch him die."

A familiar rage surged inside Little Bird, a glowing heat that pressed against her skin. She glanced at Xander, one side of his face scraped red, his eyes wide in terror. Another victim if Denisia didn't get her way. Nervous energy crackled through her like static before a storm, her breath coming in short, shallow bursts. She looked past Denisia to where the wolves and Nightsky waited, whether for her, Denisia, or Katiah, she couldn't tell. It din't matter. The sight of them gave her strength. Her gaze swept over Xander once more, then locked on Denisia's angry face. Her vision blurred. The world narrowed to a single point: the one who had stolen twenty years of her life.

Like a viper, she snatched Denisia's wrist and yanked her close. Power thrummed beneath the goddess' skin—Little Bird could feel it, sense it flowing through her blood. She squeezed hard, then reached out with her other hand and gripped one of Katiah's golden ones. Closing her eyes, she focused, drawing on every last bit of energy she could pull from Denisia. At first, the goddess looked confused, but then she started to fight, twisting and trying to break free. Little Bird held fast, pouring all her strength into her grip. Denisia wrenched and yanked, jerking Little Bird's arm so violently it felt like her shoulder might tear loose.

Little Bird clenched her teeth, forcing all her fury into the strength of her hold. Standing between the two sisters, she became a channel from one world to another, Denisia's power entering through one palm and exiting the other as if it were her own blood bleeding through her skin. She extracted mightily, willing Denisia's strength into Katiah, even as her captor tried to pull away. Soon, Little Bird's body stretched taut between them, her arms straining, tendons and ligaments crying out in pain. She held fast, her mind fixed on the flow of energy, her focus so fierce her body trembled.

Katiah's hand moved. The dark goddess' skin warmed. Conscious of the change, Little Bird opened her eyes and turned her energy around, sending it back through her right hand. A new power charged her blood, a thick and heavy force entering from Katiah's side, blazing through Little Bird's skin and pouring into Denisia's writhing form. Bending her will toward the goddess' destruction, Little Bird fixated on the woman's fair face, a furious fire pulsing within her. When Denisia attempted to break free, Little Bird released her mother and clamped both hands around the half goddess' wrist. Denisia's mouth opened in pain. Little Bird's face darkened, her lips pressed into a thin, merciless line, flames raging inside her as if her blood were boiling within.

Slowly, the jerking and pulling eased, and then the wrist in her grip withered. Denisia collapsed, dead, at her feet.

CHAPTER
FORTY-NINE

696 BC
Gordium, Capital City of Phrygia

Aster paused at the bottom of the north stairwell and peered around the corner. Something lay on the stairs about halfway up. He ducked back. When he heard nothing, he peered around again. The figure was crumpled against the wall. The pants, the jacket. Aster hurried forward, then groaned inwardly. *Timon.* The king's faithful minstrel lay dead on the stair, the front of his shirt bathed in blood. Aster lowered his head. A great sadness rose inside of him, soon replaced with a growing rage. First Rastus. Now Timon. He squeezed the minstrel's shoulder, then continued up the stairs. At the second level, he thought about checking the rooms, but the king was on the third level. Finding the stairwell clear, he kept going.

At the entrance to the hallway, he paused. The king's two guards were down and the king's door, open. He waited, listening. When all remained quiet, he stole down the hall. Both of the guards were dead, their throats slit open. His dagger drawn, he searched the room, but it was empty.

Where would the warriors take the king?

He flew back down the stairs, pausing at the second level and again at the first. There. Footsteps! He poked his head around the corner to see three warriors escorting the king past the dining hall. Midas wore a cream-colored tunic, moccasins, and his royal robe. His legs were bare. It was cold outside. Aster clenched his jaw. Who did these Gimirri think they were?

They appeared to be headed out the front doors. Once they were gone, Aster descended to the lower level and found Zoe waiting for him.

"So?" she said, meeting him at the doorway.

Aster took a moment to catch his breath. "They do not have the king," he said.

She glanced at the stairwell as if she might run after them.

"I did not see three."

"Where are they taking him?"

"They did not go out the front castle doors."

"He is their hostage," she said, gazing down. "They will use him, or . . ." She swallowed hard.

Aster had no comforting words. She was correct. Unless they took action, the warriors would kill the king.

"We have no fighting men," Zoe said.

"There is not something else," Aster said.

She searched his gaze.

"Timon."

Tears sprang to Zoe's eyes. "No. Oh, no." She turned away from him and leaned on the tall table nearby. "Rastus. Now dear Timon." She smacked the table with her fist. "Those bastards! Aster, what are we going to do?"

Not knowing what to say, he gently took her shoulders, pulled her in, and held her.

. . .

Denisia lay still, her body draped over the broken rocks. Little Bird swayed, weakened by the exchange, and stumbled toward her. The captor, the woman who had held so much power over her for so long, now appeared strangely depleted, her face withered and thin as if it had been sucked dry. Little Bird dropped beside her and put her finger under Denisia's nose.

She's dead, she murmured in her mind.

"You killed her?" Katiah said.

Little Bird glanced back at her mother. The dark goddess stood before her in the flesh, the gold having melted at her feet, the king's sword discarded behind her. Her dark hair fell in luscious waves to her shoulders, her skin as luminescent as the moon.

She stared at Denisia's body. "How did you do that?"

Little Bird's gaze dropped to the charred wrist—blackened, burned. She lifted her own right palm. It was a slightly inflamed but otherwise unharmed. *I don't know,* she said. Her vision blurred. A wave a dizziness swept over her.

Katiah came up behind her, her footsteps uneven as she picked her way over the fallen stones. "Well, I suppose she deserved it."

Little Bird pressed her fingers to her temple. When the world stopped moving, she slowly stood up. Beside her, Katiah looked curious. Perhaps even a little . . . nervous?

"Have you noticed this sort of power before?" Katiah asked.

Power? Little Bird frowned. Her blood had calmed, the heat dissipated.

Katiah glanced down once more. "Poor sister. I told her to let go of her obsession with the prince. I guess she couldn't."

Little Bird glared. *Poor?*

"Come now, you have to feel a little sorry for her, don't you?"

Little Bird narrowed her eyes, heat rising in her cheeks.

"Oh." Katiah's expression sobered, then softened. "Look at how you've grown." She lifted her hand, tentatively at first, then gently cupped Little Bird's face. "You're so beautiful."

Little Bird stepped back.

Katiah dropped her hand. Her face fell almost imperceptibly, the light in her eyes dimming as she cast her gaze around, surveying the city beyond. The smoke was blacker now, more of it polluting the sky, the breeze blowing it eastward. "Well, here it is again," Katiah said, her hair fluttering. "The land of man. It hasn't changed much, has it?" With a last glance at Little Bird, she started down the path toward the road.

Little Bird hesitated, turning back once to be certain Denisia hadn't stirred. But the body seemed even more lifeless now, the limbs slackened, the chest sinking inward. It was done. Denisia was dead. Somehow, Little Bird had taken her revenge. She relived the experience, the power still humming in her veins. In its wake came the vision—the red faces flashing behind her eyes, pleading as before. But this time, they didn't seem quite so frightening.

She turned and followed her mother, her gaze seeking the wolves, but they had disappeared. Nightsky, too, was gone. She reached the base of the hill and looked up. The city beyond pulsed with chaos—smoke twisting upward, voices crying out beneath it.

Before her, Katiah paused. "Xander?"

Little Bird looked left. There, Xander huddled just over a small rise, clutching his arms about himself. "Great goddess," he breathed, looking up from where he crouched. "The most pretty one. You have . . . returned."

"With some thanks owed to you, I suppose," Katiah said, planting a hand on her hip. "Why are you cowering there like a guilty dog?"

Xander cast a sheepish glance around. Though free of the tree limb, he looked battered and dazed.

"Afraid to see me again?"

"It was rather unpleasant when you were here last." Xander brushed dirt off his knees. "Little Bird," he said, "is that you?"

Her heart skipped. She gave a quick nod. He remembered her!

Xander smiled, his expression as joyful as a child's. "I can't believe it. After all this time. Why didn't you come sooner?"

Little Bird answered in her hand language, but Xander didn't understand.

"My dear half-sister kept her captive," Katiah said.

"Captive?" Xander's smile disappeared. "All this time?"

Little Bird caught his eye. At least he seemed to understand.

"It has been a long time for both of us," Katiah said. "And you don't have to stand there trembling. Little Bird has convinced me to give you a reprieve. For now."

Xander's eyebrows shot up. He started to say something else, but then stopped and simply bowed. "I am grateful."

"As am I. That was some trick, you breaking the stone apart."

"That wasn't me, great goddess. That was Matar Kubileya."

"Matar?" It was Katiah's turn to be surprised. "I haven't heard that name in a long while."

"She is trapped in a cave in Acharaca. Or . . . she was? She wanted me to release you. Something about restoring balance to the underworld."

"Ah." A knowing look crossed Katiah's face. "And so we shall."

Little Bird sensed her mother's gaze on her, but she was watching the burning city beyond.

"Oh no," Katiah said. "I suppose you're still worried about *him*?"

Little Bird's expression hardened. *He's my father,* she said in her mind.

Katiah sighed. "I shouldn't have told you."

Xander frowned. "Um, great goddess, told her what?"

"You know how I feel about it," Katiah said, ignoring Xander.

I'm worried about them, Little Bird signed.

Katiah rolled her eyes. "I don't see why you care. He was horrible to me."

Little Bird turned her gaze to Xander.

"She's asking about the king and the princess," Katiah said in a resigned tone.

"The princess is lost, last I knew," Xander said. "And the king . . . he has aged."

Little Bird looked from him to the city and back. *I must go*, she signed.

"We've just reunited, and now you're going to run off again?" Katiah said. "Didn't you miss me at all?"

Little Bird kept her gaze steady, her expression resolved.

Katiah shook her head. "This is why goddesses don't enjoy having children."

Xander frowned, casting a puzzled glance at Little Bird.

"So what, you want to go with him?" Katiah gestured to Xander.

Little Bird nodded.

Katiah's expression cooled. "Very well." She turned to Xander. "Little Bird will go with you. I have . . . other tasks to attend to." She began to walk away, then paused to cast Little Bird a final glance. "Remember where you came from. I'll be talking to you soon."

Little Bird watched as her mother shimmered, then vanished into the air.

"I haven't seen her do that in a long time," Xander said.

Little Bird stared at the place where Katiah had been, a strange sensation rising in her breast. Sorrow? Regret? Unable to reconcile it, she turned her attention back to Xander.

"This way," he said, and led her up the narrow path toward the castle.

The deep, dark underworld

EMIR WAS BURNING UP, the flesh on his skin sizzling and falling into ash, his muscles charring underneath. He screamed in agony, but kept running through the ever-narrowing space, the walls throbbing on either side of him, rocks cascading from overhead.

For he had heard Katiah's voice.

At least, he thought he had. It was distant. Not something he'd heard as much as sensed echoing inside his head. There was nothing like it. No sound so smooth and feminine, so self-assured. In his former life, he wouldn't have raced toward it. Now, hers was a voice from the past, one that belonged to a powerful being who had saved him twice before.

"Katiah!" he called. "Katiah, help me!"

Why would she help you? Darko asked. *You're a fool rushing head-long toward your oblivion.*

Emir was surprised. His hallucinatory alter ego had been quiet for a long while. "She helped me before," he said through gritted teeth. He dared not look down at his feet, for he was certain they were badly burned, perhaps disfigured by now. "Katiah!"

She cares nothing about you.

"Why did I hear her voice?"

Oh, I don't know, perhaps because you're going insane? Or could it be because you're burning yourself to a crisp?

The tunnel narrowed again, forcing Emir to slow to a walk to slip through the slim space. He turned sideways, doing his best to avoid touching the scalding hot stone. *You have to stop.* The words echoed in his mind. *You are rushing to your death.* But he couldn't be. Not after everything.

"Katiah!"

This is fun, Darko said. *Let's play don't touch the wall. A lovely way to end things.*

"Nothing is ending," Emir growled.

I see. And what will you do when the two sides of the tunnel join together, blocking you from going any farther?

Emir kept on, more flesh dripping off his limbs as he went, his bones boiling. The madness would overtake him. "Katiah!" he raged.

The rock rumbled suddenly and violently, hurling him against the wall. He cried out, pain ripping through him as he scrambled for balance. But the shaking didn't stop. Another violent jolt threw him the other way, his back slamming into stone, the impact searing like fire.

"Katiah, please . . ."

His cries faded to a whisper. He crumbled to the hot floor, fresh flames erupting around him. Blinking through the heat, he looked down the tunnel, but saw only red, throbbing rock.

Please, just stop.

Let it end.

"Katiaaaaaahhh!"

CHAPTER

FIFTY

696 BC
Gordium, Capital City of Phrygia

The next time she looked out the window, Elanur was wearing the princess' dark maroon dress, white fabric framing her collarbone and wrists. She'd run Zoe's comb through her hair, letting it fall loose over her shoulders, and put on some of the princess' rose perfume. As a final touch, she'd donned the cream-and-maroon necklace. The alternating beads and stones lay cool on her bare throat. She hadn't heard anymore footsteps, but she knew she had little time.

Within moments, Ilker emerged from the castle doors below her. Khogu and Kerkin marched behind him, escorting the king. Karem was still in his moccasins, but at least they had replaced his robe with his cloak. Her chest tightened as she watched. The proud, brave king she had seen twenty years before was gone. Here now was an old man, disheveled and beaten. The warriors positioned him near the statue of Prince Anchurus. Mitin, Draris, and Thom joined the group, emerging from the south side of the castle. That was all six of them. It seemed they had searched the grounds and believed themselves to be alone.

She had escaped their attention. A small blessing. Beyond, she heard shouting voices. The rest of Ilker's men were at the gate. They called for their leader to let them in. Ilker would do so soon enough, she suspected, but for now he was focused on the king, as if desiring to keep this victorious moment all to himself. He said something to Kerkin, gesturing toward the ruler. Kerkin looked from his adopted father to King Midas and hardened his expression. Elanur's heart fell. Ilker would teach her son to hate Karem. When Ilker's two men pulled the king forward, Elanur ran across the room. If she was going to act, she had to do it now.

She opened the door carefully. Finding the hall empty, she raced to the south stairwell and descended, her feet soundless on the stone. *Please, Ilker,* she thought to herself. *Please be the man I know you can be.* She hurried all the way to the front doors, encountering no one. Opening them a crack, she peered out.

"You should have given us your gold, great king," Ilker said in Elanur's language. "Now I must decide. What to do with your daughter?"

A flash of anger passed over the king's face. He uttered something inaudible.

"She is ours," Ilker said.

Midas lunged at Ilker, but the two warrior guards held him back.

"She will join us, or be killed," Ilker said.

Elanur glanced away. Zoe! Captured? But hadn't that been her coming through the gates?

Ilker droned on about how the strong defeat the weak. Elanur wished she had never taught him her language. When he paused, she squared her shoulders, opened wide the door, and strode out onto the stone landing.

No one paid her the least bit of attention. It wasn't until she had descended the stairs and started walking toward them that they glanced her way. Kerkin's expression changed from stern to surprised. When Elanur locked eyes with Ilker, she was startled to find him smiling at her.

"Ilker, please." She raised one hand to beseech him. "Do not harm him. He is my brother."

He watched her with his usual pleased look.

"When you took me," she said, "all those years ago. I was on my way back to him."

Ilker raised his eyebrows in fake surprise. "Is that so?"

Elanur came near and paused. "Do you understand what I'm saying? He is my brother. By blood. I came to warn him."

Ilker glanced around innocently. "About *us*?"

"He is my family."

Ilker's smile disappeared. "*We* are your family."

"Yes." Elanur acknowledged what she felt in her heart. "But he was my family first."

Ilker cast a glance at Midas, then smiled again. "You see, great king, I have your sister too." Then he nodded to Draris and Thom, who seized Elanur by the arms.

"Ilker?" Elanur said, her skin going clammy. "What are you doing?"

They dragged her over to stand near Midas, four warriors in a line. Khogu and Kerkin restrained the king. Draris and Thom held her, while Mitin stood off to the side. Ilker approached, studying her with open admiration.

"The perfect match for the leader of the Gimirri tribe," he said in her language, brushing her cheek with his fingers. "A king's sister." He let his hand fall, his dark eyes softening. "When the goddess told me, imagine my good fortune. You were so beautiful."

Elanur's face crumbled. *The goddess?* Her mind reeled, memories lining up in a new, terrible order. "All this time?" she whispered. "You *knew*?"

"At the great Denisia's command, we found the girl," Ilker said. "Denisia took her, but left you to me. I wasn't certain. But you are better than my dreams. And now you are here." He turned to Kerkin. "My son, you did well."

Elanur's gaze snapped to Kerkin. *He* had told his father about her? He shifted under her stare, unable to meet her eyes.

Ilker grinned, triumphant. "My Elanur. Witness my glory!" He threw up his hands and turned, striding away. "Great king," he called over his shoulder, "what say you? Will you surrender now?" He paused, then spun back around, grinning at them all.

An icy chill clawed down Elanur's spine, the truth settling over her like a dark shroud. Every memory unraveled, revealing Ilker's plan plotted with sinister care. He loved her. She knew he did. But now that love was tainted with the poison of betrayal. He had lied to her from the very beginning, manipulated his way into her heart, used her for his ambitious aims. She stood paralyzed, as if the ground beneath her had vanished, but she had nowhere to fall.

"You stole me," she whispered. "You robbed me of my life."

Ilker was taunting the king again, speaking of how Midas could surrender peacefully or condemn his people to further suffering. He moved with a kind of dance, joy erupting through him. This, Elanur saw now, was what the Gimirri leader had lived for. After years of planning, fighting, and building his tribe, he was savoring his moment of victory. Her initial shock gave way to a heat that coiled tightly around her core. She had trusted him. But it had been a horrible mistake. She glanced at Kerkin and was surprised to find his gaze on her.

"He stole you too," she said in Gimirri, "just like he did me."

Ilker stopped talking.

"He is not your real father," she said firmly. "I am not your mother."

"Don't listen to her." Ilker strode toward Elanur and bent his head to her. "You must not harm our son."

"Me, harm him?" Elanur's anger mounted. "How could you do this? To me? To him?" She gestured to the young man. "I gave you everything. I went along with your ways. And the whole time . . . the whole time!"

"It is nothing!" he said. "What care you for him?" He pointed at Midas. "An old man you no longer know. This is your family now." He gestured to himself and Kerkin. "You will be loyal to us."

She took a step toward him, pulling against her guards. "You stole him." She raised her voice to be sure her son could hear. "You wrenched him away from his real family, just like you did me. He has another family out there somewhere mourning for him, as I mourned for my brother and my niece. You didn't offer either of us a choice."

"I took care of you," Ilker said matter-of-factly. "The tribe accepted you. You gained position as healer."

"You never *asked* me," she said.

"I never forced you."

She turned away from him. It was no use. Suddenly, the distance between the two of them opened up like a canyon. She had ignored their differences before. Now, with her brother's life on the line and her son's future in question, she could no longer do that.

"You will see." He opened his hand to her. "Our tribe will be strong. You will live in a castle!" He gestured behind him. "You will want for nothing!"

He thought this would please me? "Please, Ilker. Let my brother go."

Ilker's smile faded. He looked from her to the king, then turned and headed down the stone path toward the gates. He would allow the rest of his men to come in to witness his glory. Elanur addressed her son.

"Kerkin, King Midas is my brother. He was my brother long before I came to be your mother. I plead for his life now, because we are family."

Kerkin watched his father, but she could tell he was listening.

"When Ilker brought you to me, you were just a baby. You had other parents. You may have been too young to remember, but—"

"Why do you speak this?" he mumbled in Gimirri.

401

Elanur stopped. "Because it is the truth."

He looked up at her then, his expression baffled. "You are my mother."

"Of course," she said, relenting. "Always. But before me, the woman who gave birth to you. She was your mother first."

Kerkin shook his head. "You are angry. Angry with Father."

Elanur's shoulders slumped. It was too much for him to accept. Beyond, Ilker was coming back. He hadn't yet opened the gate. She gazed at Karem, who was now watching his enemy. "You must be strong, Karem," she whispered. "It is only strength he will respond to."

Ilker stopped in front of the king, his jubilant expression replaced with determination. "I have your sister. I have your daughter. Surrender and die with honor. Or I will finish you all."

EMIR HAD EXPECTED it to be over. The fire had consumed him, the sides of the tunnel grown together into a rock wall he couldn't penetrate. There had been no river. No escape. No way out. What else could there be but the end of everything?

But he wasn't dead. Unless dead was this weightless, floating sensation. He had dreamed about it once, flying, when he was a child. In the depth of his slumber, all he'd had to do was will himself into the air and he would float along in any direction he chose. This time, he was not in control. He was floating upward at a steady pace, like a piece of pollen tossed by the wind.

After a while, the terror of the fiery tunnels receded enough to allow other thoughts in. He wondered whether this was what dying was like. Then another, less savory thought came to him. Perhaps he was in some other underworld realm where he would be forced to live out a different form of torture. His longing for his former life returned with a sharp pang. He fought to open his eyes again, but it was as if he had no eyes and traveled only as a formless shadow.

It seemed like another year had passed before he called out to

Darko. It surprised him, the mental cry. But he longed to talk to him, to anyone. The madness that had possessed him in Khar's arena licked at the corners of his mind, slithering like a snake into his consciousness, seeking control. He called again for Darko, desperate for another voice, but there was no answer. After many tries, Emir knew the snake would win, that he would succumb to his bestial nature, and that it wouldn't be long now. The thought scared him perhaps more than any other, even more than being burned alive among the molten rocks or floating forevermore through a silent darkness. He renewed his efforts to be strong, rehearsing his memories, adding the ones from his time in the tunnels, even the battles in Khar's cave. Repeatedly, he told his own story to himself.

He had just begun to relax when he awoke to a ghastly scene. Prince Anchurus was there, weakened as he had been after the fire. Emir saw himself ram his sword through the prince's heart, then turn and cut off King Midas' head. With both rulers dispatched, he marched up the stairs at the front of the castle and declared himself king. He tried to shut his eyes to the images, but they played out before him like one of Timon's theater shows, he, a powerless witness forced to watch. It was when he sensed a spark of pride at his imagined actions, along with the energy of power, that he knew he was losing it. The threads of his sanity were unraveling.

He started speaking his memories aloud. Again, he began with his childhood, announcing his mother's name. He continued from there, shouting each memory as if to drown out a crowd. His recitations sound like ravings, but he poured his energy into them, preferring anything to the madness knocking inside his mind.

The new underworld was unending, wearing away Emir's ability to resist. He didn't know how much time had passed when the realization came to him he was going to fail. What little strength he had left would soon be depleted. He would surrender to the beast inside him, and there would be nothing left of the proud warrior he had always tried to be. Grief-stricken, he called once more to the one who had saved him before, the only one with the power to release him even from this.

"Katiah, please. Before I am gone."

The words escaped him like a surrendering sigh. With a feeling similar to that of closing his eyes, he gave himself up.

The rising motion slowed. The surrounding air became heavy, like a smothering blanket. Movement scraped against his skin, silence pounding against his ears, a roar more terrible than Khar's. He trembled, a new chill seizing his bones.

Then he heard an answer.

"Hello, darling. Did you miss me?"

CHAPTER
FIFTY-ONE

696 BC
Gordium, Capital City of Phrygia

Xander couldn't stop looking at Little Bird. Beyond, the city was burning. Who knew how many the warriors had killed, or if the king, Aster, and the princess were still alive? He hurried along the narrow path, his mind racing with worry—yet his eyes kept returning to her. This was the same boy from all those years ago. The same fine features, the same shy manner. The same graceful way of speaking with her hands. But she was not the same.

And what had Katiah said about having children?

He picked up his pace, nearly running as they skirted the north wall. The warriors could be anywhere. They had to tread carefully. Reaching a swell in the ground, he crouched. "You must stay here," he told her. "It's not safe. I'll come back for you." He turned and took off, but behind him, footsteps swished through the grass.

He paused and pointed to the ground. "Stay here. Understand? I will come get you when it's safe." He jogged away again. She followed. He kept going until he reached the gnarled bush hiding the tunnel entrance, and then turned once more, thrusting his palm out. "Please. Wait until I come back."

She signed something to him, but he didn't understand. She pointed to the castle and signed something else.

"I don't want anything to happen to you," he said. "Not now, after you've just . . ."

She looked at him with a kind expression and pointed toward the castle again. She would not be swayed.

Xander relented and pushed aside the low branches, revealing the secret wooden cover on the ground.

"Hurry!" he whispered.

They ran through the tunnel, climbed the rope ladder, and emerged into the kitchen. "Stay here." Xander moved into the hall. It was no use. The young woman kept following him. He climbed the north stairwell, pausing every few steps to listen. He heard no one. No servants. No guards. He paused at the second level. Quick feet moved past him, Little Bird taking the lead. She dashed into Zoe's room, Xander on her heels. The room was empty. He walked across to the window and, taking care to shield himself, looked down at the courtyard. King Midas and another woman stood trapped among six warriors, all of them gathered at the base of Prince Anchurus' statue.

"Oh no," he murmured.

Little Bird came up beside him, but he gently pushed her back. "You don't want them to see you." He glanced around, wondering where the princess was. And Aster?

Footsteps sounded in the hallway. They ducked for cover, Little Bird behind the shelf against the north wall, Xander against the side of the wardrobe. The door creaked open. Xander held his breath as two figures entered.

"There," a woman's voice said. "By the wardrobe!"

Her companion moved swiftly across the room. "Do not reveal yourself!"

"Aster!" Xander burst forth. "In the name of the gods, am I glad to see you!"

The two men embraced. When Aster released him, Xander saw the princess standing behind him. "Your Highness!" He bowed low. "I'm so pleased you made it back."

She smiled at him. "You are a welcome sight, Xander."

Xander observed them both, his eyes gleaming, but his smile quickly faded. "Your father," he said. "They have taken him."

"You have seen him?"

Xander led her to the window. The three observed the gathering by the statue. The sun was sinking in the sky, its rays bathing Anchurus' likeness in a honey-like glaze.

"Oh, no." Zoe covered her mouth. "They have Elanur too."

"*That's* the king's sister?" Xander asked. "How did she—"

"Another time," Zoe said, focused on her father.

"I don't know how the thieves got in," Xander said. "Somehow, they got past the gate guards."

"It was not Gediz," Aster mumbled, and pointed out the still figure lying prone by the gates.

Xander stared. "Gediz? *Let* the warriors in?"

Zoe emitted a soft groan and dropped onto the couch. "They're going to kill him," she said.

Xander couldn't tear his gaze from Gediz. A king's advisor. Betraying them all! He turned to Aster, but his friend was tending to the princess. A warrior's cry went up from outside of the gates.

"Why haven't they let the rest of them in?" Xander asked.

"The leader does not want to savor his moment of victory against the king," Aster said with a grimace.

A somber heaviness settled over the room. The silence held— until soft footsteps approached from behind the shelf. Zoe glanced up to see Little Bird coming toward her.

"Oh!" Xander said. "I forgot. This is . . ."

But Zoe had already stood up. The two women stared at one another.

"She met us at Katiah's tomb," Xander said quietly.

"She . . ." Zoe looked the woman up and down. "I know you."

A gentle smile crossed Little Bird's face. She raised her hands, flattened one as if something were resting on it, and made the motion of drawing with the other hand.

Zoe's eyes widened. "The boy," she said. "The slate and rock!"

Little Bird smiled again.

"But you . . . aren't a boy?"

Little Bird laughed. There was no sound, but her mouth opened and her eyes danced.

"It is really you? Little Bird?" Zoe glanced back at Xander.

"We haven't had time to catch up," he said.

Zoe stared in awe for a few more moments, then whirled on Xander. "Katiah?"

He gave her a sheepish look. "Out. And gone. For now."

"It was difficult?" Aster said.

"The rock helped," Xander said.

"She just left?" Zoe asked.

Xander gazed at Little Bird. "She won't bother us for now."

Zoe watched him, waiting for more. When he didn't elaborate, she squeezed Little Bird's hand, then returned to the window. Ilker was gesturing toward Elanur. "Xander, Aster," she said. "Any ideas?"

The two advisors exchanged glances. "Perhaps," Xander said.

He led them down the hall to Zoe's workroom, allowing the princess to go in first. "Forgive me, Your Highness, if I may have your permission?" He retrieved Zoe's heavy crossbow from the shelf and took it to Aster. Pointing out the closed window, he said, "A well-placed shot might provide the distraction we need."

Aster shouldered the weapon and carefully opened one shutter. "It is not far," he said. "I can be sure of my accuracy."

"Even if he hits one," Zoe said from behind him, "they will come searching for us. And they will still have the king."

"If some come looking," Xander said, "there will be fewer with the king. We go out while they come in . . ."

"Then we will have only those who remain," Zoe finished for him. "But they are vicious fighters. We are no match for them."

Xander shrugged. "It's all I have."

Zoe looked at Aster, then gazed out the window again. "Aster gets a lucky shot, and one goes down. Let's say they send two in after us. That leaves three. There are weapons in Anchurus' room." She paused, observing her brother's statue. "It would be the four of us . . ." She looked questioningly at Little Bird. "Against the three of them."

"We should take our time," Aster said.

The warriors were moving, Ilker directing the ones holding the prisoners to stand apart.

"None of you has to agree to this," Zoe said. "We will probably be killed."

Little Bird signed something, but none of them understood her. She pointed to herself, then the window.

"You want to go out there alone?" Zoe asked.

Little Bird nodded.

"They will kill you!"

Little Bird shook her head. Once again, she pointed to herself, then the window. Next, she touched Aster's shoulder, pointed to the warriors, and raised her hand as if to say, "Pause."

"We can do this together," Zoe said. "You won't stand a chance alone."

Little Bird gazed at the floor, then came forward, kissed Zoe on the cheek, and raced out the door.

"Little Bird!" Zoe hissed. "Wait!"

But "the boy" was already gone.

LITTLE BIRD FLEW DOWN the stairwell. She heard no voices, so when she reached the first floor, she hurried on, headed for the castle doors. Slowly, she eased one open and peered out.

The warriors were still there, holding the king and the woman Xander had said was Elanur. Little Bird stared at her, memory stirring from their journey so long ago. Elanur looked older now, but her bearing hadn't changed, still proud, brave, and standing tall by the king.

King Midas. Little Bird's *father*. He appeared much changed. She remembered him withered and weary when he was cursed and couldn't drink, but even then he had been powerful. Now he appeared beaten. Defeated. Old. She grew angry all over again thinking about how her captor had kept her from him all this time.

The lead warrior was saying something. She opened the door a little more and hovered, one foot on the threshold. If she proceeded, the warriors would capture her and her opportunity would be lost. But there was no other way. If they killed the king, she would lose her chance to see him once more. Besides, Zoe and the others were waiting for her.

"We have your sister, your daughter, and your castle," the lead warrior said.

Little Bird frowned. They did *not* have the princess. *Your daughter.* She realized with a start that she met that description, too. Swallowing hard, she slipped through the door and closed it behind her.

"What say you, King Midas?" the warrior said. "Surrender!"

"You have killed my people and destroyed my city," Midas said. "Why have you done this?"

Ilker laughed. "Great king, look! Your homes, treasures, food. You have these. My people were forced to wander. Gordium will go to the Gimirri!"

The other warriors shouted a rousing battle cry.

"Will you protect the kingdom?" Midas asked.

"I care for my people," Ilker said, his fist on his chest, "not yours."

"Foolish," King Midas said. "You believe that through battle and conquest, you can become a great man. All you have done is bring death to your door."

Ilker's features hardened. "Save your people. Or watch them die."

Little Bird scowled, the old anger flickering inside her. She strode across the castle grounds toward her father. Her confidence seemed a shield about her, as when the warriors noticed her approach, none of them reacted. None reached for his sword. Instead, it was as if an apparition had appeared before them, and they allowed her to float unharmed right up to the king.

Her heart thumping in her ears, Little Bird bowed, and then gazed into his face. It was as if his very being rested on a deep layer of sadness. But as he looked upon her, she saw a little of the kindness that had so attracted her as a child.

"Little Bird?"

It was Elanur who spoke. Little Bird glanced at her. She meant to smile, for it warmed her heart that the woman recognized her, but the king was all she could see. There were only the two of them in the world—her and her father.

His features shifted, the wrinkles deepening around his eyes. "The boy?" he whispered.

She nodded, a spark flickering to light in her chest. He remembered!

"But you were—"

King on throne, she signed, the same words she had taught him so long ago.

"The king . . . sits on a throne," he said.

A laugh nearly escaped her, a smile spreading across her face.

He seemed awestruck. "You got away from Sargon?"

Woke up in city, she signed.

"You didn't teach me that," he said.

"She found me in Durukin," Elanur offered. "She led me out. We were on our way to you when we were taken."

Midas glanced at his sister, then turned back to Little Bird. "Where have you been?"

How to tell him when there was so little time? There was only one thing she wanted him to know. She pointed to him and signed, *Father.* He didn't understand. She tried pointing to the king, then herself, but he didn't understand that either. She looked to Elanur. *Father,* she signed.

Elanur frowned and cocked her head. "I don't know that one?"

411

"Who is this?" Ilker demanded, storming toward them.

Little Bird glanced behind her. The other warriors were closing in too, her invisible shield no longer protecting her.

"The orphan girl," Elanur said to Ilker. "We were traveling together when you . . . found me."

"This is the girl?" Ilker asked.

Denisia, Little Bird signed to Elanur. *Dead.*

Elanur cocked her head. "The goddess?"

Little Bird nodded.

"She says," Elanur explained, "that Denisia is . . . dead." She glanced at her brother.

A shadow passed over Midas' face.

Ilker laughed. "The great goddess Denisia cannot be killed."

Midas held his sister's gaze, then turned again to Little Bird. A new expression dawned on his features, a foggy veil receding from his eyes. "Denisia," he said, "dead."

"You killed her?" Elanur asked Little Bird, but before the young woman could answer, meaty hands seized her from behind.

"You have me." King Midas pulled against his guards' hold. "Let them go."

Ilker reached for his sword.

"You would kill an unarmed man?" Elanur asked him.

Ilker paused, his cheek twitching. "Arm him," he barked.

The warriors released Midas, one handing over his sword.

"Who shall fight the king?" Ilker called out.

All the other warriors withdrew their weapons.

"You have defeated him," Elanur said. "Let that be enough."

"The king's rule is over. The people must know." Ilker's gaze found the boy. "Kerkin."

"No." Elanur squirmed. "Ilker, no!"

The boy stepped forward. "Prove your worth," Ilker said, nodding toward the king. "Become a true Gimirri warrior. Prove that you are my son."

"Kerkin," Elanur whimpered, "please. He is my brother."

King Midas observed the boy, who was now approaching in a fighting stance. "I am glad we met again," he said to Elanur as he raised the sword the warrior had given him. "I see our mother's strength in you."

"He is my son," was all she could say.

Midas turned to Little Bird, gazing at her with an expression akin to pride. *King falls from throne,* he signed. At her stricken look, he smiled and said, "Remember the one who was kind to you here." He gave her a pointed look.

Little Bird's lip trembled. *Princess Zoe.* He wanted her to help the princess. She nodded, wishing she could tell him she already was.

Midas turned his attention to Kerkin. "The princess?" he asked Ilker.

"She will be spared."

"Your son!" Elanur said to her mate. "You would have him kill his mother's brother?"

"He will vanquish our enemy," Ilker said. "You will rule with me in the castle. It is the way."

"It's not *my* way!" Elanur squirmed, but the warrior was too strong. "Kerkin!"

Little Bird watched it all with a great sadness flowing through her. It was done. She had seen her father. Now she was going to lose him. She heard a caw and looked up. Nightsky circled overhead.

The king and the boy squared off. Midas gave the impression that he might truly fight, but Little Bird knew better. He wouldn't harm his sister's son. She cast her gaze upward and found the window she believed belonged to Zoe's workshop. She wanted to give Aster a sign, but dared not alert the warriors, so she lowered her head and nodded twice. Then she called Nightsky down.

The bird descended like a falling stone on the guard holding Little Bird. Using his hard beak, he got in three good strikes on the man's crown before flying off, then returned to attack again, flapping his wings and scratching at the guard's eyes with his claws. The guard lifted an arm to fight off the beast, loosening his hold.

413

Little Bird got free and bolted.

"Seize her!" Ilker called.

The wind lifted her feet. A man cried out behind her. Back in the clearing, one of the other warriors fell. Aster's shot was true. *One down, five to go.* She ran in a jagged pattern, trying to throw off her pursuer, her trajectory taking her toward the castle gates. The other warriors were there, waiting to get in, so she darted left, heading past the old oak tree with the child's swing and onto the stone path that led to the king's garden. Running as fast as she could, she didn't look up until she had almost reached the archway.

There, something caught her eye. She slowed.

A figure emerged from the garden. At first, she feared it was another warrior. But no. Something was different. Something about the stranger's gait, the dark hair. Nerves pricked along the back of her neck. Her body stilled. It was as if she had walked into a painting. The warrior would catch up. He would recapture her, or worse.

But the figure was coming toward her. She couldn't move.

CHAPTER

FIFTY-TWO

696 BC
Gordium, Capital City of Phrygia

Aster's arrow was true. Soon after the first warrior fell, Ilker sent the other one who had been guarding the king into the castle. When the nomad stormed the front doors, Princess Zoe led Xander out the back. They circled around, clinging to the south side until they could once again see the king facing off against the young man, Elanur watching helplessly nearby. Down the path, Little Bird raced away, another warrior pursuing her. That left only Ilker, the young man, and the one guarding Elanur.

Zoe worried about Aster making it out of the castle undetected, but he soon arrived, breathless and unharmed, his sword in hand. They were ready.

"Finish it," Ilker said to the young man.

Zoe burst forward, Xander on her heels. Her father lifted his gaze. The young warrior took a swing.

"Father!" Zoe cried.

The boy's blade sliced across the king's ribs. Fortunately, it did little more than tear his cloak. Midas lifted his sword in response, blocking the boy's next strike.

"Zoe?" he asked.

"I'm here!" Rushing to his side, Zoe turned toward the boy, her own small sword raised just as Xander ran by and, using a long fighting club, hit the young man hard on the back. The warrior boy dashed after him.

"Kerkin!" Ilker barked.

Kerkin chased Xander for another moment, but then relented and started back as Zoe and the king approached the guard holding Elanur. Aster, meanwhile, charged forward to challenge the Gimirri leader.

"He said he had you prisoner!" Midas said to Zoe as he raised his sword to the guard.

"Aster found me," Zoe said. "We must defend ourselves now. Defend Gordium!"

The warrior backed up, holding Elanur in front of him. As Midas came on, Zoe ran around behind. Unable to watch them both, the guard shoved Elanur down and attacked. Midas blocked. The boy tried to sneak up behind the king, but Xander ran by again, wildly swinging his club. Kerkin whirled and took a swipe at him. Xander leaped out of the way. Elanur's guard pounded hard, driving Midas back. Zoe ran up behind the brute and when he paused, stabbed her sword into his flank. He howled, turned, and backhanded her, sending her to the ground. Elanur raced forward to help while the guard renewed his pursuit of Midas. Xander and Kerkin danced around one another, Kerkin looking more confused than frightened by Xander's spastic antics.

Nearby, Aster was making a valiant go of it against Ilker. The two men hit and turned, then struck again, their blades clashing with resounding rings. They seemed evenly matched at first, but then Ilker rushed forward and barreled into Aster, catching him off guard. Aster stumbled, no match for the other man's bulk. Xander, seeing his friend struggling, abandoned Kerkin and ran toward the

Gimirri leader, readying himself for a sound swing into the nomad's back.

"Father!" the boy cried in warning.

Ilker turned in time to knock Xander's club out of his hands. He grabbed the chubby advisor by the throat and backed him across the clearing. Xander struggled, but couldn't loosen the warrior's hold. Ilker shoved him down. Aster struck from behind. Ilker whirled, and the two faced off again, Xander lying still on the stone path.

Beyond Anchurus' statue, Midas fought against the injured warrior, but even with his bleeding flank, the nomad had the upper hand. Midas was old, slow, and out of shape, his steps faltering in the loose moccasins he wore. With a leap and shove, the warrior knocked the king down and moved in for the final strike. Midas rolled away just in time and got back on his feet.

Zoe stirred, pulling her elbows underneath her.

"Are you all right?" Elanur asked.

"Father?"

"He's still fighting. Stay down." Elanur headed toward Midas and his opponent, rushing forward to grab hold of her son around the waist. He squirmed and fought against her, but she wouldn't let go, shouting at him to be still.

"You must stop!" she said. "He is my brother!"

Zoe got back on her feet. On her left, her father staggered, the warrior undeterred by the blood oozing from his wound. On her right, Aster was still blocking Ilker's blows, but the Gimirri leader was backing him toward the castle. Zoe looked from one to the other, then found her small sword and started toward the warrior fighting her father. A thick hand grasped her upper arm—the fourth nomad returned from the castle. He said something she didn't understand and dragged her back to where they had held her before. She wriggled against him, desiring to call out, but all she would do is distract the men. She glanced at Elanur, who was still clinging to her son, requiring him to drag her along like an appendage as he tried to make his way to the king.

417

The four men circled one another in an arena of death, Zoe's guard content to watch. Ilker twirled his sword and smiled. He took a hard swing and then plowed into Aster with his forearm, pushing the advisor back toward the stairs. Aster ducked and turned to strike, but Ilker easily blocked him, then struck a surprising kick into Aster's gut, sending him reeling. Aster recovered and Ilker took a few more turns with him before again used his body weight to knock the advisor down. With a heavy leg, he stepped on Aster's sword hand, pinning it underneath his foot. Aster snatched the dagger at his belt and stabbed the warrior hard in the calf. The blade slid all the way through, the point sticking out the front of Ilker's leg.

The Gimirri leader bellowed in pain. Aster jumped back to his feet.

"Enough!" Ilker withdrew the dagger and held it, dripping blood, even as he lifted his sword toward Aster. "Enough!" He barked another order in his strange language. Zoe's guard propelled her forward until she stood, defenseless, in front of the Gimirri leader.

Aster recovered his sword and approached, ready to attack again.

"I will kill her!" Ilker pointed his blade at Zoe's throat. "Do you hear me? I will kill her!"

Aster glanced across the clearing at Midas. The king, alert to the threat, dropped his sword. The wounded warrior grabbed his arm and yanked him toward the front of the steps where Ilker now stood, his face red with pain. Ilker turned to Aster next. The advisor glared at the Gimirri leader and then at Zoe's guard, but finally surrendered his weapon as well. Soon, the two guards, Kerkin, and Ilker had all three of the royal family surrounded, Elanur clinging to her son, the fifth warrior who'd pursued Little Bird still absent. Near the stairs, Xander slowly got to his feet. Ilker glared at them all, perspiration slicking his face. Turning his back, he hung his head, spitting Gimirri curses onto the stone path.

Zoe found Aster's eyes, and then her father's. "For Anchurus?" she said.

"The story of Gordium will not be told for generations to come," Aster said.

Midas gazed at his daughter. "The king's crown," he said, looking at his advisors one after the other. "It goes to the princess."

Xander drew in a sharp breath and came closer.

"Princess Zoe is to be queen of Gordium. Something I should have done long ago. Not since Anchurus has there been a more worthy heir."

Zoe gaped at him. He didn't seem confused. He looked more himself than she had seen him in ages. Speechless, she bowed her head.

"No!" Ilker limped back to the group. "She will not be queen. Gordium belongs to me. She dies today!" Dark eyes blazing, Ilker stormed toward the princess, his sword raised for a killing strike.

Zoe froze, her heart seized with terror. She was going to die. But die a queen. Like her mother before her. She closed her eyes.

The blow never came. She heard a grunt, followed by a heavy thud. Opening her eyes, she found Ilker face-down at her feet, a mighty dagger sticking out of his back. Behind him stood her father. They locked gazes. He smiled, a soft ray of sunlight catching his cheek. Then the warrior behind him stabbed him clear through with his sword.

Midas' jaw dropped, his lips parting in a silent gasp. He looked down at the blade sticking out of his stomach.

"Katiah," he said, and fell.

EMIR STRODE out of the garden and onto the stone path that led to King Midas' castle. On his left were the gates through which he had entered so long ago, holding his oud in his hand, the boy at his heels. Men's voices shouted from the other side. Unfamiliar voices. On his right stood the castle, looking much the same as it had that day, except the clouds cast it in gray rather than the creamy light he remembered. He paused, glancing behind him. He'd heard Katiah's voice and then the ground had solidified under his feet.

You are restored, she'd said. Yes. That was it. Restored. *For my daughter. Go. Protect her.*

He had been in the fiery tunnels, followed by the lifting darkness. Now it seemed he was walking in the real world, his boots stepping along the stone path. Another trick. Some other form of torture. But Katiah's voice had been clear in his head. He had seen something, too. A pale face surrounded by black hair, but it was blurry, as if he'd been staring through fog. Then the harsh air against his skin and the rush of strange sounds in his ears.

Someone was coming toward him. He blinked, uncertain. It had been so long since he'd seen anything, and now there was light and smoke and the castle and this person, gradually drawing near. A woman. Slighter than the goddess, with a more hesitant gait.

Then another shape burst forward, chasing her.

On impulse, Emir quickened his stride, his hand jutting from his side to touch the rock wall. He was surprised when he didn't find it there.

The charging man slammed into the woman, knocking her aside, and came straight for him. He was big—muscular, wild-eyed. Emir grasped the hilt of his sword, the image of Khar flashing through his mind. The attacker was nearly upon him when Emir drew the blade and, with a fierce swipe, severed the man's hand. The warrior howled and clutched the stump to his belly. Emir spun, searching, fearing he was back in Khar's arena. But there was no red rock. No mass of discarded carcasses. The castle remained on his right, the gates on his left.

The warrior recovered, grabbed his sword, shook off the injured limb, and came at him again. They traded a few blows. On the man's third attack, Emir brought his sword around and cut the warrior's head clean off. The body swayed for a moment before falling with a mighty thud onto the ground. Emir turned, breathing hard.

The woman was back on her feet, but she had come no closer.

Emir sheathed the sword and walked until he was standing in front of her. She stared at him through innocent brown eyes, her dark hair spilling in unruly waves about her shoulders. Her features were small and fine, her full lips parted as she gazed upon him with an expression that looked like awe. She wore a simple woolen dress, deerskin cloak, and tall boots, a dagger in her hand. Had she come to fight? As if reading his mind, she tucked the weapon into her belt and moved her hands in a way that triggered a long-distant memory.

Hands moving. Hands talking. Emir squinted. She repeated the motion, more slowly this time. Images tumbled over one another in his mind. Fingers twisting into different shapes. But they were smaller hands. The woman took a tentative step toward him, then made the motion again. One hand in a graceful curve. The other answering it. Both held together at the finish. A name. *His* name. He raised his gaze to her face.

"Emir," he said. The sound of his own voice startled him, raw in the harsh air against his ears.

She broke out in a wide smile and came toward him. He stepped back, his hand flying to his sword. Her smile vanished. She studied him. Then she seemed to decide and turned toward the castle, motioning for him to follow. She led him past the gates and up the path. In the distance stood a mighty statue. He paused. He didn't remember that. It took him some time to place the shape. The prince. Yes, it resembled the prince. Emir had seen him in the tunnels. But the prince had left somehow . . . on a river?

A scream sounded from up ahead.

"Karem!"

The sound tore through him—sudden, electric, undeniable. *Mother!* He bolted, rushing past the young woman and charging into the clearing ahead. A blonde woman knelt by a fallen man. He wore what looked like a king's cloak. Something stirred in Emir's memory —*King Midas?* Behind the blonde woman stood a warrior like the one Emir had killed, another nearby with his sword drawn. A third, younger fighter knelt by a dead one on the ground, grief etched across his face. A dark-haired woman hovered by his side.

Emir paused, staring at her.

The two standing warriors argued with one another. Suddenly, the one closest to the king pulled the sword from his dead body and aimed the dripping blade at the blonde woman. *The princess,* Emir thought. An unarmed man who looked like one of the king's guards stepped up to defend her. The second warrior attacked and stabbed the king's man in the side. Princess Zoe screamed.

The woman with dark hair stood up and shouted at the warriors.

Emir saw her face.

Something primal surged inside him. With a sharp pull, he drew his sword and charged the first warrior who had struck the king's guard, driving him back. The man was a brute, taller than Emir with wide, punching blows, but Emir had learned a thing or two in Khar's arena. He twisted and dodged, darted and spun, slipping in a stab here, a slice there, gradually wearing the man down. As the fight wore on, the memory of a thousand battles stirred inside him. He whirled, ran, slashed, and laughed, his eyes crazed, his steps quick and deceiving. The warrior faltered under the flurry of strikes until Emir drove his blade deep into the man's gut. The brute doubled over and collapsed in a heap, lifeless.

Emir jerked his weapon free and looked up. The second warrior was poised to strike, the young fighter blocking his path to protect the two women. Emir flew across the grounds and struck the attacker from behind. The fight didn't last long. Within five blows, the warrior fell dead at Emir's feet, his neck sliced open.

Emir gripped his sword with both hands and scanned the area. The young fighter had returned to the fallen warrior's side. Princess Zoe grieved over the king in grief, Elanur staring at Emir with a haunted gaze.

Mother. He started toward her.

A chubby man had knelt by the wounded king's guard. "Aster?" he said. "Aster, are you all right?"

Aster. The name sounded familiar.

Aster coughed and sputtered. "Glorious," he said. Blood swelled onto his shirt and jacket.

The chubby advisor pulled off his own cloak and pressed it to the wound. "I don't know why you always have to be so brave."

"The princess?" Aster asked, trying to lift himself up.

"She's all right," the chubby man said, laying a hand on Aster's chest. "Lie still."

Xander. That was the chubby man's name. The king's advisor.

"Father," the princess said, rocking back and forth. "No."

King Midas. Emir glanced at him, but then turned to his mother. Her dark hair was streaked with gray, her skin wrinkled and sagging. But her eyes. They were as he remembered.

"Emir?" She approached and, with a trembling hand, touched his face. "Are you really here?"

He took her hand and held it in his. It felt more fragile, the knuckles more prominent. "I'm sorry," he said. "I'm sorry I left."

Tears spilled down her cheeks. "How are you here? What happened?"

The memories came as he'd rehearsed them. He'd taken Katiah's blow. He'd lived in the tunnels. He'd survived Khar's arena. He'd existed in the rising nothingness. And now . . . "Katiah," he said.

She flinched. "The dark goddess?" Elanur glanced about, suddenly wary, then looked at Emir again. Slowly, she wrapped her arms around him.

He received her embrace, cautious at first. It was another mirage. But she didn't vanish or fade, her body pressing against his, her warm hands on his back. He couldn't remember the last time any human had touched him. And now his mother was holding him. He yearned for his spirit to give in, to revel in the thrill of finally having his ultimate wish come true. She'd survived. And they were reunited. She held him, her tears wetting his cloak, her voice mumbling, "Emir, my Emir."

He stood rigid as a stone, a stranger in his mother's grasp barely daring to breathe.

LITTLE BIRD WATCHED Zoe fold over the king. Her father. Gone. *Their father.* Her gaze lingered on him before shifting to Emir. He was holding Elanur in his arms, his eyes lowered. So many nights she had dreamed of seeing them again, and now here they all were. But it felt distant, surreal, as if she were still in the cave, trapped in a vision.

She shifted her gaze back to the king, lying dead under his son's statue. He had remembered her. Of all the impossible things, he had remembered. But he didn't know who she really was. She wanted to join Zoe, to be with her sister as their father passed away, but she couldn't move. She yearned to be close to Emir, too, to experience the comfort that he used to give her when she was a child, but he seemed in another world apart. She watched it all unfold, the king's death, the return of the lost son, the princess' sorrow, and sensed within herself the old loneliness that had for so long been her constant companion.

Xander burst through the castle doors, a bag full of supplies in his arms, and ran to Aster. Zoe squeezed her father's hand and, still crying, moved to join Xander at Aster's side. Emir released Elanur and stepped toward the king. Nearby, the young warrior sat in stunned silence by the fallen Gimirri leader. Xander began treating Aster with what supplies he had. Zoe whispered that he was going to be all right. Elanur knelt by the grieving boy. Emir stood over the king, his face unreadable. Little Bird looked at them all, then quietly turned and walked down the stone path.

She had reached the child's swing when she heard someone running up behind her. She whirled, nerves on edge. Her breath caught in her throat. There he came, looking every bit as powerful as he had all those years ago.

"Where are you going?" Emir asked.

She hesitated, uncertain how to begin. His face was just as she'd remembered—so familiar, like a dream drawn into daylight.

"It's not safe out there."

She made the sign for his name. *Emir.* Then she pointed to herself and signed *Little Bird.*

"Little Bird . . ." He shook his head. "Little Bird was a boy."

She repeated their names. *We came together,* she continued. *Here. Long ago.*

"No. That was . . ."

Me. I was a boy.

"You are no boy."

We escaped. You played at the gate. You won the contest. It was me.

He stared at her for a long while, muscles in his jaw clenching and releasing, his face pulled taut with emotion. "Why?" he said finally.

She shrugged. *Easier.*

He turned to check on the others, then met her eyes again. "How much time has passed?"

Twenty years, she signed.

A shadow fell over his features. Thunder growled in the distance, the air smelling of unshed rain. "Come back," he said. Tentatively, he reached out his hand.

She gazed at it, the fingers so like she remembered them, the thick muscle in the palm emanating strength. She raised her own and clasped his. At the touch of his skin, a surge of adrenaline shot up her arm. She fell in beside him and together, they walked back to the statue, the fallen king, and the wounded advisor, back to the princess and the king's sister, back to the people Little Bird couldn't yet call her own, but as she approached them, a flicker of hope stirred in her breast, like the first glimmer of dawn breaking over an uncertain horizon, promising that perhaps, one day, she might find her place among them. After all, she was holding Emir's hand, and what greater miracle was there than that?

CHAPTER
FIFTY-THREE

696 BC
Gordium, Capital City of Phrygia

"It is wise for you to worry about me." Aster lay on the couch in the guest room, his face pasty with sweat. "Particularly when your soul is not once again in jeopardy."

"There's nothing I can do about that." Xander offered him a drink of water. "Besides, it looks like Katiah had other things on her mind."

"Xander, more wine," Zoe said. She was washing her hands at the basin near the door.

Xander left. Aster groaned and closed his eyes.

"Don't worry," Zoe said to him. "The medicine woman taught me how to seal a wound. You'll be all right." She stared at the needle and thread she'd set on the corner of the table. With trembling hands, she picked it up.

The door opened and Elanur burst in. She snatched the stitching materials from Zoe and started over to the injured man. "Witch hazel and willow bark," she said.

Zoe stared at her.

"I've dealt with much worse than this," Elanur said. "Witch hazel, willow bark, myrrh, and a clean bowl."

Zoe hesitated, then dashed out. Elanur lifted Aster's shirt to check the wound. "We're going to have to move you."

When Xander returned with a jug of wine, she had him slide the long table close. Together, they lifted Aster onto it. They had just gotten him settled when Zoe returned with her arms full of clay bottles and leather pouches.

"Do they not persist?" Aster asked, referring to the Gimirri warriors outside of the gate.

"I haven't heard them for a time," Zoe said. "Not since Emir threw their leader's neck medallion and armor down from the watchtower."

Pushing her thoughts of Ilker aside, Elanur took the supplies from Zoe. Sniffing one and then the other, she combined them in the bowl.

"A small blessing," Xander said, pouring wine into a cup. "Maybe they will leave now." He lifted Aster's head and steadied the wine before his lips.

Aster swallowed. "Very safe out there," he said, before dropping his head back.

"What else can we do?" Zoe asked Elanur.

"You'll have to hold him," Elanur said.

Zoe touched Aster lightly on the shoulder.

"You should not go," he said. "Xander, don't take the princess out."

"I'm not going anywhere," Zoe said.

"We're not leaving you," Xander said, "so relax."

A heavy silence fell over the room as Elanur stirred her mixture. She added a little water and set the bowl down on a nearby stand. "More wine," she said to Xander.

Aster managed three more swallows.

"He needs to be on his side," Elanur said.

Aster groaned as they rolled him over. Elanur ordered pillows stacked behind him to give him some support while she used some of the mixture to clean the wound. When she finished, she threaded the needle, then glanced up at Xander and Zoe. "Will you be strong enough, or shall I call Emir?"

The two closed in on Aster, Xander taking hold of his shoulders.

"His hands," Elanur said. "I cannot be disturbed."

Aster raised his hands. Zoe took them in hers and squeezed.

"All right," Elanur said. "Hold still." Gently, she poked the needle into Aster's wounded side. He jerked with a grunt.

Xander squinted his eyes shut. "Hang on," he said. "We've got you."

EMIR SPENT the evening wandering the halls of the castle. He began in the undercroft. More barrels and boxes had been stacked inside, all filled with supplies, but the same mattress lay against the far wall. He stood before it for a time, remembering the boy. The boy who was no longer a boy. The water basin remained too, though the water inside had gone stale. He lingered, the silence wrapping around him like an old cloak. The faint scent of grain sweetened the air, warm and familiar. He inhaled deeply, then turned and moved quietly out the door.

After tending to Aster, Elanur had prepared a meal of dried meat, yogurt, bread, nuts, and figs. They gathered in the kitchen to eat, all but Xander, who remained with Aster. Emir kept glancing at his mother. It was still difficult to believe she was real. Sometimes, he gripped her arm just to convince himself. Elanur would inevitably end up shedding tears. Then she would smooth his hair and marvel at how he hadn't aged.

Following the meal, the others went to pack their things. They would be leaving soon. Emir had nothing to pack. Neither did the one Elanur called her son. She asked Emir to watch him, so he found a practice sword in Anchurus' quarters and approached the boy, who sat sulking near the entrance doors.

"Can you manage a sword?" he said.

"Not now," Kerkin said, his accent thick over the words.

Emir thudded him on the shoulder with his blade. "Fight, or suffer the effects of my blade."

The boy scowled. Emir waited another moment before cutting a clean nick on the boy's upper arm.

"Hey!"

"Fight." Emir tossed him the sword. It clattered onto the tile floor.

The boy heaved a heavy sigh and picked up the weapon. He tipped a bit with the weight of it. Emir danced around him. Once again, he was in Khar's arena, trying to elude the lion-man monster, darting away from the flying stingers, breathing in the hot red air.

"Prepare to die, little warrior!" he said.

Emir attacked. His opponent countered, but weakly. *Clang clang*, their swords collided. Emir taunted the boy, smiling as he twirled his blade in one hand. When Kerkin lunged, Emir easily blocked the blow and smacked him on the backside. Laughing, he readied himself for the warrior's next move. The boy charged, angry now. Emir waited until the last moment, then sidestepped. Kerkin stumbled and crashed into the wall. Emir laughed again. They continued sparring, more vigorously now, down the corridor and into the dining hall, the boy growing increasingly frustrated. Emir had intended only to rouse him from his melancholy, but the more they fought, the more the game slipped away, replaced by something raw and real. Memories of the underworld slipped in like a fever. Emir's strikes grew harder. More precise. He attacked with force, knocking the boy down—once, then again. When the enemy yelled, Emir drove him back across the arena until the boy collapsed, chest heaving. Emir touched the tip of his sword to the fiend's neck.

"Emir, stop! Stop it!"

The voice sounded far away.

Emir!

Emir glanced back to see his mother standing near the double doors. He blinked, uncertain it was truly her. She dropped her bag and rushed forward. He turned to his opponent and saw the boy lying there, staring up at him with frightened eyes. He lowered his sword as Elanur knelt to check on her adopted son.

"Leave us alone," Kerkin said to his mother. "I'm not a child." He glared at Emir, daring him to try again.

Emir hesitated.

"Come on," Kerkin said, getting to his feet. "Fight."

When the boy swung, Emir defended himself. Soon they were sparring again, but this time Emir focused on remaining in the present. It helped to give the boy tips. *Keep your shoulders down. Move your feet. Watch your stance. Center your weight.* Kerkin said nothing, but Emir could tell he was listening. That was something, at least. Meanwhile, his mother remained, watching.

They sparred until Zoe called them from the hall. Kerkin kept hold of the sword, an obvious improvement over the crude blade he'd had before. Emir had meant to ask for it back, but seeing the fierce way the boy held onto it, he let it go. It was the prince's practice sword. Surely Anchurus wouldn't have minded.

Zoe asked them to meet in the guest room. Kerkin marched on ahead. Emir joined his mother. For a while, they walked in silence.

"Was it awful for you down there?" she asked finally.

"I remember little," Emir said, their footsteps echoing down the hall. "What about you?"

"No." she answered more quickly than he expected. "In many ways, it was a pleasant life."

"That warrior?" Emir asked. "The leader?"

A cloud passed over Elanur's face. "My mate."

"I don't know how you do it," Emir said.

"Do what?"

"Survive. Everything."

She took his arm. "I don't think I would have. Not this time. But then you appeared." Her grip tightened. "I have my son back. I can survive anything."

. . .

ZOE STUFFED another dress into her bag. Her hands trembled. She felt she might never stop crying. She pulled the napkin from her pocket and dried her eyes, only to have more tears follow.

Elanur had finished treating Aster not long after sunset. Now he needed time to heal—time they didn't have. The city lay in ruins. Most of the citizens had either fled or been slaughtered. All the servants, including Elif, were gone, their fates unknown. Commander Baran had never returned and was presumed dead. Rastus was lost in Kiral's dwelling, Timon dead in the stairwell. She didn't know what the warriors would do. Elanur believed that without their leader, they would probably return to their camp in the north. They had women and children there. But she feared they would leave enough men behind to seal off the exits, hoping to capture the princess. The castle remained secure, its treasures untouched, but that wouldn't last—the Gimirri would come again. If not them, someone else, for word of Midas' defeat would spread quickly. Zoe had no army and no guards. The newly named heir to the throne was completely without protection. That meant she couldn't stay. Even if no one breached the castle walls, they had no way of replenishing their supplies. There was only one option—they had to leave, and leave now, before dawn.

Xander was packing for himself and Aster. Elanur was doing the same for herself and her two sons. They had no horses, so they were limited to what they could carry. That meant most everything had to be left in the castle. The king's castle.

Zoe made her way through the room, gathering her things. A few pieces of gold jewelry to barter with, her warmest hat, her mother's rose cologne, her dagger, an extra pair of sandals, ties for her hair, a jar of lamb's fat, extra underclothes. When she caught sight of her mother's painting, she paused. It was too large to take, but she wouldn't leave it for the Gimirri or other raiders to find. She lifted it off the wall. It would go into the tunnel, where they were putting so many other items they hoped to keep safe. The only thing they couldn't leave there was . . .

She started crying again. Her shoulders shaking, she dropped the bag, clenched her fists, and pounded the mattress. With her energy spent, she lay down and curled into a ball. Her father was dead. They couldn't forsake him, but she could think of no alternatives. That a king should be left somewhere to rot was beyond her imagination. She had to find a better solution, but she was struggling to do so.

She got up and crossed to the window. She feared seeing the Gimirri again, but the castle grounds were quiet. She returned to sit on the edge of her bed. On her nightstand rested the yellow horse Anchurus had brought for her birthday so many years ago. She picked it up and cradled it in her hands, new tears filling her eyes.

"I wish you could have come back," she told the horse, imagining Anchurus listening. "Perhaps none of this would have happened." The trinket looked at her with its cheerful face. She replaced it, gazed at it momentarily, then snatched it again and tucked it into her bag.

They would go to Lydia, the neighboring kingdom to the west. They would be anonymous there. Change their names. Find safety. If they were lucky enough to sneak out with their lives. She contemplated her mother's likeness, her father's words ringing in her ears. *Princess Zoe is to be queen of Gordium.* Not that it mattered now. What was there left to be queen of? Nevertheless, the words filled her heart. Her father, who for so long had clung to tradition, had finally shown her how much he believed in her.

A knock came at the door.

"Come," she said.

"Your Highness." Xander entered and bowed.

"You don't have to bow, Xander," she said. "It's just us, now."

He raised his gaze, his hands behind his back. "No, Your Highness," he said and emerged with the king's crown. "I mean, Your Majesty." He lowered himself onto one knee and offered the jeweled prize.

Zoe lifted it gingerly, surprised by its weight. Her fingers drifted over the inset garnets and polished gold, a quiet awe settling over her. So much responsibility her father had carried.

"Your Majesty?"

Zoe handed it back. "Take it," she said.

"But the king—"

"I know." She folded inward, twisting her fingers. "Gordium has fallen. The citizens have vanished. We are defeated with no army. I am queen of nothing."

"Your Majesty, you mustn't say that. Gordium may one day be rebuilt. Regardless, you are queen." He tried to return the crown, but she would not take it.

"Put it in the tunnel with the rest of the things," she told him. "If, one day, we return . . ." Her emotions swelled over her. She paused until they passed. "For now, we must concentrate on getting Aster out of here safely."

Reluctant, Xander tucked the crown under his arm, bowed, and stood up. He gazed at the princess for a long while. "You were so brave today," he said finally.

She gave him a sad smile. "As were you," she said.

When the door closed behind him, Zoe looked down at her empty hands, then up at her mother's portrait. "I wouldn't have worn it as well as you," she said softly. "I see that now." She sighed. "Father was right all along. It should have been Anchurus. But the goddesses took that chance away from us." Her words drifted into the stillness, weightless as dust. Looking up again, she found the painting more distant than ever, the brush strokes cold and lifeless.

Her mother was gone. And now her father was too, her brother a lingering shadow in her memory. Only Elanur remained. And Aster. Zoe wiped her eyes. A queen could not be mate to her advisor. But an ex-princess?

Lifting her bag, Zoe took one more look around her room. A sharp pang pinched underneath her ribs. Would she ever see it again? Grasping the painting, she left, the door closing heavily behind her.

CHAPTER

FIFTY-FOUR

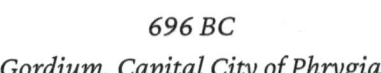

696 BC
Gordium, Capital City of Phrygia

Elanur left the guest room where Aster rested comfortably and climbed the stairs to her brother's quarters. She longed for a bath, but there was no one to heat it and bring it up, and she was too tired to do it herself. By the glow of two candle flames, she wiped herself down at the basin, changed into the long tunic Zoe had given her, and sat onto the couch near the window.

She'd wanted to rest for a few moments, but her mind was troubled. That Emir had come so close to harming Kerkin worried her. He'd recovered, but that moment had offered her a glimpse of the torment he must have endured. He was alive. He hadn't even aged. She had much to be grateful for. But he hadn't returned unscathed.

Kerkin, meanwhile, blamed her for the death of his father. Elanur had tried to explain that Ilker wasn't really his father, but he didn't believe her, his grief weighing heavily on him. He wanted to return to the tribe, he said. She didn't know what to do with that, so she had simply left, grateful for Emir's help in keeping him occupied.

Now, considering what had happened, she would have to be more careful.

A soft knock came at the door. Elanur opened it to find Little Bird. Smiling, she pulled her into a warm embrace, then led her toward the couch where the tall candles flickered on a nearby stand.

"You've grown so much," Elanur said as she sat down. "I remember you as a little girl."

Little Bird nodded.

"Zoe said that horrible goddess captured you. It must have been awful."

Little Bird drew something on the slate she'd brought and held it up.

"A cave?" Elanur looked over the drawing, noticing the water. "Near the ocean. She kept you in a cave?"

Little Bird looked at her with the same deep brown eyes.

"I shouldn't have fallen asleep that morning," Elanur said. "I've thought about it so many times."

Little Bird shook her head.

"But I could have protected you."

No. Little Bird signed the word.

"I'm so sorry."

Little Bird pointed to Elanur and raised her eyebrows, asking.

Elanur told her about her life in the camp, about Ilker and Kerkin and her work as healer. "They were my family," she said wistfully, "but he manipulated me from the beginning. More of Denisia's influence." She paused. "She's ... dead now?"

Little Bird nodded.

Elanur was curious, but she didn't ask. There would be time for that if they survived. "Did you have anyone?" she asked instead.

The girl drew on her slate.

Elanur raised an eyebrow. "Romance?"

Little Bird drew a man riding away on a horse.

"He left. You must have been so lonely."

The two women sat together, the gap of twenty years between them. The castle was quiet, the only sound the soft rustle of air around the candle flames. Little Bird extended her arm out beside her, hand flat.

"Kerkin?" Elanur sighed. "He's angry over the loss of who he thought was his father. Emir is trying to help, but . . ." She gazed at the girl. "Emir endured a lot wherever he was."

A shadow passed over Little Bird's features.

"Be careful around him," Elanur said. "Sometimes he's . . . not himself. There is something . . ." Elanur stopped, images playing in her mind. Emir standing over Kerkin, that rage in his eyes. "Twenty years," she said. "You, in a cave, him, in some terrifying underworld." She tented her hands over her nose. "My life was simple by comparison."

Little Bird drew again, a female figure coming out of what appeared to be a stone in the ground.

"Katiah," Elanur whispered. "Yes. Emir says she brought him back. She killed him, and now she brings him back." She lightly tapped the young woman's knee, then stood and checked out the window. It was still dark, but dawn hovered near. "I've packed you a few things." She handed Little Bird a bag. "Is there anything you need?"

The girl shook her head, so Elanur retrieved her own bag, and the two walked to the door. "Oh, I forgot something," Elanur said. "Go ahead. I'll be right there." The girl started out. "And Little Bird." Elanur smiled. "I'm so glad you're here. It makes me happy to see you well."

Little Bird pointed to her, then signed, *Me too.*

When the young woman had disappeared into the stairwell, Elanur returned to blow out the candles. She thought of her brother, of how much he'd missed his wife and son. Much as she didn't want to admit it, she missed Ilker, too. Part of her would never forgive him for taking Karem from her, or for manipulating her the way he had, but Ilker had been kind to her. For many years, they had been a family, as close to family as Elanur had ever had in her adult life, and her heart ached now that he was gone.

Once more, she headed toward the door, but after she opened it, she hesitated. This was her brother's room. For as long as she could remember, she had thought about him. After the Battle of Karama, she had pictured him basking in the glory of his reign as king of Phrygia. It saddened her to imagine that he had been so unhappy in his later years. She let her gaze roam over the couch, the window, the wooden chest against the wall, and the bed. She was trying to picture Karem in happier days when something caught her eye.

There, in the corner, shrouded in shadow, sat a toy. It rested atop a waist-high cabinet, barely visible behind a flower vase and empty pitcher. She set the bag down and approached, lifting it gently. The head flopped limply over the shoulder. Stepping back to the door, she opened it wider. Torchlight from the hall spilled into the room. As the glow touched the toy, she drew in a sharp breath.

It was her doll, the one she had played with as a child, the one Karem had mentioned at the battle. It had to be. No other doll looked like this. She ran her fingers over its arms and belly, memories stirring the deep recesses of her mind. The nose was missing and one eye, too, but the fabric of the dress was unlike any other. Her mother's handiwork. The stain had faded but still echoed the original yellow color. *Sunshine.* Elanur cupped the floppy head in her hand. The dress was so thin now it was nearly transparent, the little body worn soft by many years of holding. Had it brought Karem comfort or pain, she wondered? She hoped it was the former.

She clutched the doll to her chest. "Goodbye, Karem," she said to the empty room. "I'll watch over Zoe. And thank you for never forgetting about me." After another moment in the heavy silence, she picked up the bag and stepped out. The torch flickered as she passed, its flame exhaling a sorrowful sigh. Her footsteps echoed faintly down the corridor, the castle a hollow shell, whispering with the king's last breath at her back.

CHAPTER

FIFTY-FIVE

696 BC
Gordium, Capital City of Phrygia

I n the end, they hid King Midas in a secret storage room off the tunnel. Xander anointed his skin with every oil he could think of. Then he and Little Bird wrapped him in a soft nettle cloth, smoothed his cloak into place, and tied him securely to the plank/ With help from Emir and Kerkin, they lowered him through the concealed opening in the kitchen. Zoe lit a torch and led the way, a quiet procession winding through stone. The room lay about halfway between the entrance and the exit, its opening camouflaged with removable stones. They squeezed through the narrow gap and laid the king on a bench at the back. When it was done, they stood in silence around him, Zoe sniffling softly.

"He deserves so much more," she said.

Xander pictured Aster undergoing more treatment at Elanur's hands. He would be upset to have missed the king's burial, such as it was. As Xander helped replace the stones, his thoughts drifted to Gediz's dead body by the gates. The Gimirri warriors, too, littered the

439

grass by Anchurus' statue. Timon they had placed in his small room, the best they could do with what little time they had, Rastus abandoned in Kiral's dwelling in the city. That they could not properly tend to the dead was another insult they had to bear as they raced to save their own lives.

Xander returned to the guest room to find Aster sitting up. Elanur had wrapped his torso in multiple layers of cloth, so he looked stiff as he got onto his feet. Xander hoped it would be enough to prevent more bleeding. He put Aster's leather cloak on him and walked with him down to the kitchen. There, they all gathered once more around the tunnel entrance.

"I have something for you," Zoe said to Emir. A wisp of hair clung to her temple, caught in a sheen of perspiration. She stepped behind the counter, picked up a case, and passed it to him.

Emir's eyes widened as he took it. "It's still here," he murmured, his gaze locked on the object.

"We would love a tune," Zoe said, "once we've escaped the Gimirri."

Emir bowed his head, his fingers brushing the handle.

Kerkin stood by the tunnel entrance. "Are we going now?"

"We must be silent as mice," Zoe said. "If they hear us, we'll be dead." She studied Kerkin, wondering, Xander supposed, if they could trust him. If the boy called to his comrades once they were outside of the wall, they were doomed. "If we stick together," Zoe continued, "we can do this. I'm counting on you."

Xander bowed, Aster doing his best bow at his side. "We are at your service, Your Majesty," Xander said.

"None of that out there," she said. "I am Zoe Savas, as my father was Karem Savas. We can't be drawing attention to ourselves. We don't know who we're going to meet."

Xander nodded and bowed again.

"Not that either." Zoe pointed to him.

Xander stopped mid-bow, glancing nervously at Aster.

"Kerkin, lead us out," Zoe said.

Kerkin glanced at her, mildly surprised, but obeyed, dropping into the tunnel. Zoe handed him her bag and climbed down after him. Xander followed, then reached up to help Aster. Emir came next, then Elanur, and finally, Little Bird. As they trudged forward, Xander felt as if he were living someone else's life. Never had he imagined that, as King Midas' advisor, he would one day flee his own home.

"Sad to think this day has come," he said in a low voice.

"Do not take heart," Aster said.

"But we're leaving Gordium behind. And the king!"

"We do not have a new leader," Aster said, each step measured with care to avoid jarring his wound. "We may not live to see an even more glorious future."

"*If* we live," Xander grumbled.

"Your optimism is inspiring."

"I suppose. But I don't see how we're going to walk all the way to Lydia."

"You are not walking now," Aster said.

"You know what I mean!"

"You have much stamina."

"You may have to carry me."

"I would thrill to do that again."

"Especially now, in your condition," Xander said.

They paused near the room that hid the king, each bowing their heads in respect, then continued through the tunnel, a parade of sorrowful refugees. Everyone seemed to hold their breath as they emerged, but Kerkin said nothing. Under cover of darkness, they escaped the castle walls without incident and began the slow ascent into the western hills. The main road was too dangerous—no doubt watched by the warriors—so Zoe led them up a narrow wildlife trail instead, one she remembered from childhood rides with Anchurus. It made a general trek west and would get them a suitable distance away from Gordium until it was safe to turn south again and rejoin the road to Lydia.

Aster was walking without complaint, but Xander could hear his breath coming fast. He waited until the group had put some distance between themselves to drop back beside his friend once more.

"Are you all right?" he asked.

Aster didn't answer.

"Come. You can't be silent the whole way."

Aster stumbled slightly on the uneven path. "I must not protect the princess, and I'm in such good shape to do that now."

"Emir is here."

"Yes, and he's perfectly all right."

"Perhaps not, but he can handle a sword."

"He may not just as quickly cut our heads off as anyone else's."

"It must have been awful where he was."

"We ought not keep an eye on him."

"I think someone is already doing that." Xander checked on Little Bird, who seemed tethered to Emir's heels. He wondered again about what Katiah had said about children. But then, the goddess was unpredictable.

"You do not seem to be holding up well," Aster said.

"Not like I have much choice. None of us do, eh?"

"And the goddess Katiah did not visit you?"

"No, thank the gods. I mean, the . . . other gods? I have much to be grateful for."

Aster nodded. "It is comforting to know she is free again."

"At least she seems occupied at the moment."

"We must not each take a watch at night," Aster said.

"That won't help much if the Gimirri murder us in our sleep."

Aster chuckled. "We shall not meet each other in the underworld."

"That would be an adventure, wouldn't it?" Xander glanced at his friend. "But you will not go there. You will follow Prince Anchurus into the glowing spirit world."

"If you are in the underworld, I shall be glad to leave you there."

Xander smiled. "Even you, my friend, couldn't rescue me from that place."

"I did not rescue you once before."

"It is your fate," Xander said. "You are the strong one. I am the fool who gave his soul to the dark goddess."

"I wasn't the first to offer mine."

Xander raised his eyebrows at the memory. "True, but I still managed to win that round."

"A worthy prize, for certain."

They reached the first hill west of Gordium and began the steeper climb. Aster soon fell behind. Xander moved to help him, but in a flash, Emir was there. He took Aster's arm over his shoulder and, with powerful strides, propelled the advisor to the top. When the others caught up, they turned to look across the valley. Xander's heart clenched at the sight. There were always a few fires or oil lamps glowing in the city. Now, only a single flame flickered in the distance, and even that, at times, seemed imaginary. Gordium was a graveyard, exhaling wisps of ghostly smoke, the castle swallowed in shadow.

"What have we done?" Zoe asked in despair. "My father's kingdom!"

"Karem would be glad to know you are safe," Elanur said. "You were what was most important to him."

"But everything he worked for . . ."

"He gave up in the end," Elanur finished for her. "He longed for his wife, his son. In comparison, a kingdom is nothing." Elanur gazed at Emir. He stood next to her, Little Bird nearby.

Zoe stepped closer to Aster. Xander noticed the movement, then saw his friend take the princess' hand. He lifted his gaze over the city to the east, where a shimmer of light wriggled over the horizon. The day was dawning. It seemed strange, the sun coming up. With everything that had happened, it had felt to him like the sun might never rise again.

Kerkin, seemingly bored, turned to leave. Reluctantly, Zoe and the others followed. Xander lingered, then finally bade the castle a sorrowful goodbye and hurried forward until he came up alongside Aster once more.

"How are you doing?" he asked.

"Much better with you asking every few moments," Aster said.

"We might stop soon? Rest?"

"We must not put a good distance between us and them."

"But you need to heal."

"We do not have a medicine woman."

Xander glanced ahead at Elanur walking beside Zoe. "Another surprise," he murmured. It warmed his heart to see them together. The king's sister, whom Midas had spent so long trying to rescue, was finally here, now that he was gone. Not a trade Xander would have chosen, but there was comfort in it nonetheless.

Overhead, a raven circled in the sky. Xander looked up, curious. He had seen a raven with the wolves at the tomb, and later, one had attacked the warrior at the castle, giving Little Bird a chance to escape. Now here was another. Or was it the same one? It appeared to be following them. Xander glanced back at the young woman, the events of the past day replaying in his mind. Somehow, she had drawn power from Denisia to release Katiah, and then . . .

Aster stumbled. Xander stepped up to catch him. When his friend was steady again, Xander stayed close, his thoughts turning over the mysteries surrounding Little Bird's return.

"What is it not?" Aster asked.

"What?" Xander said.

"You're not doing that thing you do."

"It's nothing." When Aster glared at him, Xander glanced over his shoulder. "It's just . . . Denisia is dead, but I'm afraid we are not done with the goddesses."

"Matar?"

Xander shook his head. "I lost the rock. In the explosion. When Katiah was released."

"I enjoyed your story about that."

"It's not like we've had a lot of time to catch up."

"Time is short now."

Xander looked ahead to where Zoe had taken the lead from Kerkin. "I suppose you're right. Well, when I arrived at the tomb . . ."

Xander continued his story, recounting his adventure of releasing Katiah as they made their way along the wildlife trail. The rising sun cast their shadows before them, and the last of Phrygia's land softened beneath their feet. Their home soon disappeared from view as they bravely marched on to the life that awaited them, the weight of all they had lost pressing heavily on their hearts.

EPILOGUE

In the deep, dark underworld

King Midas awoke to darkness. For a long while, he remained still, allowing the emptiness to seep into his spirit. It was what he had longed for. Everything to stop. Everything to recede so that he could rest in peace.

Eventually, he stood up and scanned his surroundings. There was no light, no sound. The air smelled musty and damp. He explored like a blind man, his hands reaching out. Soon, they touched cold, hard rock. He felt his way along until he realized he was in what seemed to be a tunnel. The Gimirri might have thrown him in his own dungeon, but he remembered the sword penetrating his body. He winced, the pain flaring under his ribs.

When it subsided, he started walking. It was a day or maybe two before he spotted an orange light flickering ahead. This was the afterlife, he thought, or perhaps he had crossed into the underworld. A heavy sense of dread washed over him. Yes. Katiah owned his soul. He had given it to her when he was still a boy. The Gimirri had killed him, and he had ended up in *her* domain. He paused, pondering that, but the light was too compelling. He walked toward it, traveling for another indeterminable time until he heard a voice singing.

Demodica?

It seemed to come from up ahead. He didn't believe it to be real. She wouldn't be in the underworld. Yet he clung to it nonetheless, walking faster.

Time passed. Another day? Two? His thoughts were scattered. First, he focused on the light, then the image of his wife's face, but more often he was overcome with guilt that he hadn't done more for Zoe. Dear Zoe. She deserved a safe home, and he'd failed to leave her that. The thought nagged at him with a growing irritation. Demodica would be displeased.

The light grew brighter, the singing clearer. He moved faster, his legs surprisingly limber. He shifted into a run, marveling at how effortless it felt, keeping his gaze forward, his focus on his wife's voice. The orange rays blazed before him. He slowed, shielding his eyes. Up ahead, something began to take shape—perhaps a river, though it flowed red rather than blue.

The singing stopped.

"Demodica?" he called. "Is that you?" He paused. "Demodica?"

A figure shimmered within the heart of the light, gleaming like stardust suspended in air. Slowly, it began to move toward him. With each step, the brilliance behind it softened, fading into shadows, while the radiance within grew brighter—a creamy glow reminiscent of moonlight. With a pulsing energy, it drew itself into form. The goddess Katiah materialized before him, her presence both ethereal and undeniable.

"Well, Karem," she said with a seductive smile. "Here you are, at last."

THE END

ACKNOWLEDGMENTS

First and foremost, my heartfelt thanks to my family—Mary, Gerald, Jim, Nathan, and Ryan—for your unwavering support of my writing. Your encouragement and generosity in helping to bring this book to life mean the world to me.

Special thanks to Deborah Ludlam for your incredible insights (!), to Elizabeth Bauer for sticking with me through Book II of this series, and to my mom, Mary, for your thoughtful feedback and for being such a helpful sounding board when I needed to work through tricky plot points.

Thank you to Damonza for the striking cover and to BMR Williams for the updated map. To early readers and blurb writers, your enthusiasm for this series sustains me. To my newsletter subscribers, I enjoy sharing this journey with you. And to everyone who has read one of my books and left a review, THANK YOU!

∽

THANK YOU!

Thank you for reading *The Gimirri Invasion*, Book II in The Midas Legacy! If you've enjoyed reading about King Midas and his world, please consider leaving an honest review on Amazon.com, Goodreads.com, or wherever you regularly purchase your books. Get the scoop on future releases, discounts, deals, and behind-the-scenes insights at www.colleenmstory.com/newsletter.

ABOUT THE AUTHOR

Colleen M. Story writes award-winning historical fantasy, supernatural thrillers, and motivational books for writers. She grew up on a Colorado ranch making up stories on horseback, which probably explains a lot. A lifelong musician, she plays French horn in the local symphony and pit orchestras and teaches music on the side. With nearly 30 years as a freelance health writer, she's the unofficial "medical hotline" for friends and family. When she's not typing away, you'll probably find her at the movies—sci-fi, fantasy, action, or anything with a good chase scene. Find her books at colleenmstory.com and masterwritermindset.com.

linkedin.com/in/colleen-m-story-81408034

amazon.com/stores/Colleen-M.-Story/author/B016CMG616

x.com/colleen_m_story

youtube.com/ColleenMStoryteller

instagram.com/colleenmstory

goodreads.com/cmstory

bookbub.com/profile/colleen-m-story

CONSIDER THESE OTHER TITLES BY COLLEEN M. STORY

THE CURSE OF KING MIDAS: "With its engaging plot, well-developed characters, and poignant themes, *The Curse of King Midas* is a standout in the genre . . ." ~FORAM VYAS FOR READERS' FAVORITE BOOK AWARDS

THE BEACHED ONES: "Story deftly weaves the paranormal into this touching and heart-wrenching novel that will have you staying up late to accompany Daniel on his journey to the end." ~MELISSA PAYNE, BESTSELLING AUTHOR OF *THE SECRETS OF LOST STONES*

LOREENA'S GIFT: "This book sucked me in and I could turn the pages fast enough to see what was going to happen to Loreena next. I really liked how although Loreena is blind she didn't let that defeat her . . . . I absolutely loved this story and I will be on the lookout for future books from Story." ~JBRONDERBOOKREVIEWS

OVERWHELMED WRITER RESCUE: "If you read only one self help book this year – grab this one! It is not just for writers. This book is very motivating and so easy to read quickly." ~LAURA'S READING

WRITER GET NOTICED!: "A Five Star must have in your library . . . . I found her information and self-discovery processes applicable in other aspects of my life as well!" ~SUSAN VIOLANTE, READER VIEWS

YOUR WRITING MATTERS: "I wish I'd been able to read this book when I was a beginning writer. . . . It would have helped me vanquish my self-doubts, ignore naysayers, and encouraged me to develop the craft of writing." ~JOE WISINSKI FOR READERS' FAVORITE

www.ingramcontent.com/pod-product-compliance
Lightning Source LLC
Chambersburg PA
CBHW020003120726
47903CB00004B/1112